PRAISE FOR *DOOMSDAY MATCH*

"A fast-paced and enthralling thrill  and action. Once I started this boo single scene. A masterpiece of story

—*New York Ti* ᵧ ᵤutnor A. R. Torre

"Fans of James Rollins and Dan Brown will love this stunning new thriller from Jeff Wheeler. *Doomsday Match* is utterly engrossing, a dark and complex tale filled with ancient secrets, adventure, and betrayal. You won't be able to put it down."

—#1 *Wall Street Journal* bestselling author Melinda Leigh

"Jeff Wheeler knocks it out of the park with his supercharged thriller *Doomsday Match*. From the very first scene, you know you're in for an incredible thrill ride full of constant danger and relentless twists—set against a jaw-dropping conspiracy background. Just when you think you've figured out Wheeler's game, he artfully rips the rug out from under the reader, shaking up the plot. If you're a fan of fast-paced, devious conspiracies with a little more than a touch of magic and mysticism, *Doomsday Match* is for you!"

—*Wall Street Journal* bestselling author Steven Konkoly

DOOMSDAY
MATCH

DOOMSDAY MATCH

JEFF WHEELER

Text copyright © 2023 by Jeff Wheeler
All rights reserved.

Published by 47North, Seattle

www.apub.com

Amazon, the Amazon logo, and 47North are trademarks of Amazon.com, Inc., or its affiliates.

ISBN-13: 9781662505546 (paperback)
ISBN-13: 9781662505553 (digital)

Cover design by Shasti O'Leary Soudant
Cover image: © Cesar Dussac / Shutterstock; © Weredragon / Shutterstock; © PRILL / Shutterstock

Printed in the United States of America

To Robert

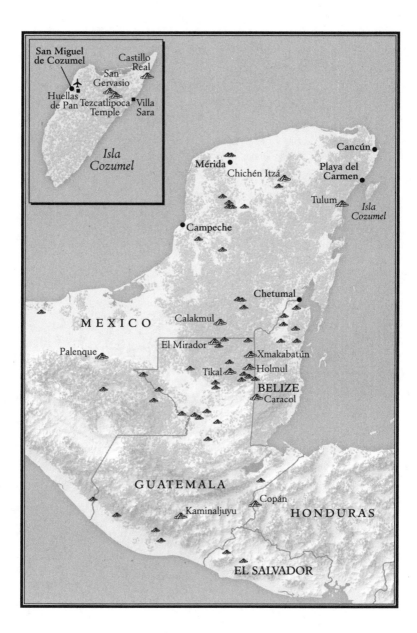

Inset map (Isla Cozumel):
San Miguel de Cozumel
Castillo Real
San Gervasio
Huellas de Pan
Tezcatlipoca Temple
Villa Sara
Isla Cozumel

Mérida
Chichén Itzá
Cancún
Playa del Carmen
Tulum
Isla Cozumel
Campeche

MEXICO

Chetumal
Calakmul
El Mirador
Xmakabatún
Holmul
Tikal
BELIZE
Caracol
Palenque

GUATEMALA

Copán
Kaminaljuyu
HONDURAS

EL SALVADOR

CHAPTER ONE

Maya Biosphere Reserve

Xmakabatún, Guatemala

December 20

The roar of the twin propellers made shouting the only way to be heard, even with the headsets. As it soared over the jungle lowlands, the plane bucked and dipped, causing various components of the LiDAR equipment to rattle, although they were secured with thick straps. The pilot's face was dripping with sweat, which leaked beneath his sunglasses and into his scraggly beard.

"That's the last run!" the pilot shouted. "Time to head back to the airport!"

Dr. Estrada shook his head, planting his palm on the cockpit dashboard to brace himself against a sudden lurch. "Let's go a little farther. We have enough fuel."

"Eh?"

"Head north!"

"We did the runs already. It's time to go back."

"We have fuel. North. Now!"

Dr. Estrada felt the sweat dripping down his ribs. The twin-prop plane was flying at an altitude of two thousand feet. That was within the ideal range for the LiDAR equipment. But it made for a choppy ride, and the blazing sun was certainly as hot at their altitude as it was down in the jungle below. The LiDAR equipment generated plenty of heat too. The strapped boxes had cables running through the plane like spiderwebs. A hole had been set into the bottom of the stripped-out plane so that the lasers pointed down at the jungle below—a tangle of cedar, ceiba, and cojon trees meshed together, so dense it was impossible to see beneath the canopy.

Data had proven that LiDAR was the next breakthrough in archaeology, capable of digitally stripping away the trees and revealing manmade structures that had been abandoned by the Maya centuries before.

Dr. Estrada was on the leading edge of the research in a joint partnership with UC San Diego in California. The lab, funded by a giant semiconductor company, processed the terabytes of data produced by the equipment in the plane. It would take a hundred years to sift through the vast amounts of data—except thanks to Moore's Law and the miniaturization of circuits, the servers were getting faster and faster, allowing the data to be mined and mapped much faster as time went on. He was excited about the work. Half of archaeology was knowing where to dig, and LiDAR provided an accurate map of what lay beneath the jungle's growth and was more dependable than the human eye.

Through the windows, he could see the scenery of the Guatemalan jungle whip below them. The plane had to avoid the occasional blizzard of startled macaws.

The pilot, Miguel Santos, had adjusted course north. The additional time meant more money for him.

"Where we going, boss?"

"We'll be there soon."

"How long?"

"What?"

"How long we going north? We'll reach the border of Mexico in minutes!"

The northern border of Guatemala was a straight line that ran through an enormous, uncharted jungle in the Yucatán Peninsula. The ruins they'd studied at Xmakabatún were on the eastern border shared by Belize, but that government didn't care if a plane wandered over the arbitrary line out in the middle of nowhere. The Mexican government, on the other hand, was a bit more testy about sharing their airspace. They looked down on Guatemalans. They didn't care that the current borders were a modern construct so steeped in history and civil war that they no longer seemed to make sense.

Two thousand years ago, the entire Yucatán Peninsula was ruled by the Maya. The vast jungle below had been ruled by a people who knew about the orbit of planets centuries sooner than their European conquerors did. They'd left behind extensive ruins, many of which had yet to be discovered. An archaeologist's dream come true.

The plane dipped again, making Dr. Estrada's stomach lurch, and he slammed his palm against the dashboard.

"We should turn back to La Libertad, sir. I don't want to get in trouble."

Flying as fast as they were, they'd probably crossed into Mexican airspace already. Miguel wiped sweat from his mouth and began to angle the plane.

"A little farther. I just want to map one other thing while we're here." He'd studied the topo maps for years and had always been intensely curious about a certain location in the heart of the jungle. Satellite images showed very little because of the tree cover, but a curious mound rose from the jungle. A mound like that was not natural. The lowland jungles were typically flat. Mounds were man-made, the sign of a pyramid built centuries, or even a millennium, ago.

Estrada believed there was an even bigger pyramid concealed beneath the jungle, the kind of prize that could make a man's career and ensure his legacy.

"I'll get in trouble!"

"You won't. I will. I'll throw in a bonus. C'mon. We're almost there."

"How much bonus?"

"Enough that you won't regret it. We'll just say we got lost."

The pilot didn't seem appeased by the thought. "Air traffic control at Cancún can probably already see us."

"We're flying too low for radar to pick us up."

Miguel scratched an itch on his chin and flared his nostrils. "I don't like this, boss."

"I don't pay you to like it. Angle northwest. Toward that mound." He could see it now, and his heart sped in anticipation.

A hiss of breath came through the pilot's teeth. "We shouldn't be here!"

Miguel was right. They'd already entered the Calakmul Biosphere Reserve, a huge swath of jungle in the southeast corner of the state and municipality of Campeche. The towns in the area were primarily along the coast. Only one highway went through the jungle, farther north. The area they were flying over was a jungle preserve, heavily wooded and almost impossible to reach by land.

Dr. Estrada had petitioned the Mexican government for permission to use the LiDAR lasers to scan the biosphere reserve. His request had been denied with no explanation. A wealthy family funded the research of the area. And since Dr. Estrada was Guatemalan, they'd not even given a sniff before saying no. The Calakmul biosphere contained a great treasure, he was certain, and the Calakmul family was keeping it a secret.

So much was concealed beneath the canopy of the jungle. Satellites couldn't see anything through the maze of trees and vegetation. Not even drones could penetrate the thick jungle. The LiDAR made all the difference. He'd seen plenty of evidence of it in the work he'd done finding the ruins of Xmakabatún. Even when he and his team were within fifty meters of the location, it was still invisible. But the technology had revealed the ruins from above—dispassionately, a series of light refractions bouncing back to the plane and revealing shapes that were clearly made by man, not by nature.

In some ways, it was like putting together a treasure map, because the Maya rulers had been buried with a wealth of jade, gold, silver, and obsidian. They were like the pharaohs of ancient Egypt, only, the Maya had disappeared one day, leaving behind clues for those who were discerning.

He had a feeling one of the richest finds would be in the Calakmul reserve. According to his research, it had once been one of the powerful kingdoms of the Maya—before the jungle had swallowed it. Besides, it was in such a remote location that any ruins were likely well preserved, untouched by modern civilization.

"Boss!"

Dr. Estrada had been lost in thought, imagining what they'd find. One pyramid temple could house untold treasures and reveal information about the Maya that had been lost for centuries. Years after Hernán Cortés had conquered the area, a group of Spaniards gathered up all of the Maya documents they could find and burned them. A few precious codices had been preserved—a small handful out of hundreds—and sent back to major cities in Europe. Like Paris, Madrid, and Dresden.

It was Estrada's dream that one of these ruins might contain an original codex even older than those that had been preserved. One that could help them fully decipher the ancient hieroglyphs. A Rosetta stone for Mayan, if you would.

"What?" Estrada looked at the pilot. Miguel's arm was outstretched, his index finger quivering.

"There's something down there," he said.

There was a gap in the jungle. They were flying low enough that Estrada could see the stone courtyard below. The light revealed ancient structures, a series of ruins hidden beneath the canopy of the jungle. Excitement bubbled inside him.

"I knew it!" he gasped. Then louder: "Fly directly over it. The LiDAR will map this place. Fly directly, then turn around for another pass." They'd need to make multiple passes so the lasers could produce enough data for the supercomputers to then unscramble. Millions of dots of light were hammering down at the trees below. Some, a small percentage, pierced the edges of the leaves and touched the ground. The varying height of that ground was what would reveal the shape of the structures. Only this time, he didn't need the LiDAR to see that something was down there. Something the Calakmul family was probably hiding and excavating without anyone else knowing.

"Turn around, make another pass!" Estrada repeated, thrilled with the discovery.

The plane banked sharply and turned, coming around for another sweep of the area, heading south again. It was a beautiful day. Perfect weather to be capturing the data. Not a cloud in the—

The plane bucked. A rumble of thunder came. Colorful jungle birds began to flee the canopy of trees as if startled by a predator.

Estrada peered out the side window of the plane. A swirl of dark clouds was gathering over the surrounding jungle, coalescing above the spot of open ground. Sudden thunderstorms were common in these jungles, but the thunderheads shouldn't be gathering this fast. The hot afternoon sun, which had been baking them in the cockpit earlier, was now blocked by the anvil-shaped clouds. In the mass of darkness ahead of them, a few flashes of lightning were already starting.

"There's someone down there!" the pilot shouted.

Estrada rubbed his eyes and saw a man standing in the middle of the courtyard. He was dressed like one of the ancient Maya, like the locals who spent their days in costume at the ruins at Chichén Itzá to pose with tourists for a price. Except there were no tourists.

"Climb, now!" Estrada said, feeling his gut clench with fear. The storm had come out of nowhere, and they were flying straight toward it. The wind shear alone could be fatal at their low altitude.

Miguel was struggling with the controls, his mouth and scrappy beard twisting with frustration as he yanked on the yoke.

The craft gave a sudden lurch, much more dangerous than the previous ones. It felt like something from the jungle had reached up and snatched their plane. Both men shouted in fear.

The yoke shook violently. Miguel gripped it hard, trying to turn, but it seemed he was wrestling a crocodile. A force was inextricably bringing them closer to the heart of the gathering storm. Thunder boomed and rain began lashing against the cockpit window.

"Turn! Turn!" Estrada shouted. "Get out of here!"

Miguel began to shout a prayer. "Hail Mary, full of grace, the Lord is with thee. *Nngghh* . . . Blessed art thou amongst women!" The sunlight had vanished behind bulging black clouds. The plane rocked and dropped again. The rain sounded like bullets against the windows. Another dip made both men gasp. The jungle. If they went into the jungle, no one would ever find them. It would swallow them whole.

"B-Blessed is the fruit of thy womb, Jesus."

Another pitch. Rain lashed the window so fast, it blurred everything except the darkness. Estrada could see the maw of the jungle out the smeared windows. It was rising to bite them.

"Pull up! Pull up!" Estrada screamed.

Miguel continued to fight the yoke. It was going right, left, up, and down as the plane was pummeled by wind. Thunder boomed through the cockpit and lightning blinded them both. It wasn't rain now. It was hail.

Hail? In a jungle?

"Holy Mary, Mother of God!" Miguel wailed.

The plane pitched violently to the left. Estrada felt his chest straining against the belt. Another lurch and he struck his face against the side of the cockpit. Stinging pain flared on his cheekbone.

"Pray for us sinners . . . !"

Estrada was a passive Catholic, but the words came to him as he waited, any moment, for the plane to crash through the canopy. Their voices joined, quavering in fear.

". . . now and at the hour of our death. Amen!"

In that moment, Estrada wasn't thinking about the value of the equipment strapped behind his seat, rattling and shaking along with the groans of the fuselage. He wasn't thinking about the lease on the plane or the immense server lab at UC San Diego.

He was thinking about dying. His body would be devoured by the jungle, his bones picked clean until they too moldered into paste. He'd seen enough skeletons in his life to know that his remains wouldn't be preserved like the Maya kings, entombed in stone.

He heard slapping noises against the hull of the plane.

The trees.

He shut his eyes, babbling in fear, propping his boot up against the cockpit dashboard to brace for impact.

And then the plane began to lift, to soar. The throttle revved, and the noise of the engines drowned out their muffled sobs.

Estrada blinked in surprise. Tears had joined the sweat on his cheeks. They were rising over the jungle, higher and higher, heading south. The yoke was calm once more.

Miguel gripped one of the yoke handles with one hand and scrubbed his cheeks with his other hand, dislodging his sunglasses. He was pale with terror.

"We . . . we almost died!"

The altimeter showed they were at three thousand feet, then four thousand, then five, rising rapidly.

A distant boom of thunder behind them was louder than the props. Estrada wished he could see out the back to look at the storm that had come from nothing and nearly hurtled them out of the sky. His pulse was still running wild.

"Th-The airport," he stammered.

"Okay, boss." Miguel glanced back at Estrada. "I'm never crossing into the Calakmul biosphere again. Ever."

Estrada nodded in agreement. They'd spent hours crisscrossing the jungles of Guatemala for this project. Already they'd found tens of thousands of structures abandoned by the Maya. There was more work than he could do in a lifetime in Guatemala.

He had no idea whom they'd seen in the heart of the jungle. Something told him it would be better if they never knew.

CHAPTER TWO

United Flight 1119

Bozeman, Montana to Cancún, Mexico

December 23

"Dad, why is the plane shaking so much?" There was a tremor in Lucas's voice. Worry.

"Turbulence. Pilots often call it 'rough air,' but it's really just sky farts." Roth noticed the way his son was clenching the armrests, squeezing them until his knuckles blanched, as the cabin jostled. He was grateful only ice was left in his cup, and he watched as the cylindrical tubes bumped around. The turbulence was bad enough to spill a drink. He hated turbulence himself—it terrified him—but calming his son's fear helped him cope with his own.

Roth's wife, Sarina, patted Lucas's hand comfortingly. The tray table in front of her was down, with her copy of the *New York Times*'s easy crossword puzzles open in front of her, the pencil wedged in the crease.

The seat in front of Roth lowered back sharply, and his daughter Suki's dyed bangs appeared in the gap, her teal-rimmed glasses partway down her nose. She gave him her typical deadpan expression. "Did you seriously just say turbulence is 'sky farts,' Dad?"

"I'm just trying to help Lucas understand there's nothing to worry about," he said, giving his daughter a meaningful look so that she wouldn't aggravate the situation. Being the eldest, she was usually helpful in these situations. But sometimes she liked to provoke the twins.

"Did you know they have categories of turbulence?" he asked Lucas, attempting to distract him from the ongoing bumps. "Like they do for hurricanes or tornados." Another sharp drop made his stomach flutter. He hated flying sometimes, especially when the plane was descending, as theirs was, toward the airport in Cancún. Out the window, he could see the Hotel Zone with the gleaming paradisiacal resorts nestled along the creamy beaches inside the reef.

"And what would this one be?" Suki asked with a twinkle in her eyes. "An F1?"

"I shouldn't have drunk the whole cup of soda," Lucas said. "I need to pee really bad."

"You'll have to wait for the airport. Just . . . hold it," Roth said. His voice quavered as another jolt of turbulence happened midspeech. Lucas grabbed his hand and squeezed really hard. It was slightly mortifying that a man of his size, girth, and with a formidable beard, should be gibbering in terror on the inside while his sixteen-year-old looked as calm as milk, and the other twin—Bryant, whom they'd nicknamed Brillante, pronounced "bree-ant-ay" in Spanish—was so distracted by his Nintendo Switch he hadn't even noticed the turbulence.

"This is just Lucas's anxiety showing itself," Sarina said. She patted their son's other arm. "We're about to land. It'll be over soon."

We're approaching a concrete runway at five hundred miles an hour, wobbling uncontrollably. What could possibly go wrong? Roth thought. But indulging his own fear wouldn't help the situation. What he needed to do was distract his son.

Sarina picked up her pencil, rubbing the eraser against her bottom lip. Her ancestors were from the Yucatán Peninsula in Mexico, which was one of the reasons they'd jumped at the chance to spend Christmas in Cozumel. Sarina's ancestors were from a more rural area, which was much more dangerous to visit because of the extensive influence of the drug cartels. A touristy place like Cozumel should be perfectly safe. As an additional incentive, they only had to pay for airfare and any food or souvenirs they bought outside the resort. The resort they were staying at was free. Another perk of being a *New York Times* bestselling author and having wealthy neighbors in Bozeman.

The shaking of the 737 felt a little like the earthquakes Roth and Sarina had grown up with in the San Francisco Bay Area in California, although not as bad as the '89 Loma Prieta quake. Lucas squeezed his hand even harder.

A story. He needed to think of a story to tell his son. It would have the added benefit of distracting Roth himself from the landing. To him, landing was the most terrifying part of flying. The only way he could bring himself to get on a plane was to sit next to the window so he could watch everything. Well, almost everything. He hated being in a seat over the wings because whenever the wings trembled, he imagined they might suddenly fall off.

He could see the jungles of Mexico outside the city limits of Cancún, just a smear of brown trees below, such a different scene from the snowy roads and mountains surrounding Bozeman that they'd left very early that morning. The layover in Denver had been snowy too.

The thought heartened him a little—Mexico was just what they needed, a little escape from the winter tundra they were living in now. He hadn't realized how much the weather affected him until they'd moved from Fremont, California, to Bozeman two years ago.

"You're looking a little green, Dad," Suki observed worriedly. "They have those little bags in the backs of the seats."

"Is Dad going to barf again?" Brillante suddenly piped in, interested. His face crowded against Suki's in the gap between the seats. She wrinkled her nose and gave him a little shove. She was off the charts on the introverted scale and didn't like anyone intruding on her personal space.

Roth frowned at his other son. It was a reference to a recent vacation to Disney World. Roth had lost his lunch after going on the Avatar ride.

"I'm *fine*," Roth said stoically. He loosened his grip, glancing out the window again. The Cancún airport could be seen in the distance, to the south of the city, along with the beautiful blue coastline. The ocean had different colors to it, based on the coral reef. It was an amazing sight. They weren't going to the nearby Hotel Zone since the resort they were staying at was on the island of Cozumel.

They were descending rapidly, the turbulence easing a little, when a story came to him. "Once I flew to Colorado for a grad-school interview." That was a long time ago. Twenty years ago. Although he'd gotten accepted, he'd decided to stay in California and teach at Hayward State. One of the reasons for that decision was because he'd met Sarina there. While he'd spent eight years getting his undergrad degree because he loved learning *everything* and kept changing his major, she was more sensible and had gotten her nursing degree and been promoted to charge nurse in the ER in the same amount of time.

"We took a 747 to Denver, and the turbulence was so bad. I mean, *really* bad. One of the engines fell off."

"Seriously?" Suki asked, pushing her glasses higher up her nose. She had short-cropped hair, dyed brown to disguise its natural black. The boys didn't care that they looked like their mom. Suki did. She preferred people to think she was half-Japanese, not Hispanic. She'd seen how Hispanic students in her school in Fremont were treated, particularly the ones with ethnic last names, and the same prejudice existed in Bozeman. It disgusted Roth. His wife had dealt with similar prejudice in her childhood, and they'd both hoped attitudes would be different by the time their children started school.

"I thought I was going to have a heart attack," Roth said, "but the guy next to me said not to worry. 'It's a 747; they have four engines. They can fly just fine with three.' Sure enough, the pilot came on and said our arrival to Denver would be delayed a half hour, but we were good."

Sarina knew the story. She smiled and said nothing, looking down at her crossword puzzle. Lucas was staring at him in surprise.

"Ma'am, tray tables need to come up," said a flight attendant, who then took their used cups with her blue-gloved hands. Sarina handed over her empty cup and clicked up first her tray table and then Roth's, while he continued the story.

"A little later, the turbulence shook us so bad another engine broke loose. Crashed on a house somewhere in Vail. A mansion, I think. No one was hurt, thankfully. Two engines gone. I was really starting to freak out. But the guy next to me said, 'Don't worry . . . it's a 747. It can fly fine on two engines.'"

Lucas's eyebrows lifted even higher. The mop of curly hair on his head shook a little from another slight bout of turbulence. "Dude!"

This was why Roth loved telling stories. He loved getting people interested and then throwing them curves. History was unpredictable, and so were Roth's books.

"The pilot came on again. You could hear the worry in his voice. He apologized for the mechanical troubles. This was a long time ago. Planes weren't as safe back then. He said that we'd be okay, but the delay was now an hour to Denver. We were flying over the Rocky Mountains, right? Imagine crashing there. We would have turned into cannibals before they'd found any survivors."

"Cringey, Dad," Suki said, wrinkling her nose. "Utter cringe."

Sarina shook her head and went back to her crossword puzzle, which was now on her lap.

"Dude!" Lucas repeated, shaking his head.

Brillante had gone back to the Switch. It was probably the soccer video game he loved to play. FIFA something. Sarina and Roth liked to call him their absent-minded professor because of how absorbed he got in whatever he was doing. When he was in the zone, playing a video game or watching TV, not even pizza could yank him out. Roth dreaded the day his son would get his first smartphone.

"Outside the window, I could see the snow-capped peaks. I thought . . . man, this is bad! We're going to crash in the mountains. Like . . . this is real. I'm going to die strapped in this seat." He looked at his kids solemnly. "Then the third engine failed. It didn't fall off. The engine failed. Quit."

The guy sitting on the aisle seat, across from Sarina, was leaning forward, looking at him too. An older guy with silver hair. Retired probably, heading to Cancún for some downtime.

"What happened?" Lucas whispered.

Roth sighed. "Three engines down. Only one left. The pilot came on again. He was terrified. You could *hear* it in his voice. 'Ladies and gentlemen, we have one engine left. I've increased the speed of our landing to compensate, but it's going to be tight. Denver is still the closest airport. There's no turning back. Crew, prepare for a crash landing if that last engine fails. We're two hours out now over rugged terrain. But if that engine holds, we'll make it there by five o'clock.'"

Roth changed the tone and speed of his voice as he told the story, techniques that drew a person in. He paused, looking from face to face. The old guy looked as if he were going to have a heart attack.

Time for the twist.

Roth leaned forward, licked his lips, and stroked his beard. Glancing outside, he could see they were about to land themselves. The turbulence had stopped. "The engine . . . held. We made it to Denver. Hours late. But we made it. When we landed, I turned to the guy next to me. 'That was the closest I've ever come to dying,' I said. 'Just think if that last engine had failed. Whew.'" Roth couldn't stop the grin. "The guy next to me was so relieved too. 'Yeah,' he said. 'We would have been stuck up there forever!'"

Ba-da-boom!

Suki frowned, folded her arms, and turned away. "That was *so* funny, Dad."

Lucas looked confused. "What? You would have crash-landed! Oh!" Now he got the joke. Each engine failure had caused a delay. So naturally, the final failure would have stranded them in the sky. Counterintuitive. The kind of punchline that Roth loved.

"Was Dad in a plane crash?" Brillante asked, his game over, his eyebrows wrinkled in confusion.

"It was just one of his stories," Sarina said. Roth liked the twinkle in her eyes.

The old guy sitting across from her was shaking his head. "I . . . I really believed you!" he said.

"My husband's an author," Sarina said to him. "He likes telling stories."

The captain made the final announcement before landing. Sarina stuffed her crossword-puzzle book into her bag. He caught a glimpse of her insulin equipment there—the extra cartridges and tubing for the pump, some bagged needles, rubbing alcohol packets, and so forth. The accoutrements of type 1 diabetes. She kept the pump in her pocket, the tube hidden beneath her shirt, and it gave her the exact dosage she needed to control her blood sugar level.

The technology to help diabetics was a lot more user friendly these days. Especially if you could afford it.

"You drank a soda," he told her. "When do you need to replace the cartridge?"

"When we get to the resort," she said. "I changed it two days ago, so I have another day before I need to refill it." She was careful about her sugar, but they were on vacation now. It was time to relax and enjoy life. Strawberry daiquiris from a hammock, that kind of thing. They were supposed to go snorkeling off Cozumel on Christmas Eve and eat fresh ceviche and chips while standing in the water. And what he was looking forward to most: they'd be visiting some of the ancient Maya ruins—now tourist locations—San Gervasio, Tulum, and Chichén Itzá . . . unless the plane broke into a bajillion flaming pieces of twisted metal on the runway at five hundred miles an hour.

He turned his face to the window, watching as the airport in Cancún loomed ever larger.

He watched the little flaps on the wing go up and down. At the back of the wing, a section detached and started to slide down with a mechanical groan. He could see the strange-looking houses and yards between the gaps, all cramped and odd-shaped—each one unique, not carbon-copy groupings of houses like the suburban neighborhoods he'd grown up in. Definitely different from the part of Bozeman where they lived, where the houses were spread far apart, nestled in the hills beneath the mountains, separated by trees and land rather than fences. They'd visited during a trip to Yellowstone for a family reunion a few years previously and had fallen in love with the raw beauty of Montana and the way it coexisted with nicely developed cities like Bozeman. The area was referred to by the locals as Sourdough, after the canyon and creek that provides water for a large portion of its inhabitants. They hadn't learned about the nickname until they'd moved in. As they were from the San Francisco area, "sourdough" had a totally different meaning for them and referred to bread, not a land feature.

Unable to look away from the view of Cancún, he stared, watching the traffic rush by. So many minibuses. Then he saw the runway. His heart was beating fast. Sweat trickled down his brow to be lost in his majestic beard.

Yes, this moment was the worst part of flying—the anticipation of the huge rubber tires meeting the unforgiving concrete.

Once, he'd flown out of San Jose International to attend Emerald City Comic Con in Seattle, his first, and they'd hit some ducks on takeoff. There'd been a noticeable thump, and then the smell of cooked fowl had filled the cabin. Because it had happened at takeoff, the pilot had no choice but to go in a circle and land so that the engines could be inspected. Roth had needed to switch planes, and he'd barely made it to the Washington State Convention Center in time for his panel and book signing. Even though it was his first, there had been quite a crowd waiting for him. That part of the memory brought a smile.

Now it felt like it had happened a long time ago, back when the book had first come out. He'd gone from being an adjunct history professor at a state college in California to a bestselling author overnight.

The distracting thoughts lasted just long enough. The tires hit the runway, and everyone lurched forward against their seat belts as the pilot applied the brakes. Roth was amazed by the physics of slowing down such a massive hunk of metal, wires, and disposable electronics.

The pilot's voice buzzed over the intercom. "On behalf of the flight crew, we'd like to welcome you to Cancún International Airport. It's 85 degrees outside, with late-afternoon clouds. Expect a little rain this afternoon. It's December 23, and local time is 2:37 in the afternoon. We're at Terminal 3. Welcome to Mexico, and thanks for flying with us. We hope you enjoy your stay in Cancún."

Suki had already unclipped her seat belt and stood and stretched. Her metallic-rose earphones hung around her neck. Her short hair would be an asset this week.

"Feeling better?" she asked Lucas.

"Still need to pee," he said, wincing.

"I'll help you find a bathroom once we get off. It's okay."

Roth smiled and gave her a nod of appreciation.

"Dude, you're starting another game?" Lucas demanded of his brother. "Come on. We gotta go!"

Brillante lifted his head from the screen. "Just one more game."

"Once we get to the resort, I want all of you kids to hand over your electronics," Roth said. "We're taking a vacation. We're climbing to the top of Chichén Itzá—if they let us—and visiting Maya ruins. Remember, there will be no cell service where we're staying on Cozumel. It's a *tortuga* sanctuary," he said, displaying his limited Spanish vocabulary.

"Sounds like you said *torture* sanctuary," Suki said with one of her eye rolls. They were practically a work of art.

"The beaches!" Brillante and Lucas said, giving each other a fist bump.

Sarina looked a little tired.

"Are you feeling okay?" Roth asked her.

"Didn't sleep well last night. I'll be okay."

All their luggage was stowed in the overhead bins. Roth didn't trust airline logistics. Each kid had a backpack and a suitcase. That was it.

"It's almost our turn. Let's go. As Grandpa says, 'You snooze, you lose,'" Suki said to her brother Brillante, who had the seat by her. The rows in front of them were nearly clear.

Roth was a little worried about getting from the airport to the island of Cozumel, but the Beasleys had promised the process was simple. They'd made all the arrangements, down to the bus that would take them from the airport to Playa del Carmen, from which they would take the ferry. Another bus would take them to the eastern half of Cozumel, away from the other resorts. The place belonged to Jacob Calakmul, a wealthy tycoon whose family owned many hotels and resorts throughout the Maya Riviera. The Beasleys had already visited it several times, and they'd raved about the amenities. They'd intended to vacation with another family this year, from Texas, but their friends had canceled at the last minute, leaving an opening the Roths had felt grateful to fill.

The invitation to Cozumel really had been too good to refuse.

Although the Roths hadn't known the Beasleys for long, their new neighbors had been surprisingly welcoming. That fact gave Roth some private amusement because there were a copious number of warning signs posted outside their property gate, from "Beware of the Dog" to "Private Drive," "No Trespassing," and a sign bearing an image of a video surveillance system saying "Trespassers Will Be Prosecuted."

Now it was time to relax, unwind, soak up the scenery, and learn more about the ancient civilization that had once occupied the peninsula. It was hard for his mind to relax. His imagination could always conceive the most horrible twists and plot devices to torment his characters. His latest book, the conclusion of a trilogy, had been turned in a week ago.

They all needed some relaxation. He was eager to get off the plane and find the Beasleys, who had flown in the first-class cabin and already deplaned.

He had no idea why a wealthy man like Calakmul was inclined to let the Beasleys and their friends stay with him for free, but the prospect was in no way displeasing.

This was going to be exactly what his family needed.

CHAPTER THREE

CARR TRANSVERSAL

COZUMEL, MEXICO

December 23

Roth startled awake when Sarina shook his shoulder. "We're almost there," she said softly.

He'd been dreaming about the first time they'd gone to the Beasleys' eclectic mansion in their Sourdough neighborhood. The Beasley boys were both into sports and had invited Brillante and Lucas to a game of poison in their indoor basketball court. Their daughter, Jane Louise, was eight and loved dolls and Disney princesses—a phase Suki, who'd always been more drawn toward anime, had never gone through. The invitation to Mexico had come after several months of getting to know each other.

Roth usually suffered from motion sickness too much to fall asleep in a moving vehicle, but the ferry ride from Playa del Carmen to Cozumel had nearly made him heave his guts out. He'd taken a Dramamine, and the heat inside the shuttle that picked them up in San Miguel had made him fall asleep. San Miguel was the main city of the island of Cozumel on the western side of the island, and the resort they were staying at was on the eastern shore.

Rubbing his eyes with the backs of his knuckles, he looked around, disappointed he'd missed most of the drive. The large Mercedes van held both families, and all of their luggage was stacked and crammed in the back. Eric sat next to his wife, Kendall, a skinny blonde who could have been on a Real Housewives episode. From what Roth understood, they'd met and married before Eric made his millions in a private hedge fund after working a few years as a Wall Street banker. It made him wonder whether the money had changed them, or they'd always been like this—sleek and fastidiously well groomed. Their boys were horsing around on different seats across the aisle. Their youngest, Jane Louise, sat next to her mom.

Roth turned his head and saw Suki in a row by herself, pushing her glasses up her nose and giving him a nervous look. She would have preferred spending the holidays back in Montana. But he'd promised that the trip would be very relaxing. Other than a few sight-seeing trips and excursions to the ruins, they'd have a lot of downtime. The twins were on the bench behind her, pointing out the window.

The road led to an isolated part of the island. Roth had looked the resort up on his browser several times prior to leaving. Cozumel was a huge part of the turtle migration, so there was no wired electricity on the eastern part of the island. Everything had to be powered by solar. Cars weren't even allowed to drive on the eastern shores after dark because the headlights could damage a turtle's eyes. The resort was on the northern half of the island near an archaeological preserve that the Calakmul family owned and ran.

Roth pulled out his phone and checked the screen. No bars and the battery had run down to less than half. They were off the grid, just as Eric had promised they would be. It would be good for them all to get away from their screens for a time.

The van stopped at a security gate. Jungle crowded through the fencing, the trees thin and narrow, the trunks speckled. That marked them as a kind of cedar. Because of the dense vegetation, they couldn't see the private resort.

A man with a uniform and automatic weapon hanging from a strap came to the driver's window and spoke to him in Spanish.

Two more guards stood at the gate. All were armed. That made Roth furrow his brow. He'd heard Cozumel was much safer than Cancún. When he'd asked Eric about it, his friend had assured him, saying that the locals resisted drug trafficking, knowing that it would seriously harm the much-needed tourist economy. At least the armed guards were on their side. But the large weapons were intimidating.

"What are they saying?" he whispered to Sarina. Her throat glistened with sweat, and he was sweating profusely himself. The humidity was bearable, but even with the air-conditioning on full blast, it was definitely warmer than what they were used to. And it was December, the coolest time of the year for this part of Mexico.

"I can't hear them very well." The air-conditioning in the van was pretty loud.

The security guard backed up and motioned for the driver to enter the compound while the other two opened the gate. Just inside the gate stood a windowed guardhouse. A mustachioed man, also in a uniform, watched as the van crept in. Roth's eyes met his as the van crept past, and he gave the man a polite nod.

The van lumbered down the long driveway and began to accelerate. Palm trees could be seen out both windows, along with the dense vegetation of the jungle. The fencing and guardhouse quickly disappeared from view.

"Can we play soccer here?" Lucas asked from behind them.

Roth was about to answer that he had no idea, but he realized his son had been talking to one of the Beasley boys.

"There's a *different* game we play down here," answered the teenager.

"Colter," said Eric coldly. There was an unspoken rebuke in his tone.

Roth turned his head and looked at Eric. His eyes were fixed on the road ahead of them. Kendall was looking down at their youngest, who was lying on her mother's lap in the shared seat. A tingle of misgiving worked through Roth when he noticed the fear in her eyes.

As they continued through the compound, passing more jungle, Roth's nerves began to worry him. He didn't know what was setting off his amygdala, but he felt hyperaware of everything around them and watched the bends of the road as if expecting armed men to jump out of the jungle with machetes and machine guns.

"You all right?" Sarina asked in an undertone, squeezing his hand.

She knew when he was out of sorts. All her life, she'd been sensitive to other people's feelings. It made her a great nurse. It was one of the reasons he'd fallen in love with her.

"You know how it is. Even if there's nothing to worry about, I try to find something. I've read that the beaches on this side of the island are more dangerous. There are crocodiles. We need to remind the boys to be careful. No wandering off."

"Okay. We'll tell them."

The jungle opened up, and they finally reached the hidden resort. There were two more Mercedes vans parked in the circular drive, both smaller than the one they were in. Roth looked up at the private resort outside the van window—white and boxy-looking, with so many windows. The van stopped in front of a huge, rectangular pool with an overflow waterfall reflecting the sunlight. Patio cushions, wide and thick, were gathered by the pool, and decorative trees lined the perimeter of the pool yard. Although it was late afternoon, the interior lights were already on.

The driver came around and opened the van door, and the Beasley kids—except for the girl—were already rushing ahead to get out. The smell of a sea breeze met Roth's nose. It was a familiar smell for one who'd grown up not far from the beaches of Santa Cruz.

Roth's nerves began to settle when he saw the resort looked exactly as it had in the photos on its website. He knew behind the resort was a series of planks and stairs that went down to the sea, where there were sitting areas and paddle boards and a view of the yacht that would be part of their transportation for excursions.

He scratched his bearded chin and rose. Sarina edged into the aisle. The back of the van was opened, and workers started to pull out the luggage stacked back there.

"You'll love it here," Eric said, gesturing for Roth and Sarina to leave first. "We're staying on opposite sides of the building. The office is in the middle if you need anything. We'll each have our own kitchens and cooking staff, but there are common areas too. Whatever your kids want to eat, they can get. Just order like it's a restaurant, and the cooks will make it. There's a tiny little town called Ixpalbarco not far from here, so if you need anything, the staff can go pick it up for you."

There was a certain dismissiveness to his words, as if he were saying he'd prefer to keep their vacations separate. Roth didn't mind per se—he *wanted* to unwind with his family—but it was a shift from the way Beasley had spoken of the trip back in Bozeman. Back there, he'd spoken of the things they'd do together. Had Eric and Kendall had some sort of argument before the trip?

"Thank you so much, Eric and Kendall," Sarina said. "It was so generous of you to invite us to join your family for Christmas this year."

Eric flashed them a warm smile. His polo shirt was literally sticking to his massive chest and shoulders. "Like I told you, it's no big deal. Our friends couldn't make it. Glad we could convince you to come on such short notice."

"I haven't been to Cozumel since I was a teenager," Sarina said. "In '97. It was very different back then. My family used to come to Cancún when I was little."

"You tried climbing Chichén Itzá and got scared halfway up," Eric said, nodding. "I remember. Your boys will love it here. But no one can climb the ruins now. Too many tourists."

Suki was ready to get off and gave Roth a look that said, *Keep Mom from talking, or I'll embarrass you both.*

"Let's go," Roth said.

They climbed out of the van, watching as the staff began dragging their luggage toward the spacious, white-walled resort. Roth had some peso bills in his pocket. Tipping was the norm in Mexico, but he wasn't sure how much was proper, and he hadn't seen Eric tip the driver. He offered the driver a hundred-peso bill, but the man held up his hand and shook his head, rejecting the offer. That was unusual, wasn't it?

He tucked the bill away, shrugging it off, and took in the resort. The smell of the ocean hung in the air, and he could hear the sound of crashing waves from the other side of the building. The wind was blowing steadily, but it was a pleasant sensation.

Suki squinted through her glasses and then shrugged as if to say it was no big deal.

"Can we go to the beach?" Brillante asked.

"Let's settle in our rooms first, then you can go," Sarina said.

"Who's the dude?" Suki muttered under her breath.

Roth turned and saw a well-dressed man approaching them. A woman holding an electronic tablet strode next to him. He was probably in his midthirties, with scruff on his face and a full head of dark brown hair that was playfully spiked and arranged. He wore glasses with no frames, or nearly invisible ones, a gray custom-made suit with a silk shirt open at the collar, and fancy leather shoes. He smiled at them, but it was a slightly predatory smile, his head tilted just a little.

"Jacob!" said Eric. The two men embraced each other, and while Eric's size dwarfed the smaller man, there was a health and vitality to the newcomer that made him every bit as intimidating if not more.

"Welcome again, old friend," said the new arrival with a Hispanic accent.

The woman next to him looked to be an assistant. She had bleached-blond hair, or so her dark roots attested, and glasses similar to Suki's, except the frames were dark brown instead of teal. Her lips and face were done up with makeup, and she wore a form-fitting business dress that went down to her knees. She was probably no more than twenty-five years old.

After the two men embraced, the newcomer approached Roth and extended his hand. "Jacob Calakmul. *Bienvenidos*."

Even Roth knew enough Spanish to recognize the greeting.

"Thank you for letting us come," Roth said as he took his hand. "It's been a long day." His hand was bigger than Jacob's, but he sensed the power in the younger man's grip. It took him aback.

"This is my assistant, Angélica," said Jacob. She bowed her head in greeting and shook first Roth's hand and then Sarina's.

"I like your glasses," the woman said to Suki. "If there is anything I can do to make your stay more comfortable, please let me know." She also had an accent, but both of them spoke English flawlessly.

"Do you have a soccer ball?" Brillante asked.

"Not soccer, I'm afraid," said Angélica. "But have you tried snorkeling? There are thousands of different fish just off the docks. And stingrays too!"

"Like in *Finding Nemo*?" Lucas asked.

"Yes. Just like in the movie." She bowed again to the boys. "Welcome to Villa Sara de Calakmul. I hope you enjoy your stay."

Roth's tension began to ebb again. Their greeting had been friendly enough, and the pool looked even more inviting than it had on the web. He recalled seeing pictures of lounge chairs overlooking the sea.

He imagined sitting on one next to Sarina, holding hands and watching their kids play in the ocean while the resort personnel fetched them drinks.

It would be perfect.

Then he saw the Beasleys' daughter, little Jane Louise, standing there gripping her mother's hand, partially concealed behind her. As if she were *trying* to hide from Jacob and Angélica. She looked up at Roth, trembling.

She was terrified.

CHAPTER FOUR

Villa Sara de Calakmul

Cozumel, Mexico

December 23

Jacob Calakmul's office in the resort had huge plate-glass windows that covered nearly every wall, front and back. There were curtains, of course, but he preferred to keep them pulled back to let in the sunlight and display the scenery. A glass door led to the helicopter pad behind the estate and provided a view of the beach. His yacht was anchored in the distance.

The tabletop of his desk was made of wood salvaged from a Maya ruin in the biosphere controlled by his family. Two square metal frames—black—supported the hefty and ancient piece of lumber.

The door to the interior hallway opened, and Angélica entered with her tablet, trailed by the intoxicating scent of her perfume—the subtle fragrance of star jasmine. He pushed aside his laptop as she passed behind him. The air seemed to prickle with tension.

Angélica came around the front of the desk and then sat on top of it, crossing her legs, the tablet cradled in one hand while she tapped the screen.

She turned to face him, her tan business dress fitting her just right, her hair coming down on each side of her face. She was so beautiful, but he kept his expression disinterested.

"Are the families settled?" he asked.

"The Beasleys are in their normal suite. Their boys are already heading to the beach. The daughter isn't feeling well. She's with Kendall. Eric wants to see you."

"Make him wait," Jacob said. "What about the Roths? Do they suspect anything?"

"Not a thing. Their twins are heading to the beach too. The daughter is wandering around inside. I don't think she likes the heat."

"She won't enjoy the heat at the temple on the mainland," Jacob said with a chuckle. "You made sure no signal could reach their devices?"

"Of course. I sent a remote text after they reached security and another one when they drove up. The signal bounced. They're out of range of the cell phone towers in San Miguel."

"Their last transmissions to family back home?"

"From the airport saying they arrived. A picture from the airplane if you want to see it."

Jacob shook his head. "The financials? Are the asset transfers ready to go?"

"All is in order, Mr. Calakmul. All of their assets, including the new Denali, are registered under the Roth family trust. All of Mr. Roth's royalties are going into the business checking account." She tapped the screen again, her brow furrowing. "For an author, he's doing very well. The royalties fluctuate from month to month, but they are consistently high."

Jacob leaned back in his chair. "What's the name of the man, the accountant, who will control the assets for the trust?"

Her nose wrinkled slightly in concentration as she switched to another screen. He knew the answer. His memory was prodigious, but he liked testing her to see how quickly she could get information. She was one of the recipients of the Calakmul family scholarship, bestowed on promising students pursuing careers in fields that might prove useful to the family. Angélica had master's degrees in computational and mathematical engineering and Latin American studies from Stanford University. She was brilliant, ambitious, and loyal.

"Bryant Westfall. CPA at Olsen-Westfall in Eagle, Idaho. He's a partner."

"He and Mr. Roth were friends at Kennedy High School in Fremont, California. Is that very far from Stanford?" He tilted his head slightly as he asked.

"Depends on traffic," Angélica answered, tilting her head to match his angle. "Fremont is on the opposite side of the bay. The two friends grew up in California, and both of them relocated out of state."

"Westfall left first for the CPA job. Mr. Roth stayed to teach at his university. They remain close, though. They trust each other."

"So it seems."

"Mr. Westfall has a wife and family."

"Yes."

Jacob thought a moment, stroking the scruff on his chin. "A car accident on Christmas Eve should do. It can happen on the way to work. Make sure the accountant is out of the equation by tomorrow night. Then position a buyout of Olsen-Westfall."

Angélica pursed her lips. "What if they win?"

"It doesn't matter. We can't have people asking questions."

"Very well. It will be done."

Jacob gave her a measured smile. "Thank you. That is all."

She slid off the desk, smoothed the wrinkles from her skirt in an unnecessarily provocative way, and then came around behind his chair.

He could feel the warmth of her through the thin fabric of the business dress.

"Is there anything else I can do for you, Mr. Calakmul?" she asked in a soft-pitched voice. The offer tantalized him. She was doing it on purpose, to test his self-control. Her interest in him was based on a total fabrication, of course. She saw him as a young widower, a man who'd lost his wife and young child in a tragic accident.

It was all part of the illusion he wrapped around himself. He never wanted anyone to look too closely, to delve too deeply.

He could feel her breath against his hair. She was still leaning in, inviting him, *coaxing* him. He looked at the jade ring on the smallest finger of his left hand.

"Yes," he said.

She leaned against the desk, right next to him, her eyes shining behind the round glasses.

Google had tried to recruit Angélica after she finished her master's degrees. He'd encouraged her to interview for a job there, a grueling process that had required multiple exhausting rounds. But she'd turned down the position to work for the Calakmul family.

That tech company had *no* idea who really controlled the world.

Her eyebrows lifted invitingly. Pinning her tablet to her chest with one hand, she lowered the other to the desktop, right next to his . . . but not touching. He felt the energy of that proximity, but still he did not give in. Not yet.

"Where is that plane that flew into the biosphere? I want to know who the pilot was and why he was flying over my land."

"I am trying, Mr. Calakmul. There were no scheduled flights at that time, and they were flying below radar. It might have been a drug plane from a cartel."

"Would they cross me? They know the rules."

"The only other registered flight anywhere nearby was for an archaeologist from Guatemala."

"Who?"

"He was making runs with the LiDAR equipment over El Mirador. They flew out of La Libertad. They were asked if they crossed the border, but both denied it."

He rubbed his palm over the rippled wood top of the desk, adorned with ancient Maya carvings. His desk was three thousand years old—and so was the magic that had frightened away the aircraft.

Their eyes met. "I want MS-13 in Guatemala to interrogate the pilot. And his family." He looked at her dispassionately. He preferred killing Americans, because they controlled the majority of the international financial scene—frankly, it was a monopoly—but he had no qualms about dispatching anyone who stood in the way of the prophecy's fulfillment. Still, he'd spare the man for now. Most people would reveal anything if their loved ones were threatened, and he didn't want to draw attention from the Americans. Not yet.

"No one intrudes on my ancestral lands without my permission. Ever."

CHAPTER FIVE

Villa Sara de Calakmul

Cozumel, Mexico

December 23

"Dad, this place has serious *Promised Neverland* vibes," Suki announced from the doorway to the living space.

Roth and Sarina turned to look at her at the same time. Sarina had just emerged from the master bathroom, where she'd put on her bathing suit and a cover-up. The door stood open, and he could see her insulin pump on the counter. The pump was a neat piece of technology, something that shouldn't be down at the beach. She must've found a sun hat in the closet because she certainly hadn't crammed one into her luggage.

"*Promised Neverland?*" Sarina said with a confused expression.

Suki looked at her and then back at Roth and sighed. "I'm not joking."

"I don't even know what that means," Sarina apologized.

Roth understood. "It's an anime series. I watched the first season with her, but it hadn't been dubbed in English yet, so we had to read the subtitles."

"We'll watch the English version when we get back," Suki said. She'd changed out of her travel clothes and into a pink tank top with some Japanese characters from another anime over brown shorts. But her expression was serious. "Dad, I'm not kidding. I'm getting the worst vibes from this place."

"Can one of you explain the *Promised Neverland* reference, please?" Sarina asked.

Roth didn't think of Suki as dramatic, though she enjoyed being in the theater arts at Gallatin High. Not as a performer. She loved the tech side of theater—the lights, sound, costumes, and stagecraft.

"Come in and shut the door," Roth said.

Suki slouched away from the doorjamb and then shut the door behind her.

The resort was pristine. The master bedroom had a king-sized bed with white sheets, a tapestry-like throw blanket folded at the base, and a fluffy stack of pillows. A wicker bench and footrest sat in the corner by the wall-length windows and door leading to a veranda, where the greenery of the jungle trees added to the mystique of the place. The air conditioner, mounted high on the wall, was quiet and efficient and glowed with the number 20, tracking the temperature in Celsius.

Sarina folded her arms, looking worriedly at their daughter.

"Since Dad has already seen it, I'll just summarize it quickly," Suki said. "It's about an orphanage with really smart kids. Everything looks perfect. Everyone *seems* happy, but the kids keep going away to get adopted, and they never come back to visit or are heard from again." She looked at Roth, since they both knew the secret revealed in the first episode, which was, in Roth's professional view, a deliciously clever and macabre twist.

"Honey," Sarina said. "I think your imagination is working overtime."

"She's not the only one who felt a weird vibe," Roth said to his wife. "The Beasleys' little girl did too. Did you see the way she reacted when we met the owner? She was terrified of him."

"I noticed that too," Suki agreed, nodding for emphasis.

Sarina looked confused. "I didn't, sorry. I was too busy noticing him and his assistant. If you ask me, there's definitely some office romance going on between those two. That was the only *vibe* I felt when we got here. It's a beautiful place. Very quiet and secluded. It's just like the Beasleys said it would be."

Roth scratched the back of his neck. Was his imagination playing tricks on him as well? "The guards at the gate had automatic weapons."

"This is Mexico," Sarina replied.

"Mom, I'm not overreacting," Suki objected. "I've been wandering around the halls. There are so few people here. The servants hardly speak at all. And the decorations are super creepy."

Roth had noticed the decorations—obsidian swords hanging from the walls, jade artwork, replicas of Maya masks. He'd thought they were kind of cool.

Sarina was sympathetic, but her tone was unconcerned. "Maybe you should go outside and play on the beach with your brothers. We're in a new place. Your anxiety—both of yours—is flaring up because we're somewhere new."

"I'm not like Dad," Suki said defensively. "I don't feel right here."

Roth knew his overactive imagination could make him ruminate about nonexistent threats and dangers. For his books, he was always looking for new ways to torment his characters, so his mind naturally went to dark places. It was an impulse he was trying to rein in. He held up his hands. "Do you really think the Beasleys invited us to Cozumel at Christmastime for some twisted reason? They vacation here every year."

"Woo-hoo for them," Suki shot back. "I wish we were back home."

"Let's just take a deep breath," Sarina said. "I can see you're upset."

But Roth's gut was starting to churn again. He rubbed his forehead. "It's not like Suki to freak out over nothing."

His teenage daughter folded her arms. "Well, I'm definitely freaking out, Dad."

He sighed and glanced at his wife. "What do we do?"

Sarina gave him a look that suggested he was being unreasonable. "Look, I'm going to go read a book, watch the boys play and snorkel, and *relax*." She picked up her book, grabbed a towel from the rack in the bathroom, and started toward the glass door leading to the veranda.

After opening it, she stopped because the twins were marching up toward the door. One of them was holding his nose, blood dripping from his hand.

She went into nurse mode instantly, tossing down the book and using her own towel to help apply pressure to Lucas's nosebleed. The boys' swim trunks were dripping, and sand stuck to their legs and feet. It rattled Roth's nerves to see them tracking sand into the pristine room.

"What happened?" Sarina asked. She ushered Lucas to the wicker bench and had him sit down.

"Shouldn't you elevate his legs?" Roth asked.

She gave him the nurse look again. "That would make the bleeding worse. What happened?"

Brillante looked upset. Almost in tears.

"What happened?" Roth pressed, not liking any part of this.

"It was Colter," Brillante said.

Sarina and Roth exchanged a look. Colter was the Beasleys' oldest son.

"What did he do?" Roth asked quietly.

"He and his brother were playing with a weird ball," Bryant said. "A lot heavier than a soccer ball. They were hitting it with their hips. Bouncing it on their knees. They were acting kinda sus."

"How did Lucas get hurt?"

"I wanna teb them," Lucas said with his pinched-nose voice.

"Dude, you're hurt. I'll tell them."

Roth's stomach twisted even more. "What happened?"

"Lucas asked what they were doing and if we could play too. I wanted to keep swimming, but I went with him. Colter said that we couldn't play the game yet. That we'd play on Christmas. It was weird. So was the look he gave us, like he hated us or something. Then he shoved the ball into Lucas's face. It's made of rubber, but it's *hard*. Did it break his nose?"

Sarina pulled the bloodstained towel away and examined Lucas's nose. "No, I don't think so." She sighed, her expression darkening with the news. "You kids go to your room and clean up."

"It hurts," Lucas whined.

"I'll get you some Tylenol." Sarina headed into the open bathroom and grabbed a small tin of medicine from one of her travel bags. She gave two pills to Lucas, who plopped them into his mouth and took a drink from a bottle of water sitting on the nightstand.

The boys left, not as exuberant as they'd been. Suki stood to the side with folded arms, giving her parents an *I told you so* look.

"Go to your room too," Sarina told her. "Dad and I need to talk."

"I think we should get out of here," Suki said forcefully, adding in a mumbled aside, *"Annoyed insistence."*

Sarina nodded to her, accepting her feelings, and then waited until she left. The kids' rooms were right next door to theirs.

Sarina shut the door and leaned against it, the sun hat folding against her forehead. She sighed again. Then she looked at Roth with a flash of anger. "I don't like what Colter did. Lucas's nose *is* broken."

"But you said—?"

"I know. I don't want the kids worrying any more than they already are. I need to set his nose so it'll heal properly." She looked upset. "What do we do, Jonny? We just got here."

Roth felt his chin itch. His mind was already working. "Kids are jerks to each other," he acknowledged.

"They were pleasant enough at the Beasleys' home."

"True. Why would they change once we got here? Doesn't make for a very pleasant Christmas break." A memory rose to the surface of Roth's mind. His eyes widened. "Remember the ride over? Colter said something about *another* game."

Sarina wrinkled her brow. "I vaguely remember that."

"Now I'm starting to get the *Promised Neverland* vibe too. It wasn't just what he said but *how* he said it. They were using the ball with their hips and knees. Doesn't that sound familiar to you?"

Sarina considered for a moment. "The Maya ball game. It was a huge part of the culture down here. Like soccer is today."

"Yeah, the game that everyone thinks is impossible to play. No hands. No feet. You have to knock a heavy rubber ball high up on a stone wall through a hoop that is barely larger than the ball itself. It's not a sport. It's insane!"

"Any sport is confusing to someone who doesn't get all the rules," she said calmly. "Like offside in soccer."

"But they don't *kill* the losing team in soccer. I remember learning about the Maya games—in fifth grade, I think? The losing side was sacrificed to the gods."

Sarina shook her head. "Jonny . . . do you honestly believe these people want to sacrifice us to the gods?"

Roth's nerves were jangling fiercely. "Look, maybe my imagination is going haywire. But Suki too? That's not like her."

"She's an introvert. She didn't even want to come."

"But she did. And she hasn't complained until now. Maybe there's a logical explanation for all of this, but I'm sufficiently creeped out to want to test the theory."

"Test what theory? I'm not getting it."

"Either this is a calm Christmas vacation, or it's something totally sus, like Brillante said."

That was a reference to *Among Us*, a popular mafia-like game teenagers were playing on their phones. "Sus" was slang for *suspicious* behavior—the player who was murdering the others on the spacecraft.

"Maybe I should take Lucas to the nearest hospital," she said.

Roth stared at his wife. "Let's all go."

"What are you going to do? Go ask Eric if his family is planning to carve out our hearts?"

"That would be brash. But no. That's also weird." He paused. "This place is a secure compound. There are three vans, and did you see the helicopter? I saw it out the windows by the office area."

"You want to steal a van, Jonny?" Sarina asked doubtfully.

"Not steal it. Borrow it. With permission. Let's see if they let us leave. That'll test our theory that something's up without calling attention to our concerns."

"And we would go . . . ? To a hospital in San Miguel?"

"Why not? Will they say no? We have the perfect pretext to leave *right now*. Our son broke his nose. We won't even say how. We'll ask to borrow the van and take him to urgent care, or whatever they have here. Tell them he needs an X-ray."

"A nose is made of cartilage."

"We'll just *say* he needs an X-ray. They'll believe you because you're a nurse. But that's not the point."

"What about our luggage?"

"We go as we are," Roth said. "Can we leave? That's the question. If they let us go to urgent care and back, then it's nothing. A misunderstanding. If they don't let us go . . . ?" He shrugged.

Sarina started pacing, her sandals clicking on the tile floor. Roth's stomach was still churning, but now that he'd thought of a plan, he felt good about it. Any normal parent would be concerned for their kids, especially an injured one. If they were forbidden to leave the Calakmul resort under such circumstances, then he'd have to come up with a plan to escape during the night. That might involve "borrowing" one of the vans. Or maybe they could follow the beach south until they passed the property line. They could reach a different resort along the coast. Sarina was fluent in Spanish. They'd get by.

Roth went to the nightstand where he'd plugged in his phone. He checked the screen and saw the battery was still low. There was no cell service.

No cell service.

He'd been warned about that, of course, but it no longer felt like a positive thing. The clenching feeling in his stomach increased. He glanced at his wife.

Her expression matched his.

"Come on," he said. "Let's give it a try. See what happens."

———

Roth and Sarina headed to the resort offices to look for the assistant they'd met earlier. Only . . . the offices were directly in the middle, but they somehow bypassed them entirely and found themselves entering the Beasleys' side of the complex. How had he managed that?

"I swear, I'd get lost in a public bathroom," Roth said, turning around, confused by the corridors. "I thought the offices were supposed to be in the middle?"

"Did we make a wrong turn?" Sarina asked. She approached a wall with some framed photos on it. Most of the decor they'd seen had been old artifacts stored in glass display cases—rubber balls, obsidian swords, spear tips, and—in one case—a flat stone with a glyph on it.

"Looks like people," Roth commented. "First photos I've seen around here."

"What was the last name of the family the Beasleys usually come with?" Sarina asked. She had a curious look in her eyes.

"Um . . . Reynolds?"

41

"Yeah. Here's a picture of the Reynoldses from last year. There's a date on the frame. But the Beasleys aren't in any of the photos." She went from one to another.

Roth joined her, looking at the display. Each photo was of a different family. One was from Texas—the Reynoldses. Another from Bozeman. One from Connecticut. The oldest one was dated 2012.

"I thought they came here every year?" Roth said, wrinkling his brow. He felt a prickle of nerves, although there was nothing overtly odd about keeping photographs of old guests. But according to the Beasleys, they *had* been there.

Sarina shrugged. "That's odd. Let's go find the offices."

They backtracked and easily found them, which made him wonder how they'd gone wrong before. Jacob Calakmul's assistant was talking to Kendall Beasley and the little girl, Jane Louise, farther down one of the decorated halls. The woman had lowered herself down to be at eye level with the little girl.

Kendall looked up at them as they approached, and Roth thought he detected a flicker of animosity in her eyes.

Paranoid. He was probably being paranoid. It made him feel better, at least, that he was doing something about it. He'd be happier than anyone if he were proven wrong.

"Are you sure there isn't anything I can get for you, honey?" the assistant asked brightly. "Some ice cream? What's your favorite flavor? They have mango, chocolate . . . ? What do you like?"

"No, thank you," said the little girl with a sniffle.

"Stop it," Kendall said impatiently. "I don't know what's gotten into her. She won't play outside with her brothers."

The assistant gave Kendall a sympathetic glance and patted Jane Louise's shoulder. "I'm sorry you're upset, *mija*." She turned her head back to look at Roth and Sarina, her blond hair swishing. Getting to her feet, she gave them an encouraging smile.

Jane Louise looked at Roth and started to tremble.

"If you're going to be like this, you can do it in your room," Kendall said sharply. She tugged her daughter's hand and led her away.

Roth had never really liked Eric's wife. She'd always been friendly enough on the surface, but she was a shallow conversationalist. Sarina was an excellent listener, and even she had struggled with Kendall's aloofness and her constant bragging about her children's accomplishments. Especially the boys'.

"Is there something I can help you with?" the assistant asked brightly.

They'd agreed that Sarina would be the one to ask. "My son broke his nose down by the beach," she said.

The assistant's expression instantly shifted to one of concern. "I'm so sorry! What happened?"

Roth watched her closely, trying to judge her sincerity. She either meant what she'd said or was a good actress.

"The kids were just horsing around," Sarina said lightly, trying to make nothing of it. "I'm a nurse, and I think it needs an X-ray. I'm so sorry for the inconvenience, but can we borrow one of the vans and take him into town? Is there a little hospital or something nearby, or are they all in San Miguel?"

The assistant's brow lowered. Her reaction seemed more wary than worried.

"All the hospitals are in San Miguel," she said. "I'll send for a doctor to come here. I can have one here in an hour or two. Would that work?"

Sarina looked at Roth, then shook her head. "I'd feel better if he had an X-ray, and a doctor can't bring the machines. It would save time if we could go there ourselves."

Roth added, "We don't want to inconvenience your staff. My wife speaks Spanish, and I used to drive vans like those. We'll go and come right back."

The assistant looked perplexed. "I'm so sorry. I'll have to ask Mr. Calakmul first. Insurance. You know how it is."

"Thank you. We really don't want to be any trouble," Sarina said.

"Not at all. I'm so sorry for your son. The boys are so cute. I love their curly hair. I imagine having twins wasn't easy."

It was something they'd heard several times after they found out Sarina was pregnant with them. Roth shrugged, and they stood there as the assistant turned and walked away. Her high heels tapped against the tiles as she approached a door painted black.

"What do you think?" Sarina asked in a low voice.

"Her response was . . . sus."

"Are we doing *Among Us* now or going back to *Promised Neverland*?"

"Both."

They watched the assistant open the door. Roth could hear her voice. Beyond her, he could see Mr. Calakmul sitting at a desk in front of an open laptop, sunlight glinting off his rimless glasses. Roth's heart was pounding double time as he waited for the outcome.

The conversation was over in moments.

The assistant came back, smiling at them.

"Of course you can borrow one of the vans if you'd like. Mr. Calakmul is sorry your son is hurt. He'll pay for the hospital bill. Just tell the admitting person you are from here, and you won't need to use insurance or pay for anything."

"That's very generous," Sarina said. "Thank you."

The answer was not what Roth had been expecting. His gut began to unclench. Maybe he had been wrong about the resort.

Or was Mr. Calakmul a man who thought three steps ahead too?

CHAPTER SIX

Villa Sara de Calakmul

Cozumel, Mexico

December 23

The tires of the Mercedes Sprinter van crunched on sand and gravel as Roth pulled away from the resort. When he was in college, he'd earned decent money—for a student—driving wine tours in Napa Valley. So he really was comfortable driving the fourteen-seater van.

"Why are we going to the hospital?" Lucas asked again in confusion. He still had that stuffy-nose sound. The swelling of his nose was more pronounced.

Sarina was in the front passenger's seat, her brow knotted with concern. "I think your nose is broken. But that's not why we're going."

"We're getting out of here," Suki said. "Are we going back to Cancún?"

"Maybe," Roth said. "First thing's first. We wanted to take care of Lucas. If the Beasley boys are jerks again tomorrow, we won't go on the snorkeling trip. Maybe we'll take off early while they're gone. Stay at one of the resorts in Cancún. There's no reason for us to have an unpleasant vacation."

"How would we leave the island?" Suki asked. "We don't have a boat."

"The ferry goes back and forth all day," Sarina explained. "We can buy tickets when we need them. It's not like flying an airplane where you need reservations."

Roth looked at his family in the rearview mirror as he maneuvered down the narrow road. The road to the main gate was only a mile or two away, with dense jungle on either side.

"I'm still surprised Mr. Calakmul let us go," Roth said to Sarina.

She nodded. "They were acting weird. But they let us leave. That's something."

"I still don't like the vibe there," Suki said.

Roth's mind was evaluating the situation fast. He wanted to talk it through to make sure he wasn't missing anything. "One thing I didn't think about is they could try to stop us at the gate," he said. "What if they don't let us leave the compound?"

"They will. We have Mr. Calakmul's permission."

"What if they don't? Should we take them up on their offer to bring a doctor here?"

"That would be a good move on our part. We can try to scope out another way to leave." He answered his own question and then thought a moment before adding, "I fell asleep on the way here. How far is San Miguel?"

"Thirty minutes," Sarina answered.

"Not if Dad gets us lost," Suki said.

"You're not helping," Sarina said, turning to look at her. Lucas and Brillante were in the first row of seats, and Suki sat alone behind them.

Roth heard his wife gasp.

"What?" he asked, looking in the rearview mirror.

That's when he saw Jane Louise peeking out from behind the very back row.

Roth slammed the brakes, then remembered his kids might not be wearing seat belts, so he released it and gently hit the gas.

"Whoa! Dad!" Suki yelped.

Brillante flew forward but caught himself. Lucas smashed into the back of Roth's seat. "Dad!"

Suki looked furious. "What the actual heck?"

Roth brought the van to a gentler stop this time, his heart thumping wildly, then put it in park and turned in his seat. Jane Louise had ducked out of sight. Sarina unbuckled her belt and hurried down the aisle to the back of the Sprinter. Leaving the engine running so the AC would keep working, Roth disconnected his seat belt and started to follow his wife.

"Um, you know you two are acting super weird, right?" Suki said.

Roth looked at Lucas, who was holding his nose with his hand again and had a pained look in his eyes.

"Sorry," Roth apologized, then made his way back. He still couldn't believe what he'd seen in the mirror.

Sarina crouched by the girl, her voice comforting. "Sweetie, why are you in the van?"

The girl looked at Roth as he approached, then shifted her attention back to Sarina. "I wanted to go with you," she said, sniffling.

Roth was dumbfounded. He didn't even know what to say. The last he'd remembered, Kendall was taking the child to her room. When had she climbed into the van? Why?

"Go where?"

"Back *home*," Jane Louise said in anguish.

Suki came down the aisle, pushing up her glasses.

"We're only going to the hospital," Sarina said.

The girl shook her head. "You need to go *home. Now.*"

Sarina shot Roth a worried look before giving the girl her attention again. "Why?"

The girl's eyes were bright with fear. "They're going to hurt you."

The words felt like a blow to Roth's stomach. The calming feeling he'd experienced leaving the compound had shifted to dread.

He put his hand on the top of the seat and looked down at her. "*Who* is going to hurt us?"

Jane Louise frowned and began to sob.

Sarina hugged the girl and stroked her hair. Roth felt the moments ticking past, his sense of fear and anxiety ratcheting higher and higher. A family vacation in Mexico for Christmas. It was supposed to be an adventure, a celebration of their successes, but it had all gone wrong. Suki was right. Getting out of there was their only course. He began to consider their options.

"It's okay, shhh, it's okay," Sarina whispered to the little girl. She was so good with kids, always had been.

Roth was deeply conflicted. His brain was screaming at him that they needed to run. Like—literally. Run into the jungle. Disappear. But what about the Beasleys' daughter? Was it right to ditch her with the van? She was just a little kid.

He squeezed the seat cushion, watching the girl cry and hoping she'd calm down enough to talk.

When Jane Louise lifted her head, Sarina gave her a broad smile and wiped the tear tracks from her cheeks.

"It's going to be okay. Do your parents know what's going on?"

The girl nodded yes.

"Do they know you know?"

She shook her head no, her bottom lip wobbling.

Rage began to flame inside Roth's heart. The Beasleys had knowingly brought them into some sort of ambush. They'd done it deliberately. Eric Beasley was a bigger and stronger man, no denying that, but in that moment, Roth was mad enough that he imagined knocking the guy out with a single punch.

"How did you find out they were going to hurt us?"

"I heard Daddy talking to Mr. Calakmul on the phone," Jane Louise said. She blinked and wiped her nose. "I was going to his office to kiss him good night. I was on tiptoes. He didn't hear me."

"What did you hear?" Sarina coaxed.

"Daddy said . . . he said . . . we'd get your money after you were dead. All of it."

Roth stared at her in disbelief. His estate attorney was the one who'd introduced them to the Beasleys after they'd updated their living trust upon moving to Bozeman. It sickened him to think of what might have led to that moment.

"Your daddy's already rich," Sarina said, then looked up at Roth with horror in her eyes. "Richer than us."

Jane Louise sniffled. "He said . . . I heard Mr. Calakmul say . . . on the phone . . . that it would look like an accident. He said . . . he said they *always* make the matches look like an accident."

The heavy rubber ball. The Maya ruins. The injury to Lucas.

Nearly every Mesoamerican culture had its own variation of the ball game. They used different names for it. But the history Roth had studied before coming on this trip, one of his rabbit-hole searches into Wikipedia, had revealed the same story over and over. It was a fierce competition, and it always ended with death for the losing side.

He couldn't believe what he was hearing.

The Calakmuls were a prestigious, wealthy family. Why risk that to mess with a family of tourists? Money couldn't be the motivation since both the Calakmuls and Beasleys had plenty of it. So why?

His mind darted to the display he and Sarina had stumbled onto within the resort—the framed photos, each marked with the year, of different families. Could they be . . . were they the winners? But no . . .

the Beasleys had insisted they'd come before, and they'd clearly survived. He was probably jumping to conclusions again.

Still, there wasn't good reason to doubt the little girl's trustworthiness. She'd clearly been traumatized by what she'd heard back in Bozeman. There were the other signs too. The weird looks he'd noticed. The attack on Lucas. The strange undercurrents he and Suki had picked up on.

"We have to get away from Cozumel," Roth whispered to Sarina. He couldn't see out the back of the vehicle from his position in the aisle, but he dreaded the idea that another van was already on the way.

The guards at the gate wouldn't let them through. Roth was certain Mr. Calakmul had already called ahead with a pretext for turning them around. And if they went back to the resort, he would be watching them day and night. For all he knew, there were cameras planted throughout the place.

"Jonny, we can't leave with her in the van," Sarina said.

"Just take me home," Jane Louise pleaded. "I want to go home. I want my mee-maw."

Roth knuckled his forehead.

"Who's your mee-maw? Your grandmother?"

Jane Louise nodded and started sniffling again.

Stolen van. Kidnapping. Did Mr. Calakmul know the girl had slipped into the van? Had he allowed it? Or had he planted the girl there?

Roth had to know. "Does your mom know you're here?" he asked her.

Jane Louise shook her head. "I heard you were going to the hospital, so I snuck out the glass door and went around to the front of the resort. I saw the driver bring the van closer and leave the door open."

"Did anyone see you?" Sarina asked.

Jane Louise shrugged. "I'm good at hide-and-seek."

So it was unlikely Calakmul knew about this unless he'd seen it on security cameras or something. Roth wiped a trickle of sweat from his temple.

Sarina stood and took the little girl's hand. "What do we do?" she asked Roth in an undertone.

He gazed out the windshield, seeing nothing but road and jungle. "We can't trust the police. They're probably in on it, or they might be persuaded to turn a blind eye. We need to reach—I don't know, the American embassy or a place like that. The consulate? I don't remember what it's called."

"Is there one nearby?"

Roth shrugged. "I'd look it up, but we don't have cell service." He grimaced in frustration.

"I doubt there's something like that on Cozumel," Sarina said.

"We've got to get off this island."

"The ferry?"

Roth nodded and knuckled his forehead again. "I need to call Moretti," he said. His best friends from high school were Bryant Westfall and Will Moretti. The three of them had always called each other by their last names, like they were part of a law firm or something. Bryant Westfall was Roth's CPA. Will Moretti was in law enforcement, on an anti–drug trafficking team in Salt Lake City. He had connections, political and in law enforcement. He could help them.

Sarina wrinkled her brow. "Will's in Utah. He can't do much for us."

"Moretti would fly down here *tonight* if he knew we were in trouble," Roth said. "He'd help us."

Sarina nodded and sighed. "We can't leave her in the van, Jonny," she repeated. "If we take her with us, we'll be charged with kidnapping."

"Unless we get to the embassy first and explain the situation. She snuck out. We can pretend we were none the wiser until we parked the van. If they have video cameras at the compound, which they *have* to have, the footage will verify our story. Once we're safe, we can contact her grandmother."

Roth glanced at the little girl, whose eyes were glassy and bloodshot. She was a Beasley, and he resented that. But the secret she'd revealed might just save them.

He looked back and saw Bryant, Lucas, and Suki staring at him with terror-stricken eyes. They'd gathered in the row of seats closest to them and were watching him silently. They'd clearly heard the whole story.

"So we're ditching the van?" Suki asked firmly.

Roth realized there was no other way and nodded. "It's about ten to fifteen miles to San Miguel. We'll have to spend the night in the jungle, but we can get there on foot tomorrow."

"They'll be watching the ferry," Sarina said.

Roth nodded. "We'll have to hire a boat. Like from a snorkeling tour or something. There are tons on this island. I've got pesos *and* an ATM card."

"So we're not getting our stuff back, are we?" Brillante said disconsolately.

Sarina ruffled his curly mop of hair and then kissed him. "No, *hijo*."

"Um . . . what about food?" Lucas asked.

"There's food in the jungle," Sarina said. "Bananas, avocados, guavas, sapodillas."

"I was kinda hoping for Chick-fil-A," Lucas said with a pout, then he smirked.

Wild fruit trees. Deadly snakes. Weren't there crocodiles in Cozumel? Jaguars? Roth couldn't remember if he'd read that or not. Bats maybe? His imagination was not enjoying the detour.

"That's all fruit. What's Mom going to eat?" Suki said worriedly.

Roth stopped, blinking. He turned to Sarina. "Did you bring your insulin pump?"

The panicked look on his wife's face revealed that she thought she'd left it back at the resort too. They hadn't heard the alarm go off, but she would have set it to "Vibrate" when she took off the pump to go down to the beach. She pulled off her sling purse and unzipped it. There was the pump inside. She let out a sigh and then reattached the tubing to the infusion site in her abdomen and tapped "Resume Delivery."

"We're good," she breathed in relief.

CHAPTER SEVEN

Villa Sara de Calakmul

Cozumel, Mexico

December 23

Jacob Calakmul had no smartphone—they were too easy to track by international law enforcement. They were also addictive, manipulative, and symbolic of the decadence of the modern age now dominated by trillion-dollar tech companies. He relied on his office phone, although it rang rarely enough. Usually a call suggested a problem, and everyone knew Jacob preferred solutions to problems. He saw the flashing light from the secure line at the guardhouse an instant before the subtle chirp of the phone sounded.

"Yes," he said after picking it up.

"Mr. Calakmul, they abandoned the van."

Victor and his family had worked for the Calakmuls for generations. They were loyal, discreet, and ambitious—traits that had been valued in the warrior caste for thousands of years of Mesoamerican history. Jacob rewarded them well for it.

His brow furrowed. "After they left the gate?"

"They never reached the gate. We were monitoring their progress on the GPS software, and it just stopped. I thought they might have been having car trouble, but the tracking software said everything was functioning. I sent a team on ATVs to see if they needed help. The family was gone. They left the engine running."

Jacob stood from his chair, planting his palm on the rippled wood of the Maya desk. Surprise was an emotion he rarely felt. He took off his glasses, set them on the desktop, then pinched the bridge of his nose. Flames of anger rose within him.

"Let me be sure I understand you, Victor. They stopped the van, got out, and went into the jungle?"

"Maybe they saw a coati or another animal and wanted to follow it?"

That was an idiotic statement, but Jacob wasn't the kind of man who ripped apart his loyal staff. He heard the engine of the helicopter roar to life, a noisy sound that always echoed through the whole complex. Turning, he saw the rotors beginning to spin outside his window.

"Did you tell Angélica this?" Jacob asked in a measured voice.

"Of course. She's the first one I called."

"Thank you, Victor. You did well. Find the family. It'll be night soon. Bring them back before they draw attention."

"Yes, Mr. Calakmul." The line clicked and then died.

Jacob squeezed the handset in his fist and then set it back down on its cradle. His gaze shifted to the display wall decorated with various artifacts that had been discovered during excavations in the preserve. An ancient *macuahuitl* sword hung there, the polish of the flat paddle part decorated with glyphs. Squares of razor-sharp obsidian nested along the edge. Back in the day, it might have been used to decapitate a charging horse or the Spaniard riding it. But his gaze skated off it and settled on the caucho-rubber ball resting on a round metal stand. Balls like this one had been used throughout the continent in the death games. The ball was heavy enough he could have smashed the window of his office with it. He was angry enough that he wanted to.

He stifled the impulse and left his office, knowing he'd find Angélica and the pilot at the helicopter. She was the only other person on the compound who had the authority to fire it up.

Before he reached the outer door, Angélica came in, her blond hair mussed by the wind from the helicopter blades. As always, she had her tablet gripped firmly against her chest. When she saw him coming intently her way, a look of guilt flashed in her eyes behind the sheen of her glasses.

"Victor told me the Roths are gone," he said, trying to keep the anger from throbbing in his voice. He failed. She flinched.

"I . . . I didn't want to bring you a problem, Mr. Calakmul. I've asked the pilot to fly over the jungle and conduct a search."

Jacob squeezed his hand into a fist. "They won't be able to see through the trees."

"I know. But I wanted to do everything I could. Victor is already sending men into the jungle."

Jacob appreciated her taking ownership of the situation, but he was still angry that she hadn't come directly to him *first*. Guests did not run away from *his* resorts.

"Did you look at the security-camera footage?" he asked her.

Her eyes widened. "There aren't cameras between the gate and the resort. Their luggage is still in their rooms."

"Of course it is," he snapped. Mr. Roth was no fool. In fact, he was turning out to be surprisingly cunning. Had the injury tipped him off that something wasn't right? Or was he like a long-tailed coati himself— clever enough to know when he was in the presence of a true predator, a man like Jacob?

"Should I tell Enrique to stand down?"

Jacob shook his head. "No, we have a little daylight left yet. Maybe he'll get lucky. Check the security footage."

Angélica nodded swiftly and returned with him to his office. She sat down on the other office chair and quickly started tapping on the screen, trying to find the video archives. He paced, his blood itching inside his veins. Raising his clenched fist, he stroked the stubble on his chin. Magic rippled from his jade ring set in Aztec gold. It heightened his senses, his instincts.

He looked over at Angélica, noticing the unsettled look on her face and the tension in her shoulders. She was a perfectionist. It was a great quality, but when things went wrong, it clouded her thinking. It made her less useful to him.

Jacob came up behind her and started to gently massage her shoulders. "It's not your fault," he said. "I underestimated Mr. Roth. It won't happen again."

"But the ceremony," she whispered, her muscles tightening more.

He dug his fingers into her neck muscles. "Shhh. We have two days. You are too worried about disappointing me. You fear failure too much." He relaxed his grip just a little and then squeezed the back of her neck, his fingers sifting through the silk of her hair. His blood began to scream, but he controlled it. He could not lose control. Not now.

He stepped away and came to stand beside her. "The footage?"

She seemed flustered by his words, his presence. When she looked up at him, he could see a reflection of himself in her glasses. He wasn't smiling. She was *right* to be worried. But neither he nor his organization could stand to lose her just yet.

Looking down at the screen, she frantically tapped on the icons. He watched the rise and fall of her breathing, the nervous motion of her fingers, the screens opening quickly as she began to rewind the footage from the security cameras.

A knock sounded on the door. Angélica started to rise, but he gestured for her to keep working, and he walked to the door and opened it.

Kendall Beasley stood in the opening, agitation flaring her nostrils on an otherwise pretty face—a face his discerning eyes could see had been under the knife many times. If only she knew about the Aztec legend of the mountain one could climb to reverse the aging process, she could have saved herself a lot of pain, scars, and money. She had flashed her eyes at him more than once, an unspoken invitation that she'd like to be seduced. Presumably, she felt this would prove she had succeeded in retaining her youth. He would prefer to drink her blood.

"Mrs. Beasley, I'm afraid now isn't a good—"

"My daughter is missing," Kendall interrupted. Both she and her husband were proud and arrogant, qualities he normally tolerated. Now the officious tone in her voice made him want to grab the *macuahuitl* and teach her the meaning of fear. She was used to ordering around those who served her family's whims, but he was not her servant. And he was far wealthier and more important than her or her cocksure husband.

"My staff is dealing with a situation right now," he said with forced patience.

"She's *gone*," Kendall said.

"Angélica will have someone look for her soon," he said and began to shut the door in her face.

She pressed the flat of her hand against it. He nearly broke her neck with his bare hands.

"Jane Louise's been acting so strangely about coming on this trip. She cried about coming, even though she's been to Cancún and Cozumel many times."

"She can't have wandered far, Mrs. Beasley."

"I know where she is," Angélica said, standing abruptly, hugging the tablet again. The look of stress had disappeared from her face. She'd calmed herself down and slipped on the persona of the gracious hostess.

"You do?" Kendall said mistrustingly.

"You'll see her soon," said Angélica. After she walked to the door, she handed the tablet to Jacob, showing him a glimpse of frozen footage. Then she drew Mrs. Beasley to safety by getting her out of Jacob's presence, speaking comfortingly to her. Her voice always had a soothing effect on others. It put people at ease.

Jacob stood at the doorway, staring at the screen. It was from the security cameras out front, fixed on the Sprinter van that had been parked there for the Roths' use. And there, captured on the screen, was Jane Louise climbing in through the van's open door.

Mrs. Beasley's words came flooding back in his mind. The girl had been acting upset. She hadn't wanted to come on the trip at all.

She knows, Jacob thought, certain of it. *And now the Roths know too.*

The helicopter left the pad and roared over the compound, the pressure from the rotor blades rattling the glass walls and making the howler monkeys in the jungle screech.

CHAPTER EIGHT

Villa Maya Natural Reserve

Cozumel, Mexico

December 23

The noise from the helicopter grew louder and louder. Roth looked up through the dense fronds of the jungle trees. He couldn't see the chopper, but it was heading right toward them.

"Get down!" he shouted. "Hide!"

Brillante, who was farthest ahead, dived into the undergrowth. Roth took Sarina by the hand and quickly ducked into a massive fern. The day was waning fast, and they still hadn't found the perimeter fence. He'd pushed them hard to cover as much ground as possible. Sarina squeezed his hand, her chin tilted up as she examined the swaying fronds, now disturbed by the rotor blades.

Suki had grabbed Jane Louise, and the two of them were crouching under a fallen tree. It wasn't wide enough to cover them, but at least it provided some cover. Roth craned his neck and spotted Lucas farther back in a shrub that seemed to swallow his whole body.

"How'd they find us?" Sarina whispered.

Roth felt his pulse throb with worry. The helicopter was coming right toward them. The wrapper of the half-full case of water he held made a crinkling sound as he adjusted it. The water and a first aid kit, now attached to the strap of Sarina's sling purse, were the only things they'd taken from the Sprinter.

Sarina's question thrummed in his mind. Was there a tracking device on the first aid kit? He hadn't noticed anything like that when they'd examined it.

He wiped his mouth and scratched his beard, thinking fast. No, the helicopter was coming their way by chance, he decided, and given the jungle canopy was too dense for them to see the helicopter, it was also too dense for the pilot or crew to see them. If they waited, it would be gone soon.

The roar of the rotors was deafening. Birds began to shriek in the jungle, and other animals made their presence known too, grunting and chirping. But the helicopter sailed away, a shadow above the thick green fronds.

Roth looked at his wristwatch—sunset would be in less than an hour—and got to his feet. Sarina went over and asked if Jane Louise was all right, and the little girl nodded her smudged face.

"Lucas?" Suki called, looking back the way they'd come. The jungle was definitely not part of her repertoire. The soft pastel pink of her shirt was already dulled with grime, and her legs showed some whip marks from the vegetation. She scratched her short hair at the nape of her neck, still gazing back. "Dude—come out!"

"Lucas! Get over here. Brillante, stay where you are," Roth said.

One of the kids' first major worries on deciding to abandon the Sprinter was Roth's bewilderingly bad sense of direction. He used GPS to drive to the local fast-food restaurants most of the time, even though they'd been living in Bozeman for two years. It was so easy for him to get turned around.

Their smartphones had compasses. He'd worried they wouldn't work without cellular data, but thankfully, the GPS chips inside the phones still functioned without data. His battery was still lower than he would like, but at least he could check their direction frequently. He believed the fencing was likely to the west, so that was their course. West was also the direction of the city of San Miguel.

He'd sent Brillante ahead to explore the terrain and make sure it was passable before the others reached it, but his son kept slowing down because he kept finding things that caught his attention, like a pair of gray iguanas.

Lucas popped out of the shrub after going to the bathroom and then jogged over to them. His nose was purple from the bruising, and he had a red mark on his forehead from a branch.

"I was hoping we'd be at the fence by now," Sarina said to Roth, touching his arm.

"Me too. We keep going."

"Do you think the fence is electric?" Lucas asked eagerly. "We could cook an iguana on it!"

"Gross," Suki said with a disgusted look. She pulled out her water bottle and took a drink, then wiped her mouth. "This is *not* how I thought Christmas break was going to go."

"That makes two of us," Roth said to her. He was furious at the Beasleys and Jacob Calakmul for putting them in this situation, but he tamped down the anger, determined to take whatever action he could to protect his family. If they could get to the highway, they could try to hail a ride from a taxi.

"Where's Brillante?" Sarina asked, her brow furrowing.

"Brillante?" Roth called.

They exchanged a worried look when no reply came.

"I hear . . . splashing," Suki said. She pointed in the direction where he'd disappeared.

They all began to run, and as they got closer, they could hear the noise of splashing water.

"Bryant? Bryant!" Sarina shouted, using his real name this time.

A ticking noise—some bird or insect—came startling close. Roth kept hoping his son would pop up and laugh at them. He didn't. So they kept crashing through the vegetation, trying to find their missing boy.

"Watch out!" cried a distant voice, the sound echoing off stone walls.

Sarina was the first to get there, and she shrieked with fear as the jungle shrubs suddenly gave way and she fell. Roth grabbed for her purse strap, missing it by inches, and watched in horror as she dropped out of sight.

He planted his foot, dropped the partial case of water bottles, and flung out his arms on either side, catching Suki and Lucas before they too fell off the cliff. Jane Louise had already stopped.

A loud splash sounded far below.

"Mom! Mom!" cried Lucas in terror.

"We're down here," called Brillante. "It's like a huge underground swimming pool!"

The fading sunlight and shadows made it difficult to see, but there was an expanse of jade-colored water about thirty feet below them. Roth could see his son treading water. Sarina was sputtering, but she was all right. The two of them gazed up while Roth's stomach shriveled. They'd gotten lucky, but how were they going to get out?

"You okay?" he called down.

Sarina wiped her face. "Yes. I wasn't expecting that."

"I dived into the bushes and went in headfirst!" Brillante said. "I think I touched the bottom!"

Roth looked around. The diameter of the pit was at least fifty feet across. It looked like a huge well shaft, but he knew better. It was a natural formation, a sinkhole filled with water.

"It's a cenote," Sarina said. "They're all over the Yucatán."

"We need to get you guys up," Roth said.

"We could lower a rope?" Suki suggested with a sarcastic tone.

"What can you see down there?" Roth asked, giving his daughter the stink eye.

"The walls are steep. I don't see a way up."

Roth scrubbed his forehead. "How deep is the water?"

"Way deep," Brillante said.

That means they'd be treading water. For hours maybe. They'd be exhausted before long.

"There are some vines hanging down," Sarina said. "But they don't make it all the way to the water."

The walls were rough, not smooth—as if they'd been quarried. But based on the research he'd done before making the trip, the cenotes were a natural feature. Repositories of fresh water, sometimes connected by underground streams, made by collapsing segments of limestone.

Roth walked around the edge of the cenote, trampling the jungle ferns and bushes. It was hard to distinguish the boundaries in the twilight, so he tested first so that he didn't fall in too. He found the vines Sarina had mentioned and pulled on them. They were slick, which would make them difficult to handle.

A flash of frustration and anger seared through him. How could his son have been so careless? But no, his son had done exactly what he'd asked him to. If he hadn't seen Sarina go over the edge, he would have tumbled over himself.

Holding the vine, he pulled against the ends to test the strength. Perhaps he could lash two of them together. Not that he knew any knots. Suki wandered over to him, gazing down into the pit of water.

"Any ideas?" she asked him. Although she looked worried, he could tell she was trying to appear calm. Suki was always attempting to mask her emotions.

"We could try climbing out?" Sarina suggested. "It won't be easy, but if we can get high enough to reach the vines?"

"I'll try!" Brillante volunteered.

"Give it a go," Roth said. He waved Lucas and Jane Louise over to the edge of the cenote, wanting them all within view.

"Is the water warm?" Lucas asked.

"Dude, it's actually cold," Brillante said.

"Can I jum—?" Lucas started.

"No!" Roth thundered at him.

After Brillante made a few attempts at reaching the vines, all of which ended with him falling back into the cenote, Roth realized this tactic wasn't going to work. Worse, Brillante was using up his energy.

He looked at his watch again. It was 6:34 p.m. Total darkness in less than half an hour. They needed to get them out of there before then.

"We need to find something to lower down to them," Roth said. "Something really—"

"Like a tree trunk?" Suki said, pointing to a fallen palm tree nearby. Her nose scrunched. "That's weird."

"Yes! Like a fallen tree trunk. Exactly. Good eyes."

"It just . . . stood out," Suki said. He wasn't sure what she meant, but he was grateful for the discovery. The fallen palm tree was about six inches in diameter, at least fifty or sixty feet long. Coconut palms were tall in general, always competing with each other for sunlight, and this one had clearly lost the fight. The trunk width was pretty uniform all the way to the bushy top. Good for climbing.

Rising, he went over to where it lay. Locking his fingers beneath it, he hefted against it. It budged. Barely.

"Help me," he called to the others. Lucas, Suki, and Jane Louise hurried over.

"A bug!" Jane Louise shrieked, jumping back.

Roth almost jumped too. It was a whip scorpion. Harmless, but the long skinny legs made it look like a spider. "It won't hurt you," he told the little girl.

Lucas used a small branch to flick it away, and then they got to work trying to move the heavy trunk. It got darker and darker as they struggled to move it toward the edge of the cenote. Roth was the largest of the group and the strongest, so he bore the brunt of the weight. He coaxed them to give it their all, and slowly the trunk began to slide in the right direction. It took time. It took too much time. But they were able to get it where they needed.

"Swim toward the other side," Roth called down. "We're going to tip this palm trunk down. It might be long enough for you to get up."

Roth's shirt was soaked with sweat, his fingers hurting from the rough bark of the tree and his arms itching from scratches. When the tree was in the right position, he hoisted the tangled root ball and angled it so it would go straight down the shaft. Then he and the kids went to the withered top and began to shove.

"Once we get it partway," Roth said through clenched teeth, "gravity will do the rest. Let go when it starts tilting." Roth put his weight into it, grunting and growling along with his kids as they pushed it into the mouth of the cenote, which was now bathed in shadow.

Once the root ball began to pull down, the top part rose.

"Back away," Roth warned the kids. He pushed again, alone this time. The palm began to slide.

Lucas ran to the edge. "It's coming!"

"We see it," Sarina said.

The palm tilted and then slid down in a whoosh of fronds and scraping bark. The top disappeared into the cenote, and they heard the splash below.

Roth rushed to the edge, worried that it hadn't been tall enough. But he could see the mess of fronds just below the lip of the cenote.

"We did it!" he said, hugging Suki, and to his surprise, she hugged him back. She usually hated showing affection, preferring an "introvert hug" to a real one. Clearly she was very worried about Sarina and Brillante.

"Dude! Climb up!" Lucas called down.

Brillante wrapped his arms and legs around the tree and began to shimmy up. It was slow going, but he made progress without falling.

"Grab a vine," Roth told his daughter.

They parted the fronds and then tossed the vine down to Brillante. He grabbed it, and with help from above, he climbed out. Roth wrapped him in a fierce hug, grateful he was safe.

When Roth released him, Lucas grabbed his brother and grinned. "I wish I'd fallen down there."

Roth tried to slow his breathing down, drained by the effort of moving the tree. He was about to check his watch when his daughter whispered to him.

"Dad," Suki warned. He looked at her and then at her pointing arm.

He followed it. Streams of light were coming from the dark jungle behind them. Flashlights or headlamps. A few seconds later, they could hear the sound of machetes whacking and biting through the growth with metallic pings and some snatches of Spanish. Men's voices.

Another pit opened up inside Roth's stomach.

His wife was still trapped in the cenote.

CHAPTER NINE

Villa Maya Natural Reserve

Cozumel, Mexico

December 23

Roth had no doubt the men who were coming had been sent by Jacob Calakmul. He couldn't leave Sarina behind, yet he also had the pressure of keeping the kids safe.

"Dad?" Suki asked worriedly, her eyes full of fear.

Roth knelt by the edge of the cenote. He couldn't risk using a loud voice. "Hey! Listen. Some men are coming."

Sarina was treading water, but she slowed her motions, which quieted the splashing. The light was nearly gone. That would make it harder on their pursuers as well. But would it be enough?

"Who's coming?" she called up to him.

"Some people. You need to hide. Can you do that down there? They have lights. They could shine one down." He glanced in the direction of the noise, hearing the machetes slice through the foliage. The sound was getting louder. Closer.

"Yes. I can get into the shadows. There are caves down here."

"Do it! I'll come back! If we get captured, you try to make it out. Get help."

"Okay, Jonny. I love you!"

"I love you too!"

Roth snatched the case of water bottles and grabbed Jane Louise by the hand, noticing her fear-stricken face. He gestured for the twins to follow him but put a finger to his lips. They nodded. Suki didn't need the warning. But where would they hide?

His gaze followed the mass of brush that had initially concealed the cenote from them. He led the kids toward the opposite end and noticed some fallen trees. At first he thought they could hide there, but he quickly judged that there wasn't enough room for everyone. And splitting up would increase their odds of being separated and lost.

He could hear the men now, snatches of Spanish floating to him on the night breeze. He knew enough of the language to know when his mother-in-law was bad-mouthing him, but he wasn't fluent by any means. Most of the Spanish literature he'd read in college had been translated into English. Like the old Spanish novel *The Life of Lazarillo de Tormes*, which had helped inspire his bestselling fantasy series. The main character, Lazarillo, was a cunning boy who had been given away by his mother. He'd learned to be a scoundrel, a trickster, from boyhood. Roth's famous protagonist was a blend of Lazarillo and the swashbuckling Cyrano de Bergerac.

He cursed his ADHD brain, realizing his thoughts had distracted him. He was afraid they were making too much noise, that the men would hear them crunching on the fallen palm leaves strewn throughout the jungle.

"Dad! There!" Suki whispered. In the dim light, he'd almost overlooked it, but there was a small ravine, hardly more than a trench, off to the right.

"Good eyes," he whispered back. The family went to the edge. It went down about six feet. A trickle of water traveled along the base, probably a natural drain that led to the cenote.

He clambered down first, feeling the silt and pebbles against his shoes.

"Oye! Poraquí!" shouted a voice behind them.

Roth's pulse thundered. After setting down the case, he reached up and lifted Jane Louise down. The boys made their own way, scrabbling on the sandy embankment, and Suki slid down next. A little farther along, he saw a small overhang in the ravine, dense with jungle growth. He motioned to it. It was barely big enough to fit all of them, but it provided deeper shadows. It would have to do.

Roth had to squat on his haunches to fit, and Jane Louise nestled alongside him, shivering and whimpering.

Suki sat at the edge, and he saw the fading light gleaming off her glasses.

Roth pulled her closer and whispered in her ear to take them off. The reflection might give them away.

"This really sucks," Brillante whispered, shivering and still wet from his plunge.

"Why'd you fall in?" Lucas scolded.

Roth gave them a warning hiss.

The men's voices were louder now. They were at the cenote. Roth's nerves were fraying. If they caught Sarina, he'd try to fight them. He didn't know how many there were, but it sounded like four or five men.

If they had guns, he was going to fail. Even the most basic security guard had more training than Roth had. Still . . . he would have to try.

He wiped the sheen of sweat from his forehead, struggling to stay still and listen for any signs that they'd found his wife.

"Qué ves?" someone called.

Roth squinted. *What do you see?* Was that it? In addition to the lectures he'd gotten from his mother-in-law, he'd practiced a little Spanish on Duolingo. But his brain was too fried with worry to be sure.

"Crap," Suki whispered.

One of the guards was standing at the edge where they'd come down. He wore a black security uniform. Roth could see him holding a black rifle with both hands, pointing it down into the trench. If he came down, he'd find them.

"Nada," the man said into his headset.

Roth's mouth was so dry. These weren't standard security guards. They were ex-military or paramilitary, like the men at the gate. There was no way he could disarm one of them, let alone the whole squad.

"Dad, I'll run and make him chase me," Lucas offered in a very low whisper.

Roth shook his head no, his stomach twisting with dread.

A streak of light shot over their heads.

A few men began to argue, although the one standing closest to them didn't join in. Roth heard another snippet.

"Está muy oscuro!"

Some more arguing happened. The light cut out.

The soldier standing at the edge started moving again, coming toward them. They could hear his boots crunching in the grit and dead palms. More arguing from farther back. They lost sight of the soldier as he approached the overhang. Roth swallowed, pressing himself back against the sandy wall. He was afraid part of him was showing. The others were as silent as mice. He couldn't even hear their breathing.

The boots came just to the edge of the overhang, directly above them. Roth held his breath because he could *hear the man's breathing*.

More snatches of Spanish.

"Oy! Ves algo?"

"Un momento," answered the soldier above them. There was a sound of him opening a pocket or a pouch.

A golden stream began to fall down into the ravine. The stench of urine was strong. The man was relieving himself? Roth heard a little snicker from Lucas or Bryant, and he looked at them and shook his head violently. Both boys clamped hands on their mouths. Suki had a disgusted look on her face, as if to say, *Really? You had to go* now?

"Qué esta pasando!" shouted another man as he approached.

"Necesito echar una meada," said the other. The stream began to weaken, and then the man zipped himself up again.

Roth knew the slang. *"Una meada"* was going to the bathroom. He could still smell the reek. It was amazing his boys hadn't lost it and given them away. Potty humor and boys. There was no stopping a giggle fit whenever someone farted.

The man backed away from the trench. Roth heard the other voices trailing off. His legs were cramping, so he sat down and stretched out. The others relaxed too.

"Can we get Mom now?" Lucas asked in an undertone.

Roth shook his head. "Not yet. We wait. We need to be sure they're gone."

The noise of the jungle began to change as night settled over them. Birds that had called during the day were quieting, their sounds replaced by the clicking and ticking of insects. The leaves swaying in the wind were a constant noise, reminiscent of the sound of the surf. Jane Louise snuggled against Roth's belly. The temperature in Cozumel dropped about ten degrees between day and night. They wouldn't be cold in the jungle, though, not at seventy-two degrees. That was one highlight. Still, he knew the jungle was prone to rain.

He'd hoped they would reach the fence before nightfall. Now he realized that wouldn't be possible. It was too dangerous to travel when they could barely see.

When he felt sure they'd waited long enough, he detached himself from the Beasleys' daughter. Standing, he listened. They were in a secluded spot along the trench. Other than the wind and insects, he couldn't hear anything else except the faint trickling of water.

"Wait here," he said. Then he hiked along the path and climbed back up. The darkness disoriented him. Which way was the cenote? The last thing he wanted was to fall in himself.

Moving carefully, making too much noise, he crept back the way he thought he'd come. The cenote was a black maw now. He'd have to include it in a book someday.

If you get out.

Tracking the edge was difficult, but he managed it by looking for the tree they'd pushed in. He knelt by the edge. "Hey," he called down. "I'm back."

Silence.

His insides squirmed. "Hey!" he called, a little louder. The smell of cigarettes wafted in the air. His instincts screamed at him to run. Instead, he gripped the log and leaned his head down into the cenote.

"Sarina!" he hissed.

"Jonny?"

Relief gripped him. "They're gone."

"It's so dark."

"I know. I'm up here. Can you find the trunk?"

"I'm holding it. I fell . . . asleep. Sorry."

"It's okay. You're okay. We're going to be okay. Climb up."

"I'm tired, Jonny. I'm really tired."

"Come on, honey. I need you up here with the rest of us."

"Okay. I'll try."

He could feel the thrum on the trunk and heard the water drip from her as she started to climb out. Like Bryant, she hugged the trunk with her whole body, arms and legs wrapped tightly around it, and pulled herself up. He couldn't see her, but he could hear her labored breathing.

He tried to be encouraging. "You got this, girl. It's like working night shift back at the ER. You can do it."

He was afraid she'd lose her strength and fall back in, but she stopped and rested multiple times, gasping.

"You're almost there, honey. A little more. Come on!"

The sound of her scraping against the trunk got louder. Then he saw a darker smudge, and finally, finally, her fingertips were reaching for him.

Roth gripped the top of the tree with one hand and stretched down. Their fingers brushed.

"Little more!" he coaxed.

"I'm . . . so . . . tired . . ."

"You got this!"

She strained and came up a little more. They locked fingers, and he helped pull her up the trunk. He lifted her off the tree and hugged her, pressing her wet clothes against him, not caring about getting wet himself. Relief surged inside him. He kissed her hair, then her mouth. It was a feverish kiss, a desperate one. He savored the familiar feeling of her and the scent of the lotion she liked to use.

They'd known each other since college. It had surprised many of their friends that they'd fallen for each other. They were opposites in so many ways, temperament and appearance. She was short, so much shorter than Roth, and while he was pale and Germanic in appearance, she looked like a native of the Yucatán: black hair, bronze skin. Whereas he'd always been big and boisterous, full of frantic energy and knots of anxiety, she was calmer and more deliberate in her actions and decisions. Which was exactly why their relationship worked. She was his tether to keep himself from the abyss of depression he sometimes wandered too close to. In turn, he'd always pushed her outside her comfort zone. Encouraged her to take risks, to not just stay with the familiar.

Sarina had loved him before he was famous. She'd always been his friend and confidante, even back when he'd stupidly chased other women, thinking she was just a friend.

A song from the '80s came to his mind.

He stopped kissing her, feeling a little ashamed of being maudlin in such a desperate moment.

"You did it," he said, hugging her again.

"Where are the kids?" she asked, still panting.

"We hid over there. I'll take you to them."

She gripped his shirt, not moving. There was little light, but he could see tears shining in her eyes.

"You'll be okay," he said. "I'll get us out of this."

Her grip on his shirt tightened.

"Jonny. The symptoms have already started."

He swallowed, feeling his stomach wrench with dread. "You're tired."

"It's more than . . . fatigue. It's diabetic . . . ketoacidosis."

He couldn't believe that was possible so soon. "But you have the insulin pump?"

She sighed, resting her head against his chest. "They're not water-proof." She pulled the pump out of her pocket and touched the screen. Nothing happened. "It's dead. It can't pump anything, and it had already run out anyway. The stress . . . it's accelerating the hyperglyce-mia. I need to rest."

"So you need a shot of insulin? Don't you have some in your purse?"

"No. The extra insulin is in the minifridge back at the resort. I can get some from a pharmacy or a hospital."

Was there a chance he could sneak back to the resort and get her insulin without being caught?

In the middle of the night? In a jungle? Without getting lost?

No chance at all.

"I'm going to need some soon. If I don't get it under control, I could go into a coma. Or worse."

Roth nearly choked on the surge of emotions that struck him viscerally. A diabetic coma? What was worse than that?

Death.

"Then we're going to get you what you need, Sarina. I promise you."

"I know . . . I know. I'm just telling you. You need to know. If I hit the coma stage, I won't be able to walk."

"I'll carry you." He would carry her across the jungle if he had to.

"I hope if I rest . . . a little . . . we can keep walking tomorrow morning. Early."

"Okay. That's fair. We have a little spot already picked out. You can rest there."

"One more thing, Jonny." Her grip on his shirt loosened. "I don't want the kids to panic."

"They know you have diabetes."

"They've never seen me . . . like I used to . . . If I start acting strange. Saying strange things. Aggressive. It's the ketoacidosis. Okay? Can you help them understand? It's not me."

"I get it. I remember what it was like before you knew you had it."

"You thought . . . I was bipolar."

"We figured it out," he said. "Together."

"One more thing." She was panting faster and faster, even though she'd been resting. "I heard the men. They're going back to the resort."

"Really? They're giving up?"

"No," she panted. "They said something strange. They said . . . they said the *haguar* would find us."

"What?"

"The *j* is an *h* . . . in Spanish. *Haguar.* 'Jaguar.'"

Roth remembered learning there were still wild jaguars in the Yucatán. And probably some in Cozumel too. Surely they didn't have a trained jaguar, though. "Maybe it was a code word for something. Let's get back to the kids," he whispered, pressing another kiss on her head.

She held him, leaning her weight against him as she walked. He pulled her close, his mind fixed on a single thought.

A hospital in San Miguel. That was his goal now. He had to get his wife help.

CHAPTER TEN

Villa Sara de Calakmul

Cozumel, Mexico

December 23

The whir of the helicopter rotors announced the pilot's return. But that didn't put Jacob in a good mood. If anyone had found the Roths, they would have trumpeted the news.

Night had fallen over the resort. The exterior floodlights illuminated the grounds, highlighting the bright colors of the plants and flowers so carefully cultivated and preserved. Insects danced within the rays of the spotlights.

Jacob left the office to head toward the helipad, but Angélica intercepted him, looking tired and stressed.

"Mr. Beasley asked to see you again," she said. The tightness around her eyes suggested that there had been a confrontation.

"I don't have time for him right now," Jacob answered curtly.

"He wants to call the police."

"Thankfully, his cell phone doesn't work out here." He said it with a sardonic tone. It wouldn't matter if the man's phone did work. The police throughout Cozumel, Quintana Roo, and the Maya Riviera answered to Jacob's family. Not Beasley's.

Both of them walked quickly, but she reached the door first and opened it for him. The pilot landed the helicopter with a practiced grace that spoke of expertise. The engine's wail made it impossible to hear anything, and the wind from the rotors blew Angélica's hair across her face.

Jacob strode up to the cockpit door as the whine of the engine began its death. The door clicked open, and the pilot slung himself out.

"No sign of them?" Jacob asked. The other spotters climbed out and shook their heads.

"No, *jefe*," the pilot reported. "I crisscrossed the preserve dozens of times. I did see some of your security force, and they directed me from the ground. The jungle has swallowed them."

Disappointed but not surprised, Jacob sighed. "I didn't think you'd have much luck from the air. We'll have to track them on the ground. But not at night. It's too dark. Victor's men could walk right past them without noticing."

It was true. Mr. Roth had left at just the right time, making it far enough away to gain the protection of nightfall. Clever man. Jacob's admiration for him had increased, albeit only slightly.

"Fuel up and then get some rest," Jacob said. "I want you out again at dawn."

"Okay, *jefe*. We'll find them."

"You *will*," Jacob said, giving the pilot a warning look. He turned, and Angélica fell in beside him as he walked back to the resort.

Once they were inside, he took hold of her arm. "You called the port authority?"

"Yes. Everyone is watching for them at the ferry in San Miguel. The Winjet and Ultramar ticketing managers have been paid to detain them."

"He's not stupid. He'll probably try to hire a local with a boat."

"You're right. I also have the hospitals being watched. We found a large supply of insulin in the room, so she probably doesn't have enough."

"Good. Get some sleep."

"What about Mr. Beasley?"

"I don't want to see him. Get his family on the yacht tomorrow morning. Have the captain bring them to Chetumal. No snorkeling. Take them directly to the temple."

She looked surprised. "He may not want to go without his daughter."

Jacob gave her an icy look. "He doesn't have a choice. The death game will start on the twenty-fifth. The prophecy has waited for five centuries. It waits for no one now."

He was gripping her arm too hard. He noticed the flash of pain in her eyes and let go. She surreptitiously rubbed her elbow, her breasts rising and falling as she steadied her breathing.

The prophecy he spoke of had been written down in a codex that had been stolen by the Spaniards and taken to Germany. However, scholars had not been able to decipher it. Although they thought it might contain information on the planets as related to plantings and harvests, they didn't know for sure. They didn't understand the nature of the glyphs.

Jacob understood.

Jacob knew . . . and the information it contained was so much more vital than the scholars had supposed.

He returned to his office to shut down his laptop. He was too on edge to go to sleep, so he decided he would work out to relieve some of the tension.

But when he opened the door, he was surprised to find Eric Beasley standing at his desk, Jacob's phone receiver in his hand. He wore a polo shirt and cinnamon-colored shorts and sandals.

A flash of guilt came across Beasley's face as he lowered the phone back to the cradle.

"You shouldn't be in here, my friend," Jacob said, trying to curb his outrage. It took a great deal of will for him to keep his gaze off the *macuahuitl* sword. If he let himself look at it, it would be too tempting to snatch it and threaten Beasley with a premature disembowelment.

"I want my daughter back," Beasley said, shifting from guilt to anger. "Call the police. Now."

"Call them? You think that will help the situation?"

"We need more *men* looking for the Roths."

"I will be the judge of what we *need*."

"And I will be the judge of what's best for my family! I don't like how this is going down, Jacob. I thought you had things under control. How am I supposed to believe you can fulfill your promises if you can't even control an overweight author?"

Jacob stared at him, wrestling to control his fury. "*You* came to *me*, Eric. You brought your family here because it was different from what your other rich 'friends' had. You've resented those people your entire life. They only care about using each other to get further ahead. Well, when the prophecy is fulfilled, *you* will be the one standing on top in your community. They will come to *your* gate begging. My promises are sacred. They are made in blood. Something you should know very well by now."

"I'm in this too deep," Eric said huskily. "Can't back off. But you better deliver. You better . . ."

He took a threatening step forward.

Beasley liked to intimidate other men with his size. He was taller than Jacob, had the physical strength to do serious damage. But Jacob felt no danger at all. He had powers that went beyond physical strength.

"I will get your daughter back," Jacob said evenly.

Beasley glared at him. "It's almost eleven. I thought the jungle belonged to you."

Another challenging statement, delivered from one alpha male to another. A provocation. Beasley was used to demeaning others, using his wealth and physique to intimidate. It was his way of compensating for not having an Ivy League education. For having played football for a small college team. He was a small-minded man, but that was for the better. It would ensure he was easily controlled when the time came.

Jacob summoned a bit of the magic from the jade ring on his finger. It made his eyes glow amber.

"I *am* the jungle!" he said forcefully, a growl in his throat.

Beasley's eyes went wide with fear as he witnessed the display of Maya magic. This man had hunted elk and even bagged a mountain lion, but Jacob had just reminded him of his place on the food chain. He had no gun. He had nothing to defend himself against teeth and claws.

The phone chirped with an incoming call. It was Victor from the security post at the gate.

Beasley looked at it, his instincts warring with one another.

"Leave," Jacob commanded. "Never come in here again. If you do, I'll kill you without hesitation."

The phone made another chirp.

Beasley fled the room, sweat dripping down his frightened face.

Jacob answered the call. "Good evening, Victor."

"Mr. Calakmul, we can't find them in the dark."

"I know. Did you bring your men back to the checkpoints?"

"Yes, sir. One team went by the cenote."

"Which one?"

"The jade one. A tree fell into it, they said. There were footprints everywhere."

Jacob frowned. "Did the Roths go into the cenote?"

"I don't think so. It was getting too dark to track them. But we'll start at the cenote in the morning if you want."

"I'll check the area myself. Keep patrolling the fence, and have your men segment and search. I'll send for a group of local marines to help us find our missing 'tourists.' We'll have all day."

"What if they've made it through the fence already?"

"Mr. Roth is too big to squeeze through the bars. But the kids could. And his wife."

"You think he'd leave them?"

"No, but it doesn't matter. They're all going to die anyway. Neither family leaves the island without my permission."

"Of course. We'll get them, Mr. Calakmul. Especially if the marines help."

"I have every confidence we'll find them tomorrow, Victor."

There was a pause.

"Do you think . . . do you think they found the waterway in the cenote, sir? They might not be in the jungle at all. They might be traveling through the underworld."

Jacob wasn't quick to dismiss the thought. It was unlikely that the family would have been brave enough to travel through the underwater caves, presuming they could figure out how to do so. Not without a light. He didn't think the first aid kit they'd taken had a flashlight, but it wouldn't work underwater even if there were one.

"It's unlikely. I'll check when I visit the cenote."

"Okay. We'll keep patrolling the perimeter during the night."

"And the beaches," Jacob added. It was illegal to use lights on the eastern edge of the island of Cozumel. Although they told tourists it was because of the turtles, the real reason was that it allowed Jacob's people to move in and out of the island secretly.

"Already have boats in place."

"Good. Thank you, Victor."

"You're welcome."

The line went dead, and Jacob settled the receiver down, then rubbed the stubble on his chin and mouth, deep in thought. How had the Roths managed to evade his security forces for this long? It was highly unusual. As if one of the gods had interceded on their behalf. He wouldn't have been surprised had a glyph of Ix Chel, the patron goddess of the island, suddenly appeared on the comforter in the Roths' guest room. Ix Chel was known for being nurturing, unlike most of the other deities. But she was too subtle in the affairs of gods and men for such an overt manifestation. If she had intervened, why? What set the Roths apart from the other families who'd come before them?

Sarina Roth.

He glanced over at the trio of jade statues on a wall display. All three were of Ix Chel, each in one of her various manifestations—princess, weaver, and crone. It almost seemed as if the figurines were grinning at him for having finally figured it out.

Sarina's ancestors were from the Yucatán. None of the other families who'd come to the island for the death games had Mexican heritage.

Perhaps, to Ix Chel, that made a difference.

Maybe it should.

Cozumel, or *Cuzamil* in Mayan, was the island of swallows. It had possessed religious distinction for a thousand years, due to its connection to Ix Chel. It was a place where bloodshed wasn't allowed, where hospitality was expected and respected. Both Grijalva *and* Cortés had visited the island during their invasions. They'd been treated with respect and provided with food and fresh water from the cenotes, as was the custom.

In return, the populace had been killed by smallpox. Over twenty thousand Maya had once lived on the island. Only several hundred men and women had survived the ravages of the disease—and then the European pirates who had come to pillage.

Thinking about the devastation still made Jacob's stomach burn with hate. Cozumel was only a small sliver of the history. The Aztec, the Maya, the Inca, the Chavín. The Europeans had inflicted a genocide that had bathed the land in blood and death. And then they'd settled America. And the same thing had happened there.

Jacob felt the familiar need for vengeance pulse within him.

The Maya Long Count calendar had ended in 2012. The fools and the ignorant had thought it another doomsday prophecy. The end of the world.

Well, they were right. But when the end times came, it would not take the form of a fiery comet or asteroid. It would come in the same way Cortés had come: in a fury of blood and violence.

Yes, Sarina Roth had blood from the Yucatán in her veins, but it couldn't matter—the Beasleys had chosen their competitors, and it was too late for another choice to be made.

The Calakmuls had already been waiting so very long for the prophecy to be fulfilled. A prophecy the West knew nothing about.

A prophecy hidden behind a glass plate in a library in Dresden, Germany.

CHAPTER ELEVEN

Jade Cenote, Natural Reserve Area

Cozumel, Mexico

December 24

It felt like a scene from a book Roth had written, only this time, the danger was real. What he didn't understand was *why.* Kidnapping a rich author and his family and holding them for ransom? That, he could understand. Greed was a common motivation. But this didn't appear to be about money—Calakmul was far richer than Roth would probably ever be, and so were the Beasleys.

Was this really about the Maya ball game? But, if so, why would someone want *them* to play it?

The kids had fallen asleep around him—he could hear their steady breathing—but he didn't think Sarina was asleep yet.

"Honey?" he whispered, nudging her with his shoulder.

She sniffed, lifted her head up, and slid her hand up to his chest. "What's wrong?" she whispered back.

"Aside from running for our lives in a jungle today? I've been struggling to figure out a motive here. Kidnapping would be easy to understand, but this? Why us? Why would the Beasleys pretend to be our friends and lure us to the resort? Is this really about playing the game?"

"I don't think we *can* know any of that for sure, Jonny." She sounded exhausted.

"I can't stop thinking about it." He wiped at an itch in his eye.

"If it is about the game, maybe only the rich are permitted to play?"

"But there are plenty of rich people in Bozeman. Why us?"

"Maybe they believed it would be an easy win. For them."

That made him angry. Was that what they thought? If so, he was determined to upset the whole thing.

"Maybe." He rubbed her neck. "It wouldn't be the first time we were underestimated, though. What about those framed photos we found in the resort? Do you think that was some sick memento of past games?"

"Maybe," she said with a sigh. "But there's no telling."

He considered that for a moment, then said, "You're right. There's no way of knowing unless we go back, and we're obviously not going back."

"No, we can't go back." She yawned.

"Get some sleep."

"You should sleep too."

He chuckled. "You know how long *that* takes sometimes."

She was asleep in minutes, but after their conversation, sleep didn't come easily to Roth. His mind kept working through different scenarios for why they were being pursued, none of them good. A looming sense of dread filled him, but coiled beneath it lay his determination to keep his family safe at all costs.

The others had fallen asleep quickly. Sarina cuddled against Roth's body on his left, her head nestled on his shoulder. The Beasley girl lay to his right, and Suki was cuddled up next to her. The boys were curled together, next to their mother. He could hear the comforting sounds of their breathing. But what little moonlight could be seen through the canopy of trees failed to penetrate the thick shadows.

When sleep did come to him, it was in short snatches, during moments when the jungle fell still. Every strange sound roused him—and there were plenty of them—his mind conjuring unseen threats and dangers from the trickling sound of water and the murmurs in the darkness of the jungle. He slept in fits and bursts. His bearded chin kept bobbing against his chest; his eyes were scratchy and leaden. In his fragmented dreams, they were on a ball court, playing the ancient game he'd discussed with Sarina.

It was the sound of the birds that roused him fully, at the first blush of dawn. Their cries and warbles and shrieks called in the new day.

His left arm had fallen asleep from the pressure of Sarina against him. The tingles in his fingertips were uncomfortable, but he didn't want to wake her yet. Jane Louise's head was on his thigh. It was probably seventy degrees. Cool. Pleasant.

He thought maybe he'd let them all sleep for another few minutes. They'd need the rest for the day ahead. Then a startled cry wrenched his eyes wide open.

He struggled to get to his feet with two others confining him and saw a black-striped boa constrictor wrapping itself around Lucas's leg.

"Get it off! Get it off!" Lucas howled.

Roth hated snakes. He was absolutely terrified of them. But with his son in its grasp, the fear was gone. He seized the first aid kit, still attached to Sarina's bag, and rushed to his son. Bryant was clawing across the scrub to get away as fast as he could.

Roth reached his son and the boa, his stomach sick with worry. The creature was six feet, maybe seven, powerful and undulating. Lucas was pinned by its weight, trying to thrash free but already constricted by the bulging knots of the snake.

Roth let out a primal scream, hefting the metal first aid kit and swinging it at the snake. He felt the impact against its sinewy body. The boa unraveled from Lucas and slunk away, slithering down the pebbled waterway.

Roth stared at it, chest heaving, kit poised in his hand.

Lucas made it to his feet, his body trembling a little. "That was so gross."

Brillante returned, holding a stick in both hands, primed like a baseball bat. He'd gone looking for a weapon, not to save himself. If Roth hadn't attacked first, Brillante would have.

Roth couldn't speak; his mouth was too dry. All the sleepiness had been purged from his system. Sarina came up and stroked Lucas's hair.

"You okay?" she asked him worriedly.

He nodded.

Roth lowered his makeshift weapon, grateful the snake had given up so easily. It had already disappeared into the growth.

"Dude," Brillante said. "It could have eaten you!"

Sarina beamed at him, her expression full of the same parental pride Roth felt. "Thanks for coming to your brother's rescue."

"Maybe it thought he was a rodent," Suki yawned, then followed the comment with a mischievous smirk. But she was just teasing.

"A rodent of unusual size," Roth quipped.

"I'm so hungry," Lucas said. "My stomach was growling all night."

"I thought that was Dad snoring," said Suki.

Roth rubbed his hands together. "I don't think this hotel serves breakfast until seven. Unless you want me to go after the boa?"

"No thanks," Suki said. "Utter cringe." Her glasses were smeared with dirt. She wiped them on her shirt, which was just as filthy as her shorts. "I was having a nightmare about the old ball-game legends. We were wearing these weird outfits. Like bark armor."

"Bark armor?" Brillante asked with a snort.

She rubbed her nose. "It was weird. Then the whole snake thing went down. I don't think I could fall back asleep now."

"Everyone else awake?" Roth asked.

Jane Louise, who'd barely said a word since they abandoned the van, rubbed her eyes and nodded. There was something so sweet and earnest about her, and he wondered how she'd managed to keep those qualities while living with her parents.

"We should get going," Roth said. He reached into his pocket and pulled out his phone. Just as he'd thought, it was dead. That meant no compass.

The direction of the sunrise told him which way was east. But it wouldn't be useful for navigation for long. He'd read an article once about the human tendency to wander in circles in the wilderness. A German research company had actually used GPS to validate the wandering instinct. Their work indicated that people walking in the woods tended to go in erratic directions and would sometimes literally walk in circles. He could only imagine it was easier to get turned around in a dense jungle. Getting lost was a real danger.

"I need to go to the bathroom really bad," Sarina said to him, motioning to a covert of jungle ferns.

He nodded. "Does your phone work? Mine's dead."

She took the pack and kit from him and then opened the pouch. She pulled out her phone and tested it. The screen stayed black. She shook her head. "It hasn't dried out yet. Let me try the pump."

He watched her retrieve the pump and try to activate it. Nothing came on the screen.

His nerves felt like they were twisted into knots. Sarina *needed* that pump. But he didn't let it show. He squeezed her shoulder and said, "Go ahead and pee."

"You peeing in the bushes?" Suki asked.

Sarina nodded.

"I'll come too," Suki said. "The boys have it easier. Jane Louise— want to come with?"

The Beasley girl nodded, and the three broke off from the group. After they'd all relieved themselves, Roth asked everyone to drink some more water. Moving the coconut tree had been a physically exhausting ordeal, and Brillante and Sarina had climbed up it. Today would bring its own host of physical challenges. Without water, they'd get dehydrated, which would cause them further problems. They each took a water bottle and then climbed up the embankment. Thankfully, their shouts earlier hadn't brought any unwelcome visitors.

Roth held the remaining plastic water bottles against his hip, watching as the sunlight pierced the trees to the east. He turned so he could see his shadow pointed in the direction they should go. Following the shadow would work for a little while. But the sun was angled differently in winter, which meant they weren't going true west. He scratched his neck.

How could they avoid the instinct to get lost? His own sense of direction was decidedly worse than the others'. He knew he couldn't rely on it to see them through.

"You ready?" Sarina asked with a slight smile. A forced smile, he knew. She looked exhausted, and he thought again of the broken pump.

He couldn't fixate, though. The only solution was to get her to safety.

"I have an idea," he said, scratching his beard. A line was made up of points. He looked at Brillante, who was still holding the stick he'd found.

"Hand me that," he said, gesturing toward the stick. After he had it, he cleared some of the brush with his shoe to expose the soft jungle dirt.

He drilled the tip of the stick into the ground in three places, then connected the dots to form a line.

"If we walk randomly, we'll probably end up back at the resort. We need to go in a straight line if possible. That's the fastest route to the fence. So this is what we're going to do." He pointed to the first divot. "Bryant stays here. The rest of us walk ahead to here." He pointed to the second divot. "Then Lucas or Suki goes ahead to this point." Tapping the final dot, he looked from face to face. "If we stay in sight of each other, we'll keep going in a straight line. We'll avoid going in circles."

"You have boss skills, Dad," said Suki with respect.

In video games, the boss level was usually at the end. They saved the toughest monster for last. You defeat the boss and win the game. He smiled at the compliment.

"Let's do this thing," Roth said with a smile of conviction. "We stay together. We stay close. We cheer each other on. That's the only way we're making it back." He looked at Brillante and winked. "And no more falling into cenotes, okay?"

———

Not far in, they found a stand of wild banana trees. They had huge green leaves and pinecone-like trunks. The bananas were growing in clusters, probably thirty or forty bunched together. It was Suki who'd found them on her rotation. When they reached her, she was waiting smugly at the tree, her hip propped against it.

"Are those safe to eat?" Bryant asked, jumping up for a better look. Lucas was behind them.

"They're in the wild. They should be," Sarina said.

The cluster of fruit was hanging down low enough that Bryant could easily reach them when Roth hoisted him up onto his shoulders. He tore bananas down and started tossing them to the others. Roth's stomach gurgled just from looking at the fruit. Bananas were a great source of calories and energy.

After Bryant stripped down several of them, he jumped down and grabbed one.

Roth liked peeling his bananas from the black end, not the stem. A friend of his named Alan Cox had taught him to do it that way, and he'd done it ever since. The fruit was firm and a little bitter and had many more seeds than what they'd found in stores, but soon the whole family was eating them. Roth's smile faded when he saw Sarina eating a second one.

"Whoa, won't that cause a sugar spike?" he asked her softly.

She shook her head. "These bananas are okay. They're not ripe, so they have much less sugar, and the fiber has starch that slows the digestion."

She looked so tired, but she was smiling, trying to remain positive. They all needed to eat to maintain energy.

The noise of a helicopter sounded overhead, revealing that the hunt was on again. But the jungle trees shielded them from sight.

"Let's bring some with us in case we don't run into any more trees," he said.

"Bananas are breakfast, lunch, and now dinner?" Lucas asked with a groan.

"I'm sure we'll be back at San Miguel in time for dinner," Roth said. The idea of street-vendor tacos made his stomach growl.

"You doing okay, sweetie?" Sarina asked Jane Louise, crouching in front of the little girl. She clung to Roth's hand and nodded without answering.

Sarina looked up. "I need to go to the bathroom again," she whispered.

Roth closed his eyes. She'd just gone. It seemed like another sign her blood sugar was off.

"Okay," he said, worrying.

When she got back, they continued westward from the banana tree. The boys carried extra fruit in the pockets of their swim trunks, and Suki had two sticking out of the back pockets of her shorts. Roth used the plastic wrapper of the water bottle case to store more bananas, and Sarina had filled her pack with them too. Off they went, heading west as best they could.

The jungle foliage altered dramatically as they continued their arduous walk. Instead of palm trees, the way was blocked by thinner, hardwood trees speckled with gray-and-brown bark. The trees grew close enough together that getting past them became difficult as the undergrowth thickened. The canopy was also thinner, which made them more vulnerable to the helicopter. Sometimes the sound of the rotors grew faint, and at other times it seemed to be right overhead. At one point, they came across a long-tailed mammal that looked like a cross between a raccoon and a badger, with a tail as long as a monkey's, a long snout, and dark patches of fur around its eyes. Its pelt was as brown as the trees. It stared at them, and when Suki cooed at it, it bounded off in the brush and vanished.

They reached the fence at noon, the sun shining directly overhead. The temperature was in the low eighties, and they were all sweating and uncomfortable.

The fence was iron, the bars close together, but not too close. Roth could only imagine the expense of putting up such a fence. It was ten feet tall, with razor wire on the top, and it came in sections that were about fifteen feet long, lashed together with chains and fixed to cement footers. The bars were coated with jungle slime.

Brillante and Lucas squirmed through the barrier and gave each other a high five. Suki, Sarina, and Jane Louise wouldn't have trouble with it either.

But Roth knew immediately that he wouldn't be able to pass. His stomach sank.

"Tire tracks," Lucas said, stomping his flip-flops.

Roth came to the fence and squeezed the bars. He wrenched against them, trying to jiggle one loose. It didn't budge. He moved to another set, then tried to force a gap between two of the fifteen-foot sections. Nothing.

Sarina looked at him worriedly. She saw the problem as clearly as he did.

"Maybe you take the kids ahead," he whispered to her. "I'll find another way out."

Sarina shook her head forcefully. "We go together."

He jerked on the bars in frustration. "Even if I could get high enough, that razor wire would cut me to pieces."

"Let's follow the fence, then," Sarina suggested. "We might find an opening."

He knuckled his forehead, then looked her in the eyes. "You *need* to get to a hospital. It's getting worse."

"I'm not leaving you, Jonny. You don't speak Spanish. I'd be worried to death about you getting caught."

"Suki, come on!" Bryant urged.

Roth looked for her and saw she was standing close to him and Sarina. She'd been listening to their hushed conversation and had a stricken look on her face. Jane Louise was nearby, watching a colorful bug crawl up a tree trunk.

Roth rubbed his mouth and then tapped his lips with his finger. He heard the sound of an engine in the distance. A motorcycle, maybe. Or an ATV.

Roth stared at the jungle on the other side. Yes, there were fallen leaves and such, but they were regularly trampled. It was a dirt path, he realized.

Or a narrow road.

Urgency pumped through his veins. "Boys," he said. "Get back on this side."

"Something's coming," Suki said nervously.

Lucas squirmed through the bars, but Brillante stayed put and stared down the road.

"Dude, don't be dumb," Suki said. "Get over here."

"What if whoever's coming can help us?" Brillante asked.

A feeling of danger prickled at Roth. He sensed the newcomers were anything but friendly. "Get back on this side. Now!"

His son came to the fence and began to squirm through, but he got stuck partway. His mouth twisted with frustration as he tried to push past the barrier. Heart pounding, Roth rushed up and pulled him through with a strong yank.

The vehicle on the road was traveling fast. They still couldn't see it, but its noise was getting louder.

How had they come so quickly?

Cameras.

There had to be motion-sensitive cameras along the perimeter. As soon as Roth's family had appeared, the security station had been notified, and they'd dispatched a vehicle.

"Back in the jungle," Roth said, grabbing Jane Louise's hand. They all raced back the way they'd come.

Thankfully, the dense jungle swallowed them in moments. Two ATVs screeched to a halt, and Roth heard men shouting in Spanish. Their words were clipped and curt and very agitated. Yes, they'd known *exactly* where to go.

Sarina pulled him close and spoke into his ear. "Let's stop and listen. They can't cross to this side either."

She was right. The boys were bolting over a tree. Roth nearly whistled to them, but he didn't want to reveal their location.

"Suki, get your brothers and bring them back here," he told her in an undertone.

She nodded and sprinted off after them.

Roth and Sarina and the Beasley girl hunkered down in the brush. They were close enough to hear the men's conversation.

Sarina hung her head, deep in concentration, listening to the words. Roth couldn't see anyone through the screen of trees.

Was there another way through the fence? Could their pursuers remove a section and get in that way?

His stomach twisted with dread. Maybe they should be running as far and as fast as they could.

"What are they saying?" Roth asked Sarina.

"They know we were there," she whispered back. "Saw us on some monitors. They're calling in reinforcements." Her fearful eyes met his. "There's another team nearby on this side of the fence. They're heading this way now to cut us off."

CHAPTER TWELVE

Tezcatlipoca Temple, Villa Maya Natural Reserve

Cozumel, Mexico

December 24

Leaves and branches from the various jungle trees slapped against Roth's face as he barreled through the brush, the water and bananas cradled in his left arm and little Jane Louise in his right. He had to dodge or leap around fallen trunks that blocked the way, as well as occasional mounds of cut stones. Maya ruins, perhaps? A sting against his cheek warned that he'd been cut, but he gritted his teeth and kept going.

Every moment, he worried that their pursuers would catch up to them. His sons were at his heels, Sarina and Suki just behind them. Although Lucas and Bryant could have easily outrun him—their soccer training gave them a natural endurance—he'd ordered them to always stay behind him.

They'd agreed the best tactic to avoid being encircled was to run as quickly as possible, constantly changing direction. It would make them lost in the middle of the jungle, but that would also confuse those pursuing them. There was, of course, the noise they were making, but speed gave an advantage against being caught.

Roth was winded from carrying the water and the little girl, but his fear for his family and Jane Louise, who'd become his responsibility, drove him past his natural endurance. Sweat streaked down his body and stung his eyes. But he pressed on, hearing shrieking calls from jungle birds overhead.

The density of the jungle was a constant problem, and the helicopter could be heard buzzing nearby. How far had they gone already? A mile? It felt like six. But in the dense undergrowth, it was impossible to determine actual distance or even where they were in relation to the fence.

Suddenly, the trees and brush gave way, and a massive stone wall loomed in front of him. Roth nearly slammed into it but managed to stop himself. Vines and growth blotted out the upper edges, but it was very tall and very old. Because of the density of the jungle, little could be seen except what was directly ahead of them.

A wall in the middle of the jungle. It made no sense.

"Dude!" cried Lucas, who appeared a moment before his brother, gazing up at the ancient wall in awe. Bryant joined him, hardly winded at all.

Roth was panting too much to speak. He set down Jane Louise and the water bottles, knelt down to rest, then pulled out a water bottle and guzzled down the entire thing. He mopped his forehead with his arm and gazed up at the wall.

"We'll have to go around it," Roth spluttered. "Where are Mom and Suki?"

"I'll find out," Bryant offered. He was about to charge back into the jungle, but Roth grabbed the waist of his swim trunks and held him back.

"No, let's wait. Don't want you getting lost."

This part of the jungle was denser than what they'd traveled the previous day. They were probably in the middle of the island.

Roth grunted as he rose to his feet again. He was itching with sweat, bug bites, and the constant slaps from the trees.

Noise could be heard from the brush behind them, and Lucas parted the screen to reveal Suki and Sarina. They were both winded, and Sarina was gasping, her eyes wide with panic.

Roth pulled out another water bottle and hurried it over to his wife. She took it gratefully and slurped it down fast, bent over in weariness.

"A stone wall?" Suki said. "I *told* you this was *Promised Neverland*!"

Roth chuckled. She was right. In that anime show, the children had been imprisoned inside the compound by a stone wall.

"We need to get around it," Roth said. "Can't rest yet. Brillante, Lucas—you stay with your mom. How you holding up, Jane Louise?"

The Beasley girl looked scared. "I'm thirsty too," she said in a small voice. He realized it was practically the only thing she'd said since asking to come with them the previous evening.

"Everyone take a drink. But we gotta move." They all obeyed, and Roth took the lead, starting to follow the edge of the wall. Except he quickly came upon a set of steps leading up.

"This isn't a wall," Suki said to him.

"You're right. It's a pyramid." Roth couldn't believe it. The wide steps led up to a series of plateaus, all overgrown by the jungle. It extended up past the jungle canopy.

"Did the Aztecs build this?" Suki asked, scuffing her sandal against the crumbling stone.

"No, the Maya. It looks just like the ruins of San Gervasio. I saw some pictures on Google."

Sarina looked up the steps toward the jungle. She was still panting. Her cheeks looked sunken.

"Can we climb to the top?" Bryant asked eagerly.

"Race you!" Lucas challenged.

"Guys. Settle down."

In the pictures he'd seen of Maya ruins, there were always layers and layers of steps, each level going higher. Some ruins, like the one in Tikal, was so steep that tourists had fallen to their deaths. This structure wasn't as steep, but it was still dangerous. Some of the steps might also be crumbling.

"Maybe we can see where to go from up there?" Suki suggested. "And if the pyramid is tall enough, we might be able to pick up a cell tower signal."

That made a lot of sense. He was proud of his daughter's thinking. There was one problem. "My phone died last night. Mom's is dead too."

Suki grinned slyly, then reached behind her and pulled her phone out of her back pocket.

He stared in surprise. "You have power?"

"About thirty percent. No signal, so I've had it powered off to save the charge."

Roth started to laugh. "I haven't seen you pull it out. I'd forgotten all about it."

He looked up the steps. "If the pyramid is tall enough, we might get a signal without obstruction."

"I'll run up and check, Dad!" Brillante offered.

Roth looked at his wife. She was sitting on the lowest step of the pyramid, her head cradled in her hands. She needed a hospital.

"We have to stick together," he said. "Let's all climb up. Can you make it, Sarina?"

His wife nodded. "I'll bring Jane Louise. You all go ahead."

"Okay," he said reluctantly. He didn't like the idea of not being beside her, there to help if she stumbled, but they needed to test the signal.

"Let's go!" Lucas shouted eagerly.

Roth hefted the water and handed it to Lucas. "You've got so much energy. You two take turns carrying this. Suki . . . take Mom's pack."

They started the ascent. Roth's legs were burning after just a few minutes, but all the hiking he'd done with Sarina over the years had helped give him stamina. He wished he weighed thirty pounds less, but his legs were sturdy, and he kept a consistent pace, even when the kids started to lag.

Once they breached the jungle trees, he could see the pyramid in detail. It was probably two hundred feet across on each side. Moss had grown over a lot of the areas, painting the gray stone with stripes of vibrant green. A massive staircase led up the center, to a pinnacle, which lay in ruins. The jungle had grown over most of the structure, but the face they were climbing was exposed to sunlight, and it began to beat down on them mercilessly.

Roth hoped that Suki's cell phone would work. But whom would he call? Back when he was a teenager, he used to memorize phone numbers. No one did that anymore with smartphones, and his own phone was dead. He might be able to restart it for long enough to find a phone number, but there'd only be one chance.

Moretti.

He'd memorized his friend Will Moretti's personal cell number because it was so easy to remember: a combination of sevens, nines, and sixes. All he needed to remember was the area code for Utah.

Halfway up the pyramid, Roth thought he was going to die. His legs were screaming in pain. Even the boys seemed winded. He glanced back, worry eating at him. Although Suki was just behind him, head down, sweat glistening on her neck, Sarina and Jane Louise were significantly behind her, taking the ascent slowly.

Each step was painful, but he kept going. Maybe they could hide amid the ruins? At last, he reached the top of the steps, which brought him to the upper portion of the pyramid. But there was still another section that crowned it, accessible by another set of pyramid stairs.

Roth paused and wiped the sweat from his face. When he looked down, he could see San Miguel in the distance. If only he could teleport his family there. That was the awesome thing about fantasy books. Magic could help the characters travel distances.

He gave the boys some encouragement, and they all started up the final stretch of stairs. After an arduous climb, they reached the very top, and Roth could see all the way to the ocean. Looking east, he thought he saw the Calakmul compound, sunlight shimmering off the glass.

Bryant and Lucas set down the water bottles and began exploring.

"Stay close," he warned them.

Looking down, he saw Suki was on the last part of the journey. Sarina and Jane Louise were still on the first stretch of steps.

When Suki reached the top, he held out his hand for the phone. She pressed the button and waited for it to power up, then quickly used her fingerprint to unlock it. They both watched the screen, waiting for the cell service to connect—if that was even possible.

His heart leaped as one bar of service popped onto the display. Suki looked at him with shining eyes.

"This is going to work."

He hoped so.

"Dad! There's a metal plate over here!" One of the boys called out.

Roth took the phone from her and glanced over at them. They stood at the middle of the top of the pyramid. Still gripping the phone, he walked over to inspect what they'd found. It wasn't an ancient thing. It was one of those temporary road covers you'd find in a construction zone. Heavy enough for a car to drive on and definitely not a Maya relic.

"Lift it," he said to the boys. Then he opened the phone app and punched in Moretti's number. It started to ring, and he felt a spark of hope.

The boys took one end of the metal and strained to lift it, their combined strength bringing it up. Roth backed up so he could see beneath it. It was a shaft leading down into the core of the pyramid. Ladderlike steps made of stone were embedded in the walls.

"A call from an unknown number in Bozeman, Montana. Is that you, Roth?"

It was such a relief to hear his friend's voice. "Moretti!"

"Hey, bud. I thought it was you." There was something off about his voice. He wasn't his usual jovial self. "So sad about Westfall."

Roth blinked in surprise. "What? What's wrong with Westfall?"

"He died in a car wreck on the way to work this morning. I just heard about it. I figured that was why you were calling."

Roth's stomach fell. "Bryant Westfall is dead?"

Westfall, their mutual best friend from high school. The third of their musketeers. His son Bryant's namesake.

"Yeah. On Christmas Eve too. You mean you didn't know? I'm sorry you had to hear it this way."

"We went to Cancún for Christmas," Roth said, his mind suddenly a fog of disbelief and grief.

"You're in . . . Mexico? Really?"

"Yeah. Cozumel. It was kind of last minute. Moretti . . . we're in trouble."

The voice on the other end went silent.

"Moretti?"

"I'm here. Where are you right now?"

"It's . . . um . . . an island off the Yucatán Peninsula. By Cancún. I'm standing on an old pyramid in the middle of the jungle."

"Wait . . . what?"

"Listen, man. We're in a serious situation here. We came with another family from Bozeman. The Beasleys. We—" His voice cracked, his mind summoning memories of Westfall: the crack in his voice after Roth told him they'd named their son after him. How they'd always sung along together at the tops of their lungs to that one song by Elf, "Carolina County Ball," when it came on the radio. And he'd never forget the road trips they'd taken in Westfall's convertible roadster. "Sorry, I'm still upset to hear about Westfall."

"You're on a pyramid? Where?"

"We had to get out of the resort we were staying at. We were at Villa Sara. It's owned by a guy named Jacob Calakmul. He's a . . . he must be some sort of a criminal. Cartel leader? I don't know. We got a bad vibe, so we took off, and they're following us. We don't know why, but the family who invited us seems to be involved."

"Give me a sec. I'll try to look him up." Roth could hear some tapping on a keyboard.

"We gotta get off the island," Roth said. "I need help, man."

"Hang in there. Just give me a second. So this guy . . . what . . . wants to kidnap you?"

"Beasley's daughter warned us that our lives were at risk." He gazed down the pyramid at the little girl. If she hadn't snuck into the van, what would have happened to them? "We tried to get away last night. We went into the jungle and got lost."

"You . . . get lost? Remember that trip we took to San Francisco?" He heard tapping on a keyboard on the line. The San Francisco story was a classic one of Roth getting lost. Maybe his friend was trying to introduce some levity to lighten the mood.

"I don't know what these guys want, Moretti, but they have these paramilitary types hunting for us. Machine guns, battle gear. That kind of thing."

"Huh? Machine guns? That's not good." There was a pause, a little whistle of surprise. "We're going to figure this out, Roth," he said, his voice serious. "I'm looking the guy up now." Another pause, then he said, "Okay, let's see. Jacob Calakmul. Don't have any records on him at all. He's never been to the United States. That means he's probably part of one of the cartels down in Cancún. This is serious stuff."

"No kidding. Is there an embassy in Cozumel? Is that where I should go?"

"Roth, listen to me," Moretti said, his tone intense. "You can't trust anyone down there. Mexico is great, but it's corrupt. The police are often working with the cartels. It's bad news. And the military shoots first, asks questions later. If they're looking for you, they're expecting to send you guys home in body bags. Got it? The reason doesn't matter."

Roth felt a wave of nausea. "What do we do?"

"Listen to me. You need to find a safe house. Not a hotel or Airbnb. They can track those through your credit card."

"Right."

"My uncle is an immigration attorney in San Diego. He's also a judge. I'll also text you his contact info and give him a heads-up. Once you get to a safe house, call him, and he'll help get you out of Mexico. He can contact the embassy for you. There's corruption there too, but he'll know exactly whom to contact."

Another spurt of relief. "Your uncle. What's his name? This phone is mostly dead."

"Mostly dead means slightly alive," Moretti joked.

Roth laughed, but tears stung his eyes. He, Westfall, and Moretti had all loved *The Princess Bride* growing up, and quoting it had been like a shared code. He rubbed his mouth, the pain in his chest growing.

"My uncle's name is Avram Morrell. He's really good. My brother Lance got messed up on a trip to Mexico a year ago. Seriously. Got arrested for being stupid, and the police were expecting bribes to get him out. Lance called me, I called Uncle Avram, and bam . . . he was out. Got three of his army buddies out too. I can't go down there. I'd be a dead man if I stepped foot in Mexico. I arrest drug dealers for a living."

Roth nodded to the phone, scrubbing his forehead. Although his friend couldn't share details, he knew Moretti was part of a SWAT team or something like that. He'd dealt with some pretty shady people in his career in law enforcement.

"Got it. Find a place to hide. Then call Avram Morrell. Text me his number. I'm hoping we can get more juice once we find a way out of the jungle."

"I'm sorry you're in this mess, bud. Sorry about Westfall too."

Roth felt his throat seize up. "Sarina needs a doctor pretty bad. Her diabetes is flaring up."

"Doesn't she take insulin?"

"Her pump is busted. We're running out of time. Need a hospital."

He heard the buzz of the helicopter getting louder. It was coming toward the pyramid.

Fast.

"Gotta run, bud. They're coming after us with a helicopter. Text me your uncle's info."

"I will. Good luck, Roth!"

CHAPTER THIRTEEN

Tezcatlipoca Temple, Villa Maya Natural Reserve

Cozumel, Mexico

December 24

Roth bounded down the steps as fast as he dared, his heart in his throat. He had to get Sarina and the others to the top—quickly—so they could climb down the other side. Suki had fallen back to help Sarina, but Roth could see the utter exhaustion in his wife's face. She wasn't even sweating, which was a terrible sign in and of itself. She'd made it to the next level of steps but not much farther.

The whine of the helicopter turned into a roar as it approached the ancient Maya temple, reminding him of how little time they had left. Then his eyes shifted to Jane Louise, who was pointing down the steps in mute horror, and his heart sank.

Toward the bottom of the pyramid, he saw three soldiers running up the steps. They had jungle-colored stripes on their faces and wore green commando fatigues, military helmets, and carried rifles with long magazines. They looked like Navy SEALs.

Going back into the jungle wasn't an option. Descending into the shaft the boys had found, the one going *into* the pyramid, was their only chance to keep from being captured immediately. Once they were inside, they might find another way out or a hiding spot.

When he reached Sarina, he hoisted her over his shoulder and then hooked Suki behind the neck with his other hand to get her attention. She was staring down at the coming soldiers, her eyes wide with terror.

"Listen to me!" he shouted over the noise of the helicopter. He didn't imagine it could land up on the broken surface of the pyramid, but he wasn't totally sure. The resources sent to hunt them down were significant. "At the top, there's a shaft leading down into the pyramid. We gotta go down it and see if we can hide or find another exit. Get down there with your brothers. Fast."

"I'm afraid of heights," Suki said, quivering.

"I need you to lead the way," Roth said, shaking his head. "I'm not giving up. You can't either. Take Jane Louise with you."

She nodded firmly, gripped the little girl's hand, and then began sprinting up the final stairs.

"Jonny, just go. Protect the kids," Sarina panted. He could hear the worry in her voice.

"I'm not leaving you," he insisted. "We go together. The kids can do this." Then, because he knew how fragile life was, he added, "Whatever happens, Sarina, you're the best thing in my life."

"Hurry," she moaned.

Roth gritted his teeth and took the steep steps two at a time. His legs screamed from the abuse, but he kept going, knowing that the soldiers would overtake them soon. The helicopter was now hovering directly over the pyramid. The blast of wind from its rotors sprayed dirt and bits of stone everywhere. Suki's jungle-stained shirt whipped with the gale, but the girl continued to the top and disappeared with Eric's daughter.

Holding Sarina on his shoulder sapped his strength, but he was determined to get both of them up to the children. The helicopter tail spun so that the windshield was facing Roth. Through the dust, he could see the pilot and his companion.

It was Jacob Calakmul, wearing sunglasses and a headset. He was pointing right at him.

Roth reached the top of the pyramid, buffeted by the wind coming from the blades. Soldiers were now coming up all four sides of the pyramid. They'd cleared the canopy of trees and were rushing to get to the summit.

Roth stared around. The kids were all gone. The metal covering had been shoved aside.

He hurried to it and quickly set Sarina down by the edge. Her black hair blew wildly in the wind from the rotors. She waved away the smoky dust and looked down into the black maw of the shaft.

"I can't," she said, shaking her head. She was terrified of heights too.

"The kids are down there!" Roth shouted to her. The tunnel had handholds of stone all around the shaft, spaced like the rungs of a ladder. But time had worn away the sharp edges of the stone. Each was rounded slightly, which would make gripping them challenging.

"Kids," he shouted down the opening. "Are you safe?" Suddenly a burst of light came from within. He saw Lucas pointing up at him and then Suki climbing down to the bottom of the shaft. Had they found a flashlight down there?

That was encouragement enough. Roth started down until he was chest-deep into the chute. He looked at Sarina.

"On my back!" he yelled at her.

She nodded and slid around behind him, wrapping one arm around his chest and the other around his neck to clasp her hands in front of him. She hugged him tightly, pressing her cheek against his sweaty back. Her weight added to the strain, but he was wide enough to brace against the interior walls. Judging from the light shining up, it was about thirty feet to the stone floor below.

Roth clenched his jaw and shuffled down, legs spread from one wall to the other. His shoe slipped on one of the rounded edges, and he felt a spasm of fear that he'd plummet and crush his kids. But he scraped his arm against the stone wall to stop the slide.

He caught his breath, tamed his charging heart, and then started down again.

"Dad!" Suki called up to him. "We're all down!"

"Good job, sweetheart!" he shouted, straining against the burden of lowering himself and his wife. His arms and legs were gray from the stone powder sticking to his sweat. His face must look the same.

Roth's grip faltered, and he began to slide again. His shoulders screamed in pain. Sarina clutched him harder. His knees were burning against the stone as he slid down, trying to stop himself, then landed on the floor with bone-jarring force.

"Dad!" the boys yelped.

Sarina detangled herself from him, and they all helped him stand. The stinging on his forearms was awful, but his legs supported his weight. At least he hadn't twisted his ankle.

"*Ahí abajo!*" shouted a voice from above.

Roth looked up and saw a shadow smudge in the bright light. The soldiers had reached the top of the pyramid.

Lucas handed him a headlamp. They were all wearing them. There was a whole crate of them at the bottom of the chute.

Roth looked for Sarina, his heart beating rapidly. She was standing behind him. The stone dust gave her a wraithlike appearance, but she was conscious and determined.

"Jonny!" she insisted. "Run!"

Little Jane Louise was roaming down the corridor toward another set of stairs, her hand grazing the wall. The ceiling was low and cramped. It felt like a tomb, but the solid stone blocked the roar of the helicopter.

"Down, we go down as far as we can," Roth said. He hoped there would be other passages. If the interior was like a maze, it would force the pursuers to split up. At least their pursuers weren't the only ones who had lights. If they'd been searching in darkness, they never would've found anything.

Roth barged ahead and took Jane Louise by the hand. He felt the grit in his mouth, sticking to his teeth, but he didn't have time to drink. They had to hide before the soldiers caught up to them. The family ran down the stone steps, vaulting down them as fast as they could. The stairs zigzagged in different directions, sometimes leading to a short hall before continuing the descent. There were no tributaries to take. The ceiling was so low that Roth had to hunch to clear it.

Soon they could hear the noise of the soldiers pursuing them. Warning voices yelled for them to stop.

"Parad! Parad!"

They continued onward until the tunnel abruptly gave way to a huge chasm leading down to another cenote. Roth staggered to a stop, afraid it was the end of the trail. But steps had been carved into the side of the cenote, leading down to the glistening water below.

The light reflected off something blue at the edge of the water. Roth squinted, hurrying down as fast as he could.

Three inflatable boats were moored on a makeshift dock in the water of the cenote. The cenote itself was at least a hundred feet wide, and it filled the middle of the pyramid. In fact, he realized that the pyramid had been built *on top* of the cenote.

More lights shone from above. The soldiers had their own lamps attached to their helmets.

Roth reached the edge of the cenote. One of the three inflatable boats had oars secured to the top. The others had outboard motors.

"Get on that one!" he said, pointing to the one with the oars.

There were black plastic crates stacked against the natural wall near the boats, and he hurried over to them. They needed supplies and weapons that could be used in defense.

When he opened the first dusty yellow lid, he did a double take. It was full of gold jewelry, ancient in make and fashion. Flashes of green jade caught his eyes too. The headlamp illuminated several rows of identical chests, and he realized they were probably all full of treasure.

Then his eyes landed on the obsidian spear propped against the stone wall near one of the boxes. He rushed to it and grabbed it, watching as his children boarded the boat. Suki had followed him to the treasure chests and looked down at them in awe.

"Get in the boat, Suki!" Sarina called to her. Jane Louise was cuddled in her lap, while Lucas and Bryant sat at the front of the craft.

Brandishing the spear, Roth rushed to the second boat and quickly jabbed it.

As he'd learned in his research before coming to Cozumel, finely cut obsidian was nearly as sharp as diamond-bladed saws. The spear slit through the boat's side and bottom effortlessly. Air began to hiss and rush out.

Roth slit a hole in the third boat as the soldiers came rushing down the final length of the stairs. He ran to his family, slicing the mooring rope with the spear head, and leaped on board with a running jump.

Having misjudged the distance, he landed too close to the edge and tipped backward. His arms flailed, and he dropped the spear into the black water, but Suki pulled him back before he fell.

The boat lurched away from the edge, going into the waters of the cenote, and Roth could hear the rush of lost air from the other two crafts as they wilted. Turning, he shifted the light from his headlamp back to the storage chests full of Maya treasure. How many had been there? A dozen or two?

He was gasping for breath but felt a little smug about outrunning the soldiers. Though they were still stuck in an underground pond. The situation was bleak. They'd managed to stay one step ahead up until now, but they were running out of steps.

"Where you going?" shouted one of the soldiers in broken English. "Come back *aquí*! We help you!"

"No way!" Roth shouted back.

Brillante unlatched one of the oars, and Lucas saw to the other.

Roth squirmed to the middle of the boat. "Brillante, Lucas, paddle together," he said, still breathing hard. "In sync, or we'll go in circles. Let's get farther away from them."

"Where are we going?"

Good question.

The cenote they'd found earlier had been like a giant well, the walls encircling it too steep to climb. Using the headlamp, he gazed at the rough walls surrounding the cenote. The water splashed against the rubbery shell of the boat as the boys started to paddle.

Roth saw a dark gap against the side of the cenote. He pointed at it.

"There," he said, his heart pounding with anticipation . . . with hope.

And he was right. As they got closer, the boat began to speed up on its own, implying there was a current. The darkness deepened. A tunnel lay ahead.

They'd found an underground river.

CHAPTER FOURTEEN

TEZCATLIPOCA TEMPLE, VILLA MAYA NATURAL RESERVE

COZUMEL, MEXICO

December 24

Jacob Calakmul leaped off the helicopter skid and landed on the edge of the moldering Tezcatlipoca temple. Six soldiers stood guard at the mouth atop the next level, shielding their faces from the blast of dust and grit caused by the blades. The helicopter veered away and took position over the jungle canopy.

As Jacob climbed the steps to reach the pinnacle, he felt sweat trickle down his chest beneath his loose-fitting shirt. The captain of the soldiers, Anselmo, who'd been summoned to assist in the jungle search but knew nothing other than that he was helping with a "search and rescue mission" for tourists who'd "gotten lost," had crouched near the opening by the metal plate that had been dragged aside. His men were talking furtively among themselves.

"So they went down, then?" Jacob said, no longer surprised at Mr. Roth's tenacity. In fact, he was more than a little impressed by it.

Anselmo stood. His face was streaked with jungle paint, slashes of greens and blacks. He was a strong man, a marine, part of the Mexican military assigned to Cozumel.

He glanced back at the shaft into the pyramid. "Yes. Three of my men went down after them."

"I know. I saw them. I told you that your men weren't permitted to go down there. That I'd get them myself."

The captain grunted. "You're a businessman. We're soldiers. We'll bring them back. Trust me. But my men discovered what you're hiding down there, Mr. Calakmul."

He referred to the treasure boxes.

Jacob didn't trust this man, but they'd needed to find the Roths quickly, which had required reinforcements to bolster his own security forces.

The soldier gave Jacob a disdainful look. He had a rank badge on his fatigues. That rank gave him the illusion that he was in charge. The fool.

Jacob rubbed the stubble beneath his bottom lip, gazing out at the view from the pinnacle. The island held so much history . . . and the bones of so many dead.

Cozumel had been a sanctuary for the goddess Ix Chel. The Maya nobility of the entire Yucatán Peninsula would visit the island to receive blessings and make marriage alliances, to touch and be touched by the magic that was special to this place. In the year 1511, a young Franciscan friar named Jerónimo de Aguilar had left his missionary post in Panama because of rivalries and factions in the colony. He was bound for Santo Domingo but had shipwrecked and been captured by the Maya. The chests of gold they'd brought had also been seized by their captors.

Aguilar was a prisoner for eight years. His survival depended on his cooperation.

The Maya warlord Nachan Ka'an would have killed him outright. Nachan Ka'an didn't rely on his own judgment, though. A special advisor helped steer the ruler, giving him a reputation for being both cunning and wise, and this jaguar priest had thought the young missionary might be useful. The young man was skilled at languages. He learned the tongues of the Aztec empire, both Mayan and Nahuatl, and taught the jaguar priest to communicate in Spanish.

While other foreigners adapted for survival, Aguilar remained true to his Franciscan vows. He kept records, hoping to be rescued one day.

And, in 1519, he was. By Cortés himself, who had learned of a bearded Spaniard being kept on Cozumel.

In the eight years of Aguilar's captivity, the jaguar priest had come to understand an important truth. Others were coming. They wanted gold, slaves, and women. There'd been barely enough time to enact a plan to defend against the plunderers who were coming with steel swords, gunpowder, and infectious diseases.

Understanding your enemy was the surest way to learn how to defeat them.

Aguilar had provided the needed insights.

When the other Spaniards arrived at Cozumel—Grijalva first and then Cortés—the jaguar priest had enticed the Maya rulers to embrace them, to assist them, to *welcome* them. Malintzin was chosen from among the ruler's many daughters to be their people's envoy to the Spanish. A pretend "slave" who could be "rescued" and thereby infiltrate the very hearts of the conquerors.

The jaguar priest had chosen her himself.

She would lead Cortés to his doom.

History was nothing if not a series of repetitions, of cycles. One civilization ascending, another descending. And there was a pattern here too.

Just as Malintzin had done, so too had other Western families, including the Beasleys, led their brothers and sisters to their doom. It amused Jacob to watch the Westerners, who always lauded themselves for their elevated ideals, turn on one another so easily, so totally.

"I'm bringing the treasures back with us. They belong to the Mexican government."

Jacob looked at the captain again and stifled his contempt for the man. Anselmo was like thousands of men who'd come before him. He thought muscles, bullets, and bravery could conquer anything. He had no idea that he'd been influenced and manipulated by those powerful combinations of intrigue that had gone on for centuries previously. Or that the government was already bought and paid for.

The captain looked away, putting a finger to his headset. The pyramid was made of dense stone. The latest military communications equipment was impressive, but it would be hampered down there.

Jacob walked to the edge of the opening and dropped down to a low squat, gazing into the darkness. He saw a soldier standing guard at the bottom.

Captain Anselmo's face scrunched in concern. He looked down at Jacob.

"They got away," Jacob said, bemused. He watched the guard at the bottom walk deeper into the tunnel, and, straightening, he closed his hand into a signal that would be recognized by the two fellows in league with the Order of the Jaguar.

Two of the other soldiers discreetly made the sign back to him. Jacob nodded and sighed.

"I'm going down," he said to Captain Anselmo. "Looks like your men botched this simple assignment."

The captain lifted a finger and jabbed it toward Jacob. "Listen, you little—"

Jacob grabbed the man's finger, torqued and broke it, then jabbed the fingers of his other hand into Anselmo's throat. The man's eyes bulged, and he dropped to one knee, choking.

The other soldiers, shocked by the sudden violence, began to turn their guns on Jacob, but they were shot in the necks by those who were part of the larger scheme. The soldiers collapsed to the ground, dead. Captain Anselmo was struggling to breathe, both hands clutching his damaged throat.

Jacob nodded in acknowledgment to the other two men. "Take him to my chief of security," he said, gesturing to Anselmo. "He'll be sacrificed tonight."

"What of these?" asked one of the others, pointing his smoking firearm at the dead men on the ground.

"Roll their bodies down the steps like in olden times," Jacob said. "The jungle will devour them."

The two men smiled ruthlessly and then used zip-tie cuffs to secure the captain's hands behind his back. The officer's swagger was gone. Although he couldn't understand what was happening, he knew enough to recognize he was a dead man.

Jacob pulled out the radio connecting him to the pilot of the helicopter. "Fly over to the ruins at San Gervasio and wait for me there. Have the police set up a checkpoint on the road back to San Miguel."

"Okay, *jefe*," said the pilot. "I'll tell Angélica."

"Over." Jacob switched off the radio to preserve the battery. It wouldn't work underground anyway. Then he climbed down the shaft swiftly, disappointment and respect warring inside him. Mr. Roth had eluded them *again*. The man's carelessness at the perimeter fencing had nearly spelled his ruin. The motion sensors had activated and revealed his entire family and the Beasley child. The first ATV had reached them within minutes, and radio communications from the team had enabled the marines to close in around the pyramid. If Mr. Roth had gone any other way than *up*, they could have been caught by Anselmo's men before reaching the cenote and the hidden treasure.

He reached the bottom of the shaft and noticed the guard he'd seen earlier walking toward him from deeper within the pyramid, likely returning from checking in with the others, since the radios didn't always work in the labyrinthian tunnels. "Where's Captain Anselmo? He's not answering his coms."

Jacob broke his neck in less than two seconds.

The marines were decent soldiers, but they were not the FES—or the Fuerzas Especiales—who were the best trained elite in the Mexican navy. They had a distinguished history, a reputation for ferocity, and a high body count against the cartels.

But the jaguar priests had been training for much, much longer. Jacob had learned the quickest ways of killing men from earliest childhood. Poisonous plants, obsidian blades, and a magic with a deeper history than the stories of the underworld.

The soldier's painted face was locked in a shocked grimace. None of the unaffiliated soldiers who'd learned about the treasure could survive. Only those loyal to the Order of the Jaguar.

Jacob began to stroll down the tunnel. He invoked the magic, feeling his eyes adjust to the darkness. Feeling his body begin to twitch, his muscles quivering with anticipation.

The soldiers would need to be dispatched before they could get out word about the golden treasures, hidden long ago in the various cenotes to protect them from the greedy conquistadors.

Those men had stolen troves of other treasures, of course, and it was time to reclaim those ancient debts. When the time came, and it was coming soon, it would be taken in gold. And slaves. And women. And they would have the pleasure of destroying their enemies with disease too.

The brutality the Maya had suffered was beyond imagination. Friars, men like Aguilar, had written of it, had *justified* the atrocities, cloaking it in the language of their god. The various natives had fought hard against the invaders, but plague, gunpowder smoke, and steel had proven to be unconquerable.

Knowing their time would come, they'd opted to wait for the fulfillment of the prophecy, at the end of the Maya calendar cycle. Rather than fight Cortés and the conquistadors directly and be overrun, they'd slunk into the underground caves with the treasures of their rulers and watched from afar.

When Jacob arrived at the steps leading down to the edge of the cenote, he saw the two shredded boats still floating on the rippling waters, tied by the mooring ropes. Two soldiers knelt by the chests of treasure, stuffing their pockets.

They didn't hear him approach, for he no longer walked as a man.

All they saw before their deaths was a pair of luminous golden eyes.

CHAPTER FIFTEEN

Underground River

Cozumel, Mexico

December 24

Beneath the island of Cozumel, the water was as clear and pristine as any Roth had seen. The light from the headlamps cut through the tunnel so they could see the ground beneath them. By Roth's estimation, the water was probably six or seven feet deep. The tunnel they maneuvered through had hanging forests of stalactites that covered its ceiling in each direction. Some kissed the water's surface or connected with the stalagmites growing from below.

"Poggers," said Lucas in awe, swinging his head back and forth to study the glittering limestone deposits.

"Totally poggers," agreed Brillante.

The raft glided easily on the surface, carrying them deeper into the dark canyons beneath the earth's surface.

Prompted by Sarina's memories of her grandmother's stories, Roth had read excerpts from the Popol Vuh, the ancient Maya record of the early inhabitants of the region, recounting the creation of the world.

He'd been intrigued by the legends of the underworld. The gods of Xibalba could unleash plagues, cause starvation, or curse mortals. One of them—Roth couldn't remember his name—had hidden in the detritus of someone's unswept home to stab the owner to death for being too lazy to clean. The Maya must have feared these underground caves and rivers and explored them with torches and small canoes. Was it any wonder they'd considered them mystical?

Roth himself was half-convinced he was experiencing another world. The underwater river was surreal.

Since he'd slashed the two other boats with the spear, there was no way the soldiers would be able to follow them easily. That gave his family a slight reprieve. But Calakmul had a helicopter and probably knew where the river went. Perhaps it led to a dead end, and they would have to go back to the temple.

"Let's treat those scrapes," Sarina suggested, opening the metal first aid kit. She was beyond exhausted, yet there she was, going into nurse mode again.

Roth hissed in pain as she cleaned his scrapes with alcohol wipes. He had large, bloody gashes and contusions on his legs and forearms, and smaller cuts on his hands. There weren't enough bandages to cover the afflicted areas, but she'd been thorough with the cleaning, her nursing training helping and hurting him simultaneously.

"This is so cool," Lucas said, gazing at the scene. The light from their headlamps reflected off the limestone, splashing the darkness with vibrant colors.

"It's epic," Suki agreed. "Totally poggers."

"What does 'poggers' even mean?" Roth asked, amused by the teenager slang.

"I dunno how to put it. It's a way of saying something's really cool."

"Like 'awe inspiring'?" Roth asked.

"Yes. That's it. Poggers."

"Do you know how these stone icicles were made?" Brillante asked his brother.

"People made them?"

"No. It's a natural thing. It's um . . . a certain kind of stone. Limestone. Right, Dad?"

"They're calcium deposits," Roth explained. "The ground is very porous. The water leaches through the limestone and then drips and forms deposits. These caves and stalactites were made over thousands of years. Remember when we did that trip to Bear Lake?"

"The caves!" Lucas said, nodding. His light bounced up and down with his head. "They were so much colder."

They'd gone as a family to visit the Minnetonka Cave near Bear Lake in southeast Idaho. The cave had a constant temperature of forty degrees. So even though they'd visited in the summer, everyone had been shivering by the end of their excursion. The temperature in this river was cool, but definitely not as cold as they'd experienced on that trip.

They were heading straight for another clump of stalactites, so Roth took over for the boys and paddled to go around it. He glanced at Sarina. The little Beasley girl was curled up in her lap, and she was stroking Jane Louise's hair.

Sarina covered her eyes, and Roth realized he'd been shining the headlamp directly at her. Turning to look straight ahead, he asked her softly, "How you holding up?"

"I feel a little better now." But she sounded exhausted. Her brow was creased, and he caught a hint of her syrupy breath. The need to find help, soon, pounded through him.

"Where'd you get that?" Bryant demanded.

Roth turned and saw Suki hiding something from sight.

"Did you grab something from one of the chests?" Lucas asked.

"Shut up," Suki said.

Roth hadn't seen Suki take anything, but the moment had been very intense.

"Let me see," he told her.

Suki glared at her brothers. "Thanks," she said flatly.

"Show me," Roth insisted.

Suki produced a bracelet. The light from his headlamp shone on her palm, revealing a bracelet made of jade spheres with little gold-plated pieces separating the individual orbs. Jade was one of the precious stones valued by the Maya. The bracelet looked old, tarnished. The little bits of gold had etchings on them, tiny little Mayan glyphs.

"It's pretty," Roth said. He should probably scold her for stealing it, but he couldn't bring himself to care if one of Calakmul's trinkets had been lost.

"It came from the glowing chest," Suki said.

Roth frowned. "What?"

"One of the chests was glowing. That's why I went over to look. It was . . . it was kinda weird."

"The chests weren't glowing," Roth said.

"One *was*," Suki said. "Like when you shine a flashlight in a very dusty room. You can see the little dust motes dancing. This was thicker, though, more like snow than dust."

Roth gave her a quizzical look, which blinded her, and she held up her hand.

"Sorry," he said, turning his gaze. He had no idea what she was talking about. There hadn't been any dust blowing around the chests. It had looked nothing like what she'd described.

"I saw it too," Sarina said. A corner of her mouth lifted in a mirthless smile. "Thought it was a fever dream."

That surprised Roth even more. "You saw it too?" he asked in shock.

"I thought it was . . . shining? It's hard to describe. When I saw Suki go to it, it . . . scared me." Her gaze shot to the bracelet. "Maybe the treasure is cursed."

"Whoa," Lucas whispered.

"Cursed gold? Are you afraid she's going to turn into the undead?" Roth asked skeptically. It was like that Johnny Depp movie.

Sarina looked at him seriously. "My great-grandmother used to tell me stories about where she grew up in the Yucatán. I think we should get rid of it."

Sarina's great-grandmother was a legendary person in the family. Her name was Socorro, but everyone had called her Grandma Suki. She'd died when Sarina was a teenager, so Roth had never met the woman they'd named their daughter after. Socorro Marie Roth. But their daughter always went by Suki.

Suki was turning the ancient-looking bracelet over in her hands. "I want to keep it."

"It's *stolen*," Sarina persisted.

"Maybe they stole it? Look, I know it's weird, I just feel like I need to keep it. I don't understand."

"What kind of stories?" Roth asked Sarina. "Are there really curses?"

Sarina sighed and stopped pressing the point with Suki. "Stories that were handed down. Ones the *Church* didn't accept."

"Like . . . ?"

"The Maya believed in magic, Jonny. The priests who came with the conquistadors, they tried to stamp it all out. But my great-grandma believed in it. She said that one of her brothers was killed by magic."

Roth paddled to avoid another nest of stalactites straight ahead. He'd been looking for any signs of a way to exit the river, but the current kept them moving lazily along.

"Like a curse?"

"No," Sarina said. "By a *nawualli*. A shape-shifter."

"You mean a *werewolf?*" Suki asked, her voice suddenly interested.

"No, it isn't the same tradition. Moonlight doesn't make them transform. It's a form of magic rather than a disease. People can *become* like animals. Or have the power of animals. The people who can do it are basically sorcerers."

Roth had a healthy dose of skepticism. As an avid player of Dungeons & Dragons, he liked mythology, but he didn't believe any of it was real.

Then again . . .

"Moretti's dad was a missionary for his church," Roth said. "He served in a Navajo reservation in the Four Corners area. He used to tell us these wild stories about the Navajo. About skinwalkers who could transform into wolves and make bad things happen to people. In Navajo, they were called the *yee naaldlooshii*. The stories used to give me nightmares."

"Which you wrote about in your books," Sarina reminded him. "The *shadow walkers*."

Roth chuckled. That was true. While he'd called them something else in his fantasy novels, the idea had come from the stories he'd heard at the Moretti house. Moretti's father would regale them with stories, and then Roth, Moretti, and Westfall would struggle to sleep, alert to every creak and groan of the old house.

As soon as the memory struck him, he remembered that Westfall was dead. His stomach lurched, and he bit his lip, trying to quell the sudden rush of grief.

"What's wrong?" Sarina asked.

Little Jane Louise lifted her head and looked at him worriedly.

Roth swallowed, fearing he might start crying. He wiped his face and looked for obstacles up ahead. The underground river continued into the blackness, past the range of his headlamp.

"Bryant Westfall d-died this morning," Roth said softly. His voice hitched as he said it.

Sarina's face registered shock and then crumpled into sadness. She reached over and laid her hand on Roth's knee. "What happened? How'd you find out?"

"I was able to call Moretti from the top of the pyramid. Suki's phone. He gave me the contact information for someone who might be able to help us get out of this mess. Westfall . . . it was a car accident on the way to work this morning. Our phones are dead, or we would have found out sooner."

"I'm so sorry, Jonny."

"I can't believe I forgot. Well . . . I didn't forget. It's just the soldiers were closing in on us, and all I could think about was getting us out of there. The boys are the ones who found the entrance to the pyramid. Good job, by the way."

Lucas grinned at the praise, but Bryant was subdued. He'd been closer to Westfall. To his namesake.

"Sorry, Dad," Suki mumbled. She reached out her hand, palm up. He pressed his against hers and their thumbs patted each other. She called them "introvert hugs."

Roth felt the first tears fall, unable to stop them. He hated crying, especially in front of his family. The tears stung his eyes, and he buried his face in his hands. Sarina edged closer and hugged him, stroking his arm, his mass of wild hair. He laughed a little, thinking the burst was over, then broke down even more. He held her tightly, feeling as if his world were crumbling. He'd found success in life, but he hadn't been able to save his friend. Nor had any of his resources been able to protect his family so far. They'd made it by their wits alone. But at least they were together. He thought of Westfall's family, his son and daughter, his wife—Stephanie—and it made him weep even harder.

He felt Lucas join the hug. When his tears subsided, they were all looking at him, except for Suki, who was too embarrassed by emotional displays. She was folding her arms, shining her light into the darkness ahead.

"Thanks," Roth said, stifling a sniffle. It had hit him hard. Then again, it was to be expected. He'd trusted Westfall enough to make him part of his living trust. If anything happened to him and his family, then Westfall and his CPA firm would control all the intellectual property rights to Roth's . . .

It slammed into him like a semitruck.

He sat there, stunned, the realization rippling through his mind. Westfall's CPA firm had the rights to all of Roth's books if the unthinkable happened. If he and Sarina died, someone needed to control those interests so that their kids would benefit from them. Since Suki and the boys were so young, a trusted adult had been appointed to the role. The estate attorney they'd met with in Bozeman had suggested that they appoint someone business savvy, not a parent or in-law. Someone who could properly weigh the benefits of licensing, say, the film rights for a certain book. Another punch of awareness followed the first. The estate attorney was the same man who had introduced the Roths to Eric and Kendall Beasley.

Had Jacob Calakmul arranged Westfall's accident? It seemed like an unlikely coincidence.

Floored by his thoughts, Roth kissed Sarina's hair and let go of her shoulders.

Little Jane Louise was staring up at him, her eyes so like Kendall's.

He stared at her face for a moment as anger slashed through his chest. The light had to be blinding her, but she didn't look away.

The Beasleys had convinced them to come on the trip. He hated them. *Hated* them. Still, their little girl wasn't part of this insanity. If she hadn't spoken up, hadn't said something, then Roth and his family might be dead already.

He tousled the little girl's hair. "Thank you, Jane Louise," he told her. "We need to get you back to your mee-maw."

A little smile brightened her face.

"Dad, I see something ahead," Suki warned.

He angled the beam and peered ahead into the gloom. Suki was right. A small dock made of wood and stone was affixed at the edge of the river. Steps carved into the wall led upward. Another inflatable raft was moored at the dock. Just one. It was a tiny landing, and the river continued on past this point.

He wondered how far they'd come. Looking at his watch, he saw it had been an hour since they'd climbed the temple at half past noon. He guessed they'd gone maybe two miles on the underground river. He had no idea what direction they'd gone, whether they were closer to San

Miguel or farther away from it. What if the river had brought them east, back toward the Calakmul resort?

Indecision clawed at him, but he rowed toward the dock so they wouldn't sail past it.

"Are we stopping?" Sarina asked worriedly.

Roth pursed his lips. Would someone be waiting for them here? Unless they were in the jungle, the helicopter could certainly have beaten them here.

Leaving the river right now was risky, but if it got them to a hospital faster, it was a risk he had to take.

Roth used the oar to glide up to the little dock. "Grab the cleat, Brillante."

"The what?" asked his son in confusion.

"The metal thing on the dock. We'll tie the rope to it."

His son reached over the front and grabbed it. The gentle current pulled the boat until it was facing backward, but they bumped against the dock posts.

Roth grabbed a water bottle and quickly chugged it down.

"We're leaving the boat?" Sarina asked.

"I'm going to scout ahead," Roth said. He sighed. "I need to know if it's safe. You all wait here."

Sarina gave him a worried look and shook her head.

He used the remains of the rope to circle around the cleat twice, then he held the end out to Suki. "You keep the boat here until I get back."

His daughter was afraid. He could see it in her eyes. "What if you don't come back?"

He pushed her glasses higher up her nose. "I'm going to get us out of this. You're just going to have to trust me."

"Maybe you should take one of the boys?" Sarina suggested.

It wasn't a bad idea. Both of the twins were faster than him, and if there was trouble, he could send a runner back.

Their hands shot up at the same time.

CHAPTER SIXTEEN

San Gervasio Archaeological Zone

Cozumel, Mexico

December 24

Roth had always had sensitive hearing and ear-ringing tinnitus. The silence of the dark tunnel accentuated every sound from their shoes, every breath they took. The twin beams of their headlamps pierced the way ahead, cutting through the pitch black. The tunnel was so low he had to bend over to walk. He'd chosen Lucas to accompany him for the simple reason that Brillante got distracted too easily. The boy's curly hair brushed against the ceiling.

Light appeared from ahead.

Roth switched off the headlamp and motioned for his son to do the same. The two were soon engulfed in darkness. Roth's whole body tensed, and he gripped Lucas's shoulder, ensuring he would stay put. He waited, trying to control his breathing so he could hear past the subtle tinnitus that was omnipresent when his surroundings were utterly quiet.

No sound came. As they stood still, Roth's eyes adjusted to the darkness. The light ahead wasn't from a flashlight or headlamp. It was angled from the ceiling. Sunlight? Roth had felt a gentle upward slope in the tunnel ever since they'd left the others at the raft.

"Hold my hand," Roth whispered to his son. The ringing in his ears increased. He felt his son grope for his hand in the dark.

Together, they started again. Roth continued forward, using his free hand to guide them along the edge of the wall, feeling the undulations of stone pieces carved and fit together to form it. The mortar had clearly deteriorated over time, suggesting the tunnel was centuries old.

The light grew brighter up ahead, piercing the tiny slits between the stones. The faint aura revealed some broken steps going up.

The ceiling met the top of the steps, the opening covered in stone.

Roth licked his lips and then scratched an itch on his chin beneath his bushy beard. The steps were as wide as the tunnel, barely enough for him and his boy to walk side by side.

"Stay put," he told Lucas. He let go of his hand and then crept forward, hearing the crunch of the gritty stone as he approached. The steps were narrow and steep, like the typical steps found in Maya ruins. Roth led with his hands, tracing them along the steps above him, feeling layers of dirt and dust on his fingertips. He smelled the damp stone and the scent of jungle beyond it.

Cautiously, he came up the steps using both hands and feet. At the top was a curved boulder. It looked heavy.

If he were a soldier or guard, the best place to wait would be just past the stone. He put his ear up to it and listened to the stillness. He could hear Lucas's worried breathing behind him, but he could discern no sound past the stone.

That made him pause and think. If he only lifted it a little, the noise would reveal him . . . but it would also reveal if someone was standing up there. They would have to pull the stone to get at him, which would give him and Lucas a chance to run back to the raft. It wasn't that far, and Lucas would get there first to warn the others.

"See anything?" Lucas whispered.

"Nope. Don't hear anything either. I'm going to try and lift this stone. I need you to be ready to run back in case someone's out there."

"What if you need help lifting it?"

"I'm pretty strong. Let me try it first. On the count of three, okay?"

"Okay."

Roth positioned himself on the steps and put his back up against the boulder so he could use his leg strength to lift it. It felt awkward and cramped, but he held himself in that position.

"One. Two. Three!"

Roth shoved his shoulder against the heavy stone. It moved slowly, grinding against the stone lip it was nestled in. After a little more effort and a lot more hard breathing, he managed to lift it high enough to see.

The light from outside nearly blinded him, and then the sounds of the jungle came rushing into the void. Birds squawked, and he saw a gray iguana dart away from him. A round opening above looked like the rim of a well. The stone shaft was rough except where green moss clung to it, but the top of the interior was coated in cut stones. A few steps led down to his current location. He pushed the boulder aside, giving him a reprieve from its weight, and left the opening just wide enough that he could squeeze through it if he crawled on his stomach.

Roth did exactly that, snaking out of the hole until he could stand up straight, though he kept low. He heard Lucas padding up the stone steps behind him. When he lifted his head higher, he saw jungle around him, but directly ahead stood a stone temple, much smaller than the one they'd climbed. It was probably only ten feet tall.

No one was there. No one but an iguana. His anxiety began to ease.

Part of the ceiling of the temple had crumbled and decayed. A dirt trail right in front of him led up to the main door of the temple. The trail looked well-traveled. Jungle trees with thin trunks and brown-and-gray speckled bark could be seen all around him. He watched as the iguana vanished around the corner of the stone temple.

Roth brushed the dirt off his arms, feeling the sting of his cuts. Lucas came up next to him and jumped so he could see over the rim of stones.

"That's a small one," he said, regarding their surroundings with wide eyes.

There was a little stone plinth about a dozen yards away with a tourist description on it.

"Cool," Lucas said, scuffing his sandal on the stone flooring. "There's a lizard!"

Roth noticed at least three more iguanas. Two were gray and one was bright green.

Tilting his head, he listened for the sound of the helicopter. He couldn't hear anything other than the shushing of the jungle trees as they swayed in the light breeze, but anxiety made him doubt his own senses. What if the soldiers were charging through the jungle at that moment, heading right for them? Time was still a problem, and not just because of their pursuers. They needed insulin for Sarina.

Should they return to the raft and follow the underground river farther? He had no idea where they were or how far they were from civilization.

Roth pulled Suki's phone out of his pocket. He saw a text message from Moretti with the contact info of Avram Morrell and a text message: *Let me know when you're at a safe house.*

There were two bars of cell service. That meant they were even closer to San Miguel. He opened the map app. He and Lucas watched the screen as it showed their position. They were in the jungle, northeast of San Miguel. But they weren't in the middle of nowhere. A name was pinned to their location: *Zona Arqueológica San Gervasio.*

It was a popular Maya ruin on Cozumel, a major tourist destination on the island.

He smiled and nudged Lucas.

"We're not lost?" Lucas asked hopefully.

"We're not lost. And we're past the fence surrounding the compound. This is a tourist stop." Roth knew there were several ruins in the park. They were at one of the points on the trail. "Go get Mom and the others. Hurry."

Lucas grinned and then ducked back under the cleft of stone at the bottom of the well, sprinted back down the steps, and torpedoed down the tunnel. Roth rubbed his hand on the stone rim and then hoisted himself out of the tiny cenote. He quickly approached the tourist marker he'd seen. There were three languages on it. He recognized the Spanish on the left and the English on the right, but the middle one was unrecognizable—probably Mayan. From the translation, he learned that the structure was the temple of Nohoch Nah, and it had been built between 830 and 950 AD.

He walked quickly around the temple, amazed that such a structure was still standing. Roth had visited Germany, his own ancestral land, once before. He'd been in awe at some of the ancient castles and cathedrals he'd seen, but this temple was older still, built by Mesoamerican tribes that had existed long before Germany was even a unified country.

"Poggers," he said with a smile, chuckling to himself. It was pretty cool.

He heard the sound of running coming from the tiny cenote.

CHAPTER SEVENTEEN

Nohoch Nah temple

Cozumel, Mexico

December 24

As the helicopter soared over the lush jungle treetops to San Gervasio, Jacob Calakmul maneuvered through the underground river. For the chase, he'd decided on a different form, one more suitable to swimming. Alligators were very fast, even more so than dolphins. He knew the river well. It led to the ruins of San Gervasio. Even on a holiday like Christmas Eve, the parking lot would be teeming with buses and vans from all the tourists. Tourists who came in planes and hulking ships, ready to spend US dollars for T-shirts, trinkets, wooden masks, drawn to the buzz of the vendors crooning, "Only a dollar, almost free!"

One day that would all change. The tourists would all be dead.

He didn't need a flashlight to see in the dark. The magic of the Maya flowed through his reptilian being, his senses boosted beyond the abilities of his human self. The boat the Roths had stolen only had paddles. They'd chosen the slowest one because starting a motor would have taken too long, and the soldiers chasing them would have caught them. The slash marks on the boats had proven once again that Mr. Roth was a quick thinker.

Jacob's alligator form wove through the limestone columns, following the current as it added to the speed. There was one trail. One destination. One outcome. The Roths would be caught. His new shape would terrify them.

Coming around a bend, he smelled something different in the air. Something man-made. The smell of rubber.

All the major temples in the Yucatán were built over rivers and cenotes. Some archaeologists were barely discovering the secret over at Chichén Itzá. That temple, dedicated to Kukulkán, had been conquered by the Order of the Jaguar, but they'd long since abandoned it. As the most popular tourist destination in the region, it had too many visitors each year. Jacob had visited many times, imagining how it had once been when the Maya had ruled the area. Back before the Spanish came with their pox and gunpowder.

In the ancient days, cedar canoes had been used to shuttle people through the underground waterways. Wooden chests had held the treasures back then, allowing them to be moved from place to place without the conquistadors finding anything. Once the temples had been sealed off, getting into the stone structures was practically impossible. Now things were different. Rubber boats with onboard motors were much faster.

Jacob saw the raft after he smelled it. It was drifting in the water at the edge of the dock leading to San Gervasio. The powerful stench of the raft obscured the other odors, but he could smell the humans as he got closer.

Swiftly, silently, he approached the raft. Most of his body remained submerged. Just his glowing eyes hovered above the water.

With a lunge, he snapped at the inflatable boat to shred into its protective barrier. The escaping air hissed noisily.

It was empty. The smell of human was stronger now. There were mud stains within from the family's dirty bodies. An empty water bottle was wedged into one of the seams. The oars were tossed haphazardly inside.

Jacob seethed with disappointment. There were multiple ways to enter and exit the underground river. Was it just bad luck that his pilot had chosen the wrong one, or was this another example of godly interference?

When he reached the edge of the dock, he transformed back to human to climb onto it. There were footprints in the dust leading to the ruins. There would be other people milling around up there. That would make it more difficult to abduct the family.

Jacob marched up the sloping corridor, bending awkwardly to avoid scraping the ceiling, observing evidence of the family's presence in the tunnel. Disturbed dust, a banana peel. His heightened senses could even smell their sweat and fear. The trail was fresh.

When he reached the stone slab leading to the cenote just outside the Nohoch Nah temple, he flung the boulder aside with the strength of his magic. The outside light blinded his eyes for a moment after he climbed out of the cenote.

A police officer in battle gear charged down the steps from the temple, aiming his rifle at Jacob's chest.

"Stop! On your knees!" he commanded in English.

Jacob closed his eyes, trying to summon enough patience that he wouldn't murder the man right then and there.

One of the guards exclaimed, *"Está Señor Calakmul, tonto!"*

The SWAT member lowered his weapon, his face blanching with fear. *"Lo siento! Lo siento, Señor!"*

Jacob's rage was barely controllable. "You didn't find them?" he asked in an icy voice.

"Lo siento, Señor. There was no one over here but some orphans."

CHAPTER EIGHTEEN

SAN GERVASIO ARCHAEOLOGICAL ZONE

COZUMEL, MEXICO

December 24

Roth hurried back to the cenote entrance as Bryant came wriggling beneath the cleft, Lucas close behind him. They were both gasping and out of breath. Then Jane Louise came up, smiling when she saw Roth again, and then Suki followed, her arm around Sarina, who looked tired and in pain.

His wife gave him a questioning look.

"We're at San Gervasio," Roth explained. "Look, there's a marker. This is public land."

"How far are we from San Miguel?" she asked breathlessly, hope shining in her eyes.

"Probably ten miles at most."

"I can't walk that far, Jonny," she said.

"We have to find a ride," he said. "It's Christmas Eve. There probably aren't a lot of tourists around, but let's see if there are any cars in the parking lot. Maybe a tourist bus? I don't know."

Sarina nodded. Suki was wearing her mom's sling purse with the first aid kit dangling from it.

Roth looked at his kids and Jane Louise. "Stay close. We're still in danger. But at least we're outside the fence. If you hear or see anything strange, tell me."

"Dude, an iguana!" Bryant shouted, pointing.

"I meant stranger than reptiles. Let's go."

The dirt path led straight ahead and also to the left. Roth thought the straight one was the way out, so he led the family that way, keeping his ears keen for other sounds. As they walked, the jungle trees became more pronounced, both taller and thicker.

They kept moving quickly. They were all filthy and bedraggled. They'd stand out in a crowd. Best to move along as fast as possible. Roth held Sarina's hand and tried to help speed her pace, but he could tell her strength was flagging.

Still. The only solution was to find a hospital or a doctor. They *had* to keep going.

Ahead, the road turned to the left but not before opening up to another part of the ruins.

"I think that's the way out," Roth said with excitement.

But he was wrong.

The tourist placard said it was the Templo Murciélagos. The *Temple of the Bats.*

He wasn't sure whether it would be quicker to go back the way they'd come or follow the dirt path on the left. They hadn't encountered anyone else yet.

"Can we rest a minute?" Sarina asked, panting.

Roth nodded and quickly checked the map app on Suki's phone to determine the correct direction. Sarina sat down on a square boulder, holding her head in her hands. Her skin looked sallow from her illness. They were all filthy from their journey, with big streaks on their clothes and grimy faces. But he loved the bunch of them, and his heart swelled with hope. They were so close . . .

"Can we go inside?" Lucas asked, pointing to the small temple. The dark entrance looked foreboding, and Roth shook his head. The steeply sloped roof reminded him of a stone beehive.

Roth heard voices coming up the trail ahead of them, not the one they'd been on.

"I heard something," Suki warned.

It was the laughter of children.

It only took a few seconds for the first children to appear, a pair of boys sprinting ahead toward the ruins at the Templo Murciélagos. Roth hesitated between rushing his family into the middle of the surrounding jungle trees or even hiding behind some of the crumbled walls. Hiding now wasn't possible. The boys saw them. They were followed by a small group, probably six children in all, ranging from five or six years old to twelve. With their darker skin and black hair, they looked like natives of Cozumel, not a group of international tourists. They had the grinning faces of children on an adventure. There were two adults, both short, walking behind the mob of kids.

Roth and Sarina watched as the group approached them from the bend in the trail. Their sons wandered closer, on edge now that they were around other people, and Jane Louise hid in Roth's shadow. Suki pushed up her glasses and looked to her parents for guidance.

The kids were prattling in Spanish as they reached the ruins. The older boys immediately began to explore, and the younger girls regarded the strangers with open curiosity. The woman had a swollen belly, but she wasn't any taller than the oldest boy.

"She's pregnant," Sarina observed in a low voice.

"*Tienes quince minutos,*" the man said.

"What did he say?" Roth asked.

"He said they had fifteen minutes."

The smallest of the children, a girl, came right up to them and smiled. *"Hola!"* she said with a little wave.

The pregnant woman approached them. *"Estás bien?"* she asked Sarina.

Sarina began to chat with her in Spanish. The man approached with a worried look and gave Roth a distrustful glance. Then he joined the women's conversation. Introductions were quickly given. The woman's name was Teresa, and the man was Antonio.

Sarina answered their questions and asked some of her own. After a while, she turned to Roth.

"They're from a Christian orphanage in San Miguel. Only two of the girls are theirs. The rest are orphans they're raising. They live in a compound paid for by donations."

An idea struck Roth. "How did they get here?"

"They have a shuttle bus," she said. "All the families share it."

Roth's heart began to pound. "Do you think we can trust them?"

The woman asked another question.

Sarina flinched. "She asked if we were staying at one of the resorts. I think we should tell them everything."

"See if they'll give us a ride to the hospital."

Sarina asked the question. The man and the woman exchanged a concerned look, and Roth's heart beat faster.

The man repeated their question.

"He wants to know what resort we were staying at."

Roth looked down at Sarina. She'd always been a good judge of people, so when she gave him a slight nod, he returned it.

"The orphanage might be a good safe house," Roth said. "I could call Moretti and his uncle once we get there. What's it called?"

"It's called Huellas de Pan."

"Tell them again that you need a doctor," Roth said pleadingly. "It's an emergency."

Sarina did so. The man looked even more uncomfortable and folded his arms. He spoke to his wife quickly in an undertone. Roth heard the word "Calakmul."

Sarina squeezed his hand. Hard.

"Let's get out of here," Roth said in warning.

"Not yet," Sarina urged. She spoke again in Spanish.

The woman looked past them and yelled, *"Bájate de ahí!"*

Roth turned and saw some of the older boys were trying to climb the roof of the temple. Glumly, they started coming back down.

The man asked a question again, but this time added the word "Calakmul."

"Sí. Necesito una doctora," Sarina said pleadingly. *"Me estoy muriendo."*

"Villa Sara?" the woman whispered in dread.

Roth swallowed. "Yes. *Sí.*"

She knew about the resort. So did her husband. The young mother began to speak. Sarina translated for Roth.

"The Calakmul family is *very* powerful. Not just in Cozumel. In all of Mexico."

"Tell them if they help us, I know a judge who can get us home," Roth said. "We just need a place to hide and a way to contact him. Tell them you need a doctor *now*."

The young mother looked at the children playing, then back at the Roth family. She bit her lip. But she looked concerned. Gentle.

The woman sighed and turned to her husband. *"Y cuándo te vimos extranjero, y te recogimos, o desnudo, y te cubrimos?"*

Roth had no idea what she was saying. He looked helplessly at Sarina. The husband's expression changed. He nodded firmly. *"Sí."*

His wife squeezed his hand and repeated, *"Y te recogimos."*

"What did they say?" Roth demanded.

Sarina's throat was tight with tears. "She just quoted from the New Testament. They're going to help us." She gave his hand another squeeze.

The man said something to Sarina, and she nodded, listening.

"Their little bus is in the parking lot. They don't want the children to know." She listened again and then said, "He wants us to go ahead and hide in the back of the bus where the luggage is usually kept. They'll tell the children they need to go back early for the piñata." Sarina listened again. "He'll drop the children and his wife at Huellas de Pan first. Then they can call for a doctor. He said they have one who comes to see their kids when they're injured or sick. Okay?"

Roth's heart clenched with relief. "Thank you," he said to the young couple.

The woman said something.

Sarina translated it. "She said to hurry. If they're chasing us, they aren't far behind."

The man fished in his pocket and removed the car key and handed it to Roth. He spoke again.

"The van has the name of the orphanage on it," Sarina said. "It's locked."

"Thank you," Roth said, taking the keys. *"Gracias."*

Sarina put her hand on Roth's arm. "I think they were meant to help us."

———

Roth and his family were walking as fast as Sarina could down the trail to the main entrance of San Gervasio. The couple had explained they'd reach the Plaza Central first, the largest tourist area of the park. Most of the tourists visited that area, and few took the longer trails to the smaller temples. It was a giant triangle, already crowded, and if they didn't go in the correct direction, they'd end up back at the Nohoch Nah temple where they'd started. The van was in the parking lot among many huge tour buses.

Each step brought them closer to freedom, but Roth still worried about what lay ahead. Calakmul's reach was longer than he'd realized, and he clearly didn't intend to stop until he found them.

"What Bible passage did Teresa say at the end?" Roth asked her. "I didn't understand the Spanish."

"From Matthew, I think. 'When did we see you a stranger and invite you in? Or needing clothes and clothe you?' When she said that passage, I knew we could trust them. They look like they're in their late twenties. So many children to care for. These are kids . . . some orphans . . . some not . . . that no one else wants."

"If we get out of here, I'm going to send a lot of money to that orphanage," Roth said. "Seriously."

"I hope they have real food," Brillante said. "I'm sick of bananas."

"I'm thirsty," Lucas chimed in.

"Didn't you hear what your mom just said?" Roth exclaimed. His heart was hurting for these poor kids, and his children were griping about bananas. But that was typical of teenagers.

They soon reached the plaza, which was indeed crowded. The tourists, mostly older, probably retired people, were gathered in small groups with English-speaking tour guides identified by lanyards and badges. The large open space was covered in various crumbled ruins, and the Roths passed a guide gesturing to one of them as he said, "This is the bathhouse where the Maya princesses were given steam baths. Their husbands were off in the jungle, trying to find a kill that they would bring back here to prove they were old enough to support a family. Boys as young as twelve got married here."

Suki snickered at the comment, and Lucas and Brillante exchanged horrified looks.

It taxed Roth's memory, but he recalled that the Spanish had set up a base of operations in this place and renamed it San Gervasio. It had once been a temple special to the Maya. In fact, the island of Cozumel had its name from the Mayan language—Cuzamil. It was an island of birds. Swallows. A religious retreat that the Maya rulers had visited in pilgrimage once per year.

He overheard another tour guide as they passed. "It was common for ruling families to try to have more than thirteen children so that one could be sacrificed to each of the thirteen gods."

That made Roth's eyebrows arch in surprise, and he gave more of his attention to the tour guide for a moment. Nothing more was said, but he registered that the tourists all wore bands around their wrists, the kind you get at an amusement park or festival to show that a fee had been paid. The Roths didn't have them, of course, and they were all dirty. Some of the tourists looked at them as they passed, reminding him of the danger of standing out.

When they reached the far end of the plaza, there was a marker indicating a path straight ahead and one to the left. Thankfully, it was clear which way led to the exit. They couldn't afford to waste time going in circles.

The path felt too exposed, but there were so many tourists coming in and out that it would be too difficult to spot their family from above, especially with all the polo shirts and cargo shorts. Their greatest danger was from forces on foot.

"I'm thirsty," Sarina whispered.

"Does anyone have more water?" Roth asked.

Jane Louise, clinging to Sarina's hand, lifted the half-full bottle clutched in her other hand. Sarina took it and drank some of it before giving it back.

The shuddering of her hands deepened Roth's alarm. How much time did they have left? He worried they were down to a matter of hours.

"Do you want me to carry you on my back?" he asked her.

"Save your strength," she murmured. She groaned and nodded back to the trail. Another tour group was headed their way. "Let's go. *Vamos.*"

Continuing on the trail, they hurried at a brisk pace until they reached the last altar. Two more shrines could be seen, each with a single group of tourists led by guides. The path veered to the right, and they could see the buildings clustered ahead: a hut and some restrooms and a bunch of gift shops. They'd reached the entrance to the park.

The path led directly to the huts, which would put them in sight of the employees, so Roth thought it best to veer off the path in case they were challenged for not having the bracelets. But if people saw them heading into the jungle, it would be equally noticeable. He hoped they could just slip past with the crowd without drawing attention.

"Stick your hands in your pockets and follow me," he told everyone and led them into the thick of the tourists. There were so many people milling about that no one challenged them. It didn't take long to bypass the huts.

The parking lot was swollen with tour buses and vans. Several of the drivers stood in a cluster, talking quickly in Spanish.

"What was the name of the orphanage again?" Roth asked.

"Huellas de Pan." Then Sarina spelled it out. "Who can find it first?"

"There it is!" Suki said, pointing. "Victory toot-toot!"

The name of the orphanage was painted on the side of one of the off-white tour vans along with a logo. The windows were dusty, and plenty of mud was splattered on the flanks.

"We made it," Lucas breathed in relief.

A lone iguana strolled through the parking lot.

Roth scratched his throat and then looked at all the drivers waiting near their buses. There was no driver at theirs. Another big bus came lumbering into the lot. Roth glanced around, then hurried over to the orphanage van, unlocked it, and pulled open the door. He motioned for the others to climb in. Suki brought Jane Louise first.

"Go to the very back," he said in an undertone, "back where the luggage is kept." He waved for the boys to come next. Sarina was following behind them, lagging, and he felt another pang of worry.

"Do we have to wear seat belts?" Lucas asked.

Roth snorted. "No. Just cram back there. They don't want the kids to know about us."

"Smells bad in here," Lucas complained after a prolonged sniff.

"Just get in the back."

Sarina was still several feet away. As she approached them, putting on a smile for the kids, he heard the crunch of tires on gravel. A smaller car was pulling into the parking lot behind the big tour bus.

Roth's heart started beating harder as he got a look at the silver-and-blue pickup truck with flashing lights, moving speedily enough that it brought a plume of dust with it. Roth hurriedly got inside. Through the dirty windows of the van, he got a better look at the truck. A dark blue section of the siding bore an unmistakable police badge with the words—"Policía Quintana Roo." The bed of the truck had thick roll bars on it. Men in uniforms and SWAT gear sat in the back.

Roth beckoned for Sarina to hurry, his face contorting with panic.

The noise of the crunching gravel stopped, and the doors of the police truck flew open.

CHAPTER NINETEEN

San Gervasio Archaeological Zone

Cozumel, Mexico

December 24

Roth realized the police would see Sarina getting into the van, and then it would all be over. Grimacing with dread, he gestured for her to go past the van and then shut and locked the door. He leaned back against it.

"Everyone get down!" he whispered harshly to the kids. "The police!"

Suki had been waiting in the aisle, whereas the boys and Jane Louise were clambering to the back. She ducked into the nearest row and flattened herself on the floor.

"Dude, hurry up!" Brillante whispered to his brother.

"Shhh!" Roth hissed. His heart was beating wildly.

He heard men's voices approaching the van. Where was Sarina?

Then he heard her voice, speaking in Spanish. Worry crowded into his throat. He itched to rise and peek through the dusty window, but he didn't want to risk bringing notice to the kids. They'd hunkered down, thankfully, and quieted down too, the seriousness of the situation not lost on any of them.

More conversation. A shadow passed the window. Roth could hear the sound of the boots on the gravel just outside the van. He slunk down as low as he could squeeze his body.

"Dónde?" the police asked.

Sarina made an answer.

An order was given, and suddenly he heard the sound of running. He waited, his nerves taut. Then a gentle tap landed on the door.

He lifted himself up and saw Sarina standing there. He unlocked the door, and she hurried inside.

"What did you tell them?" he asked, pulling her into a fierce hug.

"They showed me a picture of you," she said. "Asked if I'd seen an American and his family inside the park. I said yes and told them about the first temple we saw. They ran ahead to check it out."

Roth hugged her tighter, pressing a kiss to her neck. "I was so worried."

"I'm okay, Jonny." She rubbed his neck. "Where are the kids?"

"Some of us are lying on a smelly floor," Suki said, popping up behind a seat.

"We're in the back!" Lucas said.

Roth still kept low, but the police truck, lights flashing, looked like it was abandoned. He wondered if they should cram into the truck and make a run for it, then realized how ludicrous the idea was and how exhausted he must be for having it. Doing something that impulsive would get them killed. He wished he still had the obsidian spear and could slash one of the tires. He left the keys on the driver's seat and unlocked the door.

"Let's get settled before they get back with the kids," he suggested.

The rest of them crawled over the last row of seats. Roth was the final one and struggled to fit in the gap, so they had to lower the seat to allow room for him.

"Anyone hungry for Chick-fil-A?" he asked after squeezing onto the floor in between Sarina, Jane Louise, and Suki. He puts his arm around Sarina, and she snuggled into him. The boys had crawled under the last row, in the empty space where luggage could be stored.

"I want a milkshake so bad," Lucas moaned.

"Waffle fries," Brillante said. "I could eat three orders and a spicy chicken sandwich."

Suki wrinkled her nose. She hated spicy stuff. Roth tousled her hair, and she swatted his hand away.

"Can I take your order?" he asked.

"I'm more of a Wendy's girl," she said. "A chocolate Frosty sounds pretty legit right now."

He looked at Jane Louise. "What about you? What would you order?"

The girl blinked. "My mee-maw takes me to McDonald's. My brothers never want to go there, and Mom and Dad always let them pick."

Roth sighed. The poor kid. She looked surprised to even be asked her opinion about such a trivial matter. He had a feeling he knew what kind of parents the Beasleys were. "What do you like from McD's?"

"Pancakes and syrup," said Jane Louise. She lowered her head onto her arms, tilting it sideways.

"That sounds pretty good right now," Roth said. "I'll get you some pancakes when we get back to Bozeman. As many as you want."

The little girl smiled, and Roth felt a tugging at his heart. He also wanted to smash Eric Beasley in the face.

Sarina was still leaning against him. He pulled her closer. "What about you? What do you want to eat?"

"She's asleep," Suki whispered.

Roth craned his neck and looked down, taking in the pallor of his wife's face. Her eyelids were closed but fluttering.

She didn't need a fast-food meal. She needed insulin.

"Can I have my phone back?" Suki asked, holding out her palm.

Roth pulled it out and looked at it, seeing that the battery was really low. "I still need it to contact Moretti's uncle. Sorry." He paused and glanced at Sarina, whose eyes were open and looking wearily back at him. He tilted his head, and she gave him a slight nod. "Kids. Mom needs a doctor. Her insulin pump broke when she fell in the cenote."

Lucas and Brillante reacted with open mouths. Suki grabbed Sarina's wrist. "That long? That's bad, isn't it?"

Sarina nodded. "My body is used to getting regular spurts of insulin. Having none at all has thrown everything out of whack."

"We need to go to the hospital," Lucas insisted. Brillante nodded adamantly.

"We're trying, bud," Roth said. "We need to get out of here. We're still too far from the city. But this is the next step. I won't lie. Diabetes is serious."

Suki squeezed Sarina's wrist.

His wife patted her hand. "These people are helping us. That's a good thing."

Roth unlocked the phone to use the GPS to find a hospital. They could get out of the van midway to the orphanage if need be. Actually, maybe they should just take the van. Roth was already planning a sizeable donation to the orphanage if they made it out, but he'd feel bad about stealing their van after they'd offered to help. They clearly didn't have many resources.

And yet . . .

Time was running out.

Sarina was getting sicker and sicker. Her body was killing itself. Diabetic ketoacidosis, or DKA, had one outcome if not treated. Coma and then death.

"Hon," Roth said, jostling Sarina. "Hon, wake up."

Sarina's chin had dipped down to her chest. It sounded like her breathing was troubled.

"Hon," Roth said, jostling harder.

Suki stared at her mom worriedly, biting her lip.

"Mom?" Lucas asked.

Roth sat up and shook her more forcefully.

Sarina's head lifted, her eyes blinking. "Did I fall asleep?"

Relief gushed in Roth's heart. "You gotta stay awake, Sarina. You gotta stay awake."

Sarina nodded, then winced. "I need to go to the bathroom again."

"We have to stay in the van," Roth said.

Moments later, he heard voices approaching the vehicle. The side door was flung open, and kids began to scramble inside, chattering away in rapid Spanish. Roth's kids instantly fell silent.

"A qué huele?" said one of the kids, sniffing loudly.

The parents entered the vehicle through the driver's and passenger's doors and began to speak as well. The engine revved to life.

The van was put into gear, and the tires crunched on the gravel as the vehicle accelerated. They were bouncing a little in the back, but they tried to keep quiet as the van left the ruins and the police truck behind.

The kids from the orphanage kept chattering away. Roth caught snatches of their words but didn't know Spanish well enough to translate. Lucas began drifting off to sleep only to be poked awake by his brother. The ambient noise in the van made it possible for them to communicate in whispers.

Without being able to look out a window, Roth began to get motion sickness. Sitting on the floor in the back, he could see very little except the tops of trees as they rushed down the lonely road leading away from San Gervasio. His mind was whirring, pinging with danger from Calakmul to Sarina's condition.

If the DKA got any worse, she would need to be hospitalized. A shot of insulin would help to stabilize her, but he wasn't sure how long it had been since the pump had delivered a small dose of insulin.

He brought his mouth close to her ear so he could whisper to her. Her head was lolling with the motion of the van, but her eyes were open, staring off into space.

"When was the last time you went this long without insulin?"

She rubbed the bridge of her nose. "I'm not sure," she whispered back. "The pump adjusts the dosage based on my glucose levels, and I hadn't looked at it since I reattached it at the van. I'm going to need a glucometer to test my sugar or get my sensor app readings on my phone to know how much insulin to take."

Back when they were younger, Sarina had always carried insulin and needles in her purse just in case. The pump had saved them from that necessity, so in their rush to leave the resort, she had forgotten to pack all her supplies.

"What are they talking about?" Roth asked after the van had been moving for a while. It wasn't that far to San Miguel. Only twenty minutes or so.

Roth nudged her again to rouse her.

"I'm so tired," she whispered.

The van began to slow down. It had felt like the husband was speeding on purpose. Maybe they were reaching San Miguel.

"I think we're almost there," he whispered. Sarina nodded and looked up. Roth's stomach was roiling even more now. He was hungry and carsick. The bananas they'd eaten had not been very filling. What he really wanted was a New York steak, cooked medium well, with a baked potato the size of a Nerf football.

"*Es un accidente?*" one of the boys in the van called out.

He knew enough Spanish to know he was asking if the slowdown was caused by an accident.

The dad spoke up loudly. *"La barricada! Es la policía!"*

Sarina's hand pressed against Roth's chest. "The police set up a roadblock," she whispered fearfully.

The same emotion began to snake through Roth's chest again. They'd escaped the jungle. They'd escaped the underground river. They'd escaped the ruins and the police in the parking lot. When would their luck give?

Jacob Calakmul must have set up a checkpoint to stop traffic going into San Miguel.

The police had shown Sarina a picture of Roth. With his wild hair and long beard, he certainly stood out. People at conventions sometimes asked how he'd grown his beard so big. The question was irrational. It required no effort to grow a beard at all. He hated scraping his neck with a razor. It was pure laziness and economy of effort, not a grand strategy.

The van slowed and then stopped.

The orphans were chittering with nervousness. They asked a flood of questions until the mother finally told them to be quiet. At least, he figured that's what she'd said since her words silenced them. The van crept forward slowly.

Roth's gaze landed on the handle to the back door. Could they slip out the back of the van? If they were on the edge of San Miguel, maybe they'd be able to slip into town another way. He didn't want to get the group from the orphanage into trouble for helping them. But there were undoubtedly cars lined up behind them. If so, they'd be noticed right away.

"Suki," Roth whispered in his softest voice. "Can you peek out the back window? Any cars behind us?"

His daughter nodded and then sat up slowly, cautiously, until she had a view out a dirty window. Suki wrinkled her nose. "There's a pretty big line of them."

Roth motioned for her to get down again.

"What do we do?" Sarina whispered.

Everyone was exhausted. But amid the growing tension, he felt his adrenaline kicking in. He was grateful he hadn't stolen the van from the parking lot because they would have been nailed at the checkpoint for sure. Either they could trust the parents to talk their way past the barricade, or they could try to run for it. In Sarina's weakened condition, running was not a good option.

"Dad?" Suki asked worriedly.

"We trust this couple," Roth said helplessly. "If we're caught, we're caught."

He heard the sound of the window coming down.

"Hola," said the dad. *"Qué pasa?"*

"Estamos buscando a este hombre americano. Lo has visto?"

Roth looked at Sarina in confusion.

Her eyes sparkled with worry. She didn't need to translate it for him to understand.

They were looking for *him*.

CHAPTER TWENTY

SAN LORENZO OUTSKIRTS

COZUMEL, MEXICO

December 24

The driver of the van, the father, began to speak in low tones. Roth's pulse quickened. His gaze skated to the latch for the back door again. With the rumble of the engine and the chatter of the children, he couldn't catch what was being said.

"We might have to run after all," he said in a low voice. "Get ready."

How far could they get before the police saw them? Not far. He couldn't tell how close they were to the jungle, and surely the other cars and vans would start honking to alert the authorities.

Sarina sat up, squeezing his arm. "Wait."

Brillante and Lucas were starting to crawl out from beneath the luggage shelf, making noise.

Roth held a finger to his mouth and gave them warning looks.

Then he saw a head pop over the back seat. A little boy, looking down at them in confusion and surprise.

Sarina was listening intently, trying to overhear the conversation at the front of the bus. She leaned close to Roth and whispered in his ear. "He said they saw a man who looks like you at the ruins at San Gervasio. A family of Americans. He said the officers must have already arrested him."

The police officer said something else.

"They're going to search the van," Sarina gasped.

Roth met the eyes of the little boy looking down at them. His stomach quivered with dread. Maybe he should wait for the officer to open the back door and then kick it hard enough to knock him down.

How many police were there at the checkpoint? They were probably armed, but Roth suspected they wanted his family alive. If not, they would have already shot them.

Running might be the only way.

"I need a better position," Roth whispered. He pivoted, turning his back on the child, and pulled his legs up so he could get leverage to kick the door back.

"Suki, get ready to pick up Jane Louise. We're going to make a run for the jungle."

Suddenly, the side door of the van opened. The children had fallen quiet, and Roth could practically hear the beating of his own heart.

The driver said something, and then all the children said in unison, *"Hola."*

"Hola, niños," said the officer at the door. Sweat trickled down Roth's back. The carsickness was still building up. He felt a threatening wave of nausea. Not now! Not now!

They were all cramped in the back. Brillante and Lucas were staring at him and nudging each other. Their expressions suggested they knew he was on the verge of vomiting. Suki shook her head back and forth.

An uncontrollable spasm shot through Roth's stomach. Suddenly his ears were ringing, and his insides twisted and wrenched.

The officer spoke again. *"Hola, niño. Qué estás haciendo ahí?"*

Sarina gripped Roth's arm worriedly.

She was staring up at the child looking down at them. Had the officer asked the little boy a question? Roth didn't know. His vision began to blur.

The little boy raised his arm and pointed. *"Eso es un gran autobús!"*

The officer chuckled. *"Sí. Así es."*

Then the door slammed shut, and they heard a hand slap against the metal siding. The van started to move forward, crawling at first and then accelerating again.

"That was close. Jonny, lie down. Let's get your legs elevated."

Roth felt his stomach would erupt any minute, but he obeyed and lay flat on the bottom of the swaying van, propping his feet up on the wall. The other kids moved as far away from him as they could. Sarina stroked his hair and then looked up at the little boy.

"Gracias por no decirlo," she whispered to him.

He smiled brightly at her.

"What did you say?" Roth asked, stifling a groan.

"I thanked him for not telling."

They were past the checkpoint now, accelerating. He watched the tops of palm trees flashing past and then closed his eyes because lying down wasn't helping his queasy stomach.

Sarina lifted herself up a little and looked out the window. "We're in San Miguel," she said.

"Does that mean we're safe?" Suki asked, pushing up her glasses.

"It'll be harder for them to find us in the city," Roth said. "There are a lot of tourists."

"Dad, we look like shipwreck survivors," Suki said flatly. She wasn't wrong.

"Maybe we can borrow some clothes?" Sarina offered.

"Dad could finally *shave*," Brillante suggested.

"That would be sick. I've never seen him without a beard." Lucas grinned.

"I'd look terrifying, but thanks for the idea." Roth chuffed. He hadn't shaved off his beard since . . . actually, he couldn't remember the last time he'd shaved it off. He'd started growing one in high school.

The van slowed and then made a turn, and they began to crisscross different streets. They went up and down, left and right. Roth's stomach was beginning to heave again.

"Crap, I'm not going to make it," he moaned, clutching his stomach.

Sarina blew air on his face.

The road became very bumpy, and each pothole they shot over made Roth think he'd lose the battle with nausea. He remembered the car trips he'd taken with his parents as a kid. His dad used to have to pull over so he could throw up on the side of the road. Dramamine had been a life changer, although it made him drowsy.

The van slowed and stopped. A door opened, but the engine was still running. Then the noise of a squeaking gate could be heard outside, and the children in the van began chittering with excitement.

Some words were spoken outside, and Roth heard a new voice. The conversation was in Spanish, so he couldn't understand the exchange.

"Can you hear them?" he asked Sarina, looking up at her as she continued to blow on his face. She was breathing rapidly, as if out of breath, and it smelled fruity as it had before. Only stronger.

"It's too noisy," she said.

Then the father came back and shut the door, and the van drove in through the gate and into a shadowed area. It crept in slowly and then stopped. The engine cut.

The side door opened, and the kids spilled out, running and laughing. All except the little boy, who was still watching them with an expression of innocent interest.

Roth heard some more words spoken as two men approached the back of the van. Struggling to sit up, he watched the back door as it swung open. Roth recognized the dad who'd been driving the van. An even shorter man stood next to him—an older fellow who looked to be about sixty years old. He had a gray mustache, big glasses, a navy-blue tracksuit, and sandals. And he was wearing a purse.

"Ay," said the older man when he saw them, quickly rubbing his mouth. "Come out. Es okay. Es okay!"

Roth swung his legs over the edge of the van. For a second he just absorbed his surroundings—the fresh-smelling air and the lawn they'd parked on next to a smaller Toyota minivan—and then the buzzing in his ears nearly exploded, and Roth found himself on his knees, vomiting noisily onto the grass. Chills rushed through his body.

The older man knelt by him, hand on his back.

"Okay, okay," he soothed.

Finally, the torture ended. The relief to his stomach was pronounced. Roth sat back on his haunches and wiped his mouth on his arm. Sweat streaked down his face. He itched all over. One look at his grossed-out kids suggested this would be another memory imprinted permanently in their brains.

He felt weak from lack of food, dehydrated, and near fainting. As he tried to get back to his feet, the old man helped him up.

"*Soy muy malo* with English," the man apologized. "*Soy Jorge. Bienvenidos.*"

Roth saw the puddle of muck at the man's sandaled feet, but his host didn't seem to care. The man gripped one of Roth's arms, and Sarina helped with the other. That she hadn't come to help him sooner was further proof of her suffering.

"Are you all hungry?" Jorge asked. "*Tienes hambre?*"

"We haven't eaten much," Roth said. Jorge looked confused at the words, but Sarina translated his words into Spanish. She was still holding Roth's other arm.

The building they were parked next to was a dull yellow. Directly ahead was the gate they'd come in through. Past the gate was a building painted a yellow orange so bright it stung the eyes. Thick trees were just past a wall that appeared to be made of concrete or stucco, about eight feet tall.

Then Roth heard the sound of an airplane engine growing louder and louder. Cozumel had an international airport, although it was more expensive to fly there than to Cancún.

"*Sí, sí. Comida.* Food. Let's get some food."

"My wife needs a doctor," Roth insisted.

"*Sí.* I know. One will come. I promise." He was like a mother hen, trying to gather the chicks to him, waving his arm invitingly. "You are safe. Welcome to Huellas de Pan. It is a little *ciudad de ángeles.* A city of angels. Come. You will see."

———

Dinner was a bowl of small elbow macaroni in tepid white sauce, with chunks of ham and two small saltine crackers.

Nothing had ever tasted so good. Roth finished his first bowl in about a minute and put it aside. But Jorge insisted the cook, who was even shorter than him, with a black fishnet cap and light blue jeans, refill it from the massive bowl of pasta. Jorge brought it to Roth with a kindly smile.

"Eat. Eat."

Everyone was gobbling up the meal, especially the twins. Suki had a disaffected look—she was usually pretty picky—but even she was hungry enough to want it. Jane Louise had a glad smile as she ate hers.

The cook then brought an assortment of plastic cups, most of them different from each other, with a brown fluid in them.

"*Jugo.* Juice," Jorge explained. "Drink."

It wasn't very sweet, and Roth feared they might get sick from drinking it, but he was too thirsty to care.

"*Agua para mí,*" Sarina said, and they brought her a cup of water, which she drank down rapidly before asking for more.

Sarina's bowl sat in her lap, untouched. She looked exhausted, but she asked Jorge for more information about the orphanage, and he answered in Spanish at some length. Finally, he nodded, smiled, and clasped his hands over the little leather purse hanging on a strap in front of his tracksuit.

"The food they feed the children comes from a single resort," Sarina explained. "It's against the law in this state, Quintana Roo, to allow the tourists' leftovers to be used to feed the hungry. And there are so many hungry. But one resort doesn't throw their waste away. Jorge picks it up discreetly and uses it to feed the kids. Sometimes all they have is one meal a day."

Guilty looks came across their eyes. Roth stopped eating his second bowl. He couldn't eat the food that was supposed to feed the children at the orphanage.

"Eat, eat," Jorge implored in his kindly manner when he saw that Roth had stopped.

"I'm full," Roth said, lying. He hadn't even found the edge of his hunger yet, but he couldn't take from the kids.

Jorge looked at Roth seriously. "My English is so-so. Spanish okay?" he asked, looking at Sarina.

"Sí," she said, nodding.

Jorge began to talk again. Even though Roth couldn't understand what he was saying, he felt a strange connection to the man. This fellow reminded him of the bishop from *Les Misérables*. There was an aura of goodness, of kindness, about him. Jorge spoke passionately, using his hands as he talked, pointing and gesturing to himself, to the cook, then to Roth's family. He clasped his hands over his purse again when he was finished talking.

Sarina seemed moved by the words. She looked at Roth. "He said that God provides for them, and God will provide for us too. Everything they have here came from donations from others. The buildings. The playground. Even the little houses. He said more food will come tonight. He doesn't know how. But he will pray for it, and it will come."

"He will *pray* for food? Like what do you mean?"

Sarina clasped Roth's hand. "That's what he said. He prays for what they need. He said their van broke down, and he wasn't able to collect the food from the resort. He didn't have money to fix it, but he prayed for help. He was in San Miguel, his van at the shop. He couldn't afford to fix it. Then someone came up to him while he was praying. He asked him what was wrong. Jorge told the man that he was praying about a problem. The man asked about the problem. Jorge explained that the van was broken and they couldn't pick up food to feed hungry children. The man . . . the man had an extra van he wasn't using. He *gave* it to Jorge. To the orphanage. That's the one we rode here in."

Roth stared at her in surprise and then shifted his gaze to Jorge, who had a childlike smile on his face. His gray mustache quivered with it.

"*Sí*. I pray for help. *El Padre* helps *me*," he said, cupping his hands and pointing to his own chest. "I help you." Then he gestured to Roth with his cupped hands.

"That's pretty cool," Lucas said, wiping his eyes.

Roth looked at the man in wonder, his throat thick.

"Eat. Eat."

"Dude, they're playing soccer!" Brillante said, holding his empty bowl. He'd wandered over to the window and was looking outside. "Dad, can we play?"

Roth looked at Sarina.

"*El doctor?*" Sarina asked Jorge.

"He comes. He comes. *Tu marido tiene diabetes?*"

"No," Sarina said, tapping her chest with her palm. "*Yo la tengo.*"

"*Sí. Sí.* Let your children play. Almost dinner. *La cena.*"

"So we can play?" Lucas asked.

Roth and Sarina both nodded, and the two brothers whooped and ran outside to join the game. Suki leaned back on the bench against the table.

"Hard pass," she said with a yawn and set her bowl down.

The cook spoke no English, and she was a stern little woman, probably no more than ninety pounds, but she pointed to the bowl Roth had set aside and gestured for him to eat it all up. He drank some of the amber juice and then wolfed down the rest of the food.

"Want to watch the boys play for a little while?" he asked Sarina. "Until the doctor gets here?" He needed to call Moretti's uncle as well, but he wanted to wait until the doctor arrived to see if they'd be going to the hospital.

"Sure," Sarina said lethargically. She held on to his arm, and he brought her out to a little patio where they could see better. Suki and Jane Louise followed them.

The playing field couldn't be more different than the ones the boys played on in Bozeman. One goal was next to a pile of rocks and boulders. The other was against the outer wall of the compound. In between was nothing but gravel and dirt. But Lucas and Brillante joined in with enthusiasm, demonstrating their skill. Even though the twins didn't speak Spanish, the sport had a language all its own.

All of the kids rushed back and forth, panting, yelling to each other when they were open. Roth leaned against the doorway, watching his boys dart back and forth with the others. The other kids were good too, especially the older teenagers. There were body checks and a little roughhousing, but Brillante and Lucas joined in. No refs. No yellow cards.

He noticed Jane Louise was sitting on the ground, her back against the building, next to two other girls her age. They both had little Mead notebooks, the kind used in school, and they were drawing pictures of flowers.

"Ouch!" Suki said with concern. "That'll leave a rash."

Roth glanced back. Brillante had taken a spill, but he was on his feet again in a second, brushing off flecks of rubble, and clapped his hands and held two thumbs up to his brother after Lucas asked if he was okay.

"I missed it," Roth said.

Suki shook her head. "He just shrugged it off."

Jorge came outside and stood nearby. His gray mustache fluttered as he laughed.

"Your boys . . . play pretty good," he told Roth, pointing to the twins, who gave each other a high five.

"Thanks. They love soccer."

"Fútbol," said Jorge, smiling. "Twins?"

"Sí," Roth answered.

Jorge nodded knowingly. His blue tracksuit and sandals would stick in Roth's mind forever, as would his compassion and kindness, which had sunk into the very walls of Huellas de Pan. He was the sort of man who would end up in one of Roth's novels.

"You heard of the Popol Vuh?" Jorge asked. "Old Maya legend."

"Yes. It's the creation story some of the Maya told. Like the Old Testament."

"Sí, sí," Jorge said eagerly. "Very similar. The Popol Vuh tells a story about twins. Two boys, Hunahpu and Xbalanque."

The names didn't sound Spanish. They were probably Mayan. "What were their names again?"

"Hunahpu and Xbalanque."

Sarina chimed in. "They played the Maya ball game against the lords of death. They won. It's a famous story."

Sarina had been brought up with the legends.

Roth had not, but he remembered the story—vaguely—from when he'd looked through the Popol Vuh before. From what he remembered of the Hero Twins, as they were called, their mother had been impregnated by a plant spitting in her hand.

Apparently, the gods of the underworld hadn't appreciated the noise and commotion of the ball game being played in the living world, so they'd challenged the twins to a life-or-death match. After attending soccer games on weekends, Roth could appreciate that in his own way.

"How did the twins win?" Roth asked. All he remembered was that they'd outsmarted the gods of death somehow.

"*Sus cabezas,*" Jorge said, tapping his forefinger against his temple.

"They used their heads?"

"Not to play the game," Sarina said. "That would concuss anyone. He meant their wits."

"*Sí!* Like your family." His brow furrowed. "They say the games will start again, Señor Roth. When the jaguar priests return." He made the sign of the cross as if trying to banish a nightmarish idea.

Roth furrowed his brow. "What's the legend?"

Jorge's fingers waggled as he explained. "They were the true rulers in ancient times. Before the Spanish came, the Order of the Jaguar chose the kings. They were advisors. Warriors. Priests. Sorcerers. They warned Moctezuma about the Spanish. They knew. Took the gold, the jade, the obsidian, the silver. Hid it. Hid it in the underworld." He grinned. "Even here on Cozumel. Spanish came for the gold." He shrugged and held up his hands. "No one knows where it is. But the jaguar priests knew."

And so did Roth. His mind conjured images of those plastic chests in the cenote. Obviously, the treasure had been moved at some point, but perhaps it had always been kept down there. Surely the conquistadors would have searched the temples, though . . .

Sarina had dozed again on his shoulder, and he jostled her to wake her up again.

"I thought Cortés didn't find much gold," he said.

"No. Much war. Disease. But the jaguar priests waited. They waited in caves. Waited in the jungle. They used La Malinche to trick the Spanish."

"What's La Malinche?" Roth asked.

"A woman. A slave. She spoke the languages of the people."

"Malintzin?" Roth asked. He'd been fascinated by her story in his research.

"*Si! Si!* La Malinche! Her name means *betrayer*. Not a good thing, okay? She was sent *by* the jaguar priests, and she helped the conquistadors conquer her people."

Roth nodded, but he was still confused. He'd studied a lot of Mesoamerican history before coming on the trip, but his history degree was from the European side of the equation—how Spain had fought for its survival against competing forces. He knew a little of Aztec and Maya history, but his knowledge veered more toward the mythical than the factual. One of his favorite stories related to the legendary image of an Aztec warrior carrying a dead woman, which he'd seen on calendars in Sarina's mother's kitchen in San Jose. It depicted the classic Romeo and Juliet story of old Mexico—a warrior had fallen in love with a princess before going to war, and she died of grief after being falsely told of his death. The warrior carried her away to be buried, and the gods turned her into a snowy mountain. A romantic legend had been born.

The sputtering noise of a motorcycle or scooter registered over the noise of the children. A buzzer rang somewhere outside. Roth stiffened.

"*Es* okay. *Es* okay," Jorge soothed. "The doctor. It's the doctor at the gate." He ambled away.

A thrill of hope swelled in Roth's breast. Maybe he wasn't too late. Maybe everything would be fine. Sarina leaned against his shoulder, her hair fanning over her face, but she was staring at the soccer game, a little smile on her mouth.

"What's so funny?" he asked.

"She looks like my grandma," she mumbled.

He looked at the rocky soccer field. There wasn't an old woman there at all. The girls playing were all younger than Suki.

"Honey, wake up," he said, jostling her again. "Wake up." Sleep wouldn't stop the progression of the DKA. Only insulin would. And only if she got it in time.

Jorge's voice called from far away, *"Ayuda!"*

Sarina started in surprise. Roth looked toward the sound of the voice. He'd seen enough *Dora the Explorer* when Suki was a toddler to know what that word meant. A cry for help.

The cook hurried to the door, responding to the call. Roth peered around the corner, afraid of what he might see coming.

There was Jorge, struggling to walk with about eight boxes of Domino's Pizza in his hands.

CHAPTER TWENTY-ONE

HUELLAS DE PAN

COZUMEL, MEXICO

December 24

When considering their trip to the Yucatán, Roth had anticipated enjoying the flavors and variety of Mexican cuisine. He hadn't expected his family would have to run for their lives. He certainly hadn't expected they'd be hiding out in an orphanage on Christmas Eve, eating Domino's Pizza. But he was starting to relax after devouring a slice of the pizza, which had been delivered on a scooter, paid for by one of the university graduates of the orphanage who'd felt that Christmas Eve would be a great time to give the kids a little treat.

Roth, Suki, and the cook stood behind the kitchen counter of the eating hall. The cook scooped noodles and ham onto a plate, Roth added some crackers, and then Suki put on a slice of pizza. They had about twenty plates ready so far, and Jorge was greeting the children as they marched in to get some dinner.

"Cuál es tu saludo?" Jorge asked each child, one after one.

The child would then offer a salute of some kind, and Jorge would mimic it in response. Some kids saluted like they were in the military. Some just gave a thumbs-up. Each child had their own special salute, and Jorge took the time to respond to every last one. Lucas and Brillante, who had been playing soccer before dinner, had joined the line to get a slice of pizza. Roth had told them not to get more of the noodles since the other kids hadn't had any yet. When it was their turn to enter, Brillante did jazz hands and Lucas did a hip-hop move. The children who had already passed Jorge roared with laughter as he tried, and failed, to replicate the hip-hop move. The boys grinned and then joined a table with some of the soccer players. Although they didn't speak Spanish, the other kids had welcomed them.

"They're so derp," Suki said, chuckling.

"What does that mean?" Roth asked. "What's 'derp'?"

"It's cute . . . like in a nerdy way. You know . . . brothers. Or even pets."

There was so much teenager slang that Roth mostly just ignored it. He was glad he'd asked.

Sarina stood behind them, cleaning dishes in the vast sink with Jane Louise. She looked exhausted, but she was trying to stay awake.

The doctor would come soon. He had to.

After all the children were inside, Jorge quieted them down and began to speak to them, while the Roths continued to help prepare the plates for dinner. Jorge spoke with a delightful cadence, his *r*'s rolling effortlessly, as he addressed the children and the parents/chaperones who lived with them.

Roth couldn't make out the words.

"Are you getting any of what he's saying?" he asked his daughter.

Suddenly the kids cheered with excitement.

"I just heard 'piñata,'" Suki said. "Must be a Christmas Eve thing to set the vibe."

Jorge quieted them down again, gave some further instructions, and then the kids began to clap for the meal.

Bowing his head, Jorge offered a prayer, reciting the words stenciled onto the wall in large letters. The kids repeated each line of it. When he finished, Jorge gestured to the parents.

The parents came up to the counter to collect the plates of food and started handing them out to the kids at the tables. There were mismatched forks, all very small, but each child got a plate and fork. Once the food was served, they filled cups with the amber punch for the kids to drink.

Roth looked over and noticed that Sarina had one hand on her brow, the other bracing her body against the edge of the sink. He heard the water running, but she wasn't washing dishes. Jane Louise stared up at her worriedly, still holding out a dirty plate for washing.

Sarina started to sway, and Roth hurried over just in time to prevent her from collapsing. She was trembling violently. He gritted his teeth in frustration. Where was the doctor?

The cook had noticed Sarina's collapse, and she shouted for Jorge's attention. The older man hurried through the kitchen door to join them.

"She needs a doctor," Roth insisted. "Take us to the hospital. *Please*."

"Doctor will come."

Roth shook his head. "She's very sick. She needs one *now*."

Jorge motioned to them and led the way back out of the kitchen. The kids were still eating, but some of them watched the adults with worried expressions. The boys were sitting with the local kids, enjoying the fresh pizza. They weren't aware of what was happening to Sarina.

"Get your brothers and Jane Louise and follow us," Roth told Suki.

Suki nodded and hung back, telling Jane Louise it was time to go in a hushed voice. Jorge and the cook led them outside. They crossed the lawn to where the shuttle van and minivan were still parked and walked onto a concrete pathway alongside the building. Suki and the others caught up to them there. There was an arch that opened up, revealing another path lined with several small homes. But they passed that arch and went toward another gate.

Sarina started to moan and thrash.

Roth's patience was at an end.

"Mom?" Lucas asked fearfully.

"She'll be okay, bud," Suki said, putting her arm around her little brother.

Jorge led them into what appeared to be the main administration building. They passed a desk and an office, heading down another hall to a waiting room of sorts with some couches. Jorge pointed to one of them and then walked back to the front lobby.

Roth heard Jorge hit some keys, presumably to make a call, but his attention was fixed on Sarina. She was still shaking as he set her carefully down on the couch.

The cook hurried away and returned soon afterward with a blanket, but Roth knew her shaking wasn't from cold. He smoothed Sarina's hair, trying to calm the racing of his heart. Trying to assure himself she'd be okay. Her eyes fluttered, as if she were trying to wake up, but she couldn't open them.

"Can you hear me?" Roth asked softly.

"Y-Yes," she said, her teeth chattering.

Roth could hear Jorge speaking in the background. *"Sí . . . sí . . . muy bien."*

He gripped her hand tightly. "It's gotten worse?"

"Y-Yes," she answered again, more softly. "I'm so dizzy. F-Feels like the room is spinning."

This was all the Beasleys' fault. If the Beasleys hadn't had them over for dinner, none of this would have happened. Anger flashed through him, but he tried to tame it. Being angry wouldn't help his wife.

Jorge came back. "I called hospital. They . . . um . . . the *doctor* is coming now. There was . . . problem. Um . . . big problem. He's coming now. Ten minutes."

Roth nodded, feeling strangled by his surging emotions. The thought of losing Sarina was unbearable. Staring down at her trembling body, he pressed a fist against his mouth to stop himself from crying.

Then he felt a hand on his shoulder. Looking up, he saw Jorge gazing down at her, his face full of compassion. The older man gave a decisive nod. "I pray for her."

The cook nodded and then left. Jorge did the same. The kids gathered close. He saw the worry in their eyes. He didn't know what to say. He wanted to reassure them but didn't want to lie. The situation was serious . . . very serious.

Roth bowed his head. He'd never been religious. He didn't look down on people of faith, but he didn't trust in a power that he couldn't see, couldn't speak to. Sarina had been raised Catholic. She didn't go to mass very often, having been disillusioned by her faith as a teenager after going to a private Catholic school from elementary to high school and seeing how so many of the rich kids had disdained their religion. Going to church didn't make someone religious any more than going to a concert made someone a musician. The practice outside the halls was what counted.

A few minutes later Jorge returned, his expression full of worry. It brightened as soon as the buzzer at the gate sounded. He smiled enthusiastically and clipped away with his sandals. A minute later, he returned with the doctor.

The doctor, probably in his early thirties, with dark hair, looked like he'd been busy all day with little rest. He still wore hospital scrubs and carried a leather bag with supplies. A stethoscope was hung from his neck. The two men hurried toward the couch where Roth knelt.

"Do you speak English?" Roth asked the doctor.

The doctor shook his head. *"Un poquito,"* he declared. Sarina was still trembling from head to foot. She lifted her head slightly.

"Jonny?"

"The doctor is here. He doesn't speak much English."

The doctor rushed to Sarina and knelt by her side. He quickly took her wrist to check her pulse.

"Can he help her?" Brillante asked Suki.

Sarina began to speak to him in a low voice, in Spanish. Roth caught snatches of it. It sounded like she might be describing her symptoms, and he recognized the word "diabetes," which was the same in both languages, only pronounced differently in Spanish—"dia-bett-es."

The doctor nodded quickly, used his stethoscope to listen to her breathing, and then hurriedly opened his leather bag and withdrew a package of syringes and—thankfully—a supply of insulin.

He quickly prepared a dose of the insulin—a big one—and flicked the needle. The doctor pushed away the blanket and Sarina's shirt, revealing her swimsuit beneath it. He pinched skin on her abdomen, about a handsbreadth from her navel, and then injected the needle.

Roth almost looked away, feeling the familiar nausea creep into him again, the lightheadedness.

The doctor turned to Jorge. *"Ella necesita mucha agua. Agua embotellada."*

"Sí," Jorge said and hurried away.

"What did he say?" Roth asked.

"I've lost too much water," Sarina said, still wincing from the shot. The doctor finished depressing the syringe and then withdrew the needle. He set it down on the floor.

"No puedo llevarte al hospital," he said. *"Ellos te están buscando."*

"Does he want to bring you to the hospital?" Roth asked.

He needed to let Moretti's uncle know where they'd be.

Sarina shook her head. "He said he *can't* bring us there. They're looking for us."

The doctor gave Roth a worried look, then glanced back at her. He spoke in a low voice, and Sarina translated.

"He's only here because of Jorge, because of all he's done for the children of Cozumel. The Calakmul family is dangerous. They are powerful. The police, the military, the locals—they all fear him. He's . . . *cómo?*"

The doctor said it again. *"El sacerdote jaguar."*

A chill coursed down Roth's spine. The jaguar priests. Like the legend Jorge had told him about. They'd been involved with the ball game . . .

Roth frowned and shook his head. "Just a story. It's probably a new cartel. The jaguar is a sacred animal here. A symbol of power."

The doctor wasn't listening to the English. He gripped Sarina's wrist, testing her pulse again, and then pressed the stethoscope against her chest.

Roth looked at her worriedly. "You're going to be okay?"

Sarina asked the doctor a question.

The doctor looked deeply concerned. He answered rapidly and, to Roth, unintelligibly. Sarina closed her eyes.

"I need to rest."

"You're going to be okay?" he pressed.

"Too early to tell," she whispered.

"No," Lucas whimpered.

"What? But he gave you insulin!" Roth said. If only they'd gone straight to the hospital . . . except, if they'd done that, Calakmul's people would have found them. They'd been waiting there, which suggested a disturbing level of calculation. They'd known she was diabetic. They'd guessed she'd run out of insulin.

"Jonny, DKA is serious. It's been too long since I've had a dose. And we've been going hard. I haven't had enough food. I'm severely dehydrated. Everything in my body is out of rhythm. I need electrolytes, like Gatorade or something like that, but water and insulin are the most important."

"Wouldn't it be better if we took you to a hospital anyway? Take the risk?"

Sarina shook her head. "The treatment is simple. All they'd do is give me an IV and monitor my vitals. The doctor can do that here."

Jorge returned with a case of bottled water. He took one out and unscrewed the cap before handing it to Roth to give his wife. She sat up a little, wincing with pain, and then gulped down water.

Were they already too late to save her? The thought was like a vise clenching around his heart.

CHAPTER
TWENTY-TWO

Cozumel International Airport

Cozumel, Mexico

December 24

Frustration seethed inside Jacob. The sunlight flooding the helicopter cockpit made him sweat. The copter rushed over the lush jungle vegetation, the teeming copse of wild oak with the occasional palm. They flew to the north of the traffic snarl on the only road leading to San Miguel. The police checkpoint was stopping every vehicle, but Jacob lacked confidence in their abilities. So far, the Roths had managed to slip away undetected.

A spike of raw anger pulsed through his frustration. The archaeological zone was being searched as well: every bus, every tourist, every restroom stall. Yes, people had *noticed* the Roth family. But their reports varied to the point of being nonsensical. The police on the ground were chasing shadows.

"There is a plane coming in," said the pilot over the headset. "Air traffic control wants us to wait for it."

Another delay. Jacob clenched his hand into a fist and let out a hiss of impatience. He could see the lights from the 737 blinking as the aircraft approached the runway. The coast of Cozumel had one of the most beautiful barrier reefs in the world. Tourists loved to come snorkeling in the clear waters, and small boats led expeditions every day, especially during the holidays. At this very moment, there would be companies of tourists standing in the waist-deep waters of the El Cielo reef near the southern tip of the island, eating fresh ceviche and chips while watching the sunset dip toward the ocean. That was what the Roths and Beasleys *should* have been doing tonight. A way to lull the new family into a feeling of safety. To disorient them before the beginning of the death games.

The sun was nearly down. Jacob removed his sunglasses to watch the extinction and saw a point of light on the horizon. Not another plane coming in. It was the planet Venus, visible at either sunrise or sunset. The morning star *and* the evening star. His people had been deeply fascinated with the orbit of Venus. They'd built their temples to align with its orbit as well as the tracking of the sun. After the spring equinox, the shadows caused by the setting sun made the illusion of a fiery serpent appear on the slopes of Chichén Itzá—a representation of the god Kukulkán. Archaeologists found it confusing that the full display of the snake had been designed to appear *after* the spring equinox rather than on it. Why go through all the trouble of building an elaborate pyramid to mark the changing of the seasons only to get the dates wrong?

Jacob smirked. The Maya hadn't gotten anything wrong. Chichén Itzá hadn't been built to welcome the change of seasons. It had been built to commemorate the arrival of Kukulkán, who had descended from the heavens to visit the ancient Maya and share his magic—*after* the equinox. Most years, the full representation of the feathered serpent happened on or around April 6.

This was just one piece of knowledge that had been lost to scholars. Burned by conquistadors and the priests as they tried to destroy Maya culture and twist the survivors' minds into worshipping the Pierced God of the Spaniards.

The light of Venus on the horizon was a reminder of the glorious past. A past that had been turned to ashes. Except for the efforts of the jaguar priests, the knowledge would still be lost.

The mammoth 737 landed and began to taxi to the terminal. The pilot angled the helicopter, and it was soon landing on the tarmac outside the executive hangar used exclusively by the Calakmuls. Jacob removed his headset, opened the side door of the helicopter, and bounded out. The pavement radiated heat from the fading sunlight.

The hangar door was open, revealing Jacob's sleek Pegasus jet. The aircraft itself was rare, it was part jet, part helicopter, something only the wealthiest could afford. It was fueled and ready to take off, just awaiting its passengers . . . presuming they could find them. The slant of the wings and the twin engines at the rear gave it a unique appearance.

The door of the executive business office opened, and Angélica exited, wearing a new outfit for the travel to the humid jungles surrounding the Calakmul ruins. The ensemble included short shorts with a wide belt and a cream-colored short-sleeve top of wicking fabric with large buttons down the front. The jungles in the southern Yucatán were much warmer. The original Maya had worn very little.

"You're smiling," Jacob said, his pique from the landing beginning to ebb.

"We found them," she said triumphantly.

Jacob stopped midstride, startled by the news.

"Where?"

"They're at an orphanage, Huellas de Pan. It's five minutes from here."

"What?" Jacob exclaimed. "Let's go, now!"

"Victor is already on the way with a team. I was about to call you but heard you were landing. It's a walled compound at the borders of San Miguel." Her expression brightened further. "Three streets away from where we're standing."

Jacob felt his stomach settle with relief. The night was falling fast. He couldn't risk another delay.

"Show me," he insisted. "I'll go inside and call Victor."

She walked back toward the building with him and showed him the screen of her tablet. He saw the Google map. Indeed, the orphanage was only 1.5 kilometers away, a quick zigzag pattern. It was on the edge of town, almost surrounded by the jungle.

"Neighbor lives here. This is Huellas de Pan. It's run by a man named Jorge Jiménez." She swiped at the screen, and up came the website for the orphanage.

"I've heard that name," Jacob said, intrigued. Then he remembered. "There were some kids from that orphanage at San Gervasio today."

"Were there?"

Anger roared inside Jacob. "The police talked to them. They lied about where they saw the Roths. What do you know about the founder?"

"Very little. Their website isn't very good, but it looks like they get some funding here and from a nonprofit in Texas."

"Where is Victor right now?"

"He's on the way with a tactical team."

"I want to talk to him."

They entered the air-conditioned executive suite. Jacob's leather travel duffel was sitting on a chair.

"Change of clothes," she said, pointing to the bag.

The receptionist, another attractive woman with looks from northern Mexico, was seated there. "Welcome, Mr. Calakmul. Do you want your private office?"

"Yes," he answered, grabbing the duffel.

"We'll start refueling your helicopter," the receptionist said.

"Good."

He walked down the short corridor, Angélica matching his stride, and she used a badge to unlock the private door. There were no windows. The lights flickered on, triggered by the motion sensors. Jacob tossed the duffel onto a chair and walked to the office desk.

He picked up the handset for the phone and pushed the button for security.

He heard a few tones, then a voice answered.

"Victor here," said the voice.

"It's Jacob."

"We're at Huellas de Pan," Victor said softly. "I can see the Roth kids in the main building with binoculars. I think the whole family is in there, but I can't get closer without going in."

"Is there a van? There was a van at San Gervasio today."

"Yes. I see it. It made it past the roadblock. I spoke to the blockade, and they remember it passing."

"They didn't search it?"

"He swears they did."

Jacob was furious. If the police helped the Roths escape, they were traitors. But maybe they'd been duped.

"Have you secured the perimeter?"

"Hold, sir." Jacob heard the line go flat. After a few breathless minutes, Victor was back. "Confirmed sighting of Mr. Roth. He's in the administration building."

"Is the perimeter secure?"

"Yes. There are two gates. I have men positioned at both."

"Are you sure there are only two gates?" He gestured for Angélica to hand him her screen. She did. "There seems to be a wall enclosing it?"

"Yes."

"Have your men run the perimeter. Be sure there isn't another way out."

"There are roads on three sides of the compound, Mr. Calakmul. The fourth wall is in the jungle. I've got two men crossing the jungle wall to see if there are any doors. It's not wide."

"Good work. Wait until dark, then storm the compound. No one leaves."

"Should we call off the local police?"

"Yes. They're incompetent. You do this, Victor. You bring me that family. Bring them right here."

"I'll get them," Victor promised.

Jacob set the handset down in its cradle. He tilted his head, looking at Angélica. She had a relieved smile. She set down the tablet and then lifted up part of her tan explorer shirt, revealing the golden skin beneath as she scratched her abdomen.

She was teasing him. Inviting him. He felt lust stir in his blood.

"Good work. Are the Beasleys already at the temple?"

"Yes. They left on the yacht this morning and arrived in Chetumal. They've been taken down the hidden road."

"Did they offer any trouble?"

"Nothing that Paulo couldn't handle. Mr. Beasley has a temper."

"I know. That's the thing about wealthy Westerners. Men like him are the same regardless of where they're from." Jacob held back a chuckle. "So much bluster. They believe laws will always be tilted toward their ends. They cheat to ensure it. But in the end, they're cowards. Americans especially. Although I almost wish that the Roths would win the game now. That would be an upset. I'd enjoy watching Eric Beasley die on the altar."

"The game must be played," Angélica said.

"The game must be played," Jacob repeated.

CHAPTER TWENTY-THREE

Huellas de Pan

Cozumel, Mexico

December 24

Roth hadn't been able to reach Avram Morrell, but he'd left a detailed voice mail describing where they were and the trouble they were in and left him Suki's number to call back. He'd also texted Moretti with the news. His friend had responded after a several-minute delay that had ratcheted up Roth's blood pressure, promising he'd also try to reach his uncle. He'd suggested sitting tight at the orphanage until he heard back from Avram.

"No safer place than with a bunch of kids," he'd said, but something about it had sent an odd feeling through Roth, almost a premonition. Was Calakmul the kind of man who'd be put off by the prospect of scaring or harming children?

He didn't think so.

Darkness had fallen. Outside the window, bugs swarmed a single floodlight fixed to the building.

The doctor checked Sarina's vitals again. He'd been doing that off and on for the last hour. He frowned and shook his head worriedly, the look on his face immediately alarming Roth.

"What's wrong?"

The doctor spoke in Spanish to Jorge.

"*Sí . . . sí . . .*" Jorge said, his countenance falling. The doctor held up his hands and said something else.

"What did he say?" Roth demanded.

Suki's eyes bulged with surprise. "Mom's going to be okay, right?"

The older man regarded her with compassion and sorrow. "Her body is shutting down."

Roth felt the tears start down his cheeks as he knelt by the couch. He held Sarina's hand, but there was no strength left in it. Her cheeks were pallid, her throat glistening with sweat. Her whole body still trembled helplessly.

The boys had tears trickling down their cheeks. Suki was sobbing. Jane Louise blinked back her own tears. Roth felt paralyzed by shock. The DKA had happened too quickly. They'd waited too long.

"It's okay, Jonny," Sarina whispered. Her voice was so weak. "I can't . . . stay awake. Slipping . . ."

"It's n-not okay," Roth stammered. "You've got to hold on. Let the insulin work."

"Even if I was in a hospital, we were too late. Can't reverse it."

"What does that mean?"

"Diabetic coma. Then . . ." She swallowed. "Then I'm gone. I thought it might be heading that way."

"You're . . . not going to die," Roth stammered, choking on the words.

"The doctor has done . . . everything he can. Let me kiss them goodbye in case I don't wake up."

Roth felt a groan rip from deep inside of him. He bowed his head and wept.

Her fingers gently stroked his hair. "I've known, Jonny. I've known."

"Then why didn't you tell me?" he said in anguish.

His eyes felt swollen. The tears felt hot enough to cause blisters. Looking into her face, he saw nothing but love and peacefulness.

"My grandma came. She's here right now."

"What?" Roth said incredulously.

"Grandma Suki. I've heard . . . from other nurses . . . the ones who work hospice. When people are dying, their loved ones come to prepare them. She came to see me during the soccer game. That's how I knew I was dying, Jonny." Her voice trailed off, her eyelids fluttering.

"Sarina!" Roth said, squeezing her hand.

That roused his wife again. "Grandma Suki is here . . . to take me."

"No," Suki said with a whimper. "You can't die, Mom. No . . ."

"It's okay," Sarina said. "Sometimes . . . sometimes the coma reverses. But I could be unconscious for weeks. Months. Until the end. No matter what happens, I'll always be your mom, Suki. I got to say goodbye. That's good. Let me kiss you all. Please."

The boys looked so grief-stricken they were frozen in place. Roth wiped tears from his eyes. He was devastated. His worst fear . . . his deepest anxiety . . . had always been losing Sarina. In their living will, there was a nonresuscitation order. She didn't want to be impaired long-term. Neither of them did.

Anguish ripped him apart inside. Should he hope for a better outcome? Or would he only be giving himself more grief and heartache?

Suki dropped near the couch and hugged her mother. Sarina kissed her forehead and then released Roth's hand so she could cup her cheeks. "I love you, Socorro. You were my baby. My first. I want you to have my ring. Okay? Until I'm better. Will you wear the one I got from my grandma? The jade one?"

Suki nodded, wiping tears from her cheeks. "I've always liked that one."

"I know." Sarina tugged the jade ring off her littlest finger and then slid it onto Suki's. "You look like your grandmother, you know." Sarina smoothed her daughter's hair. "Socorro means *help* . . . *relief.* You're going to be the one who saves our family."

Suki sniffled and nodded. As she rose, the twins both came forward and hugged their mother.

"You *can't* die," Lucas pleaded.

She kissed one and then the other. "I'm so proud of you. You've been so brave. I need you to still be brave, okay?"

Brillante nodded. Lucas shook his head no.

"You can't. You can't!"

Sarina cupped his cheek. "I may not wake up. I can't control what happens. But if it's the worst . . . I want you to know I'll miss you so much. If you feel the wind on your neck while you're playing soccer . . . that'll be me. I love you so much. My boys."

The boys hugged her again, sobbing against her. Suki leaned into Roth, burying her face in his shirt.

Jane Louise was staring at Sarina, eyes wide with fear and contrition. She looked so pathetic. So conflicted. Roth pitied her.

When the boys rose, Sarina beckoned for the little girl to come forward. She rushed to Sarina's side, instantly sobbing.

Roth's throat felt so tight it was as if he were choking on something. He could hardly breathe through the pain. Westfall had died that morning. He couldn't lose someone else so soon. Especially not Sarina. Not like this.

Roth went down on his knee again after Jane Louise had said her tearful goodbye. He gripped Sarina's hand firmly, squeezing it hard.

"You are the best . . . wife . . . in the world," Roth managed to get out. He kissed her mouth. He wept in her hair. "I love you. Please wake up."

"I'll try, Jonny," Sarina whispered huskily, her eyelids fluttering. "Just a . . . breath . . . away." She put her hand on his chest, reminding him of their first kiss, at his favorite beach in Santa Cruz. They'd almost kissed once before then, but he'd wanted it to happen in a special place, not in a parked car. So he'd brought her to the beach, which had always been a special place to him—something he'd wanted to share with her.

"Please," he begged.

"Jonny. I'm so . . . tired."

She closed her eyes . . . and didn't open them. If not for her low breathing, he would have feared she was dead. Roth felt the twins hugging him, crying into his shirt. He hugged back each of his kids, kissing them too, and even comforted Jane Louise. He had to be strong for them. He had to get them out of Mexico. All of them.

Roth looked up and saw Jorge wiping away a tear. "*Todo está bien.* Doctor called an ambulance. Have to get her to a hospital now. No other choice or she dies here."

Roth straightened, trying to quell the desire to lie down next to her. He took in her peaceful expression, the gentle breathing.

The doctor approached, holding a cell phone to his ear. "*Sí. Sí. Gracias.*" He put the phone away and touched Sarina's throat, feeling for a pulse. Her chest rose and fell, but it was subtle and strained.

The doctor looked at Jorge and shook his head, sending another spike of anguish through Roth's soul.

"Can't you help her?" he whispered.

Jorge smiled comfortingly. "*Todo está bien.*"

Roth thought a moment, wondering what that meant.

He heard a whisper in his mind. *All is well.*

The door burst open, startling them all. It was a young boy of about ten.

"*Hombres con armas! Con armas!*"

CHAPTER TWENTY-FOUR

Huellas de Pan

Cozumel, Mexico

December 24

A look of dread flashed on Jorge's face. He gripped the shoulders of the child who'd brought the news and urgently gave him instructions in Spanish. Turning his head, he looked Roth in the eye.

"Follow the *niño*," Jorge said. "Hide!" Then the old man stepped out into the night, shutting the door behind him.

The boy looked worried, but he gestured for Roth and his family to follow him.

"What about Mom?" Lucas asked, his voice thick.

Roth stared down at his wife, whose every breath was an effort. She needed a hospital, and the presence of the military men lessened her chances of getting to one safely. He wanted to be the one to bring her to safety, but the need to protect their children overshadowed everything else. He had to do this for both of them.

"Where can we hide?" he asked the boy.

"*Ándale!*" insisted the boy, who had gone down the darkened corridor that led to the back of the building. He motioned again for them to follow.

The doctor began to pack his bag. Since he didn't speak English, Roth didn't know what he intended to do with Sarina. The man felt her pulse again. Looking at Roth, he jerked his head at him, signaling they should go.

"Follow that kid," Roth said to the kids.

They followed the boy down the darkened corridor to a small bedroom. There was a crucifix and some prayer beads on the nightstand, a disheveled bed, and a recognizable pair of sandals askew on the floor. It was Jorge's bedroom.

Roth heard a noise and turned, seeing the doctor heading toward the main entrance where the receptionist area was located. The boy went to the bedroom window and opened it. He peered outside, then dragged over a chair and climbed up on the sill before hopping outside. The area behind the building was bathed in darkness.

Roth heard a door open and then a gunshot. Turning, he saw the doctor collapse as black-garbed security men rushed in, leveling their weapons.

In a panic, Roth pointed to the window. Brillante quickly hoisted himself up and over the sill, followed by Lucas. Suki helped Jane Louise up next, and one of the boys lifted her down from the other side. Meanwhile, Roth shut the bedroom door and then shoved the dresser in front of it. He heard the sound of boots coming down the hall.

When he reached the window, Suki was partway out. She stumbled and fell the rest of the way. Roth planted his foot on the chair, and followed her down, barely squeezing through the gap. The bedroom door shuddered as one of the security guards struck it.

The back of the building was adjacent to a nest of uncut trees, as dense as the jungle they'd crossed earlier. It was so dark their guide disappeared as soon as he plunged into the growth.

Lucas and Brillante were right behind him. Suki had scraped her arm on her fall, but she grabbed Jane Louise by the hand, and Roth helped push both of them to hurry.

Light illuminated them from the bedroom they'd just left, and he heard a shout. Then the trees were smacking into his face and arms. He tripped, caught himself, then tripped again and went down.

"Dad!" Brillante called. "Let's get the crap out of here!"

Roth clambered back to his feet and pressed through the deep tangle. He saw Suki's T-shirt in the dark and followed her. Beacons of light began to crisscross behind the building. Men were shouting to one another.

Then suddenly the wall of trees ended, and they were in a small clearing full of construction debris. Old tires were propped against broken boards. The young boy was waiting there, holding up a piece of plywood and waving for them to come. Roth saw that the pile of materials had been fashioned into a little hideaway by the kids of the orphanage. Jane Louise and Lucas got on their hands and knees and crawled in first.

"Is it big enough for all of us?" Suki questioned.

Roth answered by shoving her toward the gap. She went down on hands and knees too and crawled inside, followed by Brillante. The boy pointed to Roth to go next. More shouts. Then the crack of a pistol in the air.

Roth's chest heaved as he got down on his hands and knees and wriggled into the gap. The boy came last and lowered the plywood down to cover them. It wasn't completely dark; the slats of wood let in light. Soon after, the area was swarming with guards, searching for the family amid the debris.

A beam shot directly at the pile of wood, and Roth held his breath until it passed.

Roth carefully moved into a sitting position, hunched over with the debris clawing through his hair. It wasn't big enough for anyone to stand in. The floor was a dilapidated pallet, the walls struts of wood arranged to hold up the bulk of the excess material. Bits of stone and broken cinder blocks had been stacked on top of each other. It was dusty.

The noise of their pursuers didn't fade. Soon, Roth judged about eight men had gathered in the area.

"Mr. Roth!"

The voice was unfamiliar. Roth angled his neck and saw a group of men with lights attached to their helmets. Jorge was thrust before them, his navy tracksuit dusty and dirty. A man forced him to his knees and then held a pistol to his head.

"Mr. Roth! I know you can hear me." The voice sounded cruel. "We can play this game for hours if you like. This compound is surrounded. There's no way out. No help is coming. I give you thirty seconds to come out, or this man dies. I'm tired of waiting."

The man lowered the barrel tip to the back of Jorge's head.

The little boy with them began to whimper.

Roth didn't know whether he could trust the man to *not* kill Jorge and the rest. Someone who was willing to murder one innocent would just as soon kill another.

"Dad?" Suki whispered in dread.

"I will do it, Mr. Roth!" shouted the man. "The doctor who helped you is dead. I think you know that. Your wife needs urgent medical attention. Come now. No more games. We can help her in ways you can't understand."

The kids were staring at him. Roth felt the moments tick away, felt the unbearable grief of the separation from Sarina. Of depending on hostile strangers to save her life. He had tried to keep his family safe, and he'd failed. He could not let the people of the orphanage die as well. They might be killed anyway, but he wouldn't let it be because he was cringing beneath a piece of plywood.

Roth pushed aside the plywood. Guns swiveled and pointed straight at him, headlamps blazing into the gap. Roth held up his hands, hunched over.

The man holding the pistol had a vicious smile. He said something in Spanish, and one of the guards hurried forward, walking with his gun aimed at Roth's chest.

"*Sí!*" he shouted to the man with the pistol.

The man lowered his gun away from Jorge. Roth crawled out first, keeping his hands in sight. Then, one by one, the kids came out.

Roth looked at the leader. "Don't kill them," he pleaded.

The man snorted. He lifted his hand to a radio on his shoulder. "Sir. We have them."

"What can you do to help my wife?" Roth demanded. "She's in a diabetic coma."

The man smirked. "You will see, Mr. Roth. You will see. Bring them to the airport."

———

The truck pulled up to the security gate at Cozumel International Airport. A guard approached the driver's window as someone wheeled the chain-link gate open.

The leader of the security force had divided up the family. Roth and Jane Louise were in the back seat of one truck, Suki and the twins in another. Roth's stomach twisted and clenched with dread.

What had the guard meant? *You will see.* What a terrible thing to say if it weren't true. Could they really help Sarina? Would they? He'd seen them carrying her into yet another vehicle, so at least they hadn't left her behind.

The man in the passenger's seat was the one who had caught them, the leader of the security team. He spoke to the guard at the gate, who then waved the trucks in. The airport was on the western side of the island, so a hint of the sun glowed through the layers of deep purple sky on the horizon.

The trucks drove in smoothly. There was a large airplane, a Boeing, waiting at the gate. Just one craft, surrounded by orange cones and crew in headgear. The sharp noise of a jet engine roared through the air.

As they drove away from the main terminal, they approached a hangar. A smaller jet, the private kind, was ferrying out of it. A dull pit formed in Roth's stomach, increasing his feelings of desolation.

What if Sarina didn't make it? Was it his fault? Had running away been pointless after all?

He gazed at the jet with darkness in his heart. Even now, he wasn't about to quit. He'd do everything he could to save the children. To save his wife.

The trucks pulled up and extinguished their headlights. Roth recognized the blond woman from the Calakmul resort, only she was wearing short shorts and a tan adventurer-style shirt, standing by the portable ladder leading up to the jet. The passenger's door opened, and the man stepped over and opened the door for Roth. He got out and nodded for the little girl to do the same. She looked like she'd prefer to stay in the car, but she followed him out, staying close.

The blonde approached them and then lowered herself to eye level with Jane Louise. "Your mom has been very worried about you."

"My wife needs a hospital," Roth demanded.

"There's no time for that," Angélica said. "You should have turned yourselves in sooner."

"Why are we at the airport?"

"Because we need to get to the Jaguar Temple. The match begins tomorrow."

So they would be playing the ball game after all. He wasn't surprised after what Jorge had told him. Only Jorge had been wrong about one thing . . . the matches had already started again. "It won't be played here on Cozumel?"

The woman looked up at him and then straightened. He saw a reflection of himself in her glasses.

"No, Mr. Roth. Cozumel is a sacred island. The game was never played here." She looked over his shoulder. "Where is Mrs. Roth, Victor?"

Roth had seen them hoist Sarina's body into the back of a truck with the guards.

"She's in the back of that truck," Roth said, pointing.

The woman nodded. "We'll bring your wife along with us to Calakmul."

"We're going back to the resort?" Roth asked in confusion.

"No, Mr. Roth. We're going to the Calakmul Biosphere Reserve. The Beasleys arrived there earlier today."

"Where is it?"

He felt Jane Louise gripping his hand. Looking down at her, he noticed her worried expression. He glanced at Suki and the twins as they were ushered out of their vehicle. Security officers stood behind him, and one of them had a hand on Brillante's.

"It's in the jungle between Guatemala and Mexico. Not a tourist experience like Chichén Itzá. It's more . . . primitive."

"No hospitals, then?" Suki snapped.

The woman smiled. "No, Suki. No hospitals."

"Take her to a hospital here, then!" Roth shouted.

"I'm afraid it's too late for that. But there are remedies from the ancient Maya that may prove better. We'll be at the ruins by midnight."

Roth sighed and then fumed. They would be hundreds of miles away from where he'd told Moretti and his uncle they would be. His friend would have no way of finding them.

"Shall we?" the woman asked, lowering the tablet and gesturing to the plane. The guards shot them menacing looks. Refusal would be met with violence.

"If my wife dies . . ." Roth said, shaking his head threateningly.

"You're *all* going to die," said Victor, the head of security. "Get in the plane." He pointed to two guards. *"Traed a la mujer."*

The woman's brow wrinkled. "They'll have their chance to win, just like the others."

Roth glared at him and then led the way.

The jet had angled wings and two fins tilted away from the engines at the back, which made it look like an F/A-18 or some military jet. The fuselage was sleek and pointed. The plane could probably hold no more than a dozen passengers.

They were escorted to the main cabin door on the right side of the jet. A wheeled set of steps had been affixed in front of the already-open door. Roth startled when he saw two guards carrying Sarina, wrapped in a blanket, out of the third truck. Her face was solemn, sickly, but she was still alive, and that man had claimed they could help her . . .

Was he a fool to hope?

Roth took a deep breath to try to calm himself. His anxiety spiking along with his heartrate, he glanced back at his children and then helped Jane Louise up the steps. As he climbed up with her, he noticed the large circles on the particularly broad wings. Vents of some kind? That was strange.

When he ducked to enter, he saw Jacob Calakmul sitting inside, his rimless glasses shining in the interior light, a smug look on his stubbled mouth. There were four seats, two facing two, in the main cockpit—the seats large and padded with thick cushions. Behind those four were two more rows of smaller seats.

Jacob motioned to the seat in the corner across from him. He wore a linen suit, the shirt collar unbuttoned to expose part of his chest and a jade necklace.

"Kids in the back," Jacob said, his eyes flashing angrily at Jane Louise.

The little girl tightened her grip on Roth's hand. "Go on," he told her gently. She released his hand and made her way to one of the seats, her eyes wide and frightened.

Roth settled into the comfortable chair, but he felt anything but comfortable. His kids started to shuffle past to seat themselves in the back rows, but Jacob stopped Lucas, who was at the end of the line.

"Does your nose still hurt?" Jacob asked the boy.

Lucas looked startled and frightened, his eyes still red from crying. "A little sore."

"Looks painful," Jacob said. He held up his hand, the one with the gold ring on its finger, depicting some ancient glyph. *"Utzirisaj,"* he muttered, his eyes narrowing. Roth watched in astonishment as the skin on Lucas's nose twitched. The dented cartilage flared out. The bruises melted away.

Lucas blinked in surprise, then reached up and gingerly touched his nose.

"It doesn't hurt anymore," he whispered.

Jacob's eyes met Roth's across the aisle. "I can be a generous man, Mr. Roth, to those who serve me."

Calakmul's assistant had boarded during the display of magical healing, followed by the two guards carrying Sarina's body.

Roth stared at his wife. Would she be healed as well? He gripped the seat, swallowing. Hoping. He didn't understand what Jacob had done, but he clearly had some uncanny sort of power, and if that power could be used to heal Sarina, he was quite all right with it.

He watched, helpless, full of horror and hope, as Jacob studied Sarina and listened to her breathing. Then he touched her forehead with the tip of his finger, tracing something on her skin. A symbol of some kind.

"Take her to the back and secure her. She's alive but incapacitated. She won't be playing in the games."

"Can't you heal her too?" Roth asked curtly.

Jacob shrugged. "She's on the verge of death. And will remain so until the gods decide her fate. And yours. Let's go." He gestured for the guards to finish their work.

They secured Sarina in the back and then left the plane. The assistant sealed the door behind them. She took the seat next to Roth, directly across from Calakmul, and crossed her legs.

Roth glared at the man. He wasn't a big person. Not like Eric Beasley. But there was a dangerous look in Jacob Calakmul's eyes. The look of a predator.

"Cross-check," said the pilot over the intercom.

A clicking noise affirmed that the door had been secured. Roth swallowed, clenching the armrests of his seat. Weariness and despair wrestled inside him. Twisting his neck, he looked back at the kids. He couldn't see Sarina because the guards had laid her down before connecting the seat belts.

The engines began to whir, and the jet thrummed with power.

Then the aircraft began to rise like a helicopter. Roth's stomach gurgled in discomfort. Looking out the window, he once again took notice of the circles on the wings.

They contained rotor blades.

"Have you flown on a Pegasus before, Mr. Roth?" Jacob asked. "Surely you appreciate the mythological reference."

The swaying of the craft as it lifted made Roth's stomach roil even more. He dug his fingers deeper into the armrests as the craft vaulted into the sky and the rear engines began to scream.

CHAPTER TWENTY-FIVE

YUCATÁN PENINSULA

December 24

Roth maintained his death grip on the armrests as a sickening feeling oozed through his stomach. Fatigue, anxiety, and despair warred within his soul. Glancing out the window of the Pegasus, he could see no lights—just the inky darkness of the jungle beneath. The moon was bright in the sky, but its silver light offered no comfort.

Would Sarina make it? He didn't know. Nor did he know if any of them would survive this trip.

"You are persistent, Mr. Roth," said Jacob Calakmul, his tone thoughtful. "It required considerable resources to locate your family."

"Are you going to tell me what this is all about?" Roth asked in a low voice. He looked back again and saw his children strapped into their seats. They stared back at him with eyes wide with fright.

"Let's start with what you've already figured out. You're a clever man. A world-renowned fantasy author. Surely you have some guesses?"

Roth scratched his neck. "The Maya ball game. We're going to play the Beasleys."

Jacob nodded solemnly.

"One of our families is going to win. The other is going to die," Roth continued. "We both have the same estate attorney in Bozeman. That's how we were introduced."

"You have significant assets, Mr. Roth. And so does Eric Beasley."

"But this isn't just about sport, is it?" No one would go through such effort if that were the main reason. Maybe it was more like a deadly version of liar's poker, a confidence game that wealthy Wall Street bankers played—risking huge sums of money to test each other's nerve and bluffing skills. Or worse, some real-life version of *Squid Game*.

"Sports are spectacles. Competitions. They are enjoyable to watch, are they not?"

"I wouldn't know. I don't watch them."

"Oh, but you do, Mr. Roth," Calakmul said with a broad smile. "I'm not talking about the Super Bowl or the World Series or the NBA Finals. You play video games on a streaming service called Twitch. Thousands of people watch you. There's a primal urge to compete, you see. Even if you're playing against other gamers. Or a computer."

Roth wondered why none of the security guards had boarded the plane. The only adults aboard appeared to be himself, Sarina, Calakmul, the attractive assistant, and the pilot. Roth was bigger than Calakmul. And yet . . .

Eric Beasley was huge. Intimidating. But there was something in Jacob's lean physique that caused a ripple of worry inside Roth's stomach. He exuded a raw anger and power that went beyond mere muscle.

"So this is how the ultrarich spend their holidays?" Roth asked. "Competing with each other for greater wealth? What's your benefit? You get a cut for arranging the match?"

"A *cut*." Jacob laughed. "You're a fantasy author, Mr. Roth. Surely you can imagine that it takes something more than *that* to drive a man like me."

"Frankly, I can't begin to imagine what would drive a man like you," Roth said, anger sizzling inside. "The Maya and Aztec believed the universe would stop moving if they didn't play the game. Obviously, that hasn't happened in the intervening years since the Spanish came here."

"Obviously. You have another theory perhaps?"

"Not really. My best friend was killed in a car accident this morning on the way to work, and my wife is critically ill. I've had more pressing matters to consider."

Jacob's eyes immediately shot to the assistant's.

That subtle cue confirmed Roth's suspicion. "His death wasn't an accident."

"Not at all. I ordered it. The control of your assets, upon your death, will be held by the accounting firm your friend partnered with. And *I* will buy it. That gives me leverage over you whether you win or lose."

"You want control of my books?" Roth asked, perplexed.

Jacob leaned forward in his chair. "I couldn't care less about your books, Mr. Roth."

"You want my wealth? My . . . royalty income?"

He saw an amused smile on the woman's face before she turned her head to look out the window. The kids were settled in the back, but he could tell they were listening intently.

"As considerable as it is, Mr. Roth, it means nothing compared to the treasures I already possess. Treasures that you have only seen a glimpse of."

He was talking about the crates of Maya treasure they'd seen by the cenote beneath the temple. Suki must still have the bracelet she'd stolen from one of the crates. Roth hoped she'd had the presence of mind to hide it well.

"You don't want my money?" he asked Jacob.

"The winner gets the spoils. If the Beasleys win the death game, *they* will claim your assets. If your family wins, you will claim theirs. Simple."

Roth leaned forward. "If you don't get a payout, then what's in it for you? The thrill of watching some of us die?"

"Thrill, Mr. Roth? You think it was simply a *thrill* that prompted Romans to gather in the Colosseum to watch the lions devour the early Christians?"

Roth's mind felt as if it had been tied into tangled knots. He imagined he looked as confused as he felt. "You lost me."

"I'm trying to help you see this another way, Mr. Roth. The Beasleys have been coming to the resort for years."

"How come their picture wasn't on the wall?"

"Not all my guests are featured in Villa Sara. Only the winners of the death games."

So Roth's leap of logic had actually been right. There was a reason for everything with this man.

"Many have come to my resorts. But why *this* resort? Why were you invited?"

"I don't know," Roth answered.

"*Think,*" Jacob pressed.

"I don't have all the clues. How can I guess something like this?"

The woman was looking at him again with interest, as if she *wanted* him to figure it out.

"I've given you enough clues. Why do people compete?"

"My kids love playing soccer. But I don't understand why someone would willingly play a game that could end in their death, no matter how much they love the sport."

"Yet Eric Beasley chose just that." Jacob tilted his head, studying Roth intently. "Why? Why play such a game?"

"There are other ways to make money. Safer ways. And as you said, it's not about the money."

"Money is part of it. Wealth is a symbol of it. What drove men like Hernán Cortés? Christopher Columbus? Andrew Carnegie? Napoléon Bonaparte? You were a history professor. You know this, Mr. Roth."

Roth was still confused, but he took a stab at it. He leaned forward in his seat. "Ambition."

"Prestige. Reputation. Distinction. These are especially strong motivations for men who have faced rejection. Who aren't invited into the elite clubs at first. These things are what drives someone. It can drive them to kill."

As he stared into Jacob's eyes, he sensed the man's keen intelligence. He was a frightening villain. He was *smart*. He was trying to help Roth understand his motives instead of concealing them. Why? It went against the Evil Overlord rules.

If he was willing to share his nefarious plan, Roth would encourage it. "So playing in these games gives Beasley a status he can't get any other way?"

"Yes. A special status. The wealth is secondary. Tell me. How did the little girl know about the death games? She warned you, obviously."

Roth wouldn't insult the man's intelligence by denying it. "She overheard you on the phone with Eric before we all left Bozeman," he said. "Her father didn't know she was there."

Jacob glanced at the woman again and nodded to her. It was an unspoken request.

"She told you in the van, and you decided to flee into the jungle."

"We were only trying to get to the hospital at first. It was a test. I wasn't totally convinced we'd make it past the guards at the gate."

"You wouldn't have. They had orders to turn you back."

"Then you would have watched us more closely," Roth replied.

"It was intended that today, *La Noche Buena*, would be spent snorkeling and eating ceviche. To relax you before our little trip to the Jaguar Temple."

"Today was anything but relaxing," Roth said tightly.

Jacob shrugged. He didn't seem to care.

"What's going to happen to the orphanage?"

Jacob's eyes narrowed. "They defied me, Mr. Roth. The doctor already paid with his life."

Roth remembered the gunshot. Then he thought about Jorge and the children at the orphanage playing soccer. Would they be murdered for this? Jorge had *believed* the Calakmuls were using the legends of the jaguar priests to hide their cartel activities. But Jacob, at least, seemed to believe the legends were real. He was probably insane, but he was powerful too, and intelligent enough to convince others to believe him. That, in itself, was dangerous.

Would he kill Jorge and the others?

"They didn't defy you, *I* did," Roth said.

"I haven't decided what I'll do to them. I'm not rash, Mr. Roth. I think through my plans. I think through the consequences. My ancestors have honed that trait like an obsidian edge."

Obsidian could be sharpened to surgery-level precision. Roth blamed his prolific memory for such an insignificant detail.

Roth shifted in his seat. The bump and sway of the plane, paired with the knowledge that Sarina lay in a coma in the back, was making his anxiety go berserk. "And this Jaguar Temple . . . it's like the Roman Colosseum? I thought the ball court at Chichén Itzá was the most famous Maya arena."

"It's open for tourists," Jacob replied blandly. "And the probing of American satellites. Someday we will hold the games there again. But for now, we must be discreet. The jungle prevents the satellites from watching us."

"You're worried about the CIA?"

"Not particularly, Mr. Roth. They're preoccupied with what's happening in China, the Middle East, and Russia. It's more important to keep their eyes on your own borders. To keep busy watching for drug traffickers and illegal immigrants. They're so preoccupied they don't even realize there's a bigger picture."

Roth couldn't believe the man was being so direct with him. Then again, there was power in being a willing listener. The average person could not bear more than fifteen seconds of silence. In fact, it often became intolerable at ten seconds. As a former college adjunct professor, Roth knew that when asking a question, it was best to wait only ten to fifteen seconds for a response. After thirty seconds of silence, the silence became destructive. The anxiety it provoked actually inhibited learning.

So he waited, staring at Jacob Calakmul with an inquiring gaze. He hoped the man would reveal something that could give Roth and his family an advantage. He inclined his head, trying to adopt a look that showed his interest.

Jacob gave him a smug smile. "You Westerners have been lazy and indolent, especially you Americans. We've watched and encouraged it. The cruise ships. The Hotel Zone buffets. The gluttony and waste. Obesity is our export to your nations. So is drug addiction. Does that remind you of ancient Rome, Professor? Before you invade a country, you destabilize it from within. You unleash internal factions to spill each other's blood. The US is the equivalent of the Holy Roman Empire today—the one controlled by the Spaniard, Charles the Fifth. Your empire is ripe for conquest, Mr. Roth. That should sound familiar . . . to a fellow historian. It's what happened to ancient Rome, after all."

"You plan on invading the United States?" Roth asked in disbelief.

"It's already begun, Mr. Roth. We're taking your wealth. We're sickening your people. We're preparing to make you our slaves. Just as you did to us."

Roth closed his eyes, shaking his head. "The Mexican-American War—"

"You're not thinking back far enough, Mr. Roth."

"Are you talking about Hernán Cortés? America didn't even exist back then."

"America," laughed Jacob. "Named after an Italian, Amerigo Vespucci. I know history, Mr. Roth. I know it far better than you. The Order of the Jaguar kept records of Cortés's conquest. Of the tactics he used to turn rival tribes and kingdoms against the Aztec rulers at Tenochtitlán. Moctezuma. Or as your books say now, *Montezuma*. Mr. Roth, we've been waiting for nearly five hundred years to collect on the debt. With interest accruing."

Roth was dumbfounded. "Five hundred years ago. This is about . . . revenge?"

"What other emotion can endure for so many centuries? The people of this peninsula, of this tortured land, no longer even remember how it began. The Spanish were thorough in their destruction of the Maya codices. They forced our ancestors to convert to your faith or be killed. And many who converted were killed anyway. Or enslaved. There's no counting the wealth stolen, husbands and sons murdered, and wives and daughters taken as slaves and even prostituted. That is your empire's legacy, Mr. Roth. Your wife's ancestors were from these lands, and I'll bet your children know nothing of the legacy of blood. Or the debt that must be repaid."

"It was five centuries ago!" Roth said in confusion.

"Time does not requite a blood debt, Mr. Roth. Only blood does. Blood for blood. The traditions of my people were mocked, condemned—spoken of as savagery. Yet all the while, in Europe, you were murdering your own brothers in war. Spain, Portugal, England . . . and your people, Mr. Roth. Germany. We feared Hitler might ruin everything by becoming strong enough to conquer the United States. Many Germans came to these lands after the war, Mr. Roth. Some to Argentina, Paraguay, Colombia, Brazil. The ratlines. You know that name?"

Roth nodded. As a historian, he did. The phrase referred to a system of escape routes the Nazis had used to flee Europe after World War II.

"And yet . . . the savagery of what Hitler did was just a tiny cut compared to the destruction heaped on my ancestors," Jacob said. "Ninety percent of my people were destroyed. Genocide, Mr. Roth. Undeserved. Unprovoked. Administered by sword, bullet, and pox instead of gas chambers or firing squads. And that is what will happen to your people. Unless they bow the knee to the Order of the Jaguar. *That* is what Mr. Beasley is playing the game for, Mr. Roth. The prestige of being in the ruling class when your world order has been toppled. *That* is what *you* are playing it for. A chance to be part of the ruling class when the tables . . . turn. To be protected when the world is culled by blood and pox again. A sickness is coming, Mr. Roth. One that will be as terrible as the plagues of ancient Egypt."

Roth was horrified by what he was hearing. This wasn't liar's poker at all. It wasn't just a game with a rubber ball in which the losers were sacrificed on an altar, their hearts ripped from their chests. He was talking about mass murder.

"You're blaming Americans for what the Europeans did five centuries ago?"

"We take one nation, and all the others will topple," Jacob said, leaning forward, his face intense with emotion. "Before you declare any innocence, reconsider. Have you ignored your own history? What did your government do to the 'native Americans' who occupied the majority of the geography? You were a *history* teacher, Mr. Roth, at California State, Hayward. *California* itself was drowned in blood when the promise of gold in Sacramento lured hordes of treasure seekers. There is no difference between the conquistadors and you. The Trail of Tears. How quaint. It was a trail of bloody snow. You are the same. And we will conquer you. We will baptize you to our gods. Or you will die if you choose."

The man was insane.

"What about the technology advantage?" Roth said, shaking his head. "Smart bombs, F/A-18s . . ."

"You keep forgetting your history lessons, Mr. Roth. The Spanish didn't defeat the Aztec emperor with European soldiers. They unleashed the kingdoms and tribes against each other. The same is happening in your country right now. And you forge the knife that cuts your own throat! We know the business of conquest, Mr. Roth. We've had brilliant teachers, haven't we?"

Jacob fell silent, scratching his finger across the leather seam of his armrest. Roth noticed the ring on his finger. The metal formed the shape of a jaguar.

"How long have these games been played? Since before Cortés?" Roth asked.

"The Spanish stopped the games. Anyone who played them was persecuted. And often killed. Those early priests were determined to alter the culture of my people. To change our language. Our traditions. *La Noche Buena*, for example. You wished to replace our ancient festivals with your own. You worship a fat god on Christmas. A red suit and magical beasts. You follow the priests of marketing now. Commercials that tell you what to think and what to do. The Order of the Jaguar did the same in our day. They invented traditions that instilled order in the populace. Even the matches. The death games began again at the changing of the calendar cycle."

"The doomsday calendar," Roth said.

Jacob snorted. "That was a marketing ploy to sell online content to the ignorant. An imagined prophecy about the 'end of the world.' That calendar date passed several years ago, Mr. Roth. The world didn't end. Nor will it. It will *transform*. Just as it has always done. Energy transfers from one state to another. So does power. It will change again. It already is changing."

Roth swallowed, his emotions teeming. "It isn't right to murder countless millions because of what was done in the past."

"Don't lecture me, Professor, on the morality of right or wrong. In the name of Christ, the conquistadors murdered and stole. They raped and tried to *breed* us out of existence. No one wants to die, Mr. Roth. I don't begrudge you your struggle to survive. We all share that primitive instinct. And I don't care which family wins at the Jaguar Temple. The Beasleys are more likely to win. They are stronger and healthier, and there are more of them, but I will honor the results. My ancestors administered the game. It is a sacred trust."

Roth was tempted to leap out of his seat and throttle the smaller man, to choke him to death right there on the plane. He didn't want to go to some forsaken temple in the middle of the Yucatán jungle where no one would know what had happened to him or his family.

"So Beasley knows about all of this?" Roth said, quivering with rage. "He *wants* to join your cult?"

"More and more of the ultrarich are learning about us," Jacob said with pride. "That is why they are hoarding their wealth. When the social upheaval begins, they'll hunker down in the fortresses they've built. Many of which are in Montana, Mr. Roth." He laughed.

If Roth was going to die, he might as well do it on his own terms. Jacob Calakmul was like Hitler. Stalin. Mao. He was no better than the men who'd prompted him to seek retaliation.

Roth reached down and unclipped his seat belt.

Jacob looked him in the eye. A growl issued from him, and then his eyes started to glow like a panther's. No . . . like a jaguar's. Fear surged in Roth's blood, spreading throughout his whole body.

"I am a jaguar priest," Jacob whispered. "I will devour you in front of your children if you try."

His tawny eyes made Roth's heart melt with fear. It was an animal instinct, his own reptilian brain announcing he was in the presence of a true predator. His will turned to jelly. Sinking back into his seat, Roth realized why Jacob Calakmul had been so forthcoming.

Because he knew Roth and his entire family were going to die. If everything happened the way Jacob thought it would, the way he'd planned, there was no one they would be able to tell the secret to.

CHAPTER TWENTY-SIX

Jaguar Temple

Calakmul Biosphere Reserve

December 24

As the Pegasus jet neared the Jaguar Temple, the propellers on the wings engaged, causing a thrum of energy to vibrate the cabin. Jacob watched Mr. Roth's eyes close in fear, his nostrils flaring as he sucked in air to calm himself. For a moment, earlier that evening, Jacob had sensed aggression from the heavyset author. But his magic had quickly annulled it.

"Open your eyes, Mr. Roth. You will want to see the City of Gold," Jacob said.

Angélica smiled, turning her neck to gaze out the window next to her. Outside was nothing but a smudge of black. The nearest village, Halatun, was nearly twenty kilometers away, and it held few amenities. Unlike the jungle within Cozumel, the biosphere was home to jaguars, pumas, ocelots, howler monkeys, spider monkeys, and margays. It was unsafe to travel through it without becoming one with it.

"I'm trying not to throw up," Mr. Roth said.

"We will be landing soon," Angélica said. Although she was looking out the window, she used her foot to stroke Jacob's leg. Her gesture filled his mind with distracting thoughts.

The voice of the pilot came on the intercom. "Ready to land, sir."

Jacob could feel the aircraft's thrust ebb, the plane beginning to rotate. The pilot was flying blindly, completely reliant on his instruments. There were no landing lights below.

Jacob invoked the magic, and the Jaguar Temple began to glow beneath them, the carvings in the stelae illuminated. The most famous stelae discovered at Calakmul was known as Stela 51—four meters tall and one and a half wide, it bore the carving of a man—King Yuknoom Took' K'awiil. Although the stone had been taken to Mexico City, another version of it remained in the temple below. All the stelae in the ancient structure were glowing now, wreathed in the magic that looked like golden dust, creating a false dawn within the deep shadows of the jungle. Several pyramids around it glowed to life too.

"Whoa! Look!" said one of the twins.

Mr. Roth, hearing the exclamations, opened his eyes. And despite his declared queasiness, he seemed transfixed by the scene he beheld. As well he should be. The ancient steps of the main temple had been painstakingly reassembled by archaeologists funded by the Calakmul family. With such resources, much of the site had been restored to its proper glory, reclaimed from the jungle after centuries of abandonment following the Spaniards' reign of terror. Popular sites like Chichén Itzá had also been renovated and repaired, but it had taken much longer because the funds for the work had been raised by the taxation of the tourists.

The Pegasus drifted lower, gliding down into the embrace of the massive jungle, landing in the main square of the ruins. The stelae rippled with the golden magic, making the carvings appear as if they were outlined with molten gold. When a conquistador had stumbled into a similar community in South America, the legend of El Dorado, a city sheathed in gold, had been born. What he hadn't realized was he'd seen a manifestation of the magic of the Maya people.

When the magic was dormant, the stones looked like stone.

"What makes it glow?" Mr. Roth asked with genuine curiosity in his voice.

"*I* make it glow," Jacob answered. He felt the magic surging through him, making him giddy with its power. "Once we land, you will not be able to leave Calakmul until after the death game is over. Magic is real, Mr. Roth. Not like the fantasies you conjure in your books. The game begins tomorrow."

Mr. Roth glared at him and pitched his voice low but full of intensity—and accusation. "They're only children!" he hissed.

Jacob leaned forward. "Tell that to the bones of Maya children slaughtered here, Mr. Roth. Of the Aztec babes ripped from their mother's arms. From their wombs. The world is a jungle. Those who realize that learn to survive."

The landing gear unfolded, and within minutes, the Pegasus jet landed on the stone walkway in the middle of the glowing city. Jacob leaned back in his chair. He resented Mr. Roth's efforts to try to appeal to his humanity, but he wasn't surprised by them. In Mr. Roth's world—his country—life was considered of such important value that the existence of the sick and diseased was prolonged through modern medicine, even if life was torture for them. A few extra weeks could be purchased for millions of dollars, then haggled and fought over by insurance companies for years. All for a few extra breaths of life. It was madness, surely. A mental weakness of the living who feared the unknown.

Death was just another phase of existence.

"I'll take them to the acropolis," Angélica said after unfastening her seat belt. She'd stowed her tablet in the storage area by the seat. There was no internet here. The electronic device would be useless.

"When will we be taught the rules?" Mr. Roth demanded.

"In due time, Mr. Roth," Jacob said. "Get some sleep. You should not try to leave this place now that the magic has been invoked. I warn you."

But Jacob didn't expect Mr. Roth to listen to him. He would try to escape. And he'd be surprised by what happened. One family had barely made it into the jungle before a pack of howler monkeys found them and scared them back into the ruins.

The pilot disengaged the engines, and the heat from the jungle began to permeate the cabin. Then he emerged from the cockpit and released the cabin door. Immediately, the noises of the jungle flooded inside. The screeches of howlers. The call of night birds. The noisy clicks of jungle insects.

Angélica made her way to the front and then turned back to smile at the children. "Come with me. There is food and a place to rest."

Mr. Roth unfastened his seat belt and rose first.

"What about Sarina? What will happen to her?"

"She will be taken to a priestess of Ix Chel," Jacob said. "The goddess of healing. If it is the goddess's will that she survive, she will. But she will not compete in the games. And if your family loses, she too will die."

Mr. Roth gave Jacob another angry scowl and then followed Angélica to the doorway. Outside, Jacob could see the Maya servants gathering, dressed in the traditional garb of slaves. Some had jewelry piercing their noses. Many had tattoo brands marking their servitude. It amused him that tattoos were so popular in America. They were preparing themselves for bondage without even realizing it.

"Come on, Jane Louise," said the teenaged girl who was now standing near Jacob's seat. *Socorro*. That was her real name.

She held out a hand to the little girl, and his gaze was drawn to the ring on her hand. It was Maya jewelry, made with jade.

"Where did you get that ring?" Jacob asked her.

"It was my great-grandmother's."

She looked frightened, which was understandable. They were all about to die. But there was also something secretive in her look. Like she was hiding something from him. His magic heightened his senses, all of them, and he always had deeper intuition under its thrall. What could she be hiding from *him*?

"Come on," Socorro urged, motioning for Jane Louise to come. The little blond Beasley girl sidled up the aisle, but she was clearly afraid of him. She didn't want to pass him, as if being within range of his breath could kill her.

"Go on," he said to the little one, motioning her forward.

Jane Louise fearfully rushed past him and gripped the teenager's hand. They walked down the aisle together, followed by the boys.

The slaves outside had brought woven crates as steps for the passengers to deplane. There were no fuel trucks or landing crews. No security checkpoints or X-ray scanners.

Once the family had left, the pilot—who'd been waiting outside the cockpit—looked at him.

"What do we do with Mrs. Roth?" he asked.

"Take her body to the temple of Ix Chel. She's at the brink of death. So is her family."

"As you command." The pilot gave a nod and remained standing at attention.

"What time is it?" Jacob asked.

"Almost midnight."

Christmas Day, which meant nothing at all on the Maya calendar. Jacob thought back to the first death game match, which had occurred at the change of the Long Count cycle.

December 21, 2012. That was the day that many had expected to bring the end of the world—the doomsday prophesied by the Maya and the Aztec. Instead, it had marked the beginning of 13 baktun, a new cycle—13.0.0.0—the date the jaguar priests had established centuries ago as the time to commence their revenge.

Two wealthy families had been invited to Cozumel to celebrate Christmas. Only one of the families had left. The game had only lasted one day because one family had given up after three hours on the court. Their minds had frozen in despair, and they'd been unable to function any longer.

Jacob remembered that day—the first human sacrifice to have been performed in this place for centuries. The throbbing heart quivering in his upstretched palm. The look of pride on his father's stern face.

The pilot was still watching.

Jacob removed his glasses and tucked them into the seat pocket.

One of the two families would be dead in the next few days.

Most of the priests and notable spectators were wagering on the Beasleys being the victors. Some were famous actors. Others, businessmen of great renown. Several political leaders from various countries, who were as ambitious as they came. To them, the outcome seemed obvious: the Beasleys had been preparing to play it for the last three years. They were physically fit and active—all of them. And Eric Beasley was supercompetitive. He was determined to win at all costs.

But something nagged Jacob's mind.

Something about Mr. Roth.

The end was not a foregone conclusion. Ix Chel must have helped them escape from the resort, just like he'd thought. That sort of divine intervention explained so much. What if the moon goddess was still interfering on their behalf? Would she actually return Sarina to health before the games began?

With such a powerful goddess, anything was possible.

He stared up at the moon and felt a prickle of apprehension go down his spine.

CHAPTER TWENTY-SEVEN

Jaguar Temple

Calakmul Biosphere Reserve

December 25

"Dad, wake up."

Roth had been dreaming about Sarina. They'd been walking along a beach hand in hand as the surf crashed. Was it Santa Cruz? She'd told him that her great-grandmother Socorro was watching over them. That she would help them face the games. It was Lucas's voice that had roused him.

The smell of delicious food startled his senses. Light streamed in through the stone windows. It was morning. Christmas day. The humidity from the jungle was still making him sweat, but the shade and coolness of the stone rooms and buildings helped mitigate the discomfort.

Disoriented by the dream and the sudden waking, he felt the images of the beach and his wife scatter. He wanted to grab them, to remain in the dream state forever. He didn't want to face a world where his wife was on the verge of death and the continued lives of his children depended on their mastery of a game they'd never played.

"Look what they're bringing in!" Lucas said.

Roth blinked. They'd slept on woven mats on sapling rods, all of them in the same room. As he sat up, he noticed the beaded door was tethered open. Small Maya people wearing Indigenous clothing were coming in carrying wooden trays covered in steaming food. There were tamales, fresh corn, sizzling pork, and an assortment of sliced fruit. The smells coming from the feast attacked his stomach.

"Dude!" Brillante said in excitement. There was no silverware, just small corn tortillas used to grab things.

"Is all you can think about food? What about Mom?" Suki said.

Brillante's excitement faded. "Sorry."

Suki patted his back. "It's okay. We're in a weird place with all sorts of weird stuff." She sniffed at a tray with wooden mugs and then brought one of the cups to her mouth for a sip.

"Be careful," Roth warned, but his daughter had already taken a swallow.

"Smells like hot chocolate," she said, smiling softly. "It tastes like it, but better."

The boys were already cramming food into their mouths.

"I'm still so hungry! And these are good!" Lucas said, crumbs from the tamale sticking to his lips. "Better than Grandma's tamales. Don't tell her I said that!"

Roth went to the little stone table in the center of the room and joined his children. He was ravenous himself, and it was true. The tamales were so fresh, still steaming, that it burned his tongue. The flavor was amazing, easily better than his mother-in-law's tamales.

Suki gave him a cup. "Try this, Dad. It must be loaded with caffeine. I'm feeling better and better. There's something strange about it."

He took the cup. It had been made from cocoa beans, but honey had been added to sweeten it. And there was just a hint of spice. An unfamiliar one.

"This is good," Roth said, taking a deep swallow. He felt its warmth glide down his throat. Energy and resolve began to bloom inside him, and the exhaustion from their journey melted away.

"This is so good," Suki said. "Way better than the Mexican hot chocolate we have at home."

Roth smiled. The hexagonal-shaped box with the grinning Mexican grandma on it had been a presence in their cupboard for years.

The boys took cups for themselves and began to drink. They experienced the same sensations as well and commented on it.

"I want to drink this before playing soccer," Brillante enthused.

Roth didn't recognize most of the fruit on the tray. Papaya? Guava? He wasn't sure, but he sampled the slices and found they each had a distinct flavor. Not acidic—mild. One tasted a little like brown sugar.

Another servant came in with a woven basket of tamales and replenished the bowl, releasing the tether on the curtain on the way in.

"Thank you," Roth said to the fellow. He was short and squat.

"Na kink'oxomaj taj," the man replied with a shrug.

"They don't speak Spanish either, Dad," Suki said. "I think they're speaking Mayan."

It sounded nothing like Spanish at all. After the fellow filled the bowl again, he ambled out past the beaded door.

It had been days since they'd enjoyed a proper meal. The noodles and ham at Huellas de Pan had tasted nothing like this. The thought had sharp edges, and Roth found himself wondering what had happened to Jorge. To the families at the orphanage. What would Jacob do to them?

After they'd arrived, the woman had taken Jane Louise to her family, and the girl had regarded Roth with an expression that had broken his heart. The Beasleys were staying in another section of the same compound.

"It's so good to have real food again," Suki said.

"Yeah," Lucas agreed. "That's Dad's third tamale."

Roth stopped midbite.

"Oooh, awkward pause," Suki said with forced humor.

Roth gave her a look. "We'd better eat while we can."

"Are we going to try and escape?" Suki asked. "What about Mom?"

Roth chewed the tamale and then washed it down with more of the spicy hot chocolate. "Even if we manage to get out of the building, we're in the middle of the Yucatán. I don't think Calakmul was joking about that. And carry Mom the whole way? I don't think that's even possible. I know Mom would want me to get you guys out of here. That's what she'd want."

"The dude is a nutjob, Dad. I heard most of your conversation last night. He's *Undertale* in genocide mode."

Roth smiled at the video game reference. When his daughter had introduced him to the game (and its companion game *Deltarune*), it had reminded him of '80s video-game culture, but the creator had an inventive and sadistic way of making his game a philosophical adventure.

"Good comparison," he said. "This isn't about the ball game. He wants to destroy the world."

"He scared the crap out of me," Lucas said, taking more of the pork.

"I'm sure that was his intention," Roth said.

"So we're just going to play the game and die?" Suki said. "He was right. There's, like, no way we can win against the Beasleys. Hate to say it, Dad, but we're not jocks."

Roth looked at his three kids. The burning protectiveness he felt was so powerful he could barely breathe. Jacob's warning came back to him. If they lost the game, they'd all die. Sarina too.

"We are *not* losing," Roth said firmly.

"Dad, I think Mr. Beasley could bench-press a Toyota," Suki said.

"Really?" Lucas asked, and she rolled her eyes.

"And the ball is way heavier than a soccer ball," Brillante said, shuffling his feet and pretending to trip over a big stone. "Remember what it did to Lucas's face!"

"I don't think he'll heal me again," Lucas said, rubbing his nose.

The beaded curtain parted again, this time revealing the woman who worked for Jacob. Her face had been painted—a thick stripe of red went from the middle of her ear across her nose and to the other side of her face, with a thin stripe of black beneath it. Triangles were painted on her forehead—or were they arrowhead shapes? Dots and patterns accentuated her eyes and her shoulders. She'd also changed into a Maya-style outfit: her top was made of a woven fabric that crisscrossed her breasts and encircled her neck, exposing her middle. A wrap skirt covered her waist, and she had feathered anklets and bare feet. She had jewelry as well: dazzling gold rings, bracelets, and several necklaces.

"Good morning, Roth family," she said.

The kids fell silent instantly.

"I'm sorry, but I don't remember your name," Roth said in a neutral tone.

She pressed a hand to her chest. "Angélica Torres, but here, I am called Malintzin."

Roth recognized the name. "La Malinche? A traitor's name? Why would you go by that?"

She gave him an appraising look. "Westerners don't know everything."

Suki looked confused.

"She was Cortés's translator," Roth explained.

"Just as I am yours," she said. "I speak Mayan, Spanish, and English. The servants here only speak Mayan. They will be coming soon to bathe you and prepare you for the game."

Roth pursed his lips. "Bathe us?"

"You've been wandering through the jungle, Mr. Roth. The games are ceremonial. You would not want to play in your regular clothes."

"Actually, I think we do," Suki said, folding her arms.

The woman shook her head. "The rubber ball weighs nearly four pounds. The players in ancient days wore armor made of wood and leather, as will you. I will teach you the rules, and you will be given a chance to practice. The game begins at noon and ends at sunset. It will go on for however many days it takes for one side to win."

"Days?" Roth asked. "I thought it was only one day."

"When a family quits and stops playing, yes. But I don't think you have any intention of doing that. Which is why you must wear the armor. It will help protect you. Otherwise, you'll break bones." She gave Suki a warning look.

"Fine," Suki said. "But I can *bathe* myself."

She shook her head. "It is a spiritual game, and we will uphold the traditions. Those who played the games have always been honored. The food you've just eaten is part of the tradition. You must also cleanse your bodies and your minds."

Roth felt impatience spike inside him. "We were tricked into coming down here. We're not volunteers."

She looked him in the eye. "Many ancient Maya were also forced to play the game for their survival. But you are determined. That will help you endure the heat and strain of the game. And the *xocolatl*, the drink before you, will help restore your energy and strength. They invented it to prepare players for the game. The ancient Maya believed the universe would stop rotating if the game wasn't played regularly. They believed every creation would die."

"What are the rules?" Roth asked.

"I will explain them when you are ready." She paused, studying him, and said, "I know a little about your family, Mr. Roth. I know you and your wife met in the Bay Area in California. I myself graduated from Stanford University."

That startled him. "You did?"

She nodded. "Mr. Calakmul's family paid for my education. So I could learn about your land's traditions and people. I've seen the homeless in San Francisco. I've seen the traffic and the pollution. The contempt people have for one another. The political and cultural fighting. It's another kind of jungle, Mr. Roth. The strong prey on the weak."

"At least we don't try to kill each other in high school," Suki drawled.

Angélica tilted her head, studying her. "They do, actually. Active shooters. Young men so lonely, so marginalized, so enraged they come to school to kill their peers. The rates of depression and suicide among your age group are the highest they've ever been. It is time for a change. The Maya who live here are happy."

"Are they servants or *slaves*?" Roth asked her.

Angélica gave him a smile. "Why think of it in dualistic terms, Mr. Roth? They have food. Protection. Order. The great democracies of the world haven't provided their people with that. People don't function well with too much freedom. When there are no longer limits or imposed structures, the people turn on each other like wild animals. You Americans do this. The Cold War was your doomsday match."

She was right, in a way. Roth wanted to debate her on the nuances of history, but he knew it would be pointless. The Cold War was a contest of ideals. But in America, people could choose to leave or stay.

"So what's next?" he asked. "A bath in a cenote?"

"A ceremony," she answered cryptically.

———

The whole ceremony was conducted in Mayan. A shaman of sorts had brushed them with plants dunked in water and then wafted smoke over each of them from a goblet of charcoal while reciting something under his breath. Then the shaman had departed, and they'd been stripped down by female servants who then washed them.

Roth had experienced the indignity of the junior high locker room in Fremont, but his kids hadn't, and the experience was mortifying even after the loincloths had been fixed to them. Suki had suggested they all turn around and not face each other, and the boys couldn't stop giggling.

The armor the woman had spoken of was made of either leather or crocodile hide.

"I thought it was wood in my dream." She looked at the rest of them. "I saw this stuff. It was just like it."

"That's sus!" Lucas declared.

The pieces had clearly been custom built for each person, which added to the bizarreness of the whole experience. How long had this been planned? How had they discovered the Roths' measurements?

Each of them was equipped with a leather belt, a kind of girdle that fit snugly around the waist but was open at the hips. Round wooden shields were attached to it on either side to protect the hips, which were essential to playing the game. Feathered decorations encircled their ankles, but they weren't allowed to wear shoes. They were equipped with knee pads and elbow pads, with curved pieces of wood lashed to one side to allow for contact with the ball. Knees, elbows, and hips. They also had wide chest pieces that covered half of their chests and backs with more round shields attached near the shoulders. Those felt like football pads. They'd also been given headgear that strapped beneath their chins. It would help prevent broken skulls if the ball flew at their heads.

After the armor was fitted, they were given jaguar-skin skirts to wear around their waists over it. Suki was also given a jaguar-skin bra.

Roth noticed she was wearing the bracelet she'd stolen from the cenote. She'd obviously snatched it from her pocket before they'd taken away her other clothes.

The servants led them outside. The heat of the day was oppressive, but it didn't feel as hot because they were wearing minimal clothing, and the wood wasn't very heavy.

They could see a massive pyramid rising from the compound, several sets of interconnected stairs leading to the ceremonial top. Roth assumed that there was a cenote beneath it, like there had been in San Gervasio. Other buildings and structures surrounded the central pyramid, however, and there was clearly a community of Maya living there. The golden flakes of magic still clung to the rock sculptures, visible even in the daylight.

The servants brought them to a narrow aisle between slanted walls, with a freshly brushed dirt floor. Angélica was there waiting for them, holding a rubber ball that was about six inches in diameter.

"This is the practice court," she said. "The arena you will play in is bigger, and it has two stone hoops fixed to the upper wall. There are two ways to win the game."

Roth felt as if he were trapped in a nightmare, but he tried to clear his mind and concentrate. Understanding the rules was vitally important. This obviously wasn't just a game of physical prowess. It was also a mental game. One of endurance. Not quitting was possibly the most important factor. And that was something he excelled at.

"Go on," he said, nodding and staring at her intently.

"There are eight main gods of the Maya. Itzamná, Chaac, Yum Kaax, Hunab Ku, Ix Chel, Kinich Ahau, Ek Chuah, and Kukulkán— the feathered serpent. There are also gods of the underworld, but we're not playing their version of the game. Eight gods. Eight points to win. On each side of the arena, there are eight statues to the gods. When a point is scored by a team, a feather will be placed in the statue to mark it. The first side to reach eight points wins."

"How do you score?" Brillante asked.

"There are two ways. The ball must be kept moving. If it comes to a stop on your side of the court, the other team gets a point. The ball is heavy, so it will bounce and roll for a while. But it cannot be allowed to stop."

"So we're not trying to get it through the stone hoops?" Brillante asked in confusion.

"That is the other way to score. If a team gets it through one of the stone hoops on either side of the court, they win a point. The stone hoops are only slightly larger than the ball, and they are positioned high up. It is very difficult to score that way. Eight points wins the game. In ancient days, when teams were very skilled, it could take two weeks before a winner was decided."

Roth looked at her. "What's the most time it's taken since the games restarted?"

She met his gaze. "The longest? Two days."

CHAPTER TWENTY-EIGHT

Jaguar Temple

Calakmul Biosphere Reserve

December 25

Roth studied the carvings in the stone walls as they made their way toward the main arena. He'd asked Angélica if they could visit the arena beforehand, and she'd said it was permitted. The imagery was of men wearing feathered headdresses with masks. The wall looked to be made of rectangular blocks of limestone, each one containing a portion of the scene, woven together like a giant puzzle. At the center of the corridor was the image of one man—a player, no doubt—holding a decapitated head. The flourishes of blood pouring from the head looked like octopus tentacles.

There were images of jaguars and various birds too, all carved in the Maya style. The canopy of the jungle blocked out the sky, but it also provided ample shade from the piercing sun.

"The carvings on the walls are from the games played before the Spanish came," she explained, looking over her shoulder at the family as she led the way.

"If I remember right, the Classic period of the Maya was the middle of the second century to about 1000 AD," Roth said. "Was this built during that period?"

"A professor to the core," Angélica answered with a smile. "During the Classic period, there were two main rival kingdoms—Calakmul and Tikal. Both were established by Kukulkán when he descended from heaven. They fought for supremacy until 385 AD, when the king of Calakmul defeated Tikal and conquered the entire peninsula. Some of the Maya were wiped out then."

Roth was confused. "What are you talking about?"

She turned to face him, walking backward. "The history you have access to is incomplete, Mr. Roth. Remember that the Spanish destroyed most of the codices. But archaeologists have found paintings done during the Classic period. Some Maya on the glyphs are represented with red skin. Others are shown with pale skin. Dark and light. A duology. There were many civilizations that lived in this region back then. Calakmul was predominant until the Aztecs came from northern Mexico and power shifted to Tenochtitlán."

"So two factions of Maya destroyed each other?" Roth asked. "It wasn't all because of the Spanish?"

"No, Mr. Roth. One of the factions destroyed the other. Modern scholars believe that many communities of Maya simply disappeared. But no. It was the war that destroyed the people. The final battle was fought farther north, near Chichén Itzá. So many were killed that it took centuries before the population returned to reinhabit many of the areas of desolation. That is why there are gaps in the history carved in the stelae."

She turned back and then directed them toward a gap in the wall.

"The arena is through there."

That meant it was perpendicular to the path they'd been following. The walls were so high, he couldn't see any of the other pyramids, so it felt as if they were in a mouse maze.

Glancing back at his children, he saw the twins staring at the carvings on the walls. Suki was looking down, sullen and fearful. It was strange seeing her and the boys dressed in the battle gear for the games. He felt more than a little ridiculous himself. But he also didn't relish the idea of being struck by one of the heavy rubber balls *without* the armor.

They approached the entrance to the arena.

"Wait a moment," Angélica said. "Do you see the golden strands?"

In the sunlight, Roth had nearly missed the effect. A mesh of golden strands of magic covered the entrance to the arena.

"What is it?" Roth asked. He began to reach out.

"Don't," she warned.

"Is it a goalie net?" Brillante asked. "Is this the goal?"

"No," she said, chuckling. "It is a weave of magic. In K'iche' Mayan, it is called *kem äm*. That translates to 'spiderweb' or 'cobweb.'"

Lucas looked fascinated. "If I touch it, will a magic spider come out and bite me?"

"No," Angélica said. "It will throw you against that wall," she said, pointing to the wall to their left, away from the arena. "There are barriers of *kem äm* on each side to keep the players inside the arena during the game."

"Can I try it?" Lucas asked eagerly.

"It would shoot you like a cannon." Angélica held up her hand and waved it in front of the glistening golden strands, and Roth watched as the magical strands coalesced around a bracelet on her wrist and hovered there.

Interesting. The bracelet was the key to disarming the barrier.

"Now it's safe?" Roth asked. He was excited to learn about how to deactivate the barrier. It reminded him of a force field from any sci-fi episode. If it could repel matter, then it operated under the laws of physics.

His mind summoned Arthur C. Clarke's third law. Any speculative fiction author worth his salt knew it. *Any sufficiently advanced technology is indistinguishable from magic.* Maybe it *was* magic: Roth's mind certainly wasn't closed to the possibility. He'd seen those glowing lights Jacob had summoned and the miraculous healing of Lucas's nose. Or maybe Jacob had access to some sort of technology unknown enough to create the illusion of magic—a secret handed down, ancestor to ancestor. Roth had seen what the Maya were capable of. He could believe that too.

"Yes. You may enter the arena."

Roth walked inside. It reminded him of the pictures he'd seen of Chichén Itzá. The lower part of the wall was at an angle, about four feet high and pitched at fifty degrees. Above that was a vertical wall that was probably twenty feet high. There were two stone rings, midcourt, fixed to the upper portion of the wall. A lot higher than a basketball standard. And the ball itself, he knew, was barely smaller than the opening. It required a perfect shot.

The kids began roaming the court. It was about as long as a soccer field and probably twice as wide as a tennis court. The ground was made of compressed sand, fine like powder, and it looked like it had recently been tamped.

"Dude," Lucas said, pointing at one of the stone rings. "That's so high!"

"And we're supposed to get a rubber ball through it without using our hands or feet?" Suki asked with a hitch of fear in her voice.

"Knees, elbows, hips, chest. Some use their heads, but I don't recommend it," Angélica answered.

"What if the ball bounces close to the midline?" Roth asked. "Do we have to wait for it to cross to hit it?"

"The teams must remain on their own sides at all times," she answered. "If someone steps on the other side, their team loses a feather."

"Where do they put the feathers?" Brillante asked, craning his neck.

"Look at each side," she said, pointing to the opposite walls.

There were statues lining the top. Roth quickly counted eight on each side of the court. Sixteen total.

Jungle trees overhung the arena, which was probably intentional since it would conceal the place from the spy satellites of the various governments. There were gaps in the trees, so the sky could be seen, but at least they wouldn't be playing under the beating sun.

"So we play until sunset?" Roth asked. That was probably five or six hours, longer than any football or soccer game. It would be brutal.

"Yes. When someone scores a point, the servants will bring the players *xocolatl*. No food, though. You will be able to eat again before the game but not during."

"And after?" Lucas asked.

She gave him a cryptic look but didn't answer.

Roth understood her hesitation. If one team scored eight points during the first day, there wouldn't be dinner for the losing team.

His stomach cramped with dread. He turned around in a full circle, gazing at the stone hoops. Scoring that way would be far more challenging. It would require accuracy and luck to get a rubber ball anywhere near the edge of the hoop. So he reasoned that most points would be scored from the ball stopping on the ground. He stopped near the wall and gazed up at the stone ring with the emblem of a serpent carved on it, its body forming a kind of Celtic knot. He couldn't see how it was attached to the wall, but that didn't matter.

"Dad," Suki said in a low voice. "We can't win. I suck at running. Even the boys are going to get tired."

Roth stared at the hoop again, trying to reason through his growing panic. "Why did they put the hoops so high on the wall?" he asked. "There has to be a reason."

"To make it insanely difficult?" Suki said as if the answer were obvious.

He walked to the edge of the wall and then counted off his steps as he'd learned in the Boy Scouts as a teenager. The court was almost exactly a hundred and twenty-five feet wide. He estimated triple that for the length.

"Crap," he whispered. "We'll be running all over the place."

"Yeah, exactly," Suki said with frustration. "I'm not a good runner."

"You're a good swimmer," Roth said.

She gave him a biting look. "This isn't a pool, Dad."

"Endurance. This is about endurance."

"We are so dead," Suki muttered.

He shook his head. "This will be hard for anyone. Even the Beasleys. I don't care how much they've been training. Remember we're fighting for Mom too. We just need to come up with a strategy for defense and then wear them down. There's four of us. Do we do zones? Each person plays a quarter of the arena?"

"How should I know?" she asked.

"I need you to help me *think*, Suki," he said. "We have a few more hours until noon. Boys, get over here."

They jogged up to him. They weren't as despairing as their sister, which was good. Roth had to keep her motivated. He had to keep them all motivated.

"We need a defensive strategy," he said. "We have to keep the ball moving and on *their* side as much as possible."

Lucas frowned. "If it's on their side, we won't score a goal."

"Look, trying to score through a hoop isn't going to be our best move," Roth said. "What happens when you bounce a rubber ball but don't touch it?"

"It bounces lower and lower," Suki said.

"Newton's law of inertia. I think our best chance of scoring points is through their errors." Roth looked each of them in the eye. They were engaging with him, thankfully, and hope was starting to brighten their expressions.

"I think I should play near the front," Roth said. "I'm the biggest, which means I can hit it the farthest. Let's make them expend energy running around the court while we conserve ours." He lowered his voice. "I'll keep knocking it as far as I can. We all should. Then, boom, just barely tap it onto their side when they're expecting it to go soaring. If they can't get to the ball in time, it stops and we get a point."

Lucas and Brillante looked at each other. "Smart, Dad!"

"You two start in the back. You've got the youngest legs. If they hit it wide, you'll need to keep it going and get it back to Suki and me up front."

"I'm playing front too?" Suki asked.

"Yes, we'll take the front, and the boys will be in back. We can adjust as we need to."

"Hey!"

It was a man's voice, shouted from across the arena. Eric Beasley. Anger surged through Roth. He wanted to annihilate the other man. To beat him to a pulp. A quick glance revealed him and his family gathered outside the other opening in the arena, behind the golden barrier. The other family was also garbed for the game. Even little Jane Louise, who was so tiny. His heart ached for her. He couldn't see her face, but she was cowering behind her mother.

Angélica hurried over to talk with them.

Eric was angry, and his voice carried across the stone court. "What's going on, Angélica? You helping them?"

"I'm not, Mr. Beasley. They asked to see the court. You've already seen it."

"We want to see it again. Is that against the rules? Let us in."

"Your teams are not supposed to interact prior to the game."

"Then get them out of there," Eric insisted.

"They just got here, Mr. Beasley."

Kendall spoke up, her nose wrinkled as if she smelled something bad. "I think she was helping them."

"That's what it looks like to me," Eric agreed.

"No fair!" shouted one of their boys.

Tension gripped Roth's insides, clawing at him, encouraging him to act. Eric and Kendall were responsible for bringing them here. It was because of them that Sarina lay in a coma. It was because of them that his entire family might be wiped out as part of a madman's cause.

"Let us in there!" shouted the older Beasley boy.

"Dude, they suck," Suki muttered.

Roth tried to regain control of his emotions. "They're doing this on purpose," he said.

"No crap, Sherlock," Suki quipped.

"It's psychological," Roth said. "Intimidation. This isn't like football where both sides tackle each other. They have to stay on their side of the court. Same with us. So they'll talk smack during the game too. Try to rile us up."

"It's working," Suki said.

"Can't let it," Roth replied, shaking his head. "We've got to play better than them. Our lives are at stake. Mom's life is at stake. We have to play not just as a team, but as a family. We can't get angry or upset with each other. We have to *help* one another."

"They have more players than us," Brillante said.

"Doesn't matter," Roth said.

"Just let us in!" Eric shouted.

"I'm sorry, Mr. Beasley, but not until they are done."

"Oh, they're *done*," Eric roared. "You hear that? You hear that? You're done, Roth! You're dead!"

"Anger-management seminar?" Suki suggested under her breath. "Or one of those squishy stress balls?"

The boys snickered. Roth smiled at her.

"There we go, that's it," he said to Suki. "That's what I'm talking about."

"They're losers," Brillante said with a snort.

Fear flickered beneath his bravado, but Roth would never call him on it. They needed to put on a brave front, if only for themselves. Believing they could win was the only way they had a chance.

"Totally," Lucas agreed as he patted his brother on the back.

It heartened Roth, the way they were supporting each other. Building each other up. Narrowing his gaze on Suki, he lowered his voice and said, "Did you notice how she took down the magic wall?"

Suki's eyes met his, and she rubbed the bracelet encircling her wrist.

"Smart girl," he whispered.

CHAPTER
TWENTY-NINE

Jaguar Temple

Calakmul Biosphere Reserve

December 25

When Roth's humorous fantasy novel about a young man who was raised by medieval con artists and pretends to be a wizard hit the *New York Times* bestseller list and took up residence there, his career was catapulted onto a new trajectory. He was no longer just an adjunct faculty member of the history department at a university in Hayward. He was a man in the arena of literature with a crowd screaming at him—some in praise and some in derision. The voice he'd come up with for his protagonist had resonated with so many people, but he'd also been publicly eviscerated by tons of haters and trolls who took him apart on the internet or in reviews.

Even so, it felt different walking into an *actual* arena, where the stakes were life and death, not just for him but for the people he loved.

As the Maya servants led his family down the chasm of stone, past the violent scenes etched into the walls, he could hear the throbbing noise of deep drums and the combined voices of thousands of spectators who had gathered in the midst of a forbidding jungle to watch the spectacle of two American families fighting their ancestral game.

"How many people do you think are here?" Suki asked as they walked. She looked seasick.

Roth glanced back at the twins. They were staring up at the walls, their expressions showing the growing anticipation of meeting the crowd behind such a ruckus. Like the excited and nervous looks of players before they began a soccer game against a superior team.

When they reached the magical barrier, the *kem äm*, there were two warriors stationed at it, both wearing feathered headdresses. They were heavily muscled and painted, with ink on their arms, legs, faces, and bare chests. They each held wooden paddles edged with razor-sharp obsidian, which made the weapons look like chain saws. The warriors stared them down as they approached, and Roth felt his blood chill.

When they reached the spiderweb of magic, he could see the crowd gathered along the walls on each side of the arena. Everyone was standing—there were no available seats except for an empty throne that hadn't been there when they had visited the arena that morning. Men and women wearing traditional Maya clothing were standing and stomping and cheering, waving feathers in the air. The heavy beat of the drums caused pressure in Roth's ears. His stomach was sick. He'd never been a sports guy in high school. He'd preferred playing D&D with Moretti and Westfall to going to Friday-night football games. Now he had to play a sport—and win—to secure the lives of his children and wife.

The two guards stood still at the entryway, not moving aside. It wasn't time to start yet.

"Dad," Suki said weakly. "I think I'm going to throw up."

Roth let out his breath in a slow, steady rhythm. That's what Sarina would have told him to do. His gut clenched with worry thinking of her. They hadn't been allowed to see her, but Angélica had assured him that her condition was stable and that she was in the temple of Ix Chel, a shrine of healing. Was she only being preserved until the game was over? Had she died during the night? He didn't know. What he did know was he couldn't let himself descend into worry and grief. Not now. He had to keep his head for all of them.

"Slow breaths," he told his daughter. "Just like Mom always says."

"What if we need to pee during the game?" Lucas asked.

Roth snorted. "I don't think we're getting bathroom breaks. And once we start playing, your body will need every ounce of moisture."

"There must be thousands of people in there," Brillante said in awe. "It sounds like thousands."

It did. From the maw behind the guards, they could see the undulating crowd.

Roth saw the Beasley family arrive at the other entrance. The two teams stood opposite each other, separated by the court and a web of magic. Roth was tempted to touch the magic strands, but he didn't. He was curious—not stupid.

Suki was breathing in gasps now. Was she trying to calm herself down or hyperventilating?

"Slower," he said. "Follow mine." He performed deliberate inhales and slow exhales, and she started copying the pattern.

A loud, hornlike blaring filled the air. Roth looked up and saw eight men holding what appeared to be elephant-tusk horns. The sound came from them, and suddenly, the noisy crowd fell silent.

The two warriors, still gripping their obsidian weapons, waved their free arms over the barrier. Roth noticed the magic adhered to the bracelets on their wrists as it had done earlier, creating an opening for them to enter the arena. The servants motioned them forward.

Roth shook his head. Then, mustering his courage, he advanced, with his children following. On the opposite side, the Beasleys stepped forward too. They had black paint adorning their faces, like the warriors at the gate. Roth noticed that the warriors on the opposite side did not have painted faces. He didn't understand the significance, but one team was painted and the other was not. Was that a reference to the two different groups of Maya that Angélica had told them about?

Once the families passed the gates, the guards invoked the magic again, and both ends were blocked. Roth gazed at the crowd gathered within the walls. Although the spectators wore a variety of costumes, feathers and jaguar skins were the predominant decoration. But they were not all Hispanic. Roth saw spectators who looked vaguely familiar, despite the ancient attire. He could swear one of them had been on the cover of *Time* magazine. Interspersed through the onlookers were individuals who were clearly previous winners. The wealthy. The proud. The ambitious. Was one of them dressed as John Galt from *Atlas Shrugged*? Another dystopian novel about wealth and a fractured society. All of them wore feathers as part of their ensembles. And jaguar pelts. It *was* the Jaguar Temple. The feathers, he surmised, represented the feathered serpent, Kukulkán, the god who had supposedly descended from the heavens to visit the Maya. Some had wooden helmets in the shape of jaguar heads, their faces visible through the jaws. There were murmurs from the crowd, but it was surprisingly quiet for such a packed space.

The trumpet-tusks were lowered. The empty throne that had been put there while they were gone was in the middle on the left side. It hadn't been there earlier, so it was put there while they'd been gone.

A line had been marked in the dirt at the half-court, running from the base of the wall below one stone hoop to the wall below the other. Roth didn't want to look at Eric Beasley's face, so he glanced at the hoops again. The height still seemed off. Besides, they weren't the same as basketball hoops, where gravity could help a ball sink into the net. These were mounted sideways, so the ball had to hit the circle dead center without touching the sides or ricocheting off the walls. Otherwise the ball was more than likely going to deflect off the stone.

Even if they'd been allowed to use their hands, it would have been nearly impossible to score through them. How had the ancient Maya done it with their hips?

Unless he was missing something, getting a ball through that hoop just wasn't practical. It wasn't going to happen.

"One family lives," Eric said in a low voice. "One family dies. You're going to eat dirt, Roth. Your wife is already halfway there."

Roth bristled but forced himself to ignore the comment. He had already known the man was despicable. That he would play mind games and shout insults and barbs. At least he and his boys weren't allowed to cross the line in the dirt.

A man began to speak at the far end of the court. Surprisingly, the acoustics were so refined he didn't even need to shout to be heard. The stone amplified his voice, but the words were Mayan, and Roth didn't understand.

After he said a few sentences, he stopped.

Angélica's voice began to echo through the arena. It took a moment for him to pick her out of the crowd, but she was standing by the throne. "Welcome to the death game. Two families, nobles from America, have come to compete."

A loud hurrah-type greeting came from the throng, startling Roth. The kids seemed startled too.

The first speaker continued, and the pattern repeated. Angélica, or Malintzin, he supposed, was the translator. Just as the original Malintzin had translated for Cortés when he met Montezuma, the Aztec emperor.

"The game will commence when Lord Calakmul releases the ball into the arena. It will end by victory or sunset. Then a feast will celebrate the occasion."

More words. More instructions.

The drums began to beat again, and the people stamped their feet.

Angélica raised her voice. "Welcome to the jaguar priest! Welcome to the heir of the Calakmul family. Welcome to the prophesied one! He whom Kukulkán spoke of who will bring us all to the land we were promised!"

The thumping grew louder and more intense. The chanting from the crowd intensified.

Roth's pulse was racing.

Then a jaguar slunk through the entrance at the far side of the arena. The cries became frenetic; the stamping shuddered the ground.

The jaguar moved down the aisle in front of the gathered mass of onlookers, and people bowed as it passed.

"That's a freaking jaguar," Suki whispered.

"Poggers," Lucas gasped.

When the jaguar reached the throne, Roth watched in amazement as the beast suddenly stood on its hind legs and transformed into Jacob Calakmul. He wore a jaguar pelt around his waist, feathered anklets, and a golden chest piece that made him look like an Egyptian pharaoh. His muscular chest lacked any hint of fat. He sat down on the throne, looking like a real king.

The servant standing next to the throne raised a wooden headdress, plumed with multicolored feathers, and placed it on his head.

The crowd went berserk.

Impassive, dignified, Jacob gazed at the gathered assembly. Then he looked at the two teams, inclining his head to Eric and then to Roth.

"Did I just see what I think I saw?" Suki whispered. "He's a freaking were-jaguar?"

Roth glanced at Eric, who was regarding Jacob with a look of fear. His wife, Kendall, stared at the jaguar priest with an entirely different emotion. She looked like she was about to faint with desire. Roth remembered the Navajo stories he'd heard from Moretti's dad. The scary stories of the *yee naaldlooshii*. The skinwalkers.

Jacob raised his palm, and the crowd fell silent.

"Players, stand ready!" Angélica shouted.

Roth turned and motioned for his kids to move. "Get into position!"

They scrambled to attention, quickly obeying. Suki went to the right half of the front. Roth would stay in the left quadrant, and the boys would both be defenders. He'd used soccer rules since those were the easiest for them to grasp. Their whole purpose was to get the ball as far from the line as possible and make the Beasleys run for it constantly. The Roths wouldn't try to shoot for a goal at all.

As soon as Jacob took the ball that was given to him and hurled it into the arena, Roth's entire plan fell apart.

———

Sweat dripped from Roth's entire body. He was covered in dust and dirt. If the heat of the sun weren't blocked by the overhanging jungle trees, he probably would have collapsed long ago. His chest was in dire need of oxygen, but there wasn't enough. Each lungful burned. The cramp had started early on.

They'd played for hours, and the Beasleys had dominated the game.

They'd been practicing as a family. They knew the rules. And they were *ruthless*.

It was six points to zero and Roth was giving it everything he could to hold off until sunset. In his peripheral vision, he saw the shadows of the arena changing, getting longer.

Every time a point was won, servants came rushing in with cups of *xocolatl*, just like Angélica had told them. The drink had an energizing effect on the players on both sides. It was a small reprieve, and Roth told his kids to drink as much as they could before the game started up again. The energy from the drink didn't last forever.

The first lost point had been Roth's fault. The next four had been the twins', who struggled to keep the ball bouncing when it went far afield. When they were down by three, Roth had switched the boys to playing front while he and Suki worked as defenders. But the Beasleys adjusted to their tactics quickly and kept making the Roths run for it. The Beasley boys also kept trying for the hoops. Each time they did, the crowd went wild with enthusiasm, but so far they hadn't succeeded.

In keeping with their strategy, Roth and his kids didn't even try for the hoops. They kept knocking the ball back as far as possible, but the Beasleys were fit and fast, and they always got to it. Several times, Eric had kneed the ball deep into their territory at the last possible moment, making them scramble after it.

Roth hadn't thought it possible, but he hated the man even more now.

With sweat dripping in his eyes, he continued to examine the game analytically. Because of their strong lead, the Beasleys were playing confidently. They took their time when they were in possession, but as it got closer to sunset, Roth saw their intensity pick up. They wanted to finish the game in one day.

"Come on, harder!" Eric shouted. His kids were tired but not nearly as exhausted as Roth's family. He wanted to shout encouragement to his kids, but he had no spit left.

The older Beasley boy, Colter, made another run for the hoop.

Or so it appeared. At the last moment, he bounced it over to Eric, who hipped it midcourt. It bounced over Suki's head. Roth sprinted toward it, his knees killing him. Suki was turning around, trying to hit it, but it was heading directly into Roth's area.

"Come on, Dad!" Lucas shouted. "Get it!"

Roth saw the bouncing diminish with each progressive movement.

"Yes! Yes!" Eric bellowed. That would make seven. Seven points on the first day.

The ball was bouncing so low now that Roth wished he could kick it like a soccer ball, but if he did so, he'd lose a point anyway. Grimacing in anticipation of how much it would hurt, he did a baseball slide to try to catch the ball with his knee. If he could hit it hard enough, it might ricochet off the back wall of the arena. Then one of the kids could keep it moving.

Roth felt the friction of the slide and then the jarring impact of the dense rubber ball ricocheting off his bent knee. The ball shot away from him, not toward the wall but the mesh of spiderweb magic. As soon as the ball struck the weave, it shot off at an angle like a cannon. Roth skidded to stop and rolled onto his chest, lifting his head.

The ball hit Eric in the chest and knocked him down as if a battering ram had struck him. Then, deflecting off his armor, it shot back onto Roth's side. Brillante rushed to it, then hipped it hard. The Beasley boys went running for it, but the ball went directly to Jane Louise, who caught it in her hands.

"No!" Colter shrieked.

Jane Louise looked confused.

A groan came from the crowd.

"Not your hands! Not your hands!" shouted the boys.

Jane Louise's face crumpled, and she dropped the ball.

Roth got back to his feet as the mesh went down and servants came running in with more of the *xocolatl*. Across from him, he saw Kendall slap the little girl's hand.

"We told you! Don't touch or kick it. Just . . . just stay out of it!" she snarled.

"Jane!" barked Eric, getting back to his feet, rubbing his sore chest.

Roth took the drink he was given and gulped it down, feeling a wave of righteous indignation on the girl's behalf. It spoke of the Beasleys' lack of character, not that he was surprised. Although points had been lost on his side, of course, he'd tried to brush it off and be encouraging. He saw the little girl's guilty expression. Her shame at being shouted at in front of the crowd.

But then she glanced across the arena at Roth, and he realized something startling.

She'd done it on purpose.

CHAPTER THIRTY

Gran Acropolis

Calakmul Biosphere Reserve

December 25

It was a sight Jacob never tired of—the glowing temples, shrouded in golden mist, illuminating the revelers spread throughout the main plaza and beyond. Temple after temple, each one painstakingly repaired. Jacob stood at the pinnacle of the highest part of the Jaguar Temple, listening to the music of the celebrants and witnessing their dancing as the warmth of the jungle caressed his skin.

Six feathers to one. The end was near.

Jacob looked down and saw Uacmitun, the chief of the warriors who guarded the ancient city and the surrounding jungle. The man came rushing toward him in the zigzag pattern that was familiar to all who traversed the narrow steps of the temple. The design made visitors ascend sideways, thereby showing respect to the one at the top. He wore the black paint and white stripes of the death god he served. One of the gods of Xibalba—the underworld.

The warrior approached on bare feet, almost soundless. When he arrived at the summit, dripping with sweat from the strenuous climb, he knelt before the jaguar priest.

"Have your men found the pilot who flew the plane over our land last week?" Jacob asked.

"Yes, Great One. He confessed. The glyphs summoned the storm to drive them off. But he knows where the temple is located, and so does the archaeologist with him. Do you want them both killed?"

"Are they both in Guatemala still?"

"The professor went back to America. The pilot is home."

"Keep watch on them both. Wait until the pilot returns and then sabotage the plane so it will crash in the jungle."

Uacmitun smiled. "As you command." He turned, about to leave, but stopped. "You were right, Great One," crowed the warrior. "The family is preparing to escape as you prophesied."

It had not required any divination on Jacob's part to foresee this, although it never hurt to add to his legend. Mr. Roth was a crafty man. He'd proven as much since his arrival in the Yucatán. He was curious as to how the author would make his attempt.

"Have your men track them in the dark," Jacob said. "I want to see where they'll try to slip past the web. Have your warriors take them." Jacob smirked. "We'll honor the legend of the Xibalban ball games. One of the twins lost his head. That should please the crowd."

The warrior bowed. "Do you care which?"

"I do not. It will demoralize the rest of the family, and they'll quit or lose the last two points. It is time to end the game. Tomorrow, we will perform the sacrifices. Be ready, Uacmitun."

"Yes, Ajwäch. As you command." The warrior bowed until his forehead grazed the stone. He was a skilled warrior they'd trained since childhood, one who had joined the Mexican special forces—the FES—on their behalf, to gain more skills. After his training, he'd returned to Calakmul to help train others at the temple. His skills were a mixture of ancient and modern assassination techniques. He could have killed Jacob in an instant. But his devotion to the family was beyond doubt.

Jacob looked past him to the throngs celebrating the games. They'd be disappointed if the games ended so soon. And, truth be told, so would Jacob. The quick-thinking author had intrigued him. The chase had been thrilling. And as with tradition, the longer the game was played, the longer the celebration afterward. In the future, the death games would take longer, especially as whispers of them began to spread more rapidly through the global network of the rich and powerful. Within a generation, there would be families who'd trained for the games since childhood. Like the Beasley sons. This wouldn't be their only game. They would be even more ruthless than their father.

Still. He had to consider the bigger picture. If he asked himself which man would be easiest to control in the future, once the prophecy had fully manifested, the answer was obvious. Beasley was a fool; Mr. Roth was wiser than he should be. Fools were easier to control.

"Go," Jacob said.

The warrior rose and then hastened down the steps in the same zigzag pattern. Back when tourists were allowed to climb the temple at Chichén Itzá, there were always one or two people each year who tumbled to their death because they didn't know how to climb the steps properly. Submission and humility were the keys to success.

After watching Uacmitun depart, Jacob retreated to the opening at the top of the temple. As with the other temples, a shaft descended to the lower reaches. There were no ropes or equipment here. Jacob didn't need them.

He invoked the magic of his ring, and a mesh disk of golden strands appeared in the opening, which he stepped on. It didn't repel *him*—it repelled his mass, absorbing it. With a thought, the disk descended rapidly down the shaft to the lower portion of the temple, where the treasures and obsidian weapons were kept, along with crates full of modern military gear.

Beneath Calakmul was another city entirely, one lit to the brightness of daylight by the magic imbued in the stone. Carvings and glyphs shining in the gloom to reveal a network of tunnels.

Jacob made his way to the palace of the high priest. *His* palace. His servants bowed and greeted him, and he took a sliced black sapote fruit from one of them and bit into the chocolaty flesh. After taking a drink of coconut milk, he retired to the palatial bedchamber. The female servants quickly gathered around him and removed the headdress, cape, and the cedar ceremonial armor across his chest. They took off the golden jewelry armbands, bracers, and anklets as well, leaving him standing in the jaguar-hide wrap around his waist.

Jacob walked to the stone doorway that led to a set of stairs carved directly into the limestone. There was a private cenote beneath the building that only he used for bathing and relaxation. The servants weren't allowed down there.

"My lord."

The voice interrupted him as he was about to depart.

It was Angélica—his Malintzin.

He paused at the threshold and turned to look at her. She'd changed into another Maya costume, one that bared enough of her skin to stir his blood. He wanted her. And he was afraid of that desire. He met her eyes, forcing himself to look at her face instead of her body.

"Yes?"

"Teach me the magic," she pleaded. "I've been loyal to you. I want to learn *more*."

He admired her ambition. It was one of the reasons he'd selected her and paid for her education and training. Some women would cringe at being separated from the trappings of modern life, from internet and cell phones, but Angélica had always relished it. She enjoyed living beyond the mores of society. Her Maya blood was awakened there. She was asking him to make her his equal. Did he dare?

"You don't know what you are asking," he said.

"I think I do," she said, coming into his private chamber without invitation. That was a risk in and of itself. He could have executed her for such an affront. But she was showing she trusted him to have mercy.

"You've done well in your role as Malintzin," he said.

"She was a princess."

"She was a *priestess*," he corrected. "She won Cortés's trust. She bore his child. All because the jaguar priests asked her to."

"What must I do to prove my loyalty?" she asked, her eyes inviting him to ask anything of her. It was tantalizing.

He gazed at her face, at the paint decorating the skin of her cheeks and forehead. She knew the traditions well. She was fluent in the language.

"There are many Mayan words for secrets," he said. "Name them and their meanings."

That surprised her. Her brow furrowed a little. "'*Ajwäch*'—*one who knows secrets*. There are two that are similar. *'Jasjatem'* and *'jasjatik.'* Those are words that mean *to whisper*, or *to speak in secret*." Her voice was low and sultry. "'*Man k'o tä -bij.' To keep* . . . *secrets*. I have kept your secrets. I have been faithful to you."

She had. He had mosquitoes that spied on her for him. The Mayan word for the buzzing sound they made, the sound that could only be heard when they were very close, was "*rininik*." They whispered her secrets to him. Some of the security men had tried to seduce her—at his request. She'd been clever enough in her refusals not to make any enemies.

"There are other words," he said. "Is that all you've learned?"

Her brow furrowed in consternation.

He stepped toward her. "'*Membal,' a secret hand signal*. One used to identify those who share the secret. *'Pa k'ask'atem.' To meet in secret. 'Q'abanik.' To blame, trick, or slander someone* . . . *in secret*. The word can also mean *sin*. The followers of Kukulkán used it thus. And they hunted our kind. They tried to destroy the great secret."

Her eyes lit with enthusiasm. She was hoping he would tell her more, but he couldn't do that until she took the oaths required.

"I want to learn," she said.

"But you are not ready to learn the secret of the *nawualli*."

She came even closer, enough that he could smell the fragrant oil coming from her skin. His thoughts began to buzz with the madness of desire. But he would not allow himself to be swayed by it.

"When?"

"That is for me to decide, Malintzin. Kukulkán asked for a broken heart as sacrifice. Do you think the lords of Xibalba demand anything less?"

Her eyes widened. "Is that . . . how your wife died?" she whispered.

She'd come very close to discerning the truth. Jacob admired that.

He reached out and grazed his finger along her cheek. "You are not ready," he said huskily.

He saw her tongue stroke the edge of her lower lip.

"Why are there so many K'iche' words for secrets?" he asked her. "Ponder that. Think on the history. Not what the scholars know, but what *you've* learned."

"If reading pleases you, I will." There was a hint of disappointment in her voice. She'd been anticipating this conversation.

"Knowledge pleases me," he said, tapping her forehead with his fingertip. The desire to wrap her in his arms and kiss her nearly overpowered him.

Her eyes roved his chest, his arms. She bowed and retreated from the room, although she paused on the threshold, turning back. Was she posing dramatically for his enjoyment? He thought so.

"What about Mrs. Roth? Will she be part of the sacrifice?"

"If her heart stops beating, she cannot be part of the sacrifice."

"Will she die?"

"She's at the gate. If I revoked the glyph I drew on her forehead, she'd be dead in an instant."

Angélica looked at him curiously. "But death is not the end. Not according to the legends."

"This is true. Ix Chel has left her footprints. If Mrs. Roth dies, I'd want to be sure Ix Chel doesn't resurrect the woman. I have warriors guarding her tomb."

"Do you fear that?" Angélica asked wonderingly. "Has it happened before?"

"The ancient ways are very strange," Jacob said. "I've asked Uacmitun to behead one of the twins tonight when the Roths try to escape. Will he be resurrected too, I wonder? Like in the legend?"

She flinched. She'd grown a little fond of the family. It was only natural. But compassion led to weakness of will.

"How do you know they'll escape?" she asked, controlling her features once more.

"Because I know Mr. Roth. You don't have to watch it, Malintzin. I don't ask it of you."

She gave him a look of unconcern. "They're all going to die anyway." As she headed down the corridor, he watched the swaying of her hips. The thin fabric of the garment hardly concealed her.

Unless Ix Chel intervened more directly, the Roths would die. But this temple wasn't her stronghold. It was *his*.

CHAPTER THIRTY-ONE

RESIDENTIAL COMPLEX

CALAKMUL BIOSPHERE RESERVE

December 25

Roth could hear the revelers from the window of the stone room. Although he was physically and emotionally spent from the exhaustion of the day and the drink having worn off, his mind would not shut off. He lay on the woven mat, hands crossed behind his head, staring at the ceiling in the semidark room. He wished he could see Sarina. Just being able to hold her hand would have eased his feelings. The ache in his chest was overpowering.

Six points to one. They'd come very close to losing the death game on the first day. If they played tomorrow, it would all be over. His family would die. Roth felt certain of it. Why couldn't he figure out a way to get out of this mess? His skull throbbed from the restless thoughts that kept exerting themselves.

He sat up on the mat, and it crunched beneath him. The gear they'd used in the arena had been taken away to be mended, and the Maya servants had equipped them with loose-fitting tunics and sandals. Some of the wooden disks had been cracked by the heavy ball. Roth's hip ached, and he'd found multiple bruises there. As he wrapped his arms around his knees, he felt the ache in his elbows too. The ball had gotten past him so many times, and he'd been unable to run hard enough to catch up to it. The boys' years of playing soccer had prepared them for such an exhaustive feat, but they were tired too. And scared.

Roth rubbed his mouth.

"Dad?"

It was Suki's voice.

"You awake too?" he asked her.

"Nothing like the dread of waking up to give you a good case of insomnia," she said. "Do you have any more ideas?"

"We need to get out of here."

"Nah. I think I'll get used to the stone toilets."

Roth chuckled. Suki was always ready with a quip, even now. "Quite a party going on out there."

"What time do you think it is?"

"I have no idea." Roth sniffed. "Do you want to hear my thoughts on escaping?"

"Okay."

Roth rubbed his forearm, feeling the ache of his muscles. His legs were strained from playing the game. "The bracelet you took. I think that's our way out."

"I don't know how to use it."

"So we'll have to figure it out. That woman and the guards, they waved their arms, and the glowing gold stuff gathered around their bracelets. It was as simple as that. I think we should try it. See if it works."

"That's your plan?" She sounded disappointed.

"That's just the first part. I'm still working on how to survive the jungle," Roth said. "We don't have light. Once we leave this . . . place . . . we'll be wandering in the dark, and that's too dangerous. That's why I think we should try to bring some of that glowing stuff with us."

"Um . . . what about Mom? We can't just leave her here."

Roth sighed. "I don't want to leave her here. But she'd want me to get you kids out if I could. So we need to test to see if that's even possible. Escaping at night is better than during the day. But it's dark. So we need a form of light."

"Okay, like a torch? What about those oil lamps the servants were using earlier?"

"How do we light them? Can't wander around with one already lit. It would draw too much notice."

"We already draw attention everywhere we go, Dad. You especially. What about Jane Louise?"

Roth's stomach clenched with dread. He'd had the same thought. What would happen to the Beasleys if Roth's family managed to make it out? He'd grown fond of the little girl.

He sighed. "Can't do anything about it. She's with her own family now."

"They're totally jerks."

"Yeah. There are other choice words I'd use to describe them. But none of this is her fault."

"I wish we could take her with us."

"Me too."

"How do we get out of the building we're in?"

Roth pointed to the window. "We slip out and then find a way back toward the ruins on that side, away from all the commotion."

"Why are you guys talking?" Lucas complained. "I'm trying to sleep."

"We're getting out of here," Suki said.

"What?" he said, sitting bolt upright.

Brillante spoke up. "Dude. It's about time. Let's bail."

The crunching of the mat rushes revealed both boys were getting up.

"It's so hot, even at night," Lucas said.

"This place is always hot," said Suki. "Dad, I think the window is a bad idea. That's the most obvious way out. The obvious way usually means trouble."

"We go out the bead door, and we're going to run into the servants," Roth said.

"The party is still going strong," Suki said. "Maybe we should wait until it quiets down?"

It was a sensible suggestion. He was about to say so when he heard a slap.

"Dang mosquitoes!" Brillante complained.

"Suki's right. We'll wait until the party quiets down."

They sat on their mats, talking quietly among themselves as they waited. It had to be close to midnight. Roth didn't know how they'd survive in a jungle filled with so many predators, but staying would almost certainly mean death. At least they'd die trying to escape instead of playing the stupid game.

They talked about the game. They'd all done their best, but the pure physicality of it had been brutal.

"It makes no sense why those hoops are so high," Lucas said. "I mean, no one got a goal through it, even though the Beasleys were trying hard."

"It is too high," Roth agreed. "The geometry of it doesn't make sense."

"Geometry?" Suki said with a huff.

"It's a parabola. You remember those from school, right?"

"I'd prefer to forget all the math I've learned in school," Suki said.

"Everyone asks when they'll ever use high school algebra," he said with a small smile. "Well. Here's your chance, kiddo. A hyperbola, instead of a parabola, might be a better description for what we'd need to do to score."

"How's that going to help?" Lucas said.

"I'm not getting it," Brillante put in. "What do you mean?"

"Think of it this way," Roth said. "We stand on the arena floor. One person hits the ball at a certain angle and a certain force. According to the physics of motion, the ball will travel up, arc, and then come down the exact same slope. That's a parabolic curve."

"So?" Suki said with exasperation.

"That means to get the ball through the stone hoop, you have to hit it from the ground, standing on the same plane as the hoop. With the right force and the right angle, the ball goes through."

"Yeah, but there are a ton of problems," Suki said. "How tall you are, whether there's any wind—"

"There was *no* wind today," Brillante interrupted.

"Whatever. Even if we practiced it day after day for weeks, it would take time to figure out exactly how hard to hit it."

"It's a bit like throwing free throws," Brillante said.

"It's not like soccer or basketball because we can't use our hands or feet!" Suki countered.

"But Brillante has the right idea. A free throw shot is a parabola. The ball has to hit its vertex above the hoop."

There was a moment of quiet.

"In this game," Suki said, "the stone hoop is positioned vertically, so . . . the hoop itself has to be the vertex. Not an invisible point above it."

"Exactly," Roth said, proud of his girl for figuring it out.

"I still don't get it," Lucas said.

"Dude, the vertex is the top of the curve," Brillante said. He'd always been better at math than his brother. "The highest point it reaches. The only way to get the ball through is . . . you know . . . hitting it hard enough to just reach the hoop."

"The ball isn't much smaller than the circle," Suki said.

"Exactly," Roth added. "It's nearly impossible. I don't think any of us are skilled enough to achieve that height with just our hips. The Beasleys kept trying to ricochet off the wall. They came close, but the hoop itself knocks the ball another way."

"We should use our knees," Brillante suggested. "Like that bouncing drill coach makes us do!"

"Okay . . . ?" Lucas said, still sounding confused. "Aren't we leaving anyway?"

It was a good point. Still, discussing it was passing the time, and they needed the diversion.

"So you're saying that the Maya were sort of good at math and they invented a game out of it?" Suki sounded skeptical.

"They were more than 'sort of good.' They built their pyramids to align with the planetary orbits. Maybe they started teaching the game to their kids when they were little. By the time they reached adulthood, they knew the geometries."

"Unless they got sacrificed first," Suki pointed out.

"Hey, it's getting quieter," Brillante said.

He was right. The ruckus outside had faded substantially.

"Where did they go?" Lucas asked. "I don't hear anyone coming this way."

He was right. Roth rose from his mat and walked to the window. Outside, he saw the moon, nearly full, through the canopy of jungle trees high overhead. He had a glimpse of a stone wall and a small walkway.

"The moon is out now," Roth said. "Lucky for us."

"Why does the moon matter?" Suki asked.

"We'll be able to see better. Hey, why don't one of you two go up on the roof to see what's out there?"

"I'll do it!" Lucas volunteered.

"I can," Brillante said, just a beat behind him.

Roth glanced at the boys. "Lucas. Your turn."

He laughed in triumph and then went to the window. Roth interlocked his fingers and made a place for Lucas to plant his foot.

"I don't think he should get up on the roof," Suki said.

"Why not?" Roth asked her.

"Got a bad vibe about it."

"He's just going to have a look," Roth said.

Lucas stepped onto his hands, and Roth hoisted him up onto the window ledge. The whole building was made out of carved limestone. Lucas crouched on the sill, filling the frame.

"Dad. This isn't a good idea." Suki sounded worried.

"I'll do it," Brillante offered.

Lucas reached his hand out the window and grabbed the edge of the roof. He twisted around so that he was facing them again.

"I might need a boost. I'm not good at pull-ups."

"Dude, let *me* do it," Brillante said.

"Dad!" Suki said sharply. "Don't let him go out there. I've got a *really* bad vibe about it."

"I got this!" Lucas said. He began pulling himself up, his legs dangling.

The sound of bare feet came from the hallway beyond the bead door. Roth turned and looked that way. They hadn't heard anyone roaming the stone house all night. Maybe some of the servants were returning from the celebration?

"Get on the mats," Roth whispered.

"What about Lucas?"

Roth knew they didn't have time to get him back inside, and he'd be safer if they didn't draw attention to him. The curtain parted, and in walked Angélica. Her bracelet glowed with the golden threads wrapped around it. She had on a different costume now, and her expression was grave.

Roth's stomach flipped. How long before she noticed the missing boy?

Roth approached her, using his larger body to block her field of view. "What's the matter?" he demanded.

Her eyes met his. "Don't try to leave," she warned. "They're watching."

"Who?" Roth asked.

"The Jasaw Chan."

He heard Lucas yelp in surprise outside the window. "Let me go! Daaad!"

CHAPTER THIRTY-TWO

RESIDENTIAL COMPLEX

CALAKMUL BIOSPHERE RESERVE

December 26

Roth rushed to the window. In his haste to climb out, he ended up falling face-first onto the stone below, bringing up his forearm to catch himself. A shiver of pain shot down to his wrist.

Grunting, he scrabbled to his feet and searched both ways. When he didn't see his son, he remembered that Lucas had climbed up to the roof. Except for the pyramids the ancient Maya had built, most of their structures and dwellings had been square or rectangular with ridges along the roofline like a castle's battlements.

As he looked up, his heart rammed into his throat.

A painted warrior with white stripes like a skeleton painted on his legs, arms, and body held Lucas by his curly hair. With his other hand, he trained the blade of an obsidian weapon at Lucas's throat.

"Wait!" Roth shouted, staring at the scene in horror.

The warrior had black or darkly colored feathers hanging from his headdress. He was muscled like a gladiator. Lucas was stiff with terror.

Brillante climbed up to the windowsill, his expression panicked. Roth held his hand up to forestall his son, but the boy came jumping out. "Lucas!" he yelled.

Then he too saw the danger and froze.

"Stop! Please!" Roth begged. There was enough moonlight for him to see the warrior's disdainful expression. Lucas began to sob.

"D-Dad!" he moaned.

"Let him go! Please! Let him go!"

"He doesn't speak English," said Angélica. She was standing at the window, her face illuminated by the glow of the golden strands clinging to her arm. Suki stood next to her, a fearful expression clouding her face.

"He's got my son," Roth said in a quavering voice.

The warrior barked out some Mayan words.

"It is dishonorable to try to flee the games," the woman said, translating.

The warrior snarled something else.

"What did he say?" Roth asked.

She frowned and paused. Was she afraid to reveal it? "He said you will have one less player. The boy must die."

No! Roth thought in despair. He reached his arms out in supplication. "Please no! No! We weren't trying to escape."

The woman said something in Mayan, her tone matching the man's, her diction precise.

The warrior yanked back on Lucas's head, exposing his throat even more. He spoke again, barking the words.

"He says you know nothing of honor. You are cowards who deserve to die."

Lucas closed his eyes, gibbering with fear.

Roth's mouth was so dry, he could barely speak. His mind was a frantic buzz of disbelief and dread. He was going to watch his son get beheaded. A choking sob threatened to strangle him. Sinking to his knees, he reached out his arms. "Please, please don't kill my son."

The woman said something else in Mayan. The man answered, and she spoke again—their words were clipped. She didn't translate.

"Lucas," Brillante moaned, crying.

The warrior barked some more words, and the woman offered up a gentle response, almost pleading.

The warrior gritted his teeth, making a horrific face, and brought the obsidian even closer to Lucas's throat. It nicked the skin.

Roth almost vomited.

But the death stroke didn't happen. In the moonlight, Roth saw a snake manifest on the warrior's arm, seemingly appearing out of nowhere. It hissed. The warrior, in reflex, released Lucas and tried to shake off the serpent.

Lucas, off balance from the shove, fell off the roof.

Roth lurched forward and caught his son in his arms. His left arm wrenched in pain at the sudden pressure, and he dropped Lucas and grabbed his injured wrist. Brillante hurried to Lucas and hugged him, and the two brothers sobbed against each other.

Roth gently cradled his injured arm with his other hand and got to his feet. The warrior gazed down at him in fury and fear, then shouted some more words and skulked from the roof's edge until he was out of sight.

Relief surged in Roth's chest. They'd avoided the worst . . . for now, but the buzz of worry in his mind was like a hive of jacked-up bees. He could hardly think straight. Rising to his feet, he slung his uninjured arm around his sons and held them close and kissed their hair.

"I will come out and get you," Angélica said. "Don't climb up the window, please."

Roth nodded to her, savoring the moment of relief. He brushed tears from his eyes. He hadn't realized he'd been crying. His breath came in gasps.

As Angélica left the room, Suki stood at the windowsill, her hands resting along its edge. Her eyes shone with emotion, but she had a small smile of relief.

In a few moments, he heard Angélica coming down the stone path between the building and the wall. Then she beckoned for them to follow her.

Roth bent his elbow and cradled his arm against his chest, worried he'd fractured his forearm in the fall. The boys walked on either side of him, each one grabbing him by the waist as they followed. She led them to the rear opening of the building, and they wove around servants who were bedded down on mats. One or two of the women lifted their heads to look at them, but no one spoke a word.

When they reached the sleeping chamber again, Angélica held the beaded curtain so they could enter and then came in after them. The rustling noises of the beads interrupted the stillness. Outside, the revels had completely ended. All was quiet except for the screeches of monkeys and the clicks of insects.

"What did you say to him?" Roth asked Angélica. She'd said something. She'd interceded on their behalf.

"He had orders from Uacmitun to kill one of the boys tonight," she said.

"Who's that?"

"Uacmitun is the chief of the warriors here at the biosphere. Like Victor back at the resort in Cozumel."

"Why did Uacmitun want to kill one of us?" Brillante asked in a shaky voice.

"Because Mr. Calakmul was certain you'd try to escape again. He told me so himself. I came tonight to warn you. I was too late, but Ix Chel intervened."

He wondered why she was speaking so openly, but it struck him that none of the servants spoke English. The warriors probably didn't either.

"She's one of the Maya goddesses, right?" he asked her, confused.

She pursed her lips. "She is. And Mr. Calakmul believes she has been helping you. Your wife, your children are part Mexican." She gave them a sorrowful look. "You're part of my culture too. Her protection is powerful."

"Can she get us out of here?" Roth asked softly, hardly daring to hope.

"You were being guarded all night in case she tried. While she has a shrine here, this city was not devoted to her. Her powers are strongest on Cozumel."

"But can *you* help us?" Roth begged.

Angélica shook her head. "I don't dare, nor do I have that kind of influence, Mr. Roth. I hope you win the death game, but it doesn't seem promising. Only two more points and the Beasleys win. I wish . . ." She sighed.

"What?" Suki asked. "What do you wish?"

Angélica looked at the teenager. "I wish you knew how to *really* play the game," she said.

"What do you mean?" Roth demanded.

"I've already said too much. I don't like the Beasleys. Especially Kendall. I knew people like that in Palo Alto. Rich and entitled. Bigots. I've seen how they treated Hispanics, especially the helpers they hired to clean their mansions or take care of their children. I was offered work, you see, by men as rich as Eric Beasley. Men who made promises to lure in the unsuspecting." Her eyes flashed with the memories.

"We're not . . . like that," Suki said, pushing up her glasses.

"I know," Angélica said. "I know a lot about your family. And theirs. Little Jane Louise is different. She's resisting Kendall's efforts to mold her. Sadly, it won't last long. A child can only take so much brainwashing, especially from her own family."

Roth swallowed. "If you want us to win, you're going to have to help us."

"You are *going* to lose, Mr. Roth. The way you're playing the game, they'll outlast you. It's just a matter of time."

"So help us!" Roth seethed.

Angélica shook her head. "I can't. If Mr. Calakmul knew I'd even said this much, he'd be very . . . displeased."

"He'd kill you?" Roth asked.

Her gaze was confident. "He wouldn't hesitate. If it were up to me, you'd win and the Beasleys would be sacrificed, like that soldier was tonight."

Roth blinked in surprise.

She gave him a pointed look. "One of the soldiers who hunted you in the jungle. He defied Mr. Calakmul. His men were shot, but the leader was brought to Calakmul on the yacht with the Beasleys. They didn't know it. He was sacrificed to Ek Chuah, the god of war, sacrifice, and violent death." She held up her hands. "It was a celebration. That's what you were listening to tonight."

Dread thrummed in Roth's chest at the horrible thought of being tied to an altar, awake, while he watched Jacob Calakmul cut out his heart. It was about as terrible a way to go as he could imagine. How many seconds would he live after his heart was gone?

"But you implied there's a way we can win the game," Roth said.

"Yes," Angélica answered. "If you can figure it out in time. But it doesn't look good. You're nursing an injured arm. Your kids are frightened. Your wife is in a coma." She looked at the boys and then at Suki and sighed again. "Get some rest. You'll need it for tomorrow."

After the mention of Sarina, Suki toyed with the ring on her finger, the one she'd been given.

"Where did you get that ring? It's jade, isn't it?" Angélica asked.

Suki lowered her hand and looked at the stone. "It's . . . my mom's," she said in a husky whisper.

Angélica nodded in sympathy. "I'm sorry she couldn't join you for the game. She might have helped you figure it out."

"What is Ix Chel the goddess of?" Roth asked.

Angélica smirked. "The Spanish teach she's the goddess of making children. So the Spaniards believed that Cozumel, which was dedicated to her, was a sex island. Bishop de Landa misunderstood."

"Who was de Landa?"

"Diego de Landa was the bishop of the Yucatán in 1572. It was his job to *convert* the Maya to Christianity. And I use that term very generously. He was the one who ran a campaign of terror that ended in millions of deaths. And he destroyed all the codices."

Roth remembered now. He'd learned about him during his research. "He didn't burn all of them, though. Some were sent back to Europe."

"Yes. The lost codices. One from Chichén Itzá was sent to Dresden. Another to Paris. Mr. Calakmul wants them back."

Roth squinted at her. "Why?"

"Because of the prophecy Kukulkán gave to the Maya centuries before the Spanish ever came. The prophecy is real, Mr. Roth. Kukulkán is *real*. And he will return once we've prevailed against the Western oligarchs."

He wanted to know more about this. Surely there was more to it. "Do you know the prophecy?" he asked, intensely curious. If he was going to die, he may as well find out why.

"Yes," she said. "It's hidden in the Dresden Codex."

"What does it say?"

"It's forbidden to speak about it to unbelievers. But there is a chance you might figure out how to win. If you truly believe Ix Chel is helping you." As she said the name, she reached out and stroked Suki's cheek with her glowing arm.

CHAPTER THIRTY-THREE

THE ARENA

CALAKMUL BIOSPHERE RESERVE

December 26

The ball rushed at Roth's face. If it struck, it would break bones. By reflex, he ducked, and the heavy ball flew past him and bounced, heading toward the back of the court. Before he could pivot on his heel, Brillante sprinted past him, arms pumping, legs stretched long.

"Get it! Get it!" Lucas yelled in encouragement. Suki was on her side of the court, much too far to make it there in time.

Roth watched with growing despair as the ball bounced a few more times, lower and lower. But Brillante slid toward it and struck it with his bent knee, and the ball shot against the golden threads of the magical webbing and cannoned back across the court.

The score was still six to one.

"Up! Up! Up!" Roth shouted to Brillante, then hurried to cover his son's position. The ball bounced twice before the younger Beasley boy,

James, deflected it with his hip. It ricocheted off the side wall of the arena, and then Colter used his hip to drive the ball toward the stone circle near Roth.

Roth positioned himself, hands spread apart. They'd been playing for several hours already, and everyone on the court was weary but determined. Since no points had been scored, there had been no more drinks of *xocolatl* to restore them. Dehydration and the heat had sapped their strength.

The cheers and shouts from the gathered crowd changed pitch now that Colter was going for a goal, something that always invigorated the crowd. Colter's face held a grimace of determination.

The angle was right. The pitch was right. Roth's throat clenched with dread as he watched the ball sail toward the opening in the stone circle.

But it bounced off the edge and shot back at Colter.

The crowd groaned. Colter swore under his breath and tried it again, but it went under the hoop, missing completely, ricocheted off the wall below, and started toward Roth.

"I'm back!" Brillante gasped, sprinting up to him.

Roth saw Eric Beasley on the other side of the line, crowding as close as he could without crossing it.

"Come on and hit it, you tub of lard!" Eric taunted. "You got nothin'!"

Roth ignored his goading.

"You should pass it," Brillante said. "Let me try for a goal."

"You think you can hit it that high, shrimpy?" Eric sneered.

"You got this," Roth said, using his hip to pass the ball to his son.

"You can do it!" Suki shouted.

"No, he can't!" Colter shot back. "He's too weak!"

Brillante's eyes were fixed on the stone hoop embedded into the upper wall. He positioned himself to hit the ball. Roth thought the angle was a little off, but he wasn't going to mess up his son's concentration.

"Shoot it!" Eric roared.

Roth wanted to punch the bigger man in the face. Sure, Eric was stronger, but he figured he could pack enough force to break a tooth or two. Except neither of them could cross the line . . .

Brillante clenched his jaw as the ball came to him and he struck it with his knee. The crowd fell silent as the rubber ball flew up. It hit the wall next to the hoop and then bounced over to the other side of the court.

Another groan came from the crowd, but there was some clapping too. Encouragement?

"Get back to your position, Dad!" Brillante said, shooing him away.

Roth realized his blunder and hurried back to his part of the court.

"It's impossible to hit it perfectly," Suki muttered when he was close enough.

The ball came at them again, but Lucas jumped up and blocked it with an elbow, sending it right back. It sailed past Eric, who couldn't hit it. Kendall Beasley lunged forward, tapping it with her knee to her younger son, James. Then it went to Colter, who drove it back toward the hoop, where it ricocheted back again.

It was amazing how adrenaline focused one's attention. Roth had felt his anxiety subside the moment the game started. He could sense a rhythm to the game now, one that he hadn't felt the previous day, and despite the sweat and the fatigue, the physicality of the sport brought a certain thrill. He felt alive in a way that reminded him of his hikes in the mountains near Bozeman.

Colter lined up for the shot again.

Roth could already tell it wouldn't stick the landing.

There was a secret that he hadn't figured out yet. Angélica had indicated as much last night. She'd left it at that—an implication, not a confirmation—yet it had hung unspoken in the air, teasing Roth's imagination.

Why were the hoops set so high on the wall when most of the game happened below? Come to think of it, why were the arena walls so high? The Maya were short people. Their tallest warriors, back then, were probably no taller than Lucas and Brillante. Why invent a game that would be best played by giants?

Instead of taking the shot, Colter pulled a fake-out and kneed the ball hard, sending it over the twins' heads, directly toward Suki. She pushed up her glasses and then sprinted not to the ball but to where the bounce would take it. Colter had tried to be sneaky, to trick them into believing he was going for the goal again.

Suki didn't like using her hips, so she bent her arm and prepared to use her elbow. "Brillante!" she called.

She hit it with her elbow, wincing at the painful impact, and the ball was redirected toward her brother and started bouncing to him. Again he prepared to line it up with the circle. The Beasleys began roasting him, calling him racial slurs too.

"Take a shot, Nacho!" Eric shouted at him.

"Take a chill pill, Cheeto," Brillante said back. He focused, then went for the stone hoop again. It went under, entering Colter's part of the court.

"Pass it!" James said as it bounced toward his brother. "Let me try!"

"No way, I got this!"

Roth could see the look of disappointment on Brillante's face, the flash of anger and frustration, but the goal was too high. Unobtainable, almost. It would have taken years of practice to be good at the ball game. Not just a day.

And yet . . .

Roth stewed with frustration. He *knew* he was missing something. If only he had time to study the glyphs carved into the walls. They obviously told a story, but it was an unintelligible one. The game had been played since the Maya ruled the peninsula. A game of glory and sacrifice.

His thoughts were interrupted by Eric's booming voice as the ball bounced closer to Colter. "To me."

"I got this, Dad!" Colter insisted.

"To me!" his father shouted again.

Colter, cowed, passed the ball to his father once it reached him. Eric maneuvered it to the other side of the court. Would Eric try to score through one of the hoops?

Roth didn't believe so, and from his positioning, the ball would fly straight at Lucas. "Be ready, Lucas!" he shouted.

"He's going to hurt Lucas," Suki warned.

Roth didn't know how she knew, but he wasn't going to distrust his daughter's wisdom a second time.

"Back away, Lucas!" Roth said.

"What?" Lucas turned to look at him in shock.

That's when Beasley struck. He kneed the ball right at the young man. The ball struck Lucas in the stomach, hard, and he crumpled and went down.

"No!" Brillante shouted in rage, rushing closer to his brother.

The ball was bouncing lower and lower as it moved toward the wall on their side.

Roth sprinted forward, but he was too far away. If Brillante slid into it, he could knock it against the wall and hopefully start it bouncing again. It was always hard to regain momentum when the ball got too low.

Brillante slid . . . and missed.

The ball rolled to a stop in the dusty courtyard before anyone could get to it.

A cheer rang from the crowd. Roth ran up to Lucas, who was struggling to breathe. The panicked look in his eyes showed he'd had the wind knocked out of him.

He turned his head and saw one of the jaguar priests coming forward with another feather to be placed in one of the stone gods.

Seven to one.

Roth clenched his eyes shut. They'd lasted a lot longer the second day. But if the Beasleys scored one more point, they were through. What else could he do?

Maya servants approached both teams with *xocolatl* to drink. Roth was so thirsty, he guzzled his down. He began to feel the effects immediately. It was different from drinking coffee, more like what he imagined a health potion from D&D might feel like.

"Come on, Lucas," Roth said, rubbing his son's back. They stood, each gaining strength by the moment.

"That h-hurt," Lucas groaned, rubbing his stomach. He'd taken only a sip of the *xocolatl* before.

"Drink it down," Roth said. He glanced at Eric Beasley, whose swagger was that of a player about to win a big game. One point from victory. He went to his kids and gave them high fives. Then he grabbed Kendall and forced a kiss on her mouth.

Jane Louise was regarding Lucas with a sorrowful expression.

"I blew it," Lucas said miserably.

"I distracted you."

"No, dude, it's my fault," Brillante said after slurping down some of the drink. "I should have had that save. My fault."

Roth appreciated that the kids weren't blaming each other. It lessened the sting of the Beasleys' cackling. He shoved his resentment and anger aside because those emotions weren't going to help them survive.

Only . . . they weren't going to survive. The momentum was all on the Beasleys' side. They only needed one more point and the game would be over.

"Dad, for the record, this really sucks." Suki took another sip of her *xocolatl*.

He looked at her and chuckled. "Yeah. I think it majorly sucks. How'd you know?"

"What?" Suki looked confused.

"How'd you know Beasley was going to hurt your brother?"

"Because he's a dipwad."

"Sure, but that's all? Last night, you warned us about Lucas going on the roof."

Suki shrugged. She rubbed her stomach as if queasy. "I just . . . felt it. I just knew Beasley was going to pull something."

"Did you ever get that feeling back home?"

That comment startled her. "No. Not really. It started when we got here."

Roth looked at her. It also occurred to him that she'd been the first one to get suspicious about the resort in Cozumel. Was it a coincidence, or something more?

The horns blew again, preparing for the last portion of the death game. One more point was all that stood between life and death.

Roth gazed up at the crowd chanting and laughing up on the wall. He saw Jacob Calakmul on his throne, overseeing the game with smug aloofness. Angélica stood beside him, her hand on his shoulder.

She was looking directly at them.

"Dad, we're going to die, aren't we?" Suki whispered.

Roth felt his chest clench with dread.

"We'll keep playing as hard as we can."

"I know. I'm not quitting. But it really sucks that Mom's fate is dependent on us. I wish she were playing with us." Her expression was both forlorn and hopeful.

"You know, Grandma Suki was a force of nature," Roth said, trying to rein in his quivering emotions. Suki's words had devastated him. "She never quit. You take after her."

"I think I've felt her today," Suki said, scuffing the dirt with one foot. "I don't know. I'm not trying to sound weird, but I can *feel* her."

"How could that sound weird with everything else that's going on?" he asked, gesturing to the arena and all the onlookers. "Ask her for help. It couldn't hurt."

"Get ready. We gotta keep playing," Brillante said. He was jumping on his toes, full of energy, like he did when he was about to play goalie. The effort to motivate them was as appreciated as it was obvious.

When the horn blew again, Jacob Calakmul threw the ball into the arena. Roth watched it bounce, intrigued by the physics of it all. Energy used and diminished. Entropy. When the kids were younger, they'd been fascinated by a science show for kids—he couldn't remember the name, but the main actor had wild hair, and another was dressed in a rat suit. There'd been episodes on gravity and inertia. For example, you could suspend a bowling ball from a rope and pull it toward your nose. If you let go, the bowling ball would swing away and then back, but it would lose momentum because of friction from the air molecules.

It wouldn't break your nose.

Physics still applied in the universe, even with the strange magic that was on display—magic that might have come from another world that could have more sophisticated science.

"Dad!" Suki cried.

He'd lost track of the game, and the ball was bouncing toward him, its trajectory lowering with each bounce. Roth hurried to it and hipped the ball to Lucas, who used his knee to send it flying onto the other side of the court.

They played as hard as they could. Each attempt to score in the hoop failed, and Roth's family was able to keep the ball moving.

Time seemed suspended as Roth played. He fell into the rhythm of the game again. Move and respond. Deflect to keep the ball going. It would have been fascinating to watch the ancient Maya play the game. How had they lined up their angles? Was it practice and muscle memory that had allowed them to get the ball through the stone hoops, or was his inkling right? Was he missing something?

The shadows were stretching on the court. He could hear Eric Beasley shouting, but Roth's mind didn't bother to register the words. Daylight was running out. If they could just keep playing until sunset, they'd have another night to rest.

Roth's imagination began to quicken. Maybe it was the *xocolatl* buzz. He recognized that he was in a flow state, the same kind he got into as a writer. "Flow" was a phenomenon described in a TED talk he'd heard years before. As an author, he counted on it. The ability to lose himself in his writing, to not be distracted by the many things in the world that vied for his attention.

Flow was how he invented his fantasy worlds. It was the creative spark that fired up his imagination. Once there, time seemed to slow down, and everything outside his focus faded away.

His breath was steady and even. His anxiety had melted away. Looking at the far end of the court, he saw the temple standing proudly, the jungle trees forming a veil behind it. The ball court was facing east and west. The sun continued its descent.

And then he noticed the pinprick of light through the trees.

Venus.

He knew it was the planet on some visceral level. The morning and evening star. The Maya had built their structures to align with the solstices, the moon, *and* with Venus. Their calendar had been meticulously arranged to track the orbits of celestial bodies.

The planets in orbit.

What if that had some relevance to the game?

His mind churned, moving faster than he could follow: a spherical ball. Played on a court arranged to harmonize with events outside the planet . . .

A feeling of giddiness bubbled up in Roth's stomach. It came from a thought that had bloomed in his mind out of nowhere. Well, not really; he'd been pondering the situation for hours. He'd studied and researched before he'd come. That had mixed with things he'd heard from Jacob Calakmul during their flight and from Angélica the night before.

Why were the goal posts so high?

The ancient Maya hadn't been playing the game on the ground.

CHAPTER THIRTY-FOUR

The Arena

Calakmul Biosphere Reserve

December 26

Impatience roiled inside Jacob's chest, but he maintained an external calm.

The sun was a fiery spark on the horizon. Once its light was extinguished, they would need to halt the game. He didn't want it halted— he wanted it finished. For some inexplicable reason, the Roths had done better the second day. They'd made fewer mistakes. If one of the twins had been executed the previous night, it would have made them so distraught they would have certainly lost. He gazed down at the arena, watching the families rush back and forth to keep the ball in play.

"My lord, the sun has set."

Jacob glanced at the horizon again. The glimmer of sunlight was gone. Frustration seethed inside him, but he held up his hand to signal the end. The large hum tahs were lifted up, their trumpeting sound blasted out to cease game play for the evening.

Seven feathers fluttered from their positions crowning the stone effigies of the gods. Plus one on the other side. The Beasleys were still going to win. Eric looked incensed that they hadn't won yet. Amid the noise and confusion of the revelry, he shoved one of his sons in the shoulder, nearly knocking the young man down. The Roth children, on the other hand, gathered around their father and hugged him. There was little question in his mind that Mr. Roth was the better man, but the outcome was inevitable, and he wished to see it done.

"My lord."

Jacob turned his head and saw Uacmitun standing next to his throne, an urgent look in his eyes.

"What's wrong?" Jacob asked.

"My lord, I fear she's betrayed you."

It was said softly, just loud enough for him to hear the message above the clamor of the cheers and revelry.

Jacob knitted his brow. The accusation was a serious one. The man could only be talking about his Malintzin.

"Speak," Jacob said. His gaze found her in the crowd, talking to the other noblewomen assembled for the games. She was too far away to hear their conversation.

"She interceded to spare the boy's life," Uacmitun said.

"I know this already."

"My man told me that she summoned a snake to attack him so he would release the boy!"

"How does your man know this?" Jacob said.

"How else did a serpent appear on the roof? If she helps them escape *tonight*, it will bring the wrath of the gods on us all!"

Jacob glared at the woman he'd trusted, unsettled by Uacmitun's news. Even the suspicion of her betraying him made his blood scald his veins. A serpent? He had not been told that part. The goddess was known for her cleverness and meddling.

Jacob rose, summoning the magic from his rings and amulets. He channeled his wrath by summoning a storm like the one that had thwarted the airplane that had ventured too close to Calakmul. He activated the glyphs with the authority of his ring. Power rippled through him as clouds popped into the evening sky, beginning to boil.

Thunder began to rumble in the distance. Then a streak of lightning flashed in the gathering blackness. The crack of thunder echoed sharply against the stones of the arena.

Jacob rose from his throne and stepped to the edge of the barrier, gazing down at the arena and then across at those gathered on the other side.

"Malintzin!" he barked. She hurried to his side, her eyes wide with surprise.

"Yes, my lord," she said, dropping to a knee.

"Translate my words for those below." He stared at her, feeling the wild urge to lop off her head with his *macuahuitl* and throw it down into the yard. But he restrained himself.

He would ask first. He would be sure.

If there was even a hint of suspicion, he'd kill her then.

Jacob lifted his voice and shouted against the noise of the rushing wind. His voice was amplified by the magic and the natural acoustics of the courtyard.

Angélica rose and spread her arms. "The lords of the underworld are displeased!" she said. "Xibalba has awakened!"

Jacob shouted again, his words short and clipped and passionate.

"They are disturbed by the noise!" she continued. Another crackle of thunder. A few heavy drops of rain began to plop down on the stones.

Gasps of fear could be heard from the Maya in attendance. Jacob had purposefully invoked their fear of the lords of the underworld. They were fearsome beings.

Jacob uttered the next phrase.

"They demand a tribute. They want appeasement!"

He heard a throb of fear in Angélica's voice. She knew what that meant as well as he did: a *sacrifice*.

Jacob shouted out the next command.

Angélica turned to look at him, and he nodded for her to make the translation.

Trembling, Angélica turned back and looked down at the players. "The lords of Xibalba demand the game be continued at midnight. It will end at sunrise. If neither side wins, *both* lose!"

Jacob stared into Eric's eyes. Then Mr. Roth's. Each family would have less than seven hours to rest. Then they'd be playing the rest of the night until sunrise. The added stakes would alter the outcome. Perhaps the Beasleys would become more reckless. Jacob didn't care if both families perished, truthfully. But neither would be permitted to escape.

"What? That's unfair!" Eric shouted.

Jacob released the rainstorm. The pent-up fury lashed down at the stones, bringing a deluge of water. The barriers blocking the ends of the court vanished, and the servants came hurrying out to lead the families back to their rooms.

Jacob felt the hot rain trickling down his body. He turned to Uacmitun.

"Bring her to my room," he ordered menacingly.

———

Jacob's servants had removed his decorative armor and wiped his body dry. He could hear the sluicing of the waters through the limestone cracks in the walls. The cenotes would be replenished after the storm he'd summoned ended.

After the servants had cleaned up, he dismissed them and waited.

Uacmitun appeared at the threshold, gripping Angélica by the arm. Her outfit was waterlogged, her hair dripping, the paint decorating her face and limbs smeared and nearly washed away. The warrior shoved her inside and then departed.

Angélica rubbed her arm, where the warrior's grip had turned her flesh red. She looked fearful.

Jacob went to the wall and brought down his *macuahuitl*. The keen edges of the obsidian pieces glinted in the light.

She stared at him in terror.

"How were you going to get them out?" he asked her. He deliberately didn't reveal which family he meant.

"I don't know what you're—"

"Don't *lie* to me!" he roared at her, his eyes flashing with fury. "I trusted you," he added more softly, emotion choking his voice.

Angélica was trembling like a leaf in the wind. She bowed before him. "I've not betrayed you, Jacob. I wouldn't!"

"How could they have turned you against me?" he said mournfully. "I gave you everything! I promised you a future in the new world."

"You did! You have! Please, I've done nothing! Nothing against you."

He started toward her. Her entire body, still dripping wet, shook violently.

"What have I done? What have I done?" She was gibbering.

He stood in front of her, looking at her damp hair. When it was wet, the bleached part looked closer to her true color. He stared at her mercilessly. Her eyes met his for only an instant before she looked down again.

"Do you think you could ever escape me?" he asked. "Do you think you'd be safe from me in *America*?"

"No! I don't want to go back there! I wasn't helping them. N-Not . . . not really!"

"'Not really?' Confess all, and I may show you mercy. Did you summon a serpent to help the boy? Did you teach them the magic of the gold?"

"No!"

"You could be lying. You must *make* me believe you!"

Desperation was in her eyes. She knew she could die at any moment. "What did Uacmitun accuse me of?" she pleaded. "He's lying!"

He tilted up her chin, exposing her throat. The blade of the *macuahuitl* was close. He saw her swallow.

"His family is loyal," he said. "You pled for the boy's life, then a serpent attacked my warrior. Now I have to wonder why you'd do that when you knew I wanted him dead!"

"I did not summon a serpent! I wouldn't know how! When I asked Uacmitun what your orders were, he said you w-wanted his men to follow the f-family. To see how they were going to escape. They couldn't have escaped onto the *roof!* The guard let himself be seen when he shouldn't have been, that's what this is about. I don't know why there was a snake up there."

Jacob squatted in front of her, his eyes level with hers. The truth, more often than not, came spilling out of a mind frozen with panic, and there was a look of truth in her eyes.

"Uacmitun conceals his error?"

"He has it out for me because I refused to sleep with him," Angélica said.

Another truth. That explained Uacmitun's feeling of rivalry with her. He began to lower the weapon. "You didn't betray me?" he asked softly.

She began to weep into her hands. "No," she said, muffled. "Never!"

He cupped her cheek with his palm. "When you joined my family's business, you swore an oath. Do you remember it?"

She nodded. "The oath of the ancients. I pledged that if I ever revealed what I knew, I would . . . suffer my life . . . to be destroyed."

"You swore it by the wounds in Kukulkán's hands and feet," he said. "You swore it by Itzamná's heavens. You swore it by Itzamná's throne. You swore it by Chaac's footstool."

"I did," she whimpered, fresh tears falling.

"Do you think there is anywhere on this world that you could go to hide from me and your promise?"

She shook her head no.

"The prophecy will be fulfilled. *I* am the one who has been spoken of. Kukulkán himself spoke of this day when he descended and visited the Maya at Chichén Itzá. He said a descendant from my house would rise up and lead. Do you believe I am the one?"

"Yes," she said urgently.

He rose to his full stature and lowered the blade.

"I want you to be there when the prophecy is fulfilled, Malintzin. Right now, you only believe. But I want you to know it. Beyond a doubt. I want you by my side when the president of the United States kneels before me . . . and when I cut out his heart and offer it to the gods!"

CHAPTER THIRTY-FIVE

RESIDENTIAL COMPLEX

CALAKMUL BIOSPHERE RESERVE

December 26

The storm had begun to abate by the time the Roth family had returned to their dwelling. The immense deluge was impressive but, like many tropical storms, short-lived. The noises from the jungle resumed— shrieking monkeys, birds of different varieties, and even the piercing cry of a jaguar.

No revelers, though.

Roth paced by the window, watching the rain drip from the stone. The humidity had increased substantially. Someone had left an arrangement of fruits and cooked meats and plenty of water and *xocolatl* on the ancient cedar table.

"So we're playing again at midnight?" Suki drawled. "As if this whole mess weren't unfair enough."

"Shhh," Roth urged, his mind still racing with the thoughts he'd had in the arena. Was a pattern emerging from the chaos, or was his brain just grasping for connections because it longed for them?

"What's up with Dad?" Brillante asked.

"He's stewing on something," Suki said. "Like he's creating a book."

"Just . . . please . . ." Roth insisted. "I need a moment. I think I've figured something out."

His brain felt as if an electric current were running through it. He stroked his beard, trying to make sense of the chaos in his mind. All along, he'd assumed the ancient Maya had played the game on the ground and that he needed to figure out the right angle and force to get the ball into the improbably high stone circle.

If the game wasn't played on the ground, that changed the physics of everything.

The kids began eating from the platters of food. Roth's stomach growled to remind him that he hadn't eaten either. The intensity of the death games had certainly driven up his appetite. The knowledge that they'd be playing again in less than seven hours should have made him urgent to eat, but he was too caught up in his thoughts.

"Did you see the look on Colter's face?" Lucas asked between bites. "When she announced we'd be playing again for the death gods?"

"That was pretty sick. He was pretty cocky until then," Brillante said.

"Mr. Beasley was in a rage too," Suki said.

Roth realized there was no way he could keep his kids quiet long enough for him to figure this out on his own.

"Okay, keep eating, but we need to talk," he said.

"About what?" Suki asked.

"About the laws of gravity."

Her nose wrinkled. "First high school algebra, and now this?"

"Isaac Newton's theory stood a long time. He said gravity is a force that happens when two masses attract each other. But then Einstein came up with something better. Relativity."

Lucas looked confused. "We're not talking about *Little Einsteins*, right?"

Roth sighed. "I'm referring to the physicist, not the cartoon. He envisioned the universe and the space-time continuum. Three axis points that set a specific location and time to show changes. I'm standing here right now," he said, holding his palms apart from each other. Then he took four steps to the table. "Now I'm over here. My location changed *and* the time changed. I'm not where I was two seconds ago."

"Yes, you *moved*," Suki said, grabbing a piece of sliced fruit and eating it.

"A few years ago, I saw this physicist on *The Late Show*. Dr. Greene, I think. He had a demo that helped me understand space-time. To represent the universe, there was something like a trampoline except the material was spandex—really stretchy—clamped around the circumference. You roll a ball across it, and it goes in a straight line. Then he put a heavy ball in the middle, representing the sun. It made the fabric sag in the middle."

"Did it rip through it?" Brillante asked.

"No—it wasn't heavy enough—but it caused a dip in the middle. Then he started tossing in other smaller balls . . . marbles maybe . . . and they traveled in circles around the sun. That's like Einstein's theory of gravity."

"Wouldn't all the balls end up in the middle like the sun, though?" Suki asked.

"Well yeah, they all did. But if they were heavy enough and were thrown in at just the right speed, and there was no *friction* caused by the spandex to suck out the energy, they'd stay in orbit indefinitely. It's um . . . it's how the NASA scientists figured out how to get ships to launch from earth and orbit the moon. Einstein's theory turned out to be predictive of how the universe works . . . except on the smallest scales . . . like quantum physics. That stuff's really weird, its own ball game. But the theory works great for big stuff."

"And this means . . . what?" Suki asked, still confused.

"Everything I learned about the Maya before coming here attested to how much they understood outer space. They had the rotations and revolutions of the planets all figured out long before the Europeans did. Before Galileo and Copernicus even. They said Kukulkán taught them. Even the temple in Calakmul is aligned with the rising and setting of the sun *and* the planet Venus."

"So?" Brillante said after gulping more *xocolatl.* He burped. "This stuff is better than Mountain Dew."

"Isn't it possible they knew about space-time before Einstein?" Roth said.

All three kids looked at him in confusion.

"There is clearly magic here. Or . . . something at work that *we* don't understand. Jacob Calakmul summoned that storm. Or did he? Was there already a storm somewhere else nearby that he *attracted* to us? Any sufficiently advanced technology is indistinguishable from magic. "

Suki still looked confused, but there was something working in her mind. He saw the wheels turning.

"The bracelet," he said. "Consider how they use those bracelets to disarm the—what's that stuff called?"

"The *kem äm,*" Lucas said. He shoved his brother. "See? I remembered!"

"Yes!" Roth said enthusiastically. "The *kem äm* repel matter. But they're also attracted to those bracelets."

Suki tapped her lips. "So that webby crap is the space-time continuum?"

"Why not? Maybe it's more than just a mathematical equation," Roth said. "Maybe it's a literal thing, not abstract."

"So you think this golden stuff is holding up our solar system? Dad, um, I don't know how to break it to you, but we've had astronauts in space," Suki said. "They didn't see anything holding up the planet. Neither did Neil Armstrong when he went to the moon."

A spike of light struck Roth's mind. "Actually, they *did* see something."

"What?" Suki said.

"I just read it last year . . ." he said, snapping his fingers. "A biography on the life of Neil Armstrong. The crew of the Apollo saw weird stuff on their trip. Lights they couldn't explain and found it difficult to describe. They didn't talk much about it in the post-mission report because they were worried about future missions being aborted."

"No way," Brillante said.

"It's true. The author *interviewed* Armstrong. That's a primary source. And there are news articles all the time about people in the military seeing stuff they can't explain."

"Area Fifty-One," Lucas said, nudging his brother again. "Maybe this place is Area One."

"All I'm saying is that we *think* we know how the universe works, but there is a crap ton we don't know. What if the Maya figured it out? What if this Kukulkán visit changed them?"

"Aliens?" Suki asked skeptically.

"That's a Roman word," he told her. "The Latin word is *'alienus,'* which means *belonging to another*. Another what? Another tribe . . . another culture . . . another place. That's where the word comes from. People who sneak into the US without using the official process are called *illegal aliens.*"

"Okay," Suki said, holding up her hands. "Maybe you're right. But I'm not seeing how any of this is going to help us win the game."

He stared at her. "Because you can control the magic, Suki."

"What? Dude!" Brillante exclaimed.

"Remember when we went down into that temple in the jungle and found those crates of treasure? The bracelet you took. You saw the chest glowing. The boys didn't."

"Mom saw it glowing too," Suki shot back. "And remember that tree we pushed into the cenote? It was sort of glowing too. That's what drew my eyes to it."

"Really?" he said in shock. "You didn't say anything."

"Duh, because I thought it would sound too weird."

"Mom can't help us with this one," he said, feeling a burning in his chest. Anger and worry and *determination*. "But she said you're the one who could. Remember? I think it's the same kind of bracelet that these people have. They invented the jewelry to help them control the magic. When the Spanish came, they thought the people of the Yucatán were devil worshippers because they saw carved images of snakes everywhere. Chichén Itzá was built to worship the feathered serpent. That's the depiction of Kukulkán."

"Snakes don't have feathers," Lucas said.

"In Maya legends, they do. Feathers are a symbol of power. Isaiah from the Old Testament described winged angels. Cherubim. And serpents are symbols of wisdom and hidden knowledge. Consider the Garden of Eden myth. Adam and Eve were tempted by the snake. The culture in Mexico is full of that stuff. Flood myths, creation stories, resurrection . . . Some of it is very similar to what's in the Bible." He looked into Suki's eyes. "Like creepily similar. You saw the magic. I couldn't. Mom's family *came* from the Yucatán. You inherited the ability from her."

Suki's brow had deep furrows in it. "Wait . . . hold on."

"Just hear me out, Suki."

"We can't leave this place without getting killed," she said with agitation. "Remember last night?"

"I'm not talking about taking out the wall and escaping. I'm talking about *winning* the game."

"How? I don't get it."

"A thousand years ago, the game wasn't played on the *ground*. That's why the goals are so high up. Why the walls are so high. We're playing it *wrong*."

"Dad," Brillante said seriously, pointing at him. "When that woman came . . ."

"She was looking at you, Suki. Not me. We have one advantage the Beasleys don't. You three are descendants of Grandma Suki. But *you* are the most like her, Suki."

Suki rubbed her mouth. She looked at the bracelet on her arm, her brow crinkling.

"How do I do it?" she asked helplessly.

"Use the Force, Luke!" said Lucas in an exaggerated tone.

Everyone laughed.

"Maybe it's a little like that," Roth said. "Jacob lifted his arm, and a storm came. I don't know. It's just . . . if we don't have to whack the ball through the goal; if you can levitate it up there somehow . . . ?"

"You're putting this pressure on *me*?" Suki said.

"I'll take the bracelet!" Brillante said. "I'll try it!"

"I want it!" Lucas complained.

Footsteps approached from the other side of the door. Roth put his finger to his lips to silence them. Suki's face was full of consternation. She was thinking about what he'd said, and he could tell she was doubting herself. That wasn't good. If this was going to work, she had to *believe* it was going to work.

The beaded curtain rippled, and standing in the gap was a terrifying man, one of the Maya warriors. His chest rippled with muscle. He wore cedar arm guards, a breast piece, as well as black feathers in a band around his head, giving him a lionlike appearance. A jaguar pelt was wrapped around his waist. The animal's eyes had been replaced with menacing shards of obsidian.

Roth felt his stomach clench. The man said something to them in the ancient tongue, but there was no Angélica to translate.

"Get behind me," Roth said to his kids, his eyes locked on the guard, who had one of the obsidian blades attached to his hip. He also had a blowgun there.

The man spoke again and then stepped aside.

Kendall Beasley came forward, her eyes livid. She wore an outfit befitting Maya royalty, definitely more elegant than what they'd been given. She had a golden band around her left arm, but she was barefoot.

Kendall nodded to the man.

"He can't understand us," she said. "He doesn't speak English."

"I figured that." Roth asked, "Is there a problem, Kendall?"

"Yes, there's a problem," she said scornfully. Then she tempered herself. "It wasn't supposed to happen like this."

"Got your first taste of actual danger?" Suki asked wryly. "Welcome to the club."

Kendall closed her eyes, taking a deep breath. "They changed the rules."

"You never learned the golden rule?" Roth asked. "Whoever has the *gold* makes the *rules*. Since the year 2000, the value of gold has quadrupled. A little better than the S&P. Or your husband's hedge fund, I think. Calakmul and his people have crates of treasure next to the cenotes. Who knows how much."

"Look," she said, swallowing. The agitation in her eyes showed her desperation. "You can't win. You'll never score enough points. We only need *one* more point. But both of our families could *die* if you don't lose."

"You want us to quit?" Roth asked incredulously.

"I know you don't care if we die. Fair is fair. But I think you'd care if Jane Louise dies. Think of her."

"Whoa," Suki said, shaking her head. "That's pretty cold. Even for you."

Kendall shot her an angry glare. "She asked me to come. I didn't want to. She thinks you're good people. She believes you'll give up so that at least one of our families can survive this nightmare. I didn't buy it, but she begged me to come."

Roth didn't believe her for a moment. But that didn't prevent a spike of pain from burying itself in his heart. She was so cold. So ruthless.

Lucas and Brillante were both gaping at her in shock. Suki shook her head no. She didn't believe Kendall either.

How dangerous a thought can be. Especially a lie.

"I'm surprised they let you come see us," Roth said in a measured tone.

Kendall's nostrils flared. "It came at a cost. But it's important," she said evenly.

"Are you done?" he asked her.

"Well? What do you say? What should I tell Jane Louise?"

Suki was furious. "You can tell her—"

Roth squeezed her shoulder. "You can tell her we miss her. She's a special little girl. We all miss her."

"So will you forfeit?" Kendall pressed.

"That's the hard thing about life," Roth said philosophically. "It's full of uncertainty. Get used to it."

Kendall glared at him and then stormed away, past the waiting guard. Roth saw a smile on the warrior's face as he slid the beaded curtain back into place.

"Uncool," Suki muttered.

It reminded Roth of a quote he'd heard Moretti say. Probably something he'd learned in his law enforcement training. *There is no pain so awful as that of suspense.*

"We have until midnight to figure this out," Roth said. He gripped Suki by the shoulders, turning her to face him. "Try to levitate that coconut off the table."

CHAPTER THIRTY-SIX

THE ARENA

CALAKMUL BIOSPHERE RESERVE

12:01AM

December 27

The arena looked different at midnight. The carvings in the stone walls were all illuminated by the iridescent magic woven through the sigils, rendering the scene as clear as daylight. The onlookers from the tops of the walls were murmuring to one another in subdued tones. A hush had fallen over the arena, caused by the invocation of the lords of death.

Roth swallowed his nerves, trying to project calm to his family. Shakespeare had written something in one of his plays that rang very true to him in that moment: *Our doubts are traitors, and make us lose the good we oft might win, by fearing to attempt.*

That was the crux of their dilemma. Roth believed that he understood how they could win the game, but until Suki believed in it, nothing would happen. She'd tried levitating the coconut. Even the tiniest fruit on the table. But each failure had filled her with more withering panic. She feared she would be the one to let them all down, that it would be *her* fault if they died.

The boys had tried it too, and neither of them could summon even a whisper of light to the bracelet.

Roth believed Suki had to calm her mind to make it work. And that just wasn't happening.

How can you make someone believe in themselves? Roth and Sarina had tried to instill in their kids the belief that the future held endless possibilities. Hadn't Roth proven that in his own career?

Then again, he understood self-doubt didn't care about logic. After the huge success of his first book, he'd been crippled by anxiety prior to launching the follow-up a few years later. People didn't understand the plaguing self-doubt that writers suffered from. It took a conscious force of will to step into the arena, knowing that some would hate your work, no matter what you did.

Now he was in a literal arena, trying to save his wife and kids, knowing that the lives of five other people hung in the balance. Kendall was right about one thing—the rules had been changed without warning. There was a term for what Jacob Calakmul had done: plot twist. The change in time and the deathly atmosphere that had come by invoking the names of the death gods had contributed to the psychological impact of the moment.

Ultimately, Roth's goal was to encourage his family to play their best until Suki could master her own mind. Until she could finally believe in herself, the power of her ancestry, and that Grandma Suki might be *literally* helping her.

The huge horns were raised and blew the dreadful tones that would instigate the games.

Angélica stepped to the edge of the arena wall, holding the ball in her hand. "The game must be played!" she said for the benefit of the English speakers below. "It will conclude at sunrise or when either team prevails."

"It's unfair!" Eric Beasley shouted, interrupting her. Everyone in the Beasley clan looked uneasy. The upheaval of expectations was haunting them.

Roth glanced at Jacob, who sat impassively on his throne.

Angélica said nothing. She pulled her arm back and threw the ball forward. Roth's mind sharpened. He and Suki were starting the game in the back half of the court. Lucas and Brillante were quicker on their feet. They'd also proven that their endurance as soccer players made them more than a match for the Beasley boys.

There was no room for error. One slip-up, and the last feather would be awarded. It would all be over. But Roth knew that adding psychological pressure to his kids would only increase their chances of failure. He'd told them just to play like it was zero to zero. To focus on keeping the ball on the Beasleys' side of the court instead of trying to get it through the hoops. The only way to win would be to play the game the ancient way—if he was right. So they needed to buy Suki time to figure it out.

The Beasleys came at them strong and kept drilling the ball deep into Roth's quarter of the arena. Roth and the kids had learned that hitting the ball into the webbing caused it to launch back, so he'd advised the kids to start sending the ball back that way instead of wasting energy by trying to send it across the court.

He kept looking at his daughter, who had an expression of intense concentration on her face. She was trying to invoke the magic. But she was missing something, and her self-confidence was struggling.

"I can't do it," she said to him.

"You can. I believe in you."

"Nothing's working," she said. "And if I can't figure it out soon, it won't matter. We'll all be dead."

"Don't think about dawn. Think about now. You need to focus on the present. Get in the moment."

"I'm trying, Dad," she said desperately.

So he stopped talking and offered encouragement to the boys. "You're doing great, Brillante. Lucas—stay sharp. You got this."

"You're going to let us *all* get killed," Colter snarled from across the way.

"Sucks to be you," Brillante shot back.

"Ignore them," Roth said. "Just keep playing. Keep it moving."

He was so proud of his kids. If only Sarina could see them . . . if only she could be here beside him. Maybe she would have figured out the game herself had she been able to play. But the only way Sarina was going to wake up again was if they won. And that was if Jacob wasn't exaggerating his powers or the gods' intentions. He'd healed Lucas, though. He'd controlled the weather. He could do miraculous things.

They intercepted the ball each time it came over, each of them intent on their goal, because winning meant surviving. The bystanders of the game were getting into it again as they watched the match unfold.

Colter lined up to go for a goal again, and Lucas stood opposite him, watching the ball.

"You got this, Colt!" Eric shouted intensely.

But Colter suddenly whacked it into the side wall with his hip, and it rebounded, shooting past Lucas near the middle line of the court. The bounces went lower and lower.

Brillante came running forward, and the two boys looked like they'd smash into each other.

"I got it!" Brillante said, then slid toward the rapidly decelerating ball.

Lucas jumped over his brother so they wouldn't collide, and Brillante hit the ball with his knee and sent it back across the line again. Jane Louise came running, her hands outstretched to catch the ball.

Kendall Beasley grabbed the little girl by the hair and yanked her back. "Don't you touch it!" she shouted.

Roth saw Brillante wincing with pain as he rose from his slide and started limping.

"You okay, Brillante?"

"Twisted my knee," he said.

"Suki, switch with him!" Roth shouted.

Suki hurried to take her brother's place, leaving Roth alone in the deep.

Eric kneed the ball hard, sending it straight at Roth. It struck him right in the chest and knocked him back a few paces. Roth winced, feeling the ache right in his center. It would leave a bruise for sure. Or some cracked ribs. They all had bruises. The ball bounced toward Lucas, who sent it flying to the far side of the court.

"Just go down!" Eric snarled at him.

Brillante was hobbling. He looked like he was in deep pain.

"Your knee cap?" Roth asked, still trying to get over the pain himself.

"No, the muscle on the side." Brillante bent over to rub the edge of it. "It hurts bad!"

"You need to sit and rest?"

"I can't, Dad. I can't!"

The younger Beasley boy, James, had run to catch up with the ball and sent it back to his father.

"Just . . . go . . . down!" Eric roared again. This time, he aimed the ball directly at Suki.

Suki twisted her hips, angling her body back, and the ball soared right past her. It almost struck her anyway, and if it had, she'd have been knocked flat. The ball soared toward the far end of the court, and Roth began to sprint to catch up with it, knowing Brillante wouldn't be able to reach it with his injured knee. The ball bounced once, twice, going lower each time. It struck the far wall, not the magical barrier, and started coming back toward Roth, its energy diminishing with each bounce.

Roth felt a sickening lurch. He wasn't going to make it in time.

Arms pumping, he prepared to slide into an intercept course to crash into the ball. He heard Lucas cry out in worry. Roth missed the ball by two yards and slammed into the side of the court. The impact stunned him. He'd missed!

Roth rolled onto his stomach, pushing up onto his arms, feeling his hip burn from the friction of the court floor.

And he saw the ball suspended in a bowl-like web of spun gold.

Suki was staring at it, hand outstretched, her legs flexed and bent. The ring on her finger was glowing. So was the bracelet.

Roth stared at the golden threads in shock. The ball was slowly spinning in the web.

"Suki!" Lucas cried out in wonder.

Suki was staring at the ball, her eyes fixed on it.

"Cheater! Cheater!" Eric roared at her.

Suki dragged her arm to the left, and the ball began to move, upheld by the science of the impossible magic. The ball gained height, heading toward the nearest goal.

"You got this, Sis!" Brillante yelled to her encouragingly.

Roth got back to his feet, aching all over, and watched as the ball went through the stone hoop fixed into the wall.

A roar and cheer came from the crowd. The sound reached a level of excitement previously unheard during the match. Was this something they'd been waiting for or hoping would happen?

"You did it!" Lucas screamed, rushing to hug his sister.

"Not yet!" Roth shouted. "Let her focus!"

Suki was in a state of deep concentration. After the ball passed through the hoop, it began to bend in an arc. No—an *orbit*. She was using her hands and her hips, bringing them around in a circling weave. The ball went around in a circle, passing over the stone hoop on the other side and then coming around again.

"Stop! Stop the game!" Eric shouted.

The ball went through the hoop a second time.

Another roar of cheers came from the crowd. Seven to three.

Suki was swaying to an increasing rhythm that Roth couldn't understand. The ball picked up its pace, following her movements. It went around again, and again went through the hoop.

"Yes!" screamed Lucas, jumping up and down relentlessly. Brillante was grinning, hobbling toward his brother.

"Stop the game!" Eric shouted again. "The game stops after each goal!"

Roth glanced up at the throne and saw Jacob leaning forward, his eyes keen, the expression on his face intent and . . . pleased.

Suki sent the ball through the hoop again, faster this time. The orbit was increasing in speed. Lucas jumped up and down excitedly.

The ball passed around him, going through the goal again. And then *again*.

Colter grimaced with fury and confusion as he tried to jump high enough to stop the orbit, but the ball was too high. No one on their team could get to it. Suki spun it faster and faster, making it come around its orbit again and again.

Roth's heart rejoiced. Somehow she'd figured it out. And that's when he noticed the moon had risen in the sky behind the Beasleys. The moon goddess. The pieces were all there, but he couldn't fit them together yet. It was all connected—the planets, the moon—the orbits of all influenced the game.

And then it was seven to six.

One more pass and the game would be tied. Then one more and they'd win.

That's when Eric Beasley broke across the line midcourt, rushing at Suki with a raised fist. He'd forfeit a point by crossing the line, but from the desperate rage twisting his face, it was obvious he was beyond caring. He was a wild man. A crazy man who realized his family was about to die.

Bellowing a warning, Roth raced forward to intercept the man.

Suki seemed oblivious to the danger, totally engrossed in what she was doing. If Beasley punched her, she'd go down.

"Suki!" Brillante shouted in fear, reaching out his arm, trying to hobble and collapsing.

Fear knifed Roth's heart. He wasn't going to make it in time. He—

And then a blowgun dart struck Eric in the side of the neck. Roth heard a hiss from the crowd. The man's face went blank as the toxin immediately entered his bloodstream. He collapsed before he could land a blow.

One of the warriors standing at the edge of the wall lowered a blowgun.

Eric lay twitching on the wrong side of the court as the ball went through the hoop again.

The trumpets blasted. Despite Eric's foul play, eight points had been achieved. The death game was over.

Roth dropped to his knees, relief gushing inside his chest. Lucas rushed to him. Brillante, hobbling still, came and hugged him, crying with joy. He wrapped his arms around both boys, staring at Suki with wonder.

Suddenly the ball was no longer surrounded by magic, and it dropped down and began bouncing wildly. The crowd was going berserk with glee at the ending of the game. Roth, still on his knees, beckoned for Suki to come to him. She still looked dazed, as if in a trance, but she walked over, her expression tranquil.

"You did it," he said to her. "I knew it! I knew you could!"

Suki reached out her palm. He pressed his against it, and their thumbs pressed against each other in an introvert's hug.

Suki was grinning. "Grandma Suki helped."

"Dude, we won!" Brillante said, hugging his sister. Lucas was crying, hugging Roth so tightly it hurt.

Roth couldn't speak. His heart was so full. Eight to six. The game was over. They'd *won*.

But the relief was quickly tempered when he looked past his daughter and saw the Beasleys weeping in terror. Eric was still twitching on their side of the line.

Then the shriek of a jaguar rent the air as Jacob Calakmul leaped down from the stands in jaguar form and slunk onto the court.

CHAPTER THIRTY-SEVEN

THE ARENA

CALAKMUL BIOSPHERE RESERVE

December 27

Eight feathers flared from the statues of the gods of the Maya representing the Roth family's score. Six were in position on the other side, one having been removed for the violation of the center line. Roth noticed these small details in a flash as he watched the jaguar cross to the center of the arena. Eric Beasley was still twitching from the toxin on the blowgun dart. His eyes were open, his cheek muscles contracting in little spasms.

Sickening fear crept into Roth's stomach. "Don't look," he whispered to his kids. He was still on his knees, hugging the twins. Suki turned her head, her eyes widening when she saw the jaguar heading their way.

The beast had glowing golden eyes, and a rasping snarl came from its muzzle. It was heavily muscled but lean and deadly, its sleek gold fur dotted with black spots. Roth had never seen such an animal up close. It opened its maw, revealing two large fangs on the upper jaw, two large on the lower, and shrieked again.

"Is it going to eat us?" Lucas whimpered, clutching his father in fear.

The jaguar padded up to Eric's body.

"Not us," Roth said.

"Dad," Suki said in growing horror.

"Look away," he warned her.

But she couldn't. And neither could he . . . until he saw the claws come down and slash into Eric's back. The shrieks of the Beasley children began to echo in his ears.

Then Roth squeezed his eyes shut, holding his boys tight. Suki joined them, wrapping her arms around Roth's face, hugging him close. His kids were all sobbing.

Roth knew it was over when the crowd began to howl in triumph. The game had ended.

Roth's feeling of helplessness was keen. There was nothing he could have done to save Beasley. And there was nothing he could do to save his own children if the jaguar turned on them next. All he could do was cling to them, wishing that the nightmare would end.

"Come, family. You've won. You may rest." It was Angélica's voice. Roth opened his eyes, and his stomach immediately quivered with nausea when he glimpsed the jaguar's hide.

He turned his head and pulled his kids with him, following the woman as she led them back to the end of the court.

"You figured it out," Angélica said to Suki. "I'm impressed."

Suki said nothing. She looked sick.

"I thought the Maya sacrificed people on altars," Roth said.

"That will happen to the rest of the family," she replied. "But Mr. Beasley dishonored the game with his actions. He deserved a dishonorable death."

His stomach lurched. "So the rest of the family will still be killed?"

"Yes. At the celebration tonight. The games are over . . . for another year."

Roth's conscience struck him hard. "Even the littlest? Jane Louise?"

She gave him a sympathetic look. "She cannot return with you, Mr. Roth. There would be too many questions. Her family died in a boating accident off the coast of Cozumel, you see. There were no survivors."

Her response infuriated Roth. He couldn't stomach the lack of mercy, even to children. "Isn't that Mr. Calakmul's decision to make? Does it really have to *end* that way?"

"The Maya believed human sacrifice was an honorable act, Mr. Roth. That the blood shed kept the universe in orbit."

"Well, that's pretty lame," Suki said, her voice trembling.

Angélica gave her a pointed look as she continued walking, her pace not changing. "How do you think the Maya felt when the Franciscan friars told them the voluntary shedding of Christ's blood had saved them from hell? That God was nailed to a cross by his enemies, a crown of thorns placed on his head, to save humanity? Why does that not sound equally strange in your ears, Suki?"

The wails of the Beasley family filled Roth's ears. Eric had already been killed, and they knew their lives were also forfeit.

When they reached the spiderweb of magic, Angélica raised the bracelet she wore, and magic coalesced around the band.

"Come, family. Your lives have been spared. Someone had to die today. It could have been you."

Roth pushed his boys beyond the barrier, Brillante limping awkwardly, and then turned around to witness the scene one last time.

Jane Louise came running toward him, and his heart clenched with dread, tears springing to his eyes. Angélica noticed him looking and turned around, her face pinched with sorrow.

Roth knelt down as the little girl barreled into him, sobbing.

"Take me! Take me home!"

Roth thought his heart would burst with pain as he stroked her hair.

"He can't, Jane Louise," Angélica said. "You're not his family."

"*No!*" the little girl wailed. She looked up at Roth's face, shaking her head. He couldn't speak. The anguish he felt was worse than anything he'd experienced. He'd promised Jane Louise he'd bring her back to her mee-maw, but there was nothing he could do to save her, no argument that would sway Calakmul.

He looked out at the arena, at the celebrating people who cared nothing for the fate of the family down below. Again, to his shock, he recognized some of them as powerful people in his own country. People who were, apparently, living a double life. How much influence did Jacob and his followers have in the US already?

Suki came back and hugged the little girl. So did the twins. It was a terrible moment. A moment that would be seared into their memories forever.

The jaguar shrieked again.

Angélica looked frightened. "I've been commanded to release the magic and seal you in if you stay. Then you'll share the fate of the Beasleys. Do you want that? This is your moment to escape. You'll be flown back to Cancún, and you can return home. I must obey."

"And Sarina?" Roth demanded.

Angélica shook her head. "If she leaves the shrine now, she'll die. The magic of the temple is keeping her alive. If she recovers from the coma, she will be returned to you in Bozeman."

"I want to see her before we go," Roth insisted. "I need to."

She shook her head. "I will ask Mr. Calakmul again. He insists she must stay. An alibi will be provided, along with evidence that she's at a world-class health institute overseas. But you and your family are to return home, as promised. If she revives and agrees to the terms, she will be reunited with you later."

Roth knew he shouldn't tempt fate. His anger and hatred toward Jacob Calakmul and his family ran deep. He rose and stared at the jaguar, which was now prowling toward his family. It was panting, its fangs bared.

"I'm sorry, Jane Louise," Roth said. "I'm so sorry."

Angélica pulled the little girl away and held her back. Her face crumpled and she sobbed, looking at Roth as if he were abandoning her. And he was. But he needed to protect his own family. He couldn't save everyone.

"I'm sorry," he said brokenly to her.

Jane Louise continued to stare at him as he backed away, his children with him. Once they were past the barrier, the magic released from Angélica's bracelet and filled in the gap.

"There is going to be a celebration today," Angélica told the little girl, holding her hand. "A feast in your honor. You'll be with your family. There will be lots of flowers and pretty feathers. You like feathers, don't you?"

It was said in a coaxing voice that only amplified the despair and horror in Roth's heart. He stared at the little girl. If there was a way to save her too, he couldn't think of it. His mind was too muddled. The servants who were waiting at the end of the ball court brought them coconuts to drink from and urged them to walk away from the arena.

Roth stood at the edge of the barrier, staring at the little girl, memorizing her face. "I'm sorry," he whispered huskily.

Jane Louise stared back at him with disappointment.

Roth's gaze shifted to the jaguar, and a resolve began to take shape in his heart. A firm, unyielding resolve.

He would do everything within his power to bring the death games to an end.

———

The shrine of Ix Chel was in a small internal garden within the golden city, surrounded by thick trees that concealed it from above and without. The smell of smoke wafted in the air as they approached, and the sound of chanting could be heard from within.

Angélica had escorted them there after they'd changed into their regular clothes. Their suitcases had been brought to the ancient city along with the Beasley family's possessions.

It had been a relief to change since they'd worn the same shorts and shirts for days. Angélica was wearing more formal attire as well—not the shorts or Maya garb she'd worn since arriving.

The entrance to the garden was a stone arch with a triangular edifice on top decorated with Maya runes. The glyphs depicted three women, sort of like the three Fates from Greek mythology, except they had a distinctive Maya look. Just past the entrance, Jacob Calakmul stood in a suit. His hair looked slick with gel.

On a stone plinth in the middle of the shrine lay Sarina's body, garbed in a linen tunic like those the ancients had worn. She had markings on her face, wrists, arms, and ankles, similar to the glyphs carved into the walls of this city. Her chest rose and fell slowly, her breathing shallow.

A man in ceremonial garb stood by the head of her bed. He held a smoking bundle of leaves over her face, uttering an incantation or prayer as he waved it.

Jacob stepped in front of the table and opened his palms. "As you can see, she's alive."

Indeed. That, at least, was a relief, but he'd hoped for more. He hated to see her like this, comatose, reliant on Jacob and his followers.

Suki sidled up and squeezed her mom's hand. The boys started sniffling. Roth's eyes stung from the smoke and gathering tears.

"Why can't we bring her back with us?" he asked plaintively.

"She'll die if you try," Jacob answered. "No modern doctor can treat her as we can. Do not cross me, Mr. Roth. You've seen who we have on our side—and what powers are available to us. Your own daughter has unique gifts." He eyed Suki with an intensity that made Roth bristle. "You were aided by Ix Chel, no doubt. She wanted you to win. Your lives have been spared, but no one is allowed to cross us. If you're smart, which I think you are, you'll wait for the Jaguar Prophecies to be fulfilled. Your family will be protected from the nightmares that are coming."

"Please let us take Jane Louise with us," Roth implored. "I promised her that we'd take her to see her grandmother."

Jacob shook his head. "You made a promise you couldn't fulfill. I refuse to do the same. Her fate isn't in your hands."

"I know. It's in yours. *Please.*"

"Do you know how many Maya pleaded with their conquerors? Fathers, sons, murdered in front of their families. Wives, daughters ravished by soldiers. You think I will be moved to pity *now*? The Beasleys were all killed in a boating accident during their Christmas vacation." He gave Roth a compelling look. "If you don't want any 'accidents' to happen to you, then keep quiet about the true nature of your visit." His gaze shifted to Suki with an *interested* look. "Keep practicing, *mija*."

Roth shuddered.

Shifting his gaze to encompass the whole Roth family, Jacob gave them an impassive stare. "Now say your goodbyes. We return you to Cancún."

With that, he stepped aside and gestured to the plinth. Roth and the kids gathered in close. It hurt Roth's heart to think of leaving her like this, but he knew there was nothing he could do. No argument he could make that would sway Jacob. Besides, part of him wondered if what the man said was true—if only the magic was keeping her alive. He had to hope she'd get better and, once she did, that Jacob would keep his word.

He bent over and kissed her cheek. The kids kissed her as well.

"Bye, Mom," Lucas said thickly.

"Bye," Brillante said, wiping his eyes.

Suki fidgeted with the ring. She couldn't speak, but she kissed her mother's cheek in farewell.

The heat of the jungle was oppressive. But Roth didn't want to leave. And even though they'd won, he still experienced the pain of getting his heart ripped out.

CHAPTER THIRTY-EIGHT

Cancún International Airport

Cancún, Mexico

December 27

"Here you are, family! The airport!"

Roth stepped out of the car while the cheery Uber driver, Pedro, hurried to the trunk, opened it, and began pulling their luggage out, piece by piece. They were wearing their own clothes again. His wallet was in his pocket, and he pulled it out and withdrew a fifty-peso bill.

Pedro finished stacking the suitcases along the curb. "There are your suitcases. Ready to go home?"

Roth handed the bill to the driver. "Thank you," he said grimly.

"*Gracias*, Dad," Suki reminded him.

"*Gracias,*" Roth said.

"Come back to Cancún!" Pedro said while closing the trunk.

Roth's chest felt unbearably heavy. The nightmare had happened around 2 a.m. that morning . . . and now they were in the middle of a busy city, as if nothing had happened. Shuttles were dropping off families returning from their Christmas vacations. It was surreal to see the mothers and fathers, the crowds of kids with AirPods and hats. Suki was wearing a T-shirt with an *Undertale* character on it. Her legs were bruised. They all were bruised, and Brillante was still limping.

Past the departures terminal, he saw a throng of taxi and shuttle drivers trying to persuade the new arrivals to use their services. It felt as if a month had passed since the Roths had arrived from Bozeman.

"Let's get out of here," Suki said.

Roth grabbed the handle of his suitcase and then Sarina's and pulled both toward the terminal. He had their passports. Angélica had had their boarding passes printed for them. Their cell phones had all been confiscated and destroyed, so they had no way of contacting anyone. They didn't have a landline at the house, so they'd need to pick up some new phones from the store on the way home from the airport.

Even as they joined the crowd entering Cancún International Airport, he didn't feel safe. He had the throb of anxiety that at any moment, a security guard might approach them and take them back to the games.

That feeling persisted as they passed through security, boarded the plane, and stowed the suitcases in the overhead bins, and it lingered even as the 737 rushed down the runway and took off.

Roth folded his arms, staring out the window and watching the Hotel Zone recede. Lucas sat next to him, eyelids drooping with exhaustion. The effects of the *xocolatl* had worn off hours ago. The plane had rocked with turbulence during takeoff, but Roth hadn't even gritted his teeth. What was turbulence after all they'd been through?

Lucas gripped his hand and squeezed.

"You okay, Dad?" Suki asked. She'd chosen to sit on the same row as him. Brillante was on his Switch already, window seat, on their same row, which was empty other than the four of them. The flight back home wasn't as crowded as the one they'd been on coming to Cancún. Most people would return after New Year's.

He gave his daughter a sad look. "I can't turn my mind off." The image of Jane Louise haunted him. So did the idea of leaving Sarina in those people's care.

Suki nodded. "Me too."

"You saved us, Suki," he told her. "You saved our lives."

She shook her head. "You heard Jacob. Maybe we had help. Besides, you get credit for figuring out the real game." She looked down at the bracelet on her wrist. "I'm surprised he let me keep it. Think it'll work in Bozeman?"

"His advice to keep practicing implies that it might."

"Not a lot of Maya ruins in Montana," she said, stifling a yawn. Suki pushed her glasses up, staring sightlessly at the back of the seat in front of her. "I miss Mom. Abuelita is going to be so upset when she finds out she's in a coma. That's how Grandma Suki died."

Roth wasn't looking forward to calling his in-laws to tell them about Sarina's condition, let alone that she had been sent, all expenses paid, to a cutting-edge research facility in . . . where was it? . . . Singapore? He'd need to inform her boss too. Their friends. The prospect was daunting.

Moretti too would need to be called. The sooner, the better. And he would need to call Westfall's wife. He hoped he hadn't missed his friend's funeral.

The warning Jacob had given him before leaving the jet was still burned into his memory.

Your wife may die of the diabetes anyway, Mr. Roth. My magic is preserving her. But if she dies, do not think about crossing me. You think you could tell people about the death games and I wouldn't know? Who would believe such a story? Especially from an eccentric author whose most popular series is about a liar. Do not defy me. Even in Montana, you are not safe from us. I could find you anywhere. If you want your family to live through what's coming, you'd better keep quiet and prepare for our return. It's up to you. When the plague comes, you'll know it is nearly time. Store food and survival supplies. You will need them. All who survive will be branded with a rune to protect them from the pox. Stay loyal.

Roth had promised he'd tell no one about the ordeal.

But already his mind was turning those words into a lie.

CHAPTER THIRTY-NINE

Villa Sara de Calakmul

Cozumel, Mexico

December 28

A strong wind blew against the gray-blue waters. Jacob felt the sand between his toes as he walked up the shore. Someone had arranged the shape of a Christmas tree in the debris on the sand near where a clutch of sea turtle eggs had been found. The wind was soothing and calming. Nests of green vegetation grew out of the sand, but his gaze was fixed on the flat horizon. The island of Cuba lay in the distance. It was invisible to his bare eyes, but his yacht was always welcome there.

Cozumel's weather was pleasant year-round, and he wore his European-style clothes—a silk shirt, casual pants rolled up at the hem, and sunglasses. Like a rich tourist visiting from Spain or Portugal. Looking westward, he saw the prick of light coming from Venus.

The hum of an engine caught his attention, and he turned to see Victor arriving on a UTV.

"You want a ride back to the compound, Mr. Calakmul?" Victor asked. "The tourists will be arriving soon. They reached Playa del Carmen and will be crossing on the Winjet."

"Yes," Jacob said. He hiked up to the road that ran along the shore. It was forbidden to use headlights after sunset, which was almost upon them.

He slouched onto the seat and dropped his sandals on the floor. Victor accelerated, and the UTV shot up to the road before leaping onto the sandy trail, roaring past the sign that warned against trespassing. In ten minutes, they were back at Villa Sara. One of the shuttles was gone, but he suspected it had already departed for the docks to pick up the next crew of ultrawealthy who'd arrive to celebrate New Year's in Cozumel. One of the families was interested in becoming a full "member" of the resort chain. They'd heard about some promising "benefits."

Victor parked near the front and then nodded to Jacob, who collected his sandals and departed. He saw Angélica in his office already, wearing professional attire, prepared to greet the new arrivals. The rooms had been freshened up. Cooks were already preparing the first meal.

Jacob took off his sunglasses and entered the office area through the glass door.

Angélica was talking on the office phone. "Thank you. Yes . . . yes, all will be taken care of. Perfect." She set the phone down in its cradle.

Jacob lifted his eyebrows at her questioningly.

"The monitoring devices have already been installed at the Roth residence. They just arrived at the airport in Bozeman and should be home soon."

"And the spyware on the computers?" Jacob asked.

"Installed and tested."

Courtesy of Ricardo, who'd worked for the NSA before he started working for the Calakmul family. He'd kept them under the Americans' radar for years. Jacob smiled and set the sunglasses down. "I want all of their internet traffic monitored. When they get new cell phones, I want a trojan virus installed."

"Of course. The daughter's phone showed a call to a man in Utah, made from the temple near San Gervasio. Will Moretti. A call also went out to Avram Morrell, an attorney in San Diego. Those were the only people Mr. Roth called or texted."

Jacob frowned. "Anything else on the phones?"

"Nothing. They've been destroyed."

"Do we have anyone with ties in Utah? FBI perhaps?"

Angélica picked up her tablet and quickly began tapping. "I'll find someone."

"Not now. We have visitors about to arrive."

"Yes, I'm prepared for them." She looked down at her tablet again and then glanced at him. "You think Mr. Roth is going to talk? He seemed pretty subdued."

Jacob had already pondered that question. He'd considered eliminating the entire family just to play it safe. In the past, the winning side had always been the family who'd gone into it knowing about the games and preparing for them in advance. This was the first time there had been an upset.

Ix Chel had intervened indeed. It was the only explanation for their sudden rise to eminence. The daughter's ability to summon and control the magic intrigued him. It was in her blood for certain. A latent gift. It was an interesting development, and he looked forward to seeing what would come of it.

"His wife is in a coma and under our control. He and his children nearly perished. He's been given another chance at life. I tried to persuade him that no one would believe such a fanciful tale. Some secrets are too outrageous to be acceptable. Some would even consider him the prime suspect if his wife dies of diabetes. He's a smart man. I like him. I don't *think* he'll talk."

Angélica was scrutinizing him. "But you kept the little girl alive."

Jane Louise. The Beasleys' youngest. She was still down at the biosphere reserve, being cared for by the servants.

"Even though I don't think he'll reveal us or what little he knows of the prophecy in the Dresden Codex, it's best to be prepared. He may surprise us. But if he dares do such a thing, *I* will have a surprise for him. What is given can be taken away."

EPILOGUE

Roth Residence

Bozeman, Montana

December 28

The tires on the Denali crunched on the snow as Roth pulled up to the steep driveway. The smell of Chick-fil-A still lingered in the air. It was cold in Montana—freezing, in comparison to the heat of the jungle they'd left in Mexico. The house was dark, but the lamps at the front of the drive were on. There were tire tracks in the freshly fallen snow. The roads in the Sourdough neighborhood had all been plowed.

Roth reached up and pressed the garage door opener. It strained but didn't open. Sometimes the rubber seal at the bottom froze to the concrete. He tried it again, and it lifted about an inch before stopping.

"Ugh, we don't have to go through the front door, do we?" Suki complained. "It's freezing out there."

Roth pushed the button again, and the door lifted this time. He saw Sarina's white Honda Pilot parked in the garage and felt a jolt of pain in his chest. Slowly, he advanced the Denali next to the Pilot. The garage heater kicked on immediately and could be heard over the rumble of the truck's engine. Once he'd parked, he pushed the button to turn off the car and then another to close the garage door.

"Dude, you didn't eat all your chicken strips!" Brillante said. "Can I have them? I'm still hungry."

"I'm full," Lucas said, handing his food over. "I miss Mom. This is weird."

"You said it, bud," Roth said with a sigh. He pushed the button to lower the tailgate before leaving the truck. "Grab your stuff, kids."

"Can someone take my suitcase? My knee still hurts," Brillante said.

"I will. Dad, can I watch MrBeast on YouTube?" Lucas asked.

Suki had already climbed out and walked around to the back. "I'll watch it with you if you want," she said.

"That's cool. Can we, Dad?"

"Sure. We all need to unwind. I know school starts up again next week, but if you need a few days to adjust, that's okay. Hopefully, Mom will wake up, and they'll let her come home."

Hopefully. But Roth wasn't sure whether to trust in that hope. He went over and grabbed his own bag. Suki was already stepping up. She'd been less sarcastic on the way back. She'd been looking for ways to help her brothers. And him.

"When are we getting new phones, Dad?" she asked him. "We need to tell Abuelita about Mom. And there are some questions about Grandma Suki I'd like to ask her."

"Tomorrow," he said.

"Will I have the same phone number as before?" she asked.

"Yes."

"Can Lucas and I get phones now?" Brillante asked.

"Yes and yes," Roth said. He and Sarina had been pretty strict about when to let their kids have phones, but he wanted to be able to keep contact with the boys now—anytime, anywhere.

Dragging his suitcase, Roth went to the door leading inside, then unlocked and opened it. The house smelled . . . off. Maybe one of the kids had left something in the trash before they'd gone. He flicked on the mudroom light and then the interior. They hadn't changed the thermostat before leaving, so the interior was warm enough.

Roth walked to the master bedroom, and when he saw the bed, his heart clenched again. They'd moved from a tiny home in Fremont to this monstrosity in Bozeman all because he'd won the publishing lottery. His persistence and hard work had paid off. But he would have given up everything to be back in Fremont again, being an adjunct professor, if it would bring Sarina home. He needed another cry. He rubbed the bridge of his nose. He needed a *therapist*.

Suki rolled up the other suitcase behind him, giving him a sad look. "Here," she said.

"Thanks." He took the other suitcase.

Suki let go of her own bag and then came up and gave him a hug—a real hug, not one of her hand holds.

She sniffed. "I'm going to get some cereal," she said. She hadn't ordered any Chick-fil-A. She hadn't wanted it.

Roth dragged the suitcases in and left them by the bed. He saw himself in the bathroom mirror and flinched. He looked like a stranger. A bruise discolored his arm beneath his sleeve. Scratches on his face showed the marks he bore from the jungle. His eyes were puffy and swollen from crying during the flight.

There was no landline, so he couldn't call anyone if he'd wanted to, but he could at least send a Facebook message to Moretti to let him know they were back. He walked down to his office. He had a bookshelf behind his desk that displayed Cheerios boxes and stuffed animals from video games. His whole family loved cereal.

Sitting down in his La-Z-Boy office chair, Roth swiveled it. He hadn't turned on the room light, but there was enough light coming in from the kitchen. He lifted the laptop lid and turned it on, stroking his beard while he waited for it to power up.

The screen came up, jiggled once, and then his facial-recognition software logged him in. The little jiggle was unusual. Had his home electronics been hacked? For all he knew, cameras had been installed too. He'd have to be very careful what he said or did around the house.

He opened a browser and went to Facebook and then Messenger. He shot a quick note off to Moretti. *Back in Bozeman. Didn't need your uncle. Getting a new phone tomorrow. Call you then. When's Westfall's funeral?*

He pressed the send button and leaned back in the chair, feeling his emotions roiling. He needed to call Sarina's folks and let them know she was in Singapore. Angélica had even provided fake documentation showing she'd been admitted and copies of medical reports on diabetic comas. Still . . . he could put it off for a little while. He needed to. He wouldn't be able to call them until he had a new phone.

He gazed around the room. The den was his private sanctuary. This was where he wrote his fantasy novels. Where he did livestreams of playing video games on Twitch. On the bottom shelf sat his D&D manuals and a small wooden box from a Mendocino chocolate company, which contained his gaming dice.

The sight of the box filled him with pain because Sarina had gotten it for him. Her touch was everywhere here.

The house felt empty without her, but he'd get her back. He would get her back, and he'd make Calakmul suffer for all the deaths he'd caused.

Then he opened his e-mail account in the browser and saw a ton of unread messages from his publisher, his rights attorney, plus a lot of random spam that had made it past his filter. The newest one was from his bank about a transfer.

He hadn't made any transfer.

Pursing his lips, he clicked on it.

Just in case it was a phishing e-mail—which he hated with a fiery-hot passion—he opened another browser tab and logged into his bank account.

And nearly fell out of his chair.

He stared at the screen in shock and disbelief. He knew about how much they'd had in their account before leaving for Cancún.

The balance now was $52,093,481.52.

Fifty-two million dollars had been added to the account.

He blinked, wondering if his eyes were deceiving him. Jacob Calakmul had said that the winner claimed the assets of the losing family. But the money wasn't why people chose to play the game. It was the prestige they'd get once the prophecy was fulfilled. Once the Calakmuls ruled again. Roth hadn't given the money a single thought until right this moment. This had to be the value of the Beasley estate. Their winnings from the death games. Roth stared at it, feeling his heart hammering. He didn't want that much money. He didn't *need* that much money.

Fifty-two million dollars. To a billionaire, it was chump change. A fraction. To him . . .

He never would have imagined earning so much in a lifetime.

Would the IRS know about the bank transfer? Was it taxable? He had no idea and no one to call, with Westfall being dead.

What would Sarina have suggested he do with it? She'd always been the philanthropist, making secret donations to schools and charities. The Westfalls could be helped. And so could others. Especially that orphanage in Cozumel. Roth reached for the keyboard and opened a new browser. He typed in the search bar: *Huellas de Pan Cozumel Mexico.*

Jacob's words haunted him. *If you want your family to live through what's coming, you'd better keep quiet and prepare for our return.*

But Roth had never been the kind of man who liked to keep quiet.

AUTHOR'S NOTE

This book began as a nightmare. It happened while my family was on vacation in Florida (where I *almost* threw up on the Avatar ride at Disney World) in June 2021. One night, I had a vivid dream that my neighbors had invited our family to a resort island. Everyone was acting pretty "sus" when we got there, and I began to realize that it was a plot to kill us. All the families against us. It was absolutely terrifying, and I woke up in a cold sweat, grateful that my neighbors are actually really nice.

Even though I'm a fantasy author, not a writer of thrillers, I sent myself an e-mail with the idea and filed it as I usually do. Except . . . the dream wouldn't go away. I kept thinking about it over and over while writing *The Dawning of Muirwood*. The idea I pitched to my editor Adrienne at 47North and Gracie at Thomas & Mercer was making this a series about different families who get caught up in these death games. After discussing the idea with them, they suggested I write instead a series about only one family and what happens to them and how they try to stop this awful thing from happening to others.

With that in mind, I needed a location for the story. It was my father-in-law, Pete, who suggested setting it on the island of Cozumel. I'd originally considered Jamaica or one of the Caribbean islands. I began researching Cozumel and the Yucatán, and soon I was deep into research about the Maya, the Aztecs, the conquistadors, Montezuma, Cortés—there was so much to dig into. A friend of mine who is a

Spanish literature professor suggested weaving some "magic" from the era too. So I did. During my research, I learned about the Dresden Codex in Germany, and all the pieces started coming together.

While this is my first published thriller, I want you to know that the first books I ever wrote were thrillers. While I was in high school, I wrote five novels—all of which could be categorized as thrillers. It wasn't until I was in college that I wrote my first fantasy novels. In order to wrap my head around the genre, I dived into some of the best thriller authors: Dean Koontz, Lee Child, Blake Crouch, Dan Brown, and many, many more. This helped me understand the nuts and bolts of the genre and convinced me there was room where my style of writing, themes that are important to me, would fit right in. I did consider using a pseudonym for this series but decided against it. As my editor Adrienne told me, my *fantasy* books are thrillers too.

This is also the first time I signed a multibook contract with Amazon Publishing when I *didn't* know what was going to happen after the first book. I gave myself a long runway just in case, with the understanding that if after book one I still didn't know what book two would look like, I could have a grace period while I figured it out. Thankfully, the plot ideas for book two, *Jaguar Prophecies*, started to flow while writing this book. And the same thing happened while writing the second book. I began to see where the whole story was going. This was challenging for someone who likes to plan things out well in advance. I'm not a pure-blooded pantser or plotter, to be sure. But having that freedom really helped me figure this out at my own pace.

If you are new to my writing, thanks for giving this book a try. I have over thirty other novels you might also like, even if you're not a regular fan of fantasy fiction. My website, www.jeff-wheeler.com, is a great place to start to figure out what to read next.

And to my awesome fans: thanks for trusting me again in a new genre. Don't worry, I have plenty more fantasy stories to tell. But I believe taking detours and pushing yourself is helpful and stretches us. I've learned a lot doing this and am so grateful for the support you've given me over my career.

You're all poggers!

ACKNOWLEDGMENTS

First off, I have to thank Adrienne Procaccini and Grace Doyle at APub for their enthusiastic support for me trying my hand at something new. That's one of the things I absolutely love about my publisher—the willingness (and encouragement) to take risks and explore new paths.

You'd think writing a book in our own world would be easier than a make-believe one, but no. It was way harder. Things have to be accurate and realistic. In my fantasy worlds, I get to make a lot of stuff up. Not so in this series, and I can't be an expert in law enforcement, international syndicates, healthcare, or transportation. So I knew I'd need more help to get this right, and I'm grateful to many friends and acquaintances who helped me navigate things I didn't know much about. First off, to Robert Colvin, who teased me with the idea of exploring Mesoamerican magic systems and history and weaving them into the story. I also got some great medical advice from Edwin Wells (an ER doctor) and Mary Galbraith (an RN) to help me understand diabetes and the symptoms of DKA. It also turns out my copyeditor, Wanda, had firsthand experience in this too and really helped increase the realism of the situation. I'd also like to recognize Chris Allison, a university professor and tour guide of the ancient Maya lands, for his in-depth input on the places where this story takes place. My family had the neat chance to hear from Chris in our home before we went to Cozumel and visited these lands ourselves. And to my buddy Bill Morell, who serves in law enforcement, and whom I called out of the blue one day and asked how he'd try to help get me out of Mexico if he had to.

To make this series as realistic as possible, I went to the Yucatán Peninsula with my family and some extended family members during Christmas. While in Mexico, we had several excellent tour guides (including Helaman Lehmann) who taught us about the rich history of the Maya. We even visited several villages, received a shaman's blessing, and swam in cenotes. During our trip, we did some humanitarian adventures as well at Huellas de Pan (in Cancún), Ciudad de Angeles (Cozumel), and Waves of Grace Church (Cozumel). Organizations like these do so much good for the people in their communities. It was fun playing soccer with them, serving food to families, and visiting with people and leaders who are truly making a huge difference in so many lives. All of these organizations are supported by the generous contributions of others. But if you're ever on a tourist trip, take time to serve too. We found our opportunities through Give A Day Global (https://www.giveadayglobal.org/). It was worth it, and my kids and their cousins loved it. By the way, Jorge is a pretty awesome guy.

I'm grateful to my regular team of first readers too. This was a different kind of book, but getting input and feedback is always so helpful. To Emily, Robin, Shannon, Sandi, Sunil—I appreciate your help and support. Even if this book wasn't what you were used to. Angela, my dev editor, provided great insight, as always, and helped me figure out some of the tricky spots to make it better. Robert contributed a plot twist that I can't reveal now but totally appreciate. Mary gave a great suggestion about Sarina using an insulin pump. I also have to credit Adrienne, my editor at APub, for really encouraging me to make Jacob a worthy villain. I'll never forget our afternoon chat on a beautiful day in May in downtown Seattle at the top of the Spheres while we talked about this book. Also, my kids played a huge role in the teenager lingo in this book. Sometimes I'd hear them talk and stop them and ask what it meant. So all the sus, poggers, chonky vocab (and general teenage angst), I'd like to thank them for too. Eye rolls included.

And last, but not least, to Kate Rudd, who does such an amazing job narrating my books and bringing them to life with her voice. She's been a wonderful partner, and I'm infinitely grateful that she was selected as my first narrator. While this book was in production, her mom got deathly ill. So grateful that she made it through and all is well. Life hits us all really hard sometimes.

Now it's time to get back to book two, *Jaguar Prophecies*. You know how I feel about second books (hint: they're often my favorite). Buckle up. You're going to need to hold on tight for this one.

ABOUT THE AUTHOR

Photo © 2021 Kortnee Carlile

Jeff Wheeler is the *Wall Street Journal* bestselling author of over thirty epic fantasy novels. The Dresden Codex is the first thriller he's written since his early years as a budding author, but his many fans think his fantasy novels are thrillers in their own way. Jeff lives in the Rocky Mountains and is a husband, father of five, and devout member of his church. On a recent trip to the jungles of Cozumel and the Yucatán Peninsula, he explored Maya ruins and cenotes, leading him to dive even further into the history of ancient South America and the Spanish conquistadors. There is more to the ball courts than meets the eye. Learn about Jeff's publishing journey in *Your First Million Words*, and visit his many worlds at www.jeff-wheeler.com.